THE
MIDNIGHT
VILLAGE

HOLLY MARTIN

CHAPTER 1

S tar drove through the quiet country lanes
jumping at shadows at every bend. Up above
thousands of diamonds peppered the night sky,
the moon shining brightly, guiding her home.

Home was a weird thing to think about a village
she'd never even set foot in before, but she'd always
felt this pull to Midnight Village, something she'd
never been able to explain. She'd grown up in the
nearby town of Whimbles and she used to play in the
woods behind Midnight and the closer she got to the
towering walls that surrounded it, the more she'd been
enveloped in this feeling of calm and a weird sense of
belonging. When she'd touched the walls, she could
feel this energy pulsating underneath her fingers, an
energy that she felt connected to somehow. Every day
she'd walk past the entrance to Midnight on her way

to school and feel a yearning to see what was beyond the village gates. Everyone was curious about what went on in there, who lived there, why they were so private, why no one was ever allowed in. But her connection to the village felt like so much more than curiosity.

And now she was going to live there.

She'd had butterflies of nerves and worry ever since Wolf Oakwood had phoned her that morning to say the house was hers. Initially she'd been excited and relieved to get the place, but now she couldn't help worrying about what she was letting herself in for.

It was the application process that had sent alarm bells ringing. It should have sent her running a thousand miles in the opposite direction.

The advert for a house to rent in Midnight had appeared in the paper right next to the article that had ruined her life and she'd wondered if it had somehow been fate that as one door had slammed in her face, another had opened. She remembered the first phone call with Wolf after she'd sent an email enquiring about the advert. He'd sounded a hell of a lot younger than she'd imagined an old, respectable mayor to sound. If she had to guess, he might even be around her age. He'd clearly been bored by having to trawl through possibly hundreds of applications; she could tell from the tone in his voice that he had no interest in her. But what he'd said had definitely caught her interest.

'I received your email,' Wolf said, idly. 'All I need is a sample of your blood.'

'What?'

'Your blood. Just prick your finger with a clean needle, wipe the blood on a piece of paper, pop it in an envelope and courier it over to me.'

There was silence then and she could hear Wolf typing away on the computer in the background, as he busied himself with far more interesting things than her. This was the weirdest conversation she'd ever had.

'I... I have the money to pay for the rent, you don't need to worry about that.'

'I have no interest in your money Miss Brightheart, just your blood.'

'What the hell do you want with my blood?'

'You can tell a lot about a person from their blood, Miss Brightheart, and if you knew anything about the village of Midnight, you wouldn't be asking that question. Thank you for your time, but I have other applicants to talk to.'

'No wait, please. I need this house, I need... to escape.'

He was silent for a moment. 'Why do you want to live in Midnight? I'm sure there are plenty of places in the world you can hide out from the press.'

She'd cringed as she realised he knew who she was.

'I grew up in Whimbles.'

'I see.'

'No, you don't. It's hard to explain but I've always felt this pull to Midnight, like I belonged there. I know it sounds ridiculous because I've never been in there but it felt like home. I used to play in the woods behind the village as a child because... being close to it made me feel calm. My mind races, like it's constantly thinking of a hundred different things at once, and whenever I was close to Midnight that just stopped, I could think clearly. I had a difficult childhood; I was socially awkward, they'd call it now. I didn't really have any friends because I just couldn't interact with them. I was... different to them.'

'Different how?'

'I... don't know.'

'You can talk freely with me, Miss Brightheart. Whatever you say to me will be held in the strictest of confidence.'

She bit her lip. This was getting weirder and weirder. What was it she was supposed to talk freely about, as if she had some big secret to tell?

'I'm not sure what you want me to say, Mr Oakwood.'

'Call me Wolf. I want you to tell me why you feel different to other people.'

How could she even begin to describe it?

He sighed. 'Star, trust works both ways. If I'm going to trust you to let you live in my village, then you have to trust me too. Get me the blood sample and then we'll talk.'

And with that he'd hung up.

And instead of finding another house to ride out the storm in as he'd suggested, she'd done as Wolf asked, pricked her finger, wiped the blood on a piece of paper and paid a huge wodge of cash to courier it directly to him. She'd tracked the package all the way out of London, along the motorways and country lanes, to deepest darkest Cornwall. He'd phoned her at eight o'clock the following day to say the house was hers, to explain the logistics of getting into the village, past the security guards, and that he would go over the village rules with her when she arrived and get her to sign a non-disclosure agreement which meant she could never tell anyone what went on in the village. It was all very cloak and dagger and it was now making her feel very uneasy as she picked her way through the dark country lanes to Midnight.

But what was the alternative? The press had been camping outside her house, pictures of her looking scared and harassed had been in every paper, and every news TV programme had covered the story too. She'd been staying in a hotel for a few days just to get away from them, but it didn't feel like this story would ever go away.

She drove through the entrance to Midnight, up a small winding lane, until she got to the top where there were no fewer than four armed guards manning a large metal gate. She pulled up in front of the gate and wound down the window to speak to one of them.

He smiled as soon as he saw her. 'Star Brightheart, we've been expecting you. Drive through the gate and take the first right. Your house is the last one at the very end of the close, Aurora Cottage. You can't miss it, it's got a huge windmill in the front garden. The previous owner loved their garden ornaments.'

He handed her a key and then he must have pressed a button because the gate rolled back of its own accord. The guard motioned for her to drive in and, just like that, she was in Midnight Village.

The feeling of calm was instant as if she'd driven through some kind of forcefield that was protecting her from the outside world. There was also a warmth that was unseasonably strange since it was the middle of December but it suddenly felt like a balmy summer's night. As she drove round the corner, she got her first ever glimpse of the village as it slept under the moonlight, its quaint little cottages with thatched roofs, cobbled streets and Victorian-style gas lamps that left puddles of gold across the ground. It was utterly perfect.

She drove slowly down her designated road and saw more charming cottages of various colours. She smiled when she spotted the windmill sitting outside the end cottage. It must have been at least eight foot tall, its sails turning slowly in a gentle breeze.

She pulled up in the drive and got out, looking around. There was a black cat with bright green eyes sitting on the end of her drive watching her astutely. She grabbed her bag and walked up to her blue wooden door, putting the key in the lock as, ironically, the village clock struck midnight.

Star pushed open the door, and the cat followed her into the lounge. She couldn't help smiling at the first thing she saw, a spectacular Christmas tree sitting in one corner. Although this tree was decorated far more traditionally than any she'd ever seen, it added a lovely cosy, festive air to the place. On its branches were cinnamon sticks tied with red twine, dried oranges decorated with star anise. There were holly leaves and berries, pinecones, garlands of dried fruits and vegetables, chains of popcorns and cranberries, and wooden stars made from twigs hung from the boughs. As she stepped closer she could see orbs or baubles with lavender, rose petals, whole nutmegs, cloves, and other herbs, spices and flowers inside. It smelled amazing and the whole tree seemed to twinkle with tiny fairy lights.

She looked around and could see the lounge had a cosy, squashy sofa up one end and a bright red log burner up the other. Over the mantlepiece was a garland of holly, berries and red flowers. It looked beautiful.

She wandered through to the kitchen which was surprisingly really big. Outside, in the back garden, she could see flowers and plants that seemed to tumble over rocks across multiple layers, all lit up by little orbs of light. There was a welcome hamper of bread, milk, scones, clotted cream, jam, biscuits and a bottle of wine on the breakfast table, which was a lovely touch.

It was such a contrast to arriving in her rented accommodation in London a few years before, which had had a sofa, bed and a few integrated white goods in the kitchen – and that counted as fully furnished. There had been no soft furnishings or welcome hamper there, not that she'd been expecting them. She had spent years making the place her home but now she could never go back. She'd already given her landlord notice that she would be ending her tenancy at the end of January and her friend, Tig, was bringing some of her stuff down when she came to Cornwall to visit her family for Christmas. She would pay a house clearing service to get rid of the rest. It was the end of an era and she couldn't help but feel sad about that. But now was the start of another.

She took some time to unload the car. She hadn't brought a lot of clothes with her but she had packed all of her cake-making things including a whole load of ingredients she hadn't wanted to throw away. After what had happened, she wasn't sure she ever wanted to make her cakes again but she did find the process very relaxing. Making cakes had always been her happy place.

The cat sat and watched her unloading her stuff with a look of amusement and disdain on its face, but then all cats seemed to have a look of disdain for the lesser mortals that looked after them so this was nothing new.

Once the car was empty, she closed the door, and looked at her new home. She felt suddenly so tired. It had been nearly seven hours of driving today, plus the exhaustion from the last few days was finally catching up with her.

The cat miaowed at her as it followed her into the kitchen. She noticed that inside the hamper were a few trays of cat food. She opened one and emptied it onto a plate and put it down on the floor. The cat ate it and then settled itself down on a furry rug.

Star climbed the stairs to bed feeling incredibly weary. There were only two rooms up here, a bathroom with a walk-in shower and a bedroom with the biggest, softest bed, already made up for her, standing in the middle. She undressed, climbed under the covers and couldn't help but smile.

She was home.

She rolled onto her side and fell instantly to sleep.

CHAPTER 2

S tar was woken the next morning by a loud knocking on her door. She grabbed her phone to see what time it was and was surprised to see it was past ten o'clock. She quickly threw on a dressing gown that was hanging on a hook and ran downstairs to answer the door.

On the other side was a lady, probably in her fifties, wearing a bright pink kaftan and gold slippers. She was also wearing a huge welcoming smile.

'Claudia Periwinkle, I'm your new neighbour,' she thrust out a hand to greet her.

Star shook it. 'Star Brightheart.'

'I'm so excited to meet you. I've been following your blog for years. Well, Celeste Bright's blog, I mean,' Claudia gave her a theatrical wink. 'I had no idea that Celeste wasn't your real name.'

Star cringed. She wondered if everyone in the village would know who she was. Celeste Bright had been a great pseudonym to keep her working life and private life separate and she had hoped coming here under her real name would help to distance herself from the bad press but it seemed she couldn't escape it. Would they vilify her? Hate her before they'd even met her, just like the press had done?

As if reading her mind, Claudia put a hand on her arm. 'I don't think anyone blames you for what happened to that horrid woman. The press loves a villain they can hate but this will all die down soon. I always wondered if you were one of us. Your cupcakes are just magnificent, I've ordered so many from you over the years. And now you're here. Will you be opening a cake shop in the village?'

Claudia was clearly one of those people who spoke at a hundred miles an hour and changed subjects faster than Star changed her underwear.

'I, erm, I hadn't really thought about that. Most of my business is online. I kind of came here in a bit of a hurry so I hadn't really thought much beyond getting here.'

'I understand that. And you've had a long drive. Why don't you throw some clothes on, and I'll make you a nice breakfast.'

That did sound lovely.

'OK, give me five minutes,' Star said.

'Just come over when you're ready,' Claudia said. 'Hazel Cottage, over there with the red front door.'

Star nodded and went back inside. She ran upstairs, had a quick wash and threw on some clothes, then walked over to Hazel Cottage.

The sun was shining brightly which felt at odds with the cold weather she'd experienced lately in London. Claudia's garden was filled with flowers that were tumbling over from an assortment of pots. In fact, as Star looked around at the quiet little road, all the gardens were teeming with flowers. While she was a big fan of herbs, she didn't know much about different flowers and when they grew, but wasn't December a bit late to have such a beautiful array of them?

The door was open when she arrived and she knocked and stepped inside.

'Hello, Claudia,' Star called out.

'In the kitchen,' Claudia said.

Star walked down the short hall into the kitchen and was assaulted with the warm, comforting scents of nutmeg, cinnamon and cardamom.

Claudia was standing in the middle of it all and it took Star a few seconds to realise that something was terribly wrong with this cosy cottage image. There was a knife slicing bread on the chopping board by itself, a spoon stirring a cup of coffee even though no one was touching it, and when a frying pan floated out of one of the cupboards by itself and onto the stove, Star found herself backing up against the wall in horror.

'Are you OK, dear? You look like you've seen a ghost.'

'What the hell is this?' Star said, backing away, her heart racing, adrenaline flooding her body so she was in full fight-or-flight mode – right now she wanted to run away, far far away.

Everything suddenly stopped moving and Claudia's welcoming face turned to one of worry and fear.

Movement caught her eye on the other side of the room and Star was shocked to see a huge snake sliding across the floor towards her. As it got close, it opened its huge mouth and hissed at her.

Star turned around and ran. She burst outside and immediately noticed a hosepipe and sponge washing the car opposite with no one else near it to touch it, a tree in another garden was having its branches pruned by a pair of shears that no one was holding. She ran back to her house and slammed the door behind her and then pushed a heavy ottoman in front of it.

She'd moved into the Twilight Zone. And right now she'd rather face the hordes of press than have to face this.

Wolf was just getting dressed when Mulberry, his owl, landed on his windowsill with a squawk.

He opened the mini fridge he kept in his bedroom and tossed Mulberry a dried cricket which he gobbled up.

'What's wrong?'

Mulberry always turned up when there was some kind of problem and Wolf would have to spend the next ten minutes or more trying to guess what the problem was.

Mulberry started twittering away, his monologue filled with the occasional hoot and squawk, flapping his wings as he tried to explain. Not for the first time, Wolf wondered about charming him to talk properly like someone had done with Viktor but his conversations with Viktor weren't exactly the highlight of his week so he was reluctant to give Mulberry the same skill. Mulberry had come into his life shortly after he'd become mayor at eighteen, twelve years before. The owl had clearly decided Wolf needed a familiar and taken on that role. But his communication skills left a lot to be desired and Wolf had spent many an hour trying to guess what Mulberry wanted to say, like a rather frustrating game of charades.

Suddenly there was a loud, urgent knocking on his door and Wolf guessed that this particular problem was about to be explained, which would save him trying to guess. He ran downstairs, his shirt flapping around him, to find a very distressed Claudia on his doorstep.

'She's a mundane.'

'What?'

'Star Brightheart. I just invited her over for breakfast and she walked in, saw my magic and she completely freaked out.'

'What exactly did she see?'

'I don't know, I was slicing bread, stirring the coffee, I was just making breakfast and she acted like she'd never seen magic before in her life. Then Colin came out from his little cubbyhole and you know what he's like, he hates everyone. Then she ran away and barricaded herself in her house.'

'Shit. She can't be a mundane. Her blood had so much power running through it, I could feel it through the bloody envelope.' He quickly did up a few buttons on his shirt.

'Could it be she used someone else's blood to get the house? She was desperate to get away from her life, maybe that desperation caused her to take extreme measures.'

'But she would have to know about witches and magic to do that. She might know a witch out there beyond the village walls and it's possible this witch told her about this village and gave her the blood to get in, but then she would have known all about magic and wouldn't have been freaked when she saw it. I need to talk to her. If she is a mundane, we need to get her out of here, quick.'

He followed Claudia out of the house. 'Did you tell anyone else before you came here?'

'Well, Tom and Maggie were outside in their garden when I came to you, I might have mentioned it to them. Oh and Phillipe too.'

'Shit.' Wolf broke out into a run. Already people were starting to gather in small groups, talking about their newcomer, and some people were clearly heading over that way to see this for themselves.

Wolf ran down Star's road and hammered on her door as people started to gather behind him.

There was no answer.

He banged on the door again. 'Star, it's Wolf Oakwood. We need to talk.'

He heard a whimper of terror inside.

Dear Gods, what a mess.

He could easily open the door, blow the thing off its hinges, but he didn't want to hurt her or scare her even more.

Viktor, the cat who lived in the house, jumped up onto the windowsill of the lounge and pushed open the window. Wolf clambered through it and saw Star sitting on the ottoman, her back against the front door, her head in her hands. She was visibly trembling and he felt such a huge surge of protectiveness towards her.

'Whose blood did you send to me?'

Her head snapped up in horror and she stared at him. But he didn't need her to answer, he could feel her power bubbling through her, surrounding her. He'd never really had the gift to see people's auras, but he could see little flecks of gold sparking out of her in arcs.

He was suddenly hit with an overwhelming sense of recognition. He knew this woman but he couldn't place from where. Had he perhaps slept with her at some point in the past? That would be bloody awkward if he had and he had no recollection of it. But surely he would remember if he'd slept with her; with her long dark hair down to her waist and her large grey eyes, she was strikingly beautiful. But to judge from the way she was suddenly staring at him, he knew she recognised him too.

Wanting to see her reaction to magic for himself, he summoned the wind and it quickly moved through the house, surrounding her and him, pulling at her hair, dragging at her clothes. She screamed and backed herself into a corner. She was absolutely terrified. He quickly let the wind die and approached her but then something surprising happened. The books flew out of the nearby shelf, smacking him all over his body and face, something that had nothing to do with him or his little storm of wind moments before. But she looked more terrified by this than she had by the wind.

In fact she got up, wrestled the ottoman out the way and, as the books continued to bombard him, she fled out of the house and to the safety of her car. She started the engine and reversed out of the driveway, nearly taking out the windmill in her haste to escape, and then accelerated up the road.

Shit.

There were people gathered on the side of the road as Star tore up it, all staring at her. She had to get out of here, she didn't belong here. She reached the large metal gate but it didn't open for her as it had to let her in yesterday and she had to slam on the brakes.

The guard who had let her in the night before came to her window. 'I'm sorry, Miss Brightheart, we're under strict instructions not to let you leave.'

'You can't keep me prisoner here, open the gate,' Star said.

'I'm sorry, I can't.'

She looked in her mirror and saw crowds gathering behind her, like some kind of zombie horror film in which they clearly wanted blood.

'Please let me go,' Star pleaded.

The guard shook his head.

She scrambled out of the car and started climbing the gate which was easily twelve foot high, maybe more.

'Umm, that's probably not a good idea,' the guard said.

Wolf was suddenly there, bursting through the crowds.

'Star, please come down, we need to talk.'

She carried on climbing.

The crowd was getting closer, with murmurings of discontent.

Wolf turned back to face them. 'Can everyone go back to your homes, I will handle this.'

'If she's a mundane we can't let her leave,' one man shouted out.

'She's not,' Wolf said. 'She's a wildling.'

Now the noises were of disbelief and interest. Star reached the top and straddled it with one leg either side.

'I will take full responsibility for this,' Wolf went on, addressing the crowds. 'But you're clearly making the situation worse, now please can you return to your homes.'

Some started walking away, some stayed, goggling at her like an animal in a zoo.

Wolf walked to the gate, so he was directly underneath her.

'Star, please come down, give me a chance to explain.'

Star shook her head. 'I shouldn't have come. I need to go home.'

'You are home,' Wolf said.

She looked down at him, his sea-green eyes locking with hers. She knew those eyes. She'd seen them before.

Suddenly Wolf rose off the ground so he was level with her, making her scream. As he reached out to grab her, she shrieked and yanked away, toppling over the other side of the gate and plummeted towards the ground. She put her hands out to stop the fall but something grabbed her foot. She looked up to see Wolf had followed her over the gate, hanging upside down and preventing her from falling. But what was preventing him from doing the same? Fear rose up in her and she wriggled and kicked in his grasp but as she did she banged her head against the side of the gate.

'Sleep,' Wolf said.

'What?' Star said, but then it was like she was a puppet and her strings had just been cut. She sagged, her arms hanging uselessly over her head, her body a dead weight she had no control over. Tiredness surged over her in a great wave.

Wolf gathered her up in his arms like she weighed nothing and landed gently on the other side of the gate as it opened to let him back through.

'No,' she muttered feebly.

But before she drifted off to sleep, she heard Wolf whisper in her ear, 'Don't worry. You're safe now.'

And then she knew nothing more.

CHAPTER 3

S tar woke a few moments before opening her eyes and knew straightaway she was home, lying in her bed in her tiny flat in Richmond which overlooked a little leafy courtyard. She could feel that safe, cosy sense of home surrounding her like a warm blanket. It had all been a horrible dream. She breathed in the peace and tranquillity of her home, happy that she was safe from deranged villagers and men with sea-green eyes.

She opened her eyes and realised she was in a lounge she hadn't been in before and gave a little yelp. She sat up and Wolf, sitting next to her on the coffee table, pushed her back down.

'Take it easy, just give yourself a few minutes. I promise you, you're safe, nothing is going to harm you.'

She looked at him. He was a beautiful man with

dark curly hair that hung around his face and sea-green eyes. He was huge though. He had towered over her when he'd come into her house and she could see how big the muscles in his arms and shoulders were. He had huge muscular thighs too. He could literally break her in half if he wanted to. But his eyes were filled with concern for her and, for some reason she couldn't explain, she trusted him. In fact, there was something so familiar about him. She'd thought that when he'd first come into her home – that she knew him – but she didn't know why.

'I know you must be scared and I am sorry for that. The village is your home and I would never want you to be terrified on your first day here. I will explain everything. But first drink this,' he offered out a mug and she looked at it sceptically. He smiled. 'It's just chamomile tea, sweetened with honey.'

She tried to sit up but she felt like all her strength had been sapped from her. She couldn't run away right now, even if she'd wanted to. He put his arm around her shoulders and helped her up. She took a sip of the tea and the warmth and sweetness did make her feel better. He offered out a plate of chocolate brownies and she took one of those and ate it and then she took a second and ate that too, feeling suddenly ravenous.

After a while she started feeling more normal. Or as normal as she could feel after what she'd just witnessed.

She looked at him, and she knew she had met him somewhere, maybe a long time ago. 'Have we met before?'

'No but I thought that too, I feel like I know you.'

They studied each other for a moment but then she shook her head. She would have remembered meeting Wolf Oakwood, he was insanely beautiful.

'Can I go home now?' Star asked.

'If by home you mean Aurora Cottage, then yes, but if you mean you'd like to leave the village then unfortunately I can't let you do that just yet.'

'When you said I could come here, you never said I couldn't leave.'

'People who live here are free to come and go as they wish, but you have stumbled across something here that you don't understand and I need you to stay here for a while, for the next week at least, so you can appreciate our way of life here and get to know us before you decide that life here is not for you. And I'm sure you want an explanation.'

'I don't understand what I saw. It was like something out of a movie.'

'Yes, I know. The simple answer is I'm a witch, in fact all of us are witches in this village. And Star, so are you.'

She stared at him in shock. It felt like someone was playing a horrible trick on her. She could feel the fear rising in her again.

'I know none of this seems real but I can prove it to you.' He looked around the room. 'Choose something on that shelf over there.'

She frowned and glanced over at the bookshelf, which had some weird and wonderful artefacts and ornaments on it. 'The crystal ball.'

Wolf held out his hand and the crystal ball zoomed straight into it.

She gasped, her heart racing again. She felt like she was in a dream and at any moment she would wake up. None of this made sense but what other explanation was there for what she had seen in Claudia's kitchen, for the wind that had come from nowhere and then died again just as quick and the books that had flown out of the shelf? How else could she explain how Wolf had floated up to the top of the gate and stopped her from falling when he was floating himself? Unless this was some big elaborate joke that everyone was in on, and there were hidden wires and remote-control devices, magical powers had to be the only explanation. She almost laughed to herself because she knew how ridiculous that sounded.

She took the crystal ball from him and examined it. There were seemingly no wires, magnets or anything else she could see which might cause it to fly. She passed it back to him. 'Put it back.'

He smiled and sent it floating over to the shelf, sitting back where it was before as if it hadn't moved.

'Wait, move it to the windowsill.'

The crystal ball moved over to the windowsill.

'Anything else you'd like me to move?'

She shook her head and rubbed her hand across her face. 'I feel like I'm going mad.'

Wolf took her hand and immediately she felt an energy, a force zapping through her. She stared at him.

'That's my magic... and yours.'

'Look, I might be able to believe that you have magical powers but I can't do anything like that.'

He smiled and released her hand. 'Those books that smacked me in the face were nothing to do with me.'

'That wasn't me?'

'I'm fairly sure that things like this must have happened to you in the past. Unexplained things that you've just put down to something weird.'

She thought about it. In every house she had ever lived in she'd had weird experiences. She'd thought the houses were haunted. Doors slammed when she was angry, pictures flew off the walls. TVs, computers, phones and other electrical equipment always played up when she was around. She'd looked into it and found that some people were extra conductive for electromagnetic waves. She'd put it down to that. Had that really been her magic?

'I'm guessing from your face you've had strange things happen to you. What about when you were a child? Children's powers are erratic and hard to control.'

'I have lots of weird memories of things happening when I was a child but my parents always convinced me it was just the wind or just my overactive imagination and it was easier to believe in that than believing magic was actually real. Believing in that felt like believing in Santa or the tooth fairy – it would be ridiculous.'

She had a sudden memory of playing with a boy called Cub on a regular basis in the woods behind the village and he had shown her some magic. She'd been around fourteen when they'd met in a towering maple tree that hung over the village wall. She had been enthralled by his magic and by him. Her parents hadn't believed her when she'd told them what he could do. The one time she had brought her mum to the woods to introduce him, her mum couldn't even see him, when he'd been sitting in the tree as clear as day. It had made her doubt everything.

She swallowed the lump in her throat because Cub had been really important to her and one day she could no longer find him. It was as if he'd never existed in the first place. It wasn't just that he wasn't there, she couldn't even find the tree they used to hang around in or the village walls where the tree was located. It was as if the whole thing had never happened. After he'd disappeared, she'd wondered for years if she had conjured him up in her mind because of the stress of her dad being sick and then dying. One of her mum's friends who dabbled in counselling had even told her mum that it was stress-induced hallucinations and Star had started to believe it too. Now it seemed he had been real, as was all the magic he'd shown her. Her whole life had been a lie and the worst part had been losing him. It wasn't just losing him physically when she could no longer find him that hurt, but losing him in her mind, thinking to herself that he – and therefore what they had shared – had never been real.

He had been a good friend and she hadn't had many of those in her life. But later that friendship had turned to love. And although it was silly to expect a young teen romance to last forever, he'd been the only person, apart from her parents, to ever tell her he loved her and that still stood today. There had never been anyone serious for her. And while she could hardly describe a childhood love as something serious, she had dismissed his existence. But if he and his magic had been real, then his feelings for her, however brief, were real too.

'You OK? You look upset.'

'I'm just realising how much I've dismissed over the years. And how much I've missed out on because of that.'

Like her first kiss and her first love and, while it was an innocent and sweet love that probably wouldn't have stood the test of time, she should never have dismissed it. It had been real. She had been loved.

'Tell me more about your family. Did any of them have powers?' Wolf said.

She shook her head trying to clear it of memories of Cub. She needed to deal with that revelation at another time. She cleared her throat. 'I was adopted. I know nothing about my birth parents. I don't even know their names.'

'And you grew up in Whimbles?'

'Yes. I lived there until I was sixteen.'

He narrowed his eyes. 'Is Star your first name?'

'No, Star is my middle name. Midnight is my first name. Brightheart is my adopted parents' name, but they were apparently told they had to keep my first and middle names.'

'You were born here,' Wolf said.

She sat up in surprise. 'What?'

'There are not many of us Midnight-born children. Every one is called Midnight. I'm Midnight Wolf.'

Her heart leapt in alarm. 'Does that mean my birth parents could still be here?'

He frowned. 'I wouldn't have thought so. If they were here then I think you would have grown up here too.'

'I was left in a cardboard box on my adoptive parents' doorstep. What if I was born here and then dumped outside the village and my birth parents just carried on living here as if I didn't exist?'

'I can't see that happening. If your parents named you Midnight and told your adopted parents they had to keep your name, they wanted you to know you were born here. Why do that if they wanted to pretend you didn't exist. We should be able to find out more about you and your birth parents easily enough. There should be a record of your birth in the village archives.'

Her mind whirled at the prospect of finding out more information on her birth parents.

'I've wondered for so long who they were, why they didn't want me, why I wasn't enough for them. But I've long ago accepted that I was never going to find out anything more about them. And there was a huge part of me that didn't even want to know. They didn't want me, why should I want anything to do with them? There was no explanation left with me in the cardboard box about why they couldn't look after me, no declaration of love, just a little note to say my name was Midnight Star and that it was important that I kept my name so one day I could find out who I was. I had no idea what that meant but now that message makes more sense. My parents wanted me to come back here, although I don't know why if they aren't here. But this explains so much, why this place felt like home, why I felt such a pull to here.'

'It also explains why you were never taught to use

your magic – presumably your adoptive parents didn't know.'

'I guess not.'

'There's kind of an unwritten rule that witch children are not adopted out to mundanes, for this exact reason. You should never have grown up without knowledge of your magic.'

'Mundanes?'

'Sorry, that's the rather harsh name we use to refer to those without magic.'

'And you called me a wildling before?'

'Yes, that's what we call someone with magic who doesn't know they have it – or they might know they have it but were never taught how to use it. We might see wildling children who didn't know they were witches, but it's very rare to get to your age and not know. Your magic gets stronger as you get older; I'm surprised you've never met another witch before who didn't realise what you were.'

'There are more of you out there?'

'Yes, thousands of us, in every country in the world. We have to be discreet about when and how we use our magic in front of mundanes for obvious reasons. This village was set up hundreds of years ago for those that don't want to live a secret life anymore. Here, we can do what we want without fear or judgement. Hence the reason we get all newcomers to sign NDAs and the only visitors we allow in are relatives.

We obviously don't want our way of life here to get out.'

She shook her head. It was all so much to take in. Her life had changed in seconds and there would be no going back.

'Can I talk to my mum about this, my adopted mum?'

'If you can trust her, you can tell her you're a witch and ask her any questions about your childhood. She might be able to fill in some gaps or explain a few things. But don't mention Midnight Village.'

She nodded.

'Tell me about your cakes,' Wolf said.

'What?'

'I recognised you from your photo on your application, so I looked you up. You're quite the celebrity.'

'It was never supposed to be that way. I just started making cupcakes to help people, using different herbs for different reasons. Cakes that would cure headaches or help people feel less anxious or to heal a broken heart.'

'You made magic cakes.'

'No, it was just herbs and spices. Coriander, rose petals, lavender, that kind of thing.'

'Herbs do have their place in witchcraft and spells, but there's a lot more to magic than just sprinkling a few herbs. Tell me what you were thinking when you made a cake to reduce anxiety.'

'Well, calming thoughts, I suppose.'

'And what do you think about when you make a cake for a woman who was cheated on by their husband?'

'I say things like, you're a strong, powerful woman and you are going to be much better off without that person in your life, you will be happier, more successful, more content.'

'And your cakes work, I've seen the reviews. Thousands of them all saying how they did the job. Taste pretty good too if the reviews are to be believed. That's because you add magic to your cakes. You've been making magic cakes for the last five years.'

She stared at him in shock. 'No, I can't have been.'

'And your career took off, even celebrities endorsed your cakes. You've been on TV pushing your magic cakes on the world and you had no idea what you were doing. That's quite incredible really. You were completely self-taught and you didn't even know you were doing it.'

'I thought it was just the herbs,' Star said, quietly, feeling incredibly naïve.

'And tell me what happened with Cleo Walsh, the celebrity food critic.'

Star blushed. 'I don't know what happened. She ate one of my cakes and nearly died from food poisoning, or so she says. I think she must have had an allergic reaction to one of the ingredients, though I can't think what. It was just normal stuff, sugar, butter, flour, milk, eggs, and she would know if she was allergic to eggs. I've done a ton of research into the herbs and I know which ones are safe to use and which parts of the plant are good and which are not, so I know it can't be the herbs either.'

'Which herb did you use?'

'Ginseng.'

'Vitality of life.'

'Yes exactly. She wanted a cake for success. Vile, horrible woman. She has reviewed food and restaurants all over London and her reviews are so horrible and damaging. She gets invited on TV shows just because her reviews are so nasty and it always causes contro- versy. One of my friends, Tig, owned a restaurant and Cleo came one night to review the food. The review was so damning that Tig had to close the restaurant as no one came after that, despite thousands of five-star reviews from previous customers. Cleo literally ruined her life. When Cleo came to me to ask for a cake for success, a huge part of me wanted to say no. I didn't want her to have success and I didn't want her to review my cakes.'

'What made you change your mind?'

'I have no idea. But I've never turned down a request for a cake before and I thought she might leave me a bad review if I refused so I made it and sent it to her. Within seconds of her eating it, she was vomiting so hard she could barely breathe, she bled from her eyeballs, she had seizures. I mean, really horrible stuff. The whole thing was caught on a live video, well the start of it until the paramedics arrived. It was awful. But there's no way my cake could have done all that. The police were called because they believed she'd been poisoned with rat poison or something horrid. They analysed the cake and found nothing untoward. But once she was better Cleo spared no time going to the press and telling them I tried to kill her. And the story and video just blew up.'

Wolf frowned, 'I'm afraid I believe your cake was responsible. What were you thinking about when you were making that cake?'

'I don't know, probably how vile and evil she was.'

'You poured hate into the cake, that was the thing that poisoned her.'

Star's stomach twisted with horror and she stood up in shock. 'No! She nearly died. I... almost killed her. I hate the woman but I would never...'

'It's OK.'

'It really isn't.' She started pacing the room. Her cakes had always been intended to help people. She'd obviously met a lot of people in her life who had upset her or made her angry, it was horrible to think she might have inadvertently caused them pain too. Tears sprang to her eyes as she remembered the horrific video of Cleo after eating her cake. She had done that to her. She was a horrible person.

Wolf stood up and snagged her arm as she paced past him, putting his hands on her shoulders.

'It's not your fault,' Wolf said. 'You won't be the first witch that accidentally hurts someone with your magic nor the last. But we need to make sure this kind of thing never happens again.'

'It won't happen again because I'm never making a cake for anyone ever again. Christ, I had no idea what I was doing, I could have done some serious damage to other people too.'

'Judging by the reviews, you've helped thousands of people with your cakes. You're a good person Star, don't let one little blip put you off.'

'It's a bit more of a blip, she nearly died.'

'But she didn't. Now you know, you can make sure you're more careful when making cakes in the future. You need to learn how to handle your magic.'

She let out a heavy breath. It *was* an accident. She would never deliberately hurt anyone, no matter how hateful they were. She couldn't punish herself over this. She just had to learn how to be better.

'OK, is there some kind of school?'

'No, sadly there are no magical academies or schools, despite what the movies depict. But I can teach you. I'd really like you to stay here in Midnight, at least until you have a better understanding of your magic. The village is a friendly supportive place, there are lots of people here that can help you. Then if you wish to leave the village after that you will of course be free to go.'

She thought about it for a moment. Her cupcake business was gone. Almost everyone she knew in London hated her. The door on her life before she came here was well and truly closed, so she needed to embrace her new existence. She'd always felt so different from everyone and now she knew why. She wanted to understand this way of life: even if she never used her magic, she wanted to make sure she had control of it.

She nodded. 'OK. I'll stay.'

Wolf smiled and for the first time she really felt like she'd made the right decision in coming here.

CHAPTER 4

Wolf closed his front door and started walking Star back to her house. Charles, his elderly neighbour, glared at them both as they walked past, something that Star couldn't help but notice. His dog Frankie yapped at them incessantly too.

'That's Charles,' Wolf muttered under his breath. 'He complains about everything.'

'Really?'

'He knocked on my door a few weeks ago to complain that the winter solstice is on the twenty-second this year instead of the twenty-first, as if I have control over such things. He seemingly doesn't like anyone so don't take it personally.'

To his surprise, Star waved and smiled at him. 'Morning Charles, nice to meet you.'

Charles's scowl deepened and Wolf had to suppress a bubble of laughter.

'Well I think you've made an enemy for life there.'

'I'll win him round.'

'I wouldn't pin your hopes on that,' Wolf said. With her sunny disposition, Star was everything Charles hated in the world, but Wolf had to admire her positive attitude. In fact, there was quite a lot to like about Star Brightheart.

Something had happened when he'd touched her. When he'd caught her from falling off the gate, when he'd held her hand, there had been this weird feeling he couldn't shake. He'd thought what he was feeling was their magic touching, which was quite normal, especially when two witches had great strength. But it was more than that and he didn't know what it was. Something in her called to him, their connection much stronger than that he'd ever felt with any other witch before.

He was attracted to her; he couldn't deny that. But as soon as he'd entered her house, he'd felt this incredible pull to her that went way beyond a physical attraction. It was something else, something more.

He needed some space away from her for a few days. For his sake and for hers.

It was so much for her to take in and he just wanted her to spend a day or two settling into the village, meeting people, getting used to the way of life here, before he started teaching her about her magic. It was also important that the villagers got to know her so they could see she wasn't a risk to them. She hadn't had the best of starts here but Midnight was such a lovely community and he wanted her to be a part of that, he wanted the villagers to want her to be a part of it too.

He watched Star as she walked through the village, spotting the little bits of magic that were happening in people's day-to-day lives: a dog lead taking a dog for a walk, the morning post being delivered, envelopes flying through the air, Mrs Kendle picking fresh flowers from her garden from the comfort of her sunlounger. Now that Star understood what Midnight was, she was clearly finding the whole thing charming. And he found her wonder so endearing. He'd never looked at the village through new eyes before. It must be exciting and scary all at the same time.

'What's with the hot weather? It's the middle of December and it's like a hot day in the height of summer. Is that some kind of witchy magic too?'

'In a way, yes. But actually the village was cursed around thirty years ago.'

He realised how blasé he sounded about a curse. Because he'd grown up here, the weird weather had always been a way of life for him. But as Star's eyes widened in shock he thought he'd better explain.

'Not cursed as in a plague of locusts, blood in the water or the death of a firstborn child – it's nothing that sinister or scary. The witch who cursed us was a weather witch. She had the power to change the weather at will. She lived here and there was a bit of a situation and she was forced to leave so she gave us this as a parting gift. It snows in the summer, rains in the spring and we have scorching hot sunshine in the winter. We get a lot of storms here too, high winds, torrential rains. We adapt. It could be worse. We could have been cursed with boils or eternal fleas.'

She smiled. 'What did you lot do to piss her off?'

He was ashamed of the answer to that. The mayor at the time had completely taken advantage of his position and of the witch who cursed them.

'It was before my time,' he said, trying to distance himself from that disaster.

'And none of you could ever break it, in thirty years? That's some powerful magic.'

'We've tried but no. Curses are funny like that. They generally can only be lifted by the person who placed the curse or until they reach its conclusion. And weather is a powerful thing to play with. I can call the wind temporarily, but I couldn't impact on the weather for a whole village – believe me, I've tried. Weather witches are very rare. And we've never had one in the village since she left. So it is what it is. It's been like this my whole life so I don't know any different except when I leave the village wearing shorts and t-shirt and realise it's raining outside the gates.'

'How does something like that even work – is there some kind of magical bubble around the village with its own internal ecosystem?'

'Honestly, I don't know. Being a witch doesn't mean we're all-knowing in every type of magic and spell. Lots of magic has been lost over the years as sometimes only one or two witches will know how to do something and the magic and knowledge from hundreds of years ago was never written down. We all have our specialities, there are some people that are particularly good at potions, for example. A lot of our magic is to do with the elements and most witches will have one element they are better or stronger at than the other elements. So there are those that are good at controlling water and others that are better with wind. There are some in the village that can simply look at something and it will burst into flames if they so wish. We all know how to charm a lawnmower to mow our own lawns, that stuff is easy, but changing the weather is very complex. I wouldn't even know where to start.'

They walked on as she continued to look around.

'I made it snow once.'

He stopped dead. 'What?'

She turned to look at him, laughing, her hair blowing in the wind. 'Not really, but I thought I did. I was a child and I was desperate for a snow day from school. The weather had been threatening to snow for the whole week before but, apart from a few tiny feeble flakes, the big six-foot snow drifts were nowhere to be seen. So, when I went to bed, I envisaged freezing wind and snow from the North Pole, the tallest mountains and the coldest places I could imagine, tearing across the seas and hills towards us and pouring out of the sky above me. When I woke up the next morning, we were snowed in. Three foot of the stuff and no chance of any vehicle getting in or out. I had three snow days in a row. It was brilliant and I was convinced for so long that I was the one responsible.'

'You... you summoned the snow?'

'No,' she laughed. 'Of course not. You said that's powerful witch stuff and that weather witches are really rare. I couldn't have done that. I make magical cakes and I didn't even know I was doing that, but it's safe to say I'm not going to be changing the world.'

'You have incredible power Star, I'd venture that you're probably one of the strongest witches I've met in a very long time.'

He could feel that just by standing near her.

'I don't know what could possibly make you think that. You wait until I try and charm a lawnmower or a saucepan, I imagine you'll be putting out fires left, right and centre, metaphorical and literal.'

'Great power doesn't mean great skill. It will take time to learn these things, it doesn't take anything away from your strength. I can feel it. Every witch has an energy and we can all feel each other's power. Some can even see that power like an aura. I can't do that, but when your emotions are heightened, like this morning when you were scared, I could see it then, sparking out of you like little fireworks. I've never seen that before. With the power you have, it's entirely possible you summoned the snow.'

'Are you saying I'm a weather witch?'

'I don't know – like I said, I don't fully understand that kind of magic. But those that have great power can do incredible things. Maybe you don't have to have full control of all the weather to be able to summon the snow.'

'Or it could have been a complete coincidence and I had nothing to do with the snow at all.'

'It's possible. But from my experience there are no coincidences when it comes to magic.'

They carried on walking, Wolf's mind whirling at the prospect of her being a weather witch. If she was, the other villagers would be wary of her, a few might even be scared. Some would see it as a good thing but whenever he'd heard or read about a weather witch from history, it was never tales of good. In fact, as a child, his bedtime stories, or the fantasy kids' books he'd read, were always filled with evil weather witches and great battles in which they destroyed whole armies by summoning terrible weather with a wave of their hands. And while that was fantasy and he was sure there were hundreds of weather witches who lived simple, quiet lives, he would have to keep the possibility that Star was one to himself and he needed her to keep it quiet too.

'I have a ton of questions,' she interrupted his thoughts.

'I'm sure you do and I'm happy to answer them.'

'What's the winter solstice?'

'It's a celebration of light. The solstice, the twenty-second of December this year, is our shortest day so we celebrate the sun and light returning. We have a few days of village festivities coming up. We have a garland ceremony the day after tomorrow and then a Yule tree ceremony where everyone will make decorations and ornaments for the tree. The winter solstice is the day after that and in the morning we'll have a procession of light which as the newest member of the village you'll be taking part in. The winter solstice marks the start of Yule or Yuletide, which is twelve days of celebrations. Everyone here will celebrate differently but in general most people will decorate their homes and the village with evergreen trees and foliage as a symbol that even in the darkest days there is still life. There are lots of candles and lanterns and fairy lights. There is feasting. Some will sing and dance.'

'Do you dance?'

'No.'

She snorted her laughter and tried to turn it into a cough and he felt his mouth tugging up into a smile. 'Why are you amused by the thought of me dancing?'

'You're very serious. I can't imagine you dancing.'

He couldn't imagine himself dancing either.

'Is that why my house is decorated with a tree and other greenery, for the solstice not Christmas?'

'That's right. Witches were celebrating winter festivals like the solstice and Yule long before Christmas came along. There are some of us that still celebrate Christmas alongside our Yuletide celebrations as they grew up outside the village but a lot of us don't have a special day on the twenty-fifth. Nithya decorated your house for you. She's kind of appointed herself as a welcoming committee for any new arrivals and, while I would never think of decorating someone's home or doing a welcome hamper like she does, I think it's a lovely thing to do.'

'It was. It made me feel so at home. I will have to thank her when I meet her. So if the solstice is a celebration of the shortest day, does that still stand now the seasons have reversed because of the curse?' Star asked.

'Yes. Which feels especially frustrating as normally we'd enjoy long summer days but our days enjoying the warmer weather in December are the shortest.'

'That weather witch really did hate you lot with that gift.'

45

'Yeah, she had a lot to be angry about. I suppose I should be grateful really because she could have done much worse.'

She could have wiped out the entire village with a tsunami or a hurricane, her powers were that strong.

'As mayor of the village, are you the most powerful?'

He blinked at the sudden change in subject. 'No, at least I don't think so. There is no ranking of power here, and I wouldn't know how we could do that even if we wanted to as everyone has their strengths and weaknesses when it comes to spells and charms. And for the most part, I can't feel if someone is stronger or weaker than me. Occasionally, you meet a witch and you can feel it then, this great reservoir of power, like I can feel with you, but it doesn't happen very often. But to answer your question, the mayor is always a descendant of one of the eight village founders, so it's not a hierarchy of power that gave me the position of mayor, more like a hereditary thing. Plus the power of the vote just like in any normal election.'

They walked onto the village green.

'This is the centre of the village,' Wolf said. 'If you imagine the village being laid out like a giant tree, all the branches or the roads lead back to this point. So if you ever get lost, just follow the road back to the centre and you should be able to find the right road to your home or anywhere else in the village. All the road names are displayed quite clearly at the start of each road. You'll find the village hall at the end of Holly Lane, if you need it. The shops are down Stardust Street,' he pointed to a street on the opposite side of the green. 'If you go to the shops, Ezra will help you set up your account. I live in Rowan Street and you live in Ivy. But it won't take you long to get the lie of the land.'

'I didn't realise there were shops here, what kind do you have?'

He smiled as he thought about the shops. As a child he'd always wanted to be an architect so he could design buildings, homes, hotels and shops. His childhood sketchpads were filled with weird and wonderful drawings of different buildings. When the opportunity had arisen for him to design and build, magically of course, a street of shops, he had let his imagination get a bit carried away. And partly it had been for his brother Lynx and some of the other children in the village at the time, a desire to create a place that was truly magical. But a big part of it had been for him too. While there had been those in the village who thought the road of shops was not in keeping with the cosy cottage feel of Midnight, it was still his favourite part of the village, even after all these years.

'You're probably best checking that out for yourself. There's a wide range. You can get most things from Stardust Street. Stardust, in magic, is largely used for making hopes and wishes come true so it seemed a good name for the road, as you can get pretty much anything you need or wish for down there.'

'So is the village largely self-sufficient? Does everyone just move here and then never leave? What do people do for money and food?'

'Our way of life here is pretty much the same as that in any mundane village. Some people retire here, some work from home or work in the shops here in the village, some have normal mundane jobs outside of the village. There are some food shops in the village but a lot of people will go out to the shops or supermarkets in Whimbles or other neighbouring towns or have their shopping delivered from the big supermarkets. We have deliveries from Amazon or other retailers every day for the various needs of the villagers. The only difference really is that all deliveries are made to the gates and then the village logistics team delivers everything to the relevant houses.'

'You mean magically?'

'Sometimes. Some people get funny about having their food shopping flying through the air and landing outside their house. Eggs have sometimes got broken or fruit has got bruised with an overexuberant charm. Some people prefer the food to be hand-delivered to their front doors.'

'So magic isn't always the be-all and end-all?'

'As I said before, having magical abilities doesn't

necessarily mean you're skilled in those abilities; some people's magic leaves a lot to be desired.'

As they walked towards Tom and Maggie's house, he could see them in the garden tending to their plants. Apart from his gran, Zofia, they had lived here the longest and were probably some of the biggest gossips in the village. Once Maggie had heard something, it took less than four hours for the whole village to know and, with a population of nearly seven hundred people, it was quite impressive. They would be the perfect people to introduce Star to. Maggie might also be able to shed some light on Star's parents as she was the village secretary and had been for more years than he'd been alive.

He caught Star's arm to get her to stop. 'Let me introduce you to a few people.'

She nodded and turned to greet her new neighbours, but he snagged her arm again.

'Maybe don't mention the huge amount of power you have. To anyone.'

Her eyes widened in alarm. 'Why?'

'Well, weather witches are like that pot of gold at the end of the rainbow. They're incredibly rare and some of the villagers will get very excited. If they believe you are one, you'll be hounded every day with stuff like, "I'm having a barbeque this afternoon, can you make sure it's sunny," or "I'm entering my cucumber into the biggest cucumber competition, I need lots of rain," or 'Could we have snow for the winter solstice." That wouldn't be much fun for you. But also there's that fear of the unknown. Some people might be scared of someone who has that much power.'

A lot of people would be scared but he didn't need to tell her that.

'Why would they be scared of me? I'm not going to hurt them.'

'They don't know you, they don't know what you're capable of.'

'Well neither do I, but I really don't think I'm anything to be feared. Unless they eat one of my poisonous hate-filled cakes, then they might have something to worry about.'

'Yeah, maybe we don't mention that either.'

She rolled her eyes. 'Surprisingly, I wasn't going to lead with that. If you can sense that I have this power, what's stopping other people from sensing it too?'

'Some of them won't recognise it. And those that do, we'll just tell them it's because you're a wildling and the power has gone unused all these years.'

'Is that true?'

'I guess it's possible, I've never met an adult wildling before and I'm willing to bet none of the villagers have either, so they won't know any different.'

'Christ, I really am a freak of nature.'

'I'd say you're unique. Now plaster a smile on your

face and let's sell your new neighbours the best version of yourself.'

She did as she was told, smiling in a way that was slightly inane and unhinged. He rolled his eyes.

'Morning Tom, Maggie,' Wolf called out and they looked over from squabbling over whether to deadhead the roses.

Maggie's eyes lit up once she saw who he was with. Tom, too, was obviously curious.

'Got yourself a wildling, have you?' Tom said, bluntly.

They started wandering closer.

'Yes, let me introduce you. This is Star Brightheart, Midnight Star,' Wolf said, meaningfully.

They both gasped and Maggie rushed over to shake her hand. 'You're Midnight-born, how wonderful. We don't get many of those round here. Who are your parents, maybe I know them?'

Star shook both their hands. 'Hello, nice to meet you. I'm afraid I don't know, I was adopted.'

Maggie put her hand to her chest in shock. 'By mundanes?'

'By non-witches, yes,' Star corrected. 'My adopted parents were wonderful people, but they obviously had no clue about magic or how to teach me how to handle my powers.'

'Oh how awful. I wonder why your birth parents let

you get adopted by mundanes. Thank goodness you've come home. We can help you.'

This was what Wolf wanted, he wanted the village to rally round Star, not be scared of her or resent her because she was a wildling.

'That's very kind,' Star said. 'I'm finding it all very intimidating right now. All of this is so new to me, I feel like I'm in some kind of bizarre dream. Any help you can give me would be very much appreciated.'

Tom was looking at her suspiciously. 'If you're Midnight-born, we would have a record of it in our village archives. There would also be a record of your parents too.'

'Yes. I have the archive files in my house, let me dig out the right year. How old are you?' Maggie said.

'Thirty,' Star said.

'Same as me,' Wolf said.

Maggie clicked her fingers and, with a puff of gold sparks, an old leather book appeared in her hand.

'This is a record of all the births, deaths and marriages in Midnight that year,' Maggie said, flicking through the book. 'The current book is kept in the village hall and maintained by the village secretary and the mayor,' she nodded in Wolf's direction. 'You can see that when there is a birth, we write down the date, time of birth and name of the baby and of course the name of the parents. What month is your birthday?' Maggie said, flicking through the pages.

Star put her hand on the book to stop her. 'Wait, so this record will have the names of my birth parents in?'

'Yes,' Maggie nodded, clearly keen to find out Star's heritage, although Star didn't look as enthusiastic.

Star let out a heavy breath. 'Sorry, I just wasn't expecting to find out their names today. I've only just found out I was born in Midnight so it's all come as a bit of a shock.'

'We don't have to look at this now,' Wolf said.

'No it's OK, it's just their names. I suppose it would be good to at least have that. And to find out if they're still here.' She nodded at Maggie. 'I was born in June.'

Maggie flicked through to the right month.

'Oh look, there you are: June twentieth, born at half past eleven at night. You were a summer solstice baby.'

Wolf's heart sank and Maggie gasped theatrically as she suddenly spotted what he already knew.

'That's your birthday too, isn't it Wolf?' Maggie said, excitedly. 'Do you know what that means?'

'Yes, that we can both have a joint birthday party.' He was well aware of the stupid tradition that witches born on the same day in the same place were betrothed. But he certainly wasn't going to tell Star that, nor was he going to do anything about it. Silly stupid traditions, it was utter rubbish. Just because you shared the same birthday with someone, it didn't mean you shared anything else in common with them and being born on the same day was not a good enough reason to spend the rest of their lives together. He cringed because of all the people to discover he was betrothed with Star, Maggie was one of the worst. He had no doubt that before he could escort Star back to her house, half the village would already know. He needed to change the subject and fast. 'What does it say about Star's parents?'

Maggie peered at the writing and shook her head. She snapped her fingers again and her glasses appeared in her hand. Star blinked at the magic.

Maggie put her glasses on and then gasped again before snapping the book shut. She looked aghast as she stared at Tom.

'What does it say?' Tom said, though the colour was already draining from his face as if he knew.

'Star is Rose Blaketon's daughter,' Maggie said, quietly.

Wolf cursed under his breath. Everyone knew who Rose Blaketon was.

'You knew my birth mum?' Star said quietly.

Tom's mouth pulled into a thin line and then suddenly he stormed off into the house and slammed the door.

Wolf wracked his brain as to why Tom would have such a strong reaction to Star's connection to Rose. And then the penny dropped. If the rumours were true, Tom was Star's grandad. He swore again; this was getting worse.

Maggie looked after Tom anxiously. 'Maybe now isn't the best time to talk about this. But if you wanted to know more about your parents, Tom is out tomorrow for most of the day, you could come for a chat then and I'll tell you everything I know.'

Star chewed her lip. 'It's obviously not a happy story.'

Maggie shook her head. 'It's not, I'm afraid. Your dad...' she looked back at the front door. 'He was not a good man.'

Star looked at him. 'Do you know what happened?'

'I know of your mum and a little about what happened, but it was before my time.'

'Are my parents still here in the village?'

Maggie shook her head. 'They both left many years ago, well thirty to be exact. Come and see me tomorrow and I'll explain everything.'

Wolf put his hand on Star's back. She looked like a rabbit in the headlights. 'Come on, let's get you back home.'

Star nodded. 'Thanks Maggie, I'll see you tomorrow.'

They started walking away.

'Wolf, can I have a quick word before you go,' Maggie called after them.

Wolf came back to her, leaving Star on her own.

'I think you should come with her tomorrow.'

Wolf shook his head. 'I don't think I need to be there.'

He glanced over at Star, looking a little lost and scared, and right now he just wanted to wrap her in his arms and protect her from the world. But he didn't want to be there for her in a comforting capacity. He wanted things to stay professional between them and he'd already crossed that boundary by holding her hand.

'She needs someone with her,' Maggie insisted.

'She has you.'

'Rose left a blood memory for her.'

Wolf swore again. If Star accessed the blood memory, she would get to see her mum for the first time.

'I'll be there. What time is best?'

'Ten. Tom will be gone for most of the day so she can take as long as she needs.'

He nodded and walked back to Star.

'What was that about?' Star asked as they started walking towards her house.

Wolf knew he had to tell her about the message, even though her day had already been overwhelming. 'Your mum left you a blood memory. It's a message forged with your blood and hers. Only you and your mum can access it so no one else will know what it says. There is a smudge of blood on your birth record.

When you touch it, you'll be able to see your mum, like a video message playing in your head.'

'Oh Jesus Wolf, this day is just getting weirder and weirder. Did I hit my head really badly when I fell off the gate and this is all just some kind of concussion-induced hallucination? My mum left me a message in her blood?'

'Your blood and hers. She would have pricked both of your fingers, held them together when she gave you the message and then wiped both of your fingers on the record, sealing it there forever.'

By the look on Star's face he probably didn't need to have gone into the specifics of how the blood message was done.

Star let out a heavy sigh. 'I spent so many years of my life filled with anger and resentment over my parents. They never came to see me, never wrote, never made any contact and I told myself I was better off without them. I don't know if I want to see this message.'

'And that's absolutely fine. That message will always be there for you to see it if and when you're ready – and if that's never then that's OK too. I can't begin to imagine what it's like to live with knowing you were abandoned in the way that you were. I don't know what it was like to grow up without knowing who your birth parents are and who you really are. So you handle this in the way you need to handle it.'

Star shook her head. 'I guess I'll go along to see what Maggie has to say. Living in a village this size, someone is bound to talk to me about my parents whether I want to hear it or not. I don't want to pop into the local shop and suddenly find out my dad is an axe murderer. At least this way, I'm choosing to find out my history rather than have it thrust on me unexpectedly. I guess I'll make a decision tomorrow whether to hear this message or not.'

'That's a good plan. And while your dad wasn't an axe murderer, he wasn't... kind or respectable so you need to prepare yourself for that.'

'Thanks for the doom-mongering.'

'I don't think I can dress this up with a fancy ribbon. I wish I could. I wish there was some chink of light I could share with you, but your dad was an asshole.'

'And my mum?'

He thought about the best way to describe her mum after what she had done. 'I didn't know her but I think she was a little... misguided.'

'What does that mean?'

'Why don't we talk about this tomorrow with Maggie, she'll be able to answer your questions better than I can. She was actually here when your mum was living here. My knowledge is based on rumours and hearsay from many years ago. I certainly don't know all the ins and outs like Maggie does.'

And Wolf certainly didn't know why Tom had

reacted the way he had when meeting his grand-daughter for the first time. This wasn't what he wanted for Star's first day in the village.

'Are you OK?'

'I think I'm a million miles away from being OK right now.' She sighed. 'Why did Maggie get so excited about us sharing a birthday?'

He was not going to add that particular cherry to the disaster that was her day.

'Just the coincidence of it.'

She looked at him. 'You're lying. It pissed you off and I don't think it's because you don't like to share.'

He sighed. 'I am lying but let's leave that ridiculousness for another day. I think you've had enough crazy for one day.'

'I'd agree with that.'

His head was buzzing with all this himself, he couldn't begin to imagine what she was feeling. She was Rose Blaketon's daughter. How would the villagers react when they found that out? Would they want Star to leave? His priority had always been to ensure the safety of the villagers but, now she was one of them, her safety was his priority too.

And then, to top off his crappy day, he spotted Jessica walking towards them. The bane of his life. She saw them and crossed over the street to talk to them, or specifically him.

'Oh Wolf, how lovely to see you,' Jessica said,

twirling one strand of hair round her finger. 'I hear you've got yourself a little pet to train.'

He watched Star frown and with good reason. He was angry about that on Star's behalf.

'Wow, that's rude,' Star said. 'I've had a really crappy start to my first day in Midnight and if I'm going to stay here, and I haven't decided whether I will, I really need support from the villagers, not sarcasm.'

'Star's right,' Wolf said. 'That was rude and not what I expect in this village.'

Jessica stared at him with wide eyes and then let out a nervous giggle. 'I was just joking.' She turned to Star. 'I'm Jessica Proudfoot, welcome to Midnight.'

Star gave her a half smile and stuck out her hand. 'Star Brightheart.'

'Lovely to meet you.'

Jessica turned her attention back to Wolf. 'I could help you train her if you like. Maybe you'd like to come round for dinner tonight and we can talk about it.'

'No,' Wolf said and with that he snagged Star's arm and walked away.

'Wolf, *that* was rude,' Star said, once they were far enough away. 'You could at least let the woman down gently.'

'Let me tell you something about Jessica: she's not to be trusted. The snidey comment she made when she came over here, that's her all over, and the smiley greeting after I reprimanded her was completely fake.

She wants to go out with me because if we were to get married she would be mayoress of the village and she would love nothing more than to laud it over everyone. But apart from the fact that Jessica is absolutely not my type, I never date anyone from the village, because of my position.'

'Is that another of the rules of the village?'

'No, it's one of mine. Dating someone from the village would just get messy and awkward. It also feels a bit like an employer–employee relationship, it would be an abuse of my power and could compromise my position. Let's just say I like to keep things separate. I only date people from outside the village.'

She clearly thought about this for a moment. 'So you're rude to her to stop her asking you out?'

'I'm rude to her because she once gave me a love potion.'

She stopped dead and he turned round to look at her.

'What?' Star said.

'I should have kicked her out the village for that. That kind of magic is forbidden.'

She carried on walking next to him. 'Did it work? Did you and her...?'

'No. There is no magic that can make someone do something they don't want to do. Now if I had been attracted to her, if I'd fantasised about having sex with her, but had never taken it any further than that, there is a chance it could have worked, it could have brought forward my deepest desires and I could have acted on it. Temporarily. It's not like I would have been like a man possessed with no control over what my body was doing. But that's why that kind of magic is forbidden. Just because I might have thought about having sex with someone doesn't mean I actually want to do it. There's a big difference.'

'So what happened?'

'She invited me round to discuss something important with regards to the village. Gave me a cup of tea which obviously had this potion in it. And then started undressing ready to have sex.'

'Oh my god.'

'Yeah.'

'It had no effect on you at all?'

'Oh it did, it's kind of the witchy equivalent of Viagra, it made me horny as hell, but not for her. I'm not in the least bit attracted to her, so I definitely didn't want her any more than I did before. But I knew exactly what she'd done. I was furious. I still am, if truth be told.'

'That's awful,' Star said.

'Yes it is.'

'So... you're not allowed to make someone do something they don't want to do.'

'No.'

'But you made me go to sleep. I can assure you sleep was the very last thing I wanted right then.'

He pulled a face. 'Yes, that's a different kind of magic but I am sorry, I was worried you were going to get hurt. And you were so scared, I just wanted to get you away from everyone so I could explain everything to you calmly.'

'It's OK, I'm glad you did. I've always been good at climbing up, not so good at climbing down. I used to get stuck up in so many trees as a child. If you hadn't been there to catch me, I'd have got seriously hurt. And I'm happy I'm here, at least for now.'

They arrived back at her house and he snagged her arm again.

'There's something else you need to know,' Wolf said.

'My bucket is already overflowing.'

'It's about your cat. Well, the cat that lives here. His name is Viktor – as in door, not Vikta, which is the normal pronunciation. One easy way to piss him off for months is to get his name wrong.'

'I think I have bigger things to worry about than offending a cat,' Star said.

'Trust me on this. Viktor,' he said, overemphasising the 'tor' part. 'They say a cat has nine lives, well Viktor has had over a hundred of them and he remembers every single one of them. He is most dissatisfied with this one.'

She stared at him. 'Are you telling me Viktor can talk?'

'Oh yes, he can be very vocal if he wants to be. Sometimes he says nothing, it's just the look of disdain he gives you.'

They reached her front door and she let herself in, leaving the door open for him and he followed her down to the kitchen. Viktor was there curled up in front of the stove. The cat opened one green eye to look at them then he stretched and stood up.

'I presume she knows she's a witch now?' Viktor said.

Star stopped dead.

'You knew she didn't know she was a witch last night when she arrived?' Wolf said, while Star stared at the cat in horror. Maybe this was too much on her first day.

'Of course I knew, she spent an inordinate amount of time unloading her car by hand,' Viktor said disdainfully. 'Twelve journeys it took for her to bring everything in. Any other witch would have unloaded the car in seconds.'

'Why didn't you come and tell me last night?' Wolf said, in exasperation. At least he could have had a calm conversation with Star rather than her being scared to death this morning.

'It is not my problem. And I am not going to be gallivanting round the streets after dark to sort out your lack of diligence. And I didn't tell her because I guessed she might start screaming and I can't abide screaming.'

'You really can speak?' Star said.

Viktor looked at her as if she was stupid and then back at Wolf. 'Is she a nincompoop?'

'Viktor, be kind. She had no idea about magic or witches before she came here. Today has been over-whelming. And you have to admit, a talking cat is pretty unique.'

'I am unique. I'll give you that,' Viktor turned back to Star. 'Yes I can speak. The witch who lived here before the previous occupant charmed me so I can do so, which I was very thankful for. It meant I could finally tell her how I like my tea. I like it warm not hot, served with cream and a half teaspoon of honey. I also like a fresh sprig of lavender on the top. There is a bush outside but you must clean the lavender before placing it in the tea, I will not drink my tea if there are dead bugs floating around in the top of it. I have standards even if you don't,' he looked her up and down disdainfully.

'Viktor!' Wolf said. 'I can kick you out of this village just as easily as any of the residents. Be kind.'

'I'm just saying, has the girl even heard of an iron.'

Star looked down at her clothes. 'I just grabbed something out of my suitcase this morning. I didn't realise there was a dress code.'

Viktor nodded his head with approval. 'She's a snarky one. I like her.'

With that Viktor disappeared out of the cat flap, leaving them alone.

'Is he for real?'

'Unfortunately so.'

'Do any other animals in the village talk?'

'No, some witches have familiars who help or guide in some way but they don't talk. I have an owl, called Mulberry. I wish he would talk sometimes. As familiars go, he's pretty useless.'

She blew her hair out of her face with an impatient huff and started making a pot of tea. He took the kettle off her, waved his hand and let his magic make the tea for her.

'You OK?'

She put down the mug she was holding with a sigh. 'I don't know. My head is buzzing, it's so much to take in. I'm a witch in a village of witches and to top it off my birth parents lived here and I was born here. And apparently my dad was a bit of an ass, which just fills me with that warm fuzzy feeling. I just thought I would come here and live in a quiet little village making cakes for the rest of my life and my entire world has changed. I can't even make cakes ever again in case I accidentally kill someone. I still can't get my head round the fact that Cleo Walsh nearly died because of me, because my hate for her was so powerful. I have a talking cat who has a whole lot of attitude and this village is just unreal and... it scares me a little if I'm honest. If you hadn't been there would the villagers have hurt me to stop me leaving with their precious secret?'

He shook his head and she raised an eyebrow.

He sighed. 'If you had been a mundane, they probably would have stopped you from leaving, physically if necessary, and then modified your memory before dropping you many miles from here.'

'What? And that's supposed to make me feel better?'

'No one would have hurt you, but the life we lead here is too important to let the secret out. And let's face it, most mundanes would have a similar reaction to you if they found out what goes on in here beyond the village gates. They'd be coming for us with pitchforks and burning torches next.'

She sighed. 'There's a huge part of me that just wants to go home and by that I mean not here. But I know I need to learn to control my magic even if it's purely so I don't use it ever again.'

He frowned. 'Your magic is nothing to be ashamed of. You need to accept who you are and celebrate it.'

'I just feel so... lost,' Star said and his heart went out to her. 'All of this was not what I expected when I came here. I thought I'd come here to escape the attention of the press and the public and instead the villagers are looking at me like I'm some kind of freak – or, as Jessica said, an animal in need of training.'

Without thinking, Wolf pulled her into a hug. 'It's going to be OK.'

She stood there in his arms for a few seconds before she tentatively hugged him back, her head leaning against his heart.

Feelings for her slammed into him like a wrecking ball destroying a house. It was instant and painful and oh so wonderful. Lust, need, want, all fought for attention, topped with a need to wrap her in bubble wrap and make sure nothing ever hurt her again. And there was that familiarity again. He'd done this before. He'd held her like this before.

He quickly stepped back. 'Sorry, I shouldn't have done that.'

'I...' she was blushing.

Shit. Had she felt his feelings too?

'I'm glad you did,' she cleared her throat. 'You have a way of calming me down.'

But she went and sat down away from him, which he was thankful for.

'I'm so glad I have you here. Thank you for being just so lovely.'

He frowned slightly; he needed some distance between them. He didn't want her to think he was lovely. 'I should probably go. Get some rest, explore the village, speak to people and when you're ready we can start your lessons in a few days' time. I'll see you tomorrow at Maggie's.'

'OK, thank you for coming with me to do that.'

He nodded and hurried out of the house, because the longer he spent with her the more he wanted to stay.

Maybe it would be a good idea if someone else trained her because being in such close proximity was a recipe for disaster.

CHAPTER 5

Star stepped outside her front door and looked around. There didn't appear to be any neighbours waiting for her with pitchforks so she presumed she was safe for now. She wanted to explore her new home and now seemed as good a time as any. She'd always been fine with her own company before, but she felt so alone in the house, even more so because although she was a witch like all the other villagers, she wasn't one of them. Being a wildling made her different and she'd had a lifetime of being different. This was supposed to be her new home and she didn't want to feel like an outsider here.

'Hello, Star!'

Star looked over to see Claudia in her front garden waving at her and Star wandered over.

'I'm so sorry I scared you earlier, that absolutely wasn't my intention,' Claudia said.

'It's OK, it was just very unexpected but Wolf has explained everything to me now, although it will still take a while to get used to.'

'I can imagine,' Claudia nodded sympathetically, although Star didn't think anyone could really understand what it was like to wake up in a village of witches and find out you're one yourself. 'So you're really a wildling? You had no idea at all about magic?'

'Not really. A lot of weird stuff happened to me as a child but my adopted parents kept on telling me it was my imagination or dismissed it as something else, and out there in the non-magical world it's easier to believe in that than believe in a teapot which can make a cup of tea by itself.'

'Yes of course, it all must be a big shock. And I'm sorry if Colin scared you too.'

'Your snake?'

'Yes, he's a grumpy old man, doesn't like anyone. Don't take it personally.'

'Does he talk?'

'No, only Viktor does that. That's more than enough for one village. While your house was empty, he kept on knocking on my door expecting me to make him a cup of tea every morning. He's so demanding and grumpy if he doesn't get his own way. Rude, too.'

'I heard that.'

Star and Claudia turned round to see Viktor sitting at the end of Claudia's driveway. He scowled at Claudia, lifted his paw and appeared to give Claudia the middle finger – or claw –before sauntering away.

'Did he just swear at you?' Star laughed.

'Yes he did. Little shit. I'd set Colin on him but the poor snake is terrified of him. Never mind that he's an eight-foot python that could crush him to death, every time Colin sees Viktor, he hides in his little cubbyhole and doesn't come out for hours.'

Star shook her head. What kind of monster had she inherited?

'I'm off for a wander round the village, anywhere in particular I should start?'

'You must go and have a look at the fountain in the village green. It's marvellous. And the shops of course. They are certainly something to look at.'

'Thank you, I will.'

She waved goodbye to Claudia and walked up the street, feeling a tiny bit better already. She soon reached the village green and noticed the fountain straight-away. She was surprised she hadn't seen it before but her mind had been buzzing too much. It was a cast-iron work of art with a giant cauldron at the bottom and various potion bottles pouring the water into it. It was right at home in a witchy village. She walked across the green until she got to the entrance to Stardust Street.

The road sign was an arched wrought-iron gate with the name in curly writing at the top. She stepped through and stopped because it was snowing. She looked back at the village green to see it was glorious sunshine beyond the street; the snow was just on this street and it looked magical.

Star felt like a child as she stared at the snow floating gently around her. It wasn't settling, it was dissolving before it hit the ground, but it still looked beautiful, sparkling in the unseasonable sunshine.

'It's just an enchantment,' Charles said, as he stomped past her. 'Everyone always wants snow for the solstice and Yuletide so Wolf has enchanted the street to snow. Silly nonsense if you ask me.'

'Come on Charles, not even you can hate snow,' Star said.

He muttered something that sounded like 'Humbug' and walked off.

And that's when she noticed the shops. They were like something out of Disneyland. The buildings themselves were made from brick and towered two or three storeys above the street. But it was the store fronts that were the most impressive.

The nearest shop to her presumably sold clocks and watches as the doorway was made up with a giant clock face with hands that were turning with the correct time. It was so big she wouldn't even be able to reach the centre pin if she walked inside. Two grandfather clocks stood sentry either side of the doorway, but they were bent and twisted as if they had giant knots in the middle of their trunks. The clocks in the shop looked like little works of art too.

The shop next to that sold candles and two giant six-foot red ones were burning away quite happily either side of the door.

There was a festive feel everywhere, shop windows decorated with green garlands, berries and dried fruits. Little lights twinkled in the windows and there were even lights strewn between the buildings too, which were still sparkling brightly despite the sunshine. There was also the scent of toffee apples, cinnamon and chestnuts floating in the air.

'Hello, I see you're not wearing your bracelet,' a young man with a clipboard came hurrying over to her. 'Are you a relative of one of the residents?'

'Umm no, I'm new in the village. What bracelet?'

'Ah, you're the wildling everyone has been talking about,' the man said. 'You caused quite the commotion this morning, I hear. I was here working so I didn't get to see it. But it was the most excitement we've had around here in years.'

'I'm pleased to provide the entertainment.'

The man laughed, completely missing her sarcasm.

'I'm Ezra and you are?'

'Star Brightheart.'

Ezra consulted his clipboard and she could see it

was more like a tablet or iPad than a clipboard but the screen seemed to change at his will rather than with him touching it.

'We get so many relatives arriving for the winter solstice and the Yule celebrations, it's hard to keep track of them all. Ah here we are, Star Brightheart. Did Wolf explain how all this works?'

'No but he said a nice man called Ezra would help me,' Star said, giving him a winning smile.

It seemed to do the trick.

'Well of course I can.' He clicked his fingers and a bracelet appeared in his hand in a shower of gold sparkles. It was a simple chain with what appeared to be a mood stone in the middle although this stone was already swirling around inside, changing colours rapidly. He handed it to her and she studied the ever changing colours for a moment before putting it on. 'It seems you've already been allocated a hundred pounds on your account so you can go crazy today.'

'A hundred pounds. Where did that money come from?'

'Well, I presume it would have come from you.' He looked at his magical clipboard again. 'Oh actually, it's come from Wolf but I presume that's just until we can sort out your bank details. Anyway, you'll see lots of the shops' wares floating around the street: drinks, sweets, potions, that kind of thing. These aren't freebies – if you take one, the cost of it will automatically be deducted from your account. The shops will be able to read your bracelet and you'll be charged accordingly. Same if you go into the shops to buy anything, you don't need to worry about queuing up at a till or bringing your purse whenever you come to Stardust Street, just take whatever you want from the shops and you'll be charged from your bracelet.'

'So just walk in, take what I want and walk back out again?'

'Yes exactly.'

Star grinned. 'I like the sound of that. What if I run out of money?'

'That's OK, you can still buy the stuff, you'll just get a bill posted through your door at the end of the day and you have a week to pay it. And if you buy lots of things, or any big heavy things, come and see me and I'll get it delivered to your house, although a lot of the shops will deliver it for you too.'

'Ezra, I have to say, this is all very efficient.'

Ezra beamed with pride. 'I try my best. Now go and enjoy yourself, and be sure to try the cronuts. They're delicious.'

'I will.'

'And you must try the magic stars. Those are chocolate stars with sprinkles of magic on the outside. When you eat them they will be whatever flavour you want them to be, strawberries, cheese, pumpkin, toffee apple – whatever you can dream, that's what they will be.'

'Now that I have to try.'

She started walking down the road and couldn't help smiling at the amazing-looking shops, she wanted to visit them all. She felt like a kid in a sweet shop and she didn't know which one to visit first. The one selling potions had a giant cauldron as its doorway, with a spoon stirring some purple bubbling liquid. Glass bottles of various colours moved around inside the shop, many of them sparkling, presumably with magic that made them seem almost alive.

Next to that was a seafood restaurant which was shaped exactly like a tall ship with white sails billowing in the breeze.

There was a bookshop with a giant open book as its doorway, the pages turning. Beyond the windows she could see dusty leather tomes alongside the latest crime or romance books.

A mug of steaming hot chocolate floated out of a nearby shop with a large teapot at the front door. It came towards her and she could see it was topped with lashings of whipped cream, marshmallows and chocolate sprinkles. It floated temptingly under her nose and without thinking she grabbed it to stop it from hitting her in the face. Her bracelet vibrated and she laughed that she had just been charged for a drink she didn't particularly want. As she'd paid for it, she took a big sip and closed her eyes. It was the most perfect gingerbread- and cinnamon-flavoured hot chocolate she'd ever tasted.

No sooner had she taken a sip than a large cup of churros came floating out of another shop, complete with a little pot of chocolate sauce. The shopkeepers had clearly spotted an easy target but as churros were her favourite thing in the world to eat, she had no qualms at all about grabbing one. Her bracelet vibrated again as she dipped the churro into the chocolate sauce. It tasted wonderful, light and fluffy on the inside and that perfect crispiness on the outside. The cup of churros floated along next to her quite happily until she had finished them off and then the cup and the pot of sauce disappeared back into one of the shops again.

A few minutes later a small box of chocolate stars floated across the street towards her. She knew she couldn't accept everything that was offered to her but she was here to experience all Midnight could offer so she picked up the box and her bracelet vibrated again. The stars had sprinkles on the outside so she knew these were the magic ones Ezra had talked about. She closed her eyes and imagined a sweet juicy pineapple and then popped the chocolate in her mouth. Immediately she could taste the wonderful flavour of a freshly sliced pineapple. It tasted amazing. She closed her eyes again and this time imagined a fruity mince pie and then ate the chocolate. She laughed when she could taste the fruitiest mince pie and even the sweetest pastry too. She could see why these were so popular.

As she wandered up the street, she stopped when she saw what looked like a garden gate, and beyond that something resembling a wild garden. But she could see that it was one of the shops as it still looked part of a three-storey brick building. Intrigued, she pushed open the gate and stepped inside. She realised immediately it was a herb garden. The smells were incredible. There was no ceiling above her, or any other floors, the height of the room was the top of the three-storey building. It was like a giant warehouse. There were real, towering trees in here, along with some great big bushes and tiny little shrubs too.

She moved over to a mint plant and ran her fingers over one of the leaves, sniffing her fingers and smiling at the smell.

A basket suddenly appeared in the air in front of her and a small pair of garden snips.

Star smiled at the efficiency. She took the basket, pleased to see there were inserts in the basket to keep each herb separate. She plucked the snips from the air too.

'Hello!' Star called out, wondering if all the shops worked as a help yourself and there was no need for any shopkeepers.

A small woman with bright purple cat-eye glasses came scurrying out. 'Hello, hi, good afternoon,' she said, breathlessly. 'Oh it's you.' She started shaking Star's hand quite vigorously. 'Welcome to Midnight. I'm Tabitha.'

'Hello Tabitha, I'm Star.'

'I know who you are, you're Celeste Bright. I've been following your blog for quite a while. Are you here to buy some herbs for your cakes?'

'I'm not sure I'll be making any cakes for a while.'

'Oh but you must. Your cakes have helped so many people. I love reading the reviews from your customers, how you've changed their lives. It honestly makes me so happy. There's kind of an unwritten rule that witches shouldn't help mundanes because it can draw unwanted attention to the witch community. Of course there's no one to enforce it and many witches help them every day, although most are more discreet than you. You, very publicly, are making and selling magical cakes and people are buying them in their droves.'

Tabitha pushed her glasses back up her nose. 'It just kind of makes me excited that maybe eventually our kind will be more accepted by the mundanes. Maybe one day we can coexist, use our magic openly without fear or hate. Nowadays, there's so many YouTube videos of people doing magic and most people think it's some cool special effects or camera trickery and most of it absolutely is. That's why when you stumble across a video of a real witch doing some magic, everyone just accepts it, no one freaks out. Of course they probably would if they knew it was real but maybe one day they won't. With people like you and some of the other celebrity witches in the public eye, waving the flag for us, sometimes subtly but, nonetheless, waving it, maybe times are a changing.'

Star smiled. 'I like the sound of that.' She thought back to how she'd reacted when she'd seen Claudia's magic. 'I think we have a long way to go, but I do think that people are a bit more blasé about it now.'

Tabitha nodded, her eyes huge behind her glasses. 'And I know that this thing with Cleo Walsh has put a dampener on it. But it will pass, it always does. There will be a new hot potato story soon enough. And you must find a way to carry on with your cakes, not just for the mundanes who need our help but for our community too. You need to keep flying the flag.'

Star nodded. 'Everything is still raw at the moment. What happened to Cleo was horrific but I've always loved baking so it will be good to get back to it somehow. But for now I can still use these herbs in my own meals. This shop is amazing.'

'Thank you.'

'I can't believe you have cinnamon trees growing here.'

'Oh, anything is possible with a little magic.'

Star smiled at that thought. 'Is it just fresh herbs you sell?'

'Oh no, as you know, some herbs like oregano and

rosemary are better dried whereas parsley and basil are better fresh. But it depends what you want it for. While dried rosemary is infinitely better in a meal than fresh, in magic where rosemary is used to banish negative thoughts or bad energy, fresh is sometimes best. We have dried herbs and spices at the back of the shop so we can meet all of your needs: cooking, magic or even magic cakes.'

Star grinned.

'I'll leave you to look around. Help yourself to whatever you want and if you leave the basket at the till, I'll have them all individually wrapped and sent to your house.'

'Thank you so much.'

Star took some time to get some of her favourite herbs and spices, plus some herbs she had never used before or in some cases even heard of. She left the basket at the till and called goodbye to Tabitha who was floating near the top of one of the tallest trees, collecting what looked like giant bananas the size of marrows.

She stepped outside the shop and walked straight into Wolf.

'Oh sorry,' Star said, bouncing off his hard chest.

'No, I am, I wasn't concentrating on what I was doing,' Wolf said. He suddenly reached out and stroked the corner of her lips and the feel of his fingers there gave her a kick of desire.

His eyes widened in horror and he quickly snatched his hand away.

'I'm so sorry, you had a bit of chocolate on your lips, but I had no business touching you like that, I'm really sorry.'

'It's OK,' she tried to laugh it off when the truth was she'd liked it too damn much. 'I had churros. My favourite thing in the world is churros.' She was chattering away, trying to fill the awkwardness of him touching her so intimately. 'That chocolate sauce is to die for, you should try it.'

She'd meant that he should get some churros too so she was surprised when he licked the finger that he'd used to wipe the sauce from her face.

'It does taste good.'

Good lord, it had suddenly got a hell of a lot hotter.

He cleared his throat. 'I need to go, I have some stuff to take care of. Are you finding everything OK?'

'This place is wonderful. And Ezra gave me a bracelet, although we need to sort out the money as I think I'm spending yours right now.'

'We can worry about that later. Have fun.'

And with that he hurried away.

She was staring after him trying to figure out what just happened when a lady in her seventies came over to her.

'There you are, I've been waiting for you,' the lady said.

Star stared at her in confusion. She was wearing cropped leggings and a flowery blouse, and her silvery hair was in a sleek bob.

'Sorry, I'm not sure what you mean.'

'I'm Zofia. I'm Wolf's grandmother, for want of a better word.'

'Oh hello. I'm Star Brightheart.'

'I know who you are.'

'From my blog?'

Star cringed that everyone in the village knew who she was and would therefore know about her drama with Cleo Walsh. Would they hate her for it before she'd even unpacked?

'Oh no, I have the gift of foresight and I've seen you, many times. I've seen you coming here and your future.'

Star felt her eyes widen. 'You know my future?'

'Oh yes,' Zofia grinned. 'It's a big, bright, happy one. It's a shame your mum left when she did. If she'd stayed and you'd grown up here, you'd have been married with children by now. But I knew, when the time was right, you'd come back. You and Wolf share...' Zofia paused. 'Has he told you?'

'That we share the same birthday?'

'Yes, and what that means.'

'What does it mean?'

'Ah well, that isn't my place to say. I'd have thought Wolf would have told you but with you only finding out you're a witch today, maybe he thought it was too much for one day.'

'It has been an overwhelming day but I'm not keen on secrets either, I'd rather just know all the facts.'

Zofia nodded. 'I would too but that sort of thing really needs to come from him. I'm sure he'll tell you in due course. Do you like our shops?'

Star recognised she was changing the subject but decided to let it go. She had stepped through the looking glass into this strange new world and it was a lot to get used to. She didn't need any more added to her plate.

'I love it. It's enchanting.'

Zofia linked her arm and started walking up the street with her. 'Wolf built it all, when he was just eighteen years old. There were no shops here at that stage and everyone would just go out of the village to buy everything. It was something that had been talked about in the village for many years but no one actually did anything about it. Wolf recognised that more money needed to be spent in the village. A lot of people who come here didn't want to leave the village for work, so they did work-from-home jobs. Building these shops gave people a job here and many of them have now set up successful online businesses selling their wares to the outside world too. But it also means people spend their money here rather than out there.'

Zofia waved at someone. 'There are a lot of celebrations throughout the year and a lot of the residents used to go and see their relatives for the important events because there wasn't a lot to do here. Now these shops are a focal point, we have cafés, restaurants, bookshops, potion shops, shops for your every magical need. Relatives love to come here and spend time wandering round the shops, which in turn brings more money into the village too. And there were quite a lot of children in the village at the time so Wolf wanted to make it a special place for them too, which is why it kind of looks like it belongs in a big theme park.'

'What a wonderful thing to do for the village and the shops are just... magical. I've just been inside Tabitha's herb garden. She has banana trees in there, it's like something out of another world.'

'Wolf worked with the shop owners to give them what they wanted. But he wanted something elaborate for the road. When he was a kid, and even when he was designing this place, he thought magic was wonderful and exciting. We have an incredible gift and I think over the years he's lost sight of that. He needs to have fun with his magic again and I reckon you might be the person to help him do that.'

'Oh I don't think—'

'Trust me on this. For one reason or another, you're going to be very good for Wolf. Now I must go, I'm meeting Beryl for tea and cake. See you later.'

Zofia waved at another lady across the road and walked over to join her.

Star watched her go. It was weird to think that Zofia could see her future so clearly and Star had no clue what lay ahead for her. But it seemed, as far as Zofia was concerned, that it was linked with Wolf whether Star wanted that or not.

CHAPTER 6

S tar stepped outside of the bookshop after spending an inordinate amount of time perusing all the books. There were some books on sale in there that were hundreds of years old. She'd bought a few on the history of witchcraft and one that was all about weather witches, just in case Wolf was right and she did have that power – she wanted to know more about what she was dealing with. She also picked up a few books by her favourite romance authors.

She was looking around, wondering which shop to go in next, when she saw Jessica Proudfoot making a beeline for her. She had a smug smile on her face.

'I've realised where I know you from. You're the woman who nearly killed Cleo Walsh,' Jessica said, a bit too loudly for Star's liking.

'Well that was an accident, I—'

'An accident that happened because you're a wildling that can't control your magic,' Jessica said, again too loudly.

A few people started to gather to watch the commotion and Star could see Jessica was relishing the audience. This was what Star feared, everyone finding out who she was and what had happened with Cleo and hating her for it.

When the news about Cleo Walsh and her videos about it went viral, there had been so many nasty comments directed at Star. People had started leaving one-star reviews on her website saying horrible things and they weren't even customers. For years Cleo had been hated by the public for her vile comments about different eating establishments but now she was the victim who had been brutally attacked and everyone loves a victim. The public and the press had rallied behind her and Star was most definitely the villain in all of this. And while, apparently, Star had been at fault, she certainly didn't deserve the hatred. She'd hoped to get away from it all here but now it seemed it might have followed her.

'Midnight Village is no place for a wildling. It's not safe. We have children here. What if there are more *accidents*?' Jessica said.

There were one or two nods from the other villagers.

'There won't be. Wolf is going to teach me how to use my magic safely,' Star said.

'Teaching you about magic is not a quick fix. It will take many years for you to become proficient. And in the meantime, you're putting us all at risk.'

'Oh shut up,' said a woman in the crowd.

Jessica turned to face her. 'How dare you speak to me like that.'

'I'll speak to you however I want. You're talking out of your arse.'

'As descendant of one of the village founders, I deserve respect.'

'I don't care who you are, respect is earned and you've done nothing to earn the respect of the people in the village.'

'You're just a bully and this little stunt just proves that,' another woman said.

'I'm looking out for the village,' Jessica said.

'You're looking out for yourself, as always,' said the second woman.

Suddenly a tomato seemed to come out of nowhere and splatted against Star's face. She stood there in shock for a moment, humiliation and sadness washing over her.

Jessica looked at her and burst out laughing.

Thunder suddenly rumbled in the skies nearby. The sun had been shining moments before but now the sky was turning a shade of slate grey. As the heavens opened and rain lashed down on top of them, people scattered to get inside and Star did too, before anyone could make the connection with her and the sudden change in the weather.

Wolf banged on Jessica's door. Anger was bubbling inside him and he needed to calm down because his reaction to what Jessica had done was not rational. He had no idea why he felt so damned protective over Star, he was pretty sure she could fight her own battles if she wanted to. Yet here he was. He kept telling himself he was acting on a complaint from another village member but that didn't explain why he was so angry.

After a few moments Jessica answered it.

'Wolf, what a lovely surprise.'

He stamped down on his anger and tried to talk to her calmly. 'I heard about your little confrontation with Star. I expect more from you than that. I would hope everyone would treat all newcomers with kindness.'

'I only did what you should have done. You know she caused what happened to Cleo Walsh because of her untamed magic. Yet you're happy for her to just walk the streets as if she isn't some kind of ticking timebomb.'

'That's ridiculous. What happened was an accident, she had no idea what she was doing.'

'That makes it worse.'

'What the hell are you up to? You normally stomp around here like a bear with a sore head, but you've never singled someone out for your unkindness before. And trying to rally people against her, she's been in the village for five minutes.'

She folded her arms. 'I hear the two of you are betrothed. Is that why you brought her here?'

'I had no idea who she was when I offered her a place here. She applied to come because she's always felt a connection to the village and it turns out she's Midnight-born. But our connection is nothing more than a shared birthday.'

'But I saw the two of you today, outside Tabitha's herb garden. You stroked her face. And the way she looked at you was like a puppy looking at its beloved owner.'

Wolf cursed under his breath. He had no idea what had compelled him to touch Star earlier that day. He had always been adamant not to get involved with the women of the village and he'd never been tempted to break that rule. And then Star arrived and turned his world upside down. He wanted her with a desperate need he'd never felt before. But regardless of his feelings towards her, it was important to keep things professional between them and he absolutely should not have touched her lip to wipe the chocolate away. Anyone could have seen and they did. He didn't want any of the villagers to think he was abusing his position as mayor. Most importantly, he didn't want to encourage any feelings from Star.

'I'm trying to protect you from her,' Jessica said. 'I know you don't like to get involved with women from the village and you have your reputation to think of, too.'

'I can take care of myself. And who I touch or talk to or have any kind of friendship or relationship with is nothing to do with you.'

'It would be a shame though if everyone in the village found out what happened to Cleo. I'm not sure they would be quite so welcoming if they knew Star nearly killed someone.'

The noise that came from his throat was nothing short of a growl and it surprised him. Jessica even took a step back.

'Stay away from her, do you understand me?'

She nodded, her eyes wide.

'And stay away from me too.'

With that he walked away. And now he needed to go and see Star too. His plan of staying away from her for a few days was clearly not working.

Wolf knocked on Star's door but there was no answer. He felt sure, after what had happened, she would have gone home.

Viktor suddenly jumped up on the lounge windowsill and opened the window. 'She told me to tell you she isn't in.'

Wolf sighed. He really was too big to keep climbing through the window. He peered through the crack and saw Star lurking in the kitchen.

'Star, open the door, we need to talk.'

She hesitated for a moment then came to open it. He stepped inside before she could stop him.

'Are you OK?' Wolf said, leaning over her to close the door and then realising he was too damned close. He quickly moved back, but the wall was behind him and it didn't leave much space between them.

'I had a tomato thrown at me, what do you think?'

'I had a word with Maxine about that. She absolutely shouldn't be throwing anything at other villagers, especially when she's such a lousy shot.'

'Lousy shot, she hit me in the face.'

'She was aiming for Jessica.'

'Oh.'

'Maxine and Jessica have a history which I normally try to stay away from but when Maxine resorts to throwing vegetables I had to give her a warning. Jessica is not well liked in the village, by anyone. She certainly wouldn't have won any friends for her little stunt with you today.'

Star let out a heavy sigh. 'I just thought I would come here and escape from all the uproar surrounding the incident with Cleo. But of course most people would know who I am.'

'And most people don't care. You're new here, that's more exciting than some gossip in the paper.'

'But Jessica has a point. Cleo nearly died because I'm not in control of my magic. Aren't you just a bit worried about having me here in case I hurt one of the villagers?'

'Not one single bit. You're not a malevolent person. A lot of magic is about intent and you never intended to hurt her. But if you're worried I can start teaching you how to use your magic tomorrow.'

'I think that's a good idea. I'm never going to fit in here until I can do some magic.' She sighed and then looked at him as if waiting for him to say something else. He wasn't sure what he was supposed to say. 'Are we not going to talk about what happened after Maxine threw a tomato at me?'

He frowned. 'I wasn't there so I'm not sure what you mean. Erin and Maxine came to see me after to tell me what Jessica had done. Maxine was mortified about the tomato. They didn't mention anything else.'

'They didn't mention the thunder and rain?'

'No. I mean, I know we had a little shower and a bit of thunder. Where are you going with this?'

'I'm worried I caused it.'

He felt his eyebrows shoot up.

'The thunder happened straight after I was hit in the face with a tomato. The sun had been shining seconds before, not a cloud in the sky.'

'You know we have weird weather here all the time because of the curse. Freak storms are not unusual. And from what I know of weather witches, it takes a lot of concentration and skill to summon the weather. It doesn't just happen because you're angry or sad.'

He wondered if he was trying to convince himself more than her because there was a very real possibility she was a weather witch.

She let out a small sigh of relief and his heart went out to her. She so desperately wanted to fit in here and she had so much worry hanging over her head. He just wanted to hug her and take away all this stress.

He put her hand on her shoulder. 'It's going to be OK.'

She nodded and he noticed she had a few tomato seeds stuck in her hair. He had moved his hand to remove them before he realised what he was doing and snatched it back but she had already noticed and looked at him in confusion.

Now was the time to address it, to apologise for

touching her earlier and to ensure she knew that nothing was going to happen between them.

Just then there was a knocking on the door and Star jumped as if she was expecting a rampaging mob outside.

'I'll get it,' Wolf said and she stepped back to let him open the door. He sighed when he saw Maxine there.

'Is she there? I want to apologise,' Maxine said.

Star gingerly poked her head round the door.

'I am so sorry,' Maxine said. 'I just wanted to wipe that stupid smirk off Jessica's face and I hit you instead. I should have used my magic to hit the target but I was so angry at what she was doing that I didn't even think.'

'Star, this is Maxine. Maxine, this is Star.'

'I would have come earlier, but Ezra wouldn't tell me where you lived and neither would Wolf – as if I was going to knock on your door and throw more tomatoes at you. I had to do a lot of asking around until I found out where you were. Are you OK?' Maxine said, barely drawing breath.

'I didn't tell you where she lived as I wasn't sure that Star would want to see you after what happened.'

'Of course she would,' Maxine said, completely unfazed. 'She'd want to know I'm on her side.'

'I'll leave you two to it,' Wolf said and stepped outside.

'I really am very sorry,' Maxine said.

'It's OK,' Star said.

Maxine stepped forward and gave her a big hug and Star smiled and hugged her back. Wolf walked away, wishing he had been the one to hold her and make her smile again.

CHAPTER 7

Star climbed into bed with a mug of hot chocolate, which felt a little odd to drink when it was still so warm outside. It had been an odd day and she hoped to calm her mind before she went to sleep. Her mind was so full. She was a witch, living in a village full of witches. She didn't even know where to begin with that. Finding out her birth parents had lived in the village had been another shock.

She looked at her phone to see there was a text from her friend Tig, asking how her new home was. How could she begin to explain what had happened today? Was she even allowed to tell people she was a witch? She supposed that a lot of witches confided in non-magic people about their skills, those they could really trust, and while she could probably rely on Tig not to say anything to anyone, Star didn't know where to even start that conversation. Like anyone, Tig would probably want some kind of proof if her friend suddenly claimed to have magical powers and her first request would probably be for Star to turn Cleo Walsh into a toad, as if nearly killing her wasn't enough.

She quickly typed out a reply.

STAR:

> The house is lovely and the village is very pretty.

There, that was all true.

TIG:

> Oh good can't wait to see it.

Star quickly sat up in bed. Oh god, she was supposed to be coming up on Christmas Eve with the rest of Star's stuff. Tig wouldn't even get past the gates and Star didn't want her to see the armed guards. They had been a big enough shock for Star to see even when they were friendly and letting her in, it wouldn't be a very nice experience for Tig to be turned away by them. She couldn't risk Tig seeing anything magical so she'd have to meet her at the end of the driveway and transfer all her stuff into her car away from the village. She quickly typed her reply.

STAR:

> Unfortunately, it's a private village, you won't be allowed in. When you come on Christmas Eve, I'll meet you at the end of the drive to collect my stuff or I can meet you in the nearby town for a coffee and a cake.

TIG:

> It's private? What have they got to hide? Oh wait, do you have a celebrity living there? Is it Tom Cruise? Is it Johnny Depp?

Star sighed. Of course Tig's interest would be piqued. Star had always been curious about the village too. Although now the privacy made so much sense but it was one thing telling Tig that Star was a witch, quite another telling her she now lived in a whole village of witches. That wasn't her secret to share. She cast around for an excuse as to why a village would be so private. Her eyes fell on a framed photo on the wall of Michelangelo's *David* in all his naked glory.

Star smiled and quickly typed her reply.

STAR:

> No celebs here. Nothing that exciting. If I tell you, you've got to promise not to laugh or tell anyone?

TIG:

> Of course.

Star smirked as she wrote her reply.

STAR:

The village is for naturists. Everyone walks around naked at all times. That's why they're so private.

TIG:

Even in the winter?

Star cursed that she hadn't really thought this lie through.

STAR:

Some do, they're used to the cold. Some only go nude in the warmer months

TIG:

Are you going naked too?

Star thought of the old adage: what a tangled web we weave when first we practise to deceive. She typed her reply.

STAR:

Yes, me too. I am a closet nudist. I've always loved being naked, I've just never been brave enough to do it in public before. Now I can be free to be who I really am.

At least there was a fragment of truth in that message.

TIG

> I had no idea. I'm so pleased you've found somewhere you can truly be yourself.

Star smiled.

TIG:

> Are there any hot men there?

It was followed by an emoji that had wide bulging eyes.

Star laughed. At least this was a topic she could be honest about.

STAR:

> The mayor is pretty hot.

TIG:

> And you've seen him naked?

Star smiled.

STAR:

> Not yet.

TIG:

> You'll have to let me know when you do.

Star laughed and put her phone down while she thought about Wolf, although now the idea was in her head, it was really hard not to think about him naked.

There was something between them that she couldn't place.

Of course she was attracted to Wolf – what woman wouldn't be, he was hot as hell – but that didn't mean she wanted to get involved with him. If this was going to be her new home she didn't want to complicate things by starting something with Wolf that would invariably end and then have the awkwardness of seeing him every day. He'd said the same thing himself, he would never date anyone from the village. He was going to be her teacher and she was desperate to learn it all. She didn't want things to be weird between them.

But her attraction to him was caused by something more than just his appearance. She felt like she knew him and she didn't know why. When he'd hugged her, she knew she'd been held in his arms before. When he'd touched her lips, held her hand, she'd felt a kick of recognition and familiarity.

Viktor leapt up on the bed, licking his paws after drinking the warm milk she'd made for him.

'You're thinking about him,' Viktor said.

'Who?' Star said, in alarm. Could he read minds?

'Wolf. You have love hearts in your eyes.'

'I do not. You're being ridiculous.'

'"The lady doth protest too much, methinks."'

'You're quoting Shakespeare now?'

'I wrote half of Shakespeare's plays for him, including *Hamlet*.'

'What? Seriously?'

Viktor snuggled down. 'You think ghost writers are just a thing in today's culture, where some poor author gets paid pittance to write the story while the big celebrity gets paid the big bucks to simply have their name on the front of the book? That kind of thing has happened for hundreds of years. Because he was so celebrated, Will would get paid around eight pounds when he sold one of my plays. That's a year's salary for some people. Out of that he'd pay me ten shillings. It was most unfair. But I was a woman then. No one wanted plays from a woman writer, especially not one who was what you might call a lady of the night. He paid me more for sex than he did for my plays. I'm not sure what that says about my sexual prowess when my plays are known, performed and loved around the world hundreds of years after I wrote them. I must have been some kind of sexual demon between the sheets.'

Star didn't know what to do with this information or whether to believe it.

'How old are you?'

'I have walked this earth for one thousand eight hundred and seventy-six years. I have been a king, a queen, a president, an emperor, a warrior, a doctor, a teacher, a scholar, an inventor, and now a cat. I have been in this body for fifteen years. It is not the life I am used to. But it is a peaceful one so I should be grateful for that at least. But my experience on this earth has taught me many a thing about love or lust. You, young lady, are lusting after our young mayor. I can see it.'

'It's not that. I know him. I don't know from where, but I know I do.'

'Maybe a previous life then. Soul mates often find each other in the next life and the next. You are bound to your soul mate through the passing of time and the turning of the wheel. Maybe you are soul mates, destined to be together.'

She sat back and sipped her drink as she thought. 'Have you always been around witches?'

'I've always been one. My magic is somewhat limited in this body. But when the time calls for it, I can muster a bit.'

'Over a thousand years' experience of magic and witches?'

'I've seen it all.'

She let out a little sigh. 'I have so much to learn.'

She'd spent some time looking into witchcraft on the internet and fallen down a rabbit hole of witch trials and how accused witches had been burned, drowned and hanged in the past. Then after scaring herself she'd started reading the book she'd bought on weather witches. History had not been kind to weather witches, people inevitably were terrified of those with great power. One witch in the past who had been able to command the weather at will had been horribly tortured before she died. What if some of the villagers realised how strong Star apparently was? What if they feared her and threw her out? Or worse?

'Do you know much about weather witches?'

'I know that they are always tarred with the same brush. People fear the weather witches will murder them in their beds, wipe out entire villages, even if the weather witch in question has done nothing to deserve that fear. So they pre-empt it. Kill the weather witches before the witches can kill them. Or in some cases they've tried and the witch has wreaked his or her revenge, compounding the fear for future generations. But the stories never tell what was done to the weather witch to deserve that revenge, only how evil the weather witch was. It's quite sad really.'

That didn't fill her with joy. She had no idea if she was one, but Wolf had got quite worried about her being able to summon the snow. Not that she really thought she had but Wolf was adamant she had great power. This afternoon, when it had thundered seconds after being hit in the face with a tomato, that had worried her too.

She wanted to know more about her past and only her mum could answer those questions.

'I'm going to give my mum a call,' Star said.

'I suppose you want some privacy.'

'If you don't mind. Maybe come back in half an hour.'

Viktor stretched and yawned and slinked out of the room.

She picked up the phone and called her mum, Carys. She'd moved to Australia a few years before to be closer to her sister. Her mum would be awake now, probably having breakfast in the sunroom, reading her favourite crime novel over a cup of Earl Grey.

'Hi Mum,' Star said, when she answered the phone.

'Seren Annwyl,' her mum said, fondly and Star smiled at the Welsh nickname her mum always called her. 'How is everything there? Has all the stuff in the news calmed down?'

Star hadn't even looked in the news today to see if the story was still doing the rounds. She'd spent the last week or so poring over every article and comment online to see what people were saying about her. But it hadn't occurred to her to look today. While a lot of people here knew who she was, she was hopeful that now she'd disappeared the press would forget her and move on.

'I think it will all be forgotten eventually,' Star said. 'Mum, I have a question for you and I don't want you to dismiss it or avoid answering it. I would really appreciate your honesty.'

'OK,' Carys said, carefully, clearly with no idea what was coming next.

Star paused over what she was about to say. Once she'd said it out loud there would be no going back.

'Did you know I was a witch?'

There was silence on the other end of the phone and Star wondered if her mum had heard her or what she was thinking.

'Mum?'

'Of course we knew, honey. We found you floating two feet above your cot when you were six months old. You couldn't walk or crawl but you could fly.'

Star's breath caught in her throat.

'You'd make your toys float around you, make things zoom across the room into your hands. We knew you were special. Well, we thought at first you might be possessed or that there was some kind of poltergeist visiting you. But we talked to a priest and he came to visit and he explained you were a witch. He was quite excited about it. He said he'd met a few adult witches in his time but never a child. He also told us that we must never tell anyone and that we were to stop you doing magic whenever you tried it.'

Star's voice broke when she spoke. 'Mum, why would you do that? That's a part of me, a huge part, and I lived not knowing who I was all these years.'

'He said that no one would understand what you were, that they'd try and take you away, do tests on you to find out more about your powers. We didn't want that. We didn't want anyone to think you were some kind of freak. You were our baby. So when you used your powers, we used to tell you off, stop you. I hated trying to deny who you were but your dad was so worried about others finding out. You soon stopped using them. But things happened around you all the time as if your magic was out of control. Stuff was happening when you were asleep and we didn't know how to handle it.'

Star heard her mum sigh.

'The priest put us in touch with a witch who lived in the next village and when the witch came she was furious that we had adopted a witch, she said you should be raised by your own people and that she would have to speak to the mayor about taking you back. We were horrified. You were our daughter and no one was going to take you away from us. The witch came back, brought two of her witchy friends. Apparently the mayor of their little village had said he didn't want to interfere and they weren't allowed to take you from us so they offered to teach you instead. They wanted to take you into the village every day and train you but of course we weren't allowed in there with you. We didn't want anything to do with them after their threats so we refused but we were always scared they would come back and take you anyway.'

Star's heart melted. 'Oh Mum, I never knew any of this. I didn't know you were scared of losing me. Why didn't you tell me this?'

'We thought it was easier to deny it, dismiss your observations of magic as an overactive imagination or the wind or something else. But as you grew older you were so obsessed with that bloody village next door. I didn't like them. Every time I'd meet any of them down the shops, they'd always look at us like we were bad parents. Then you started talking about playing with a boy in the woods behind the village and about his magic and I knew he was one of them too. One day you came home and said he'd told you he was going to marry you. Not asked you, but told you, and I wondered if the village was actually some weird cult and that they were encouraging child marriage. I came down to meet him to tell him to stay away from my daughter and I couldn't even see him. It freaked me out and I didn't want you anywhere near that place. And after your father died, I didn't know what to do for the best to protect you. That's why we moved away.'

Star shook her head. It had been so hard for her parents, always trying to keep her magic a secret to protect her. Her parents had lived with that fear all their lives while she had been blissfully ignorant of it all.

'God, I understand your fears, especially when I was a child and with the way the other witches treated you, but why didn't you tell me when I was older? I deserved to know the truth about who I am.'

'It all seemed so scary and dangerous. One day you

came home from playing with that boy and your hair was singed, your clothes smelled of smoke like you'd walked through a fire, and I just thought maybe you were better off never dealing with that side of you. I thought you'd be safer.'

Star remembered that day and it had been so unreal, so terrifying, she'd never told her mum the truth about what had happened. She'd spent so many years thinking about her time with Cub as some kind of fantasy that had never really happened and now it seemed it had all been true. She wondered what had happened to the boy who had told her one day they would get married. He had probably grown up and moved away many years ago.

'The problem is, these powers are in me whether we like it or not and unless I learn to use them correctly, I could end up hurting myself or others.'

'Oh Star, I'm worried about you playing with this stuff.'

'I have a very patient teacher and I have to do it. Wolf thinks that I've been making magical cupcakes all these years and the effect the cake had on Cleo Walsh was because I poured hate into her cake. Mum, I could have killed her. And this is who I am, I need to embrace that not run away from it.'

Her mum was silent for a while.

'I can't wrap you in cotton wool forever.'

'No you can't, though I do understand why you tried to protect me.'

'I love you, Seren.'

'I love you too. I'm going to bed now. I'll be in touch soon.'

They said their goodbyes and Star hung up.

She sighed, rubbing her hand across her face. Her life could have been so different if she'd known who she was.

She thought about Cub. That had been the first time someone had told her magic was real.

She remembered how they'd met and that magic had been the thing that had brought them together in the first place. She had been wandering through the trees in the woods behind Midnight Village, climbing the big maple tree so she could peer over the top of the ten-foot wall, but the houses had been too far away to see anything. She'd been surprised when the leaves from the tree had started dancing around her, doing loops and twirls, and she'd thought it was magical. She'd gone back three times to see the magic leaves but, on the third time, Cub had been there. He'd told her she wasn't allowed in the tree so she kept coming back just to annoy him. Then he would criticise, saying she wasn't making the leaves move right, though she didn't think it was her who was moving them in the first place. He was always rude to her until the day her dad had died. He'd found her crying in the tree and when she told him why, he'd floated up to sit next to her and held her in his arms while she cried.

After that they had become friends. He'd sit next to her in the tree holding her hand and shared his magic with her. Back then, as a child, it had felt like she'd stepped into Narnia or Hogwarts and was being shown this tantalising glimpse into a magical world. He'd make the leaves dance, birds and insects would sit in his hand. He could conjure fire and make sparkles of light circle around them. He would call the wind and fly around the tree. He was... enchanting. One day he told her his gran had said he was going to marry her when they were older and she'd been surprisingly OK with that. Being with him made her feel so excited.

She'd told her mum the things he could do and Carys had always dismissed it as some kind of conjuring trick, like a magician in a show might perform. Her mum had told her she had a vivid imagination and when Star wasn't with Cub, she had started to doubt the things she'd seen. But when she was with him, she didn't want to question the things he could do. She wanted to believe in magic and wonder and hope. Things were always dark and sad at home, but with Cub there had always been this light. He'd made her so happy and for the first time in her life she'd known what it felt like to be in love. And although it would have been easy to dismiss it as a meaningless childhood romance, he had risked his life to save hers.

She remembered the day her mum had spoken about, when she'd come back home with her hair smelling of smoke because that had been the last time she'd seen him. Her last kiss when she had no idea it was going to be a kiss goodbye.

She drank the last of her hot chocolate and snuggled down in bed. She went to sleep quickly and dreamed of a boy with sea-green eyes.

Star ran through the woods, across the stream and took the path behind the old broken-down shack. As she rounded a corner, she could see the towering maple tree ahead of her, the wall of the village going straight through the middle of it. The tree always made her laugh, like it could never make up its mind which season it was in. The half of the tree that was in her side of the woods had leaves of red and gold, in keeping with the rest of the autumn foliage, but the leaves overhanging the village side were fresh and green.

She swung herself up onto the lowest branch, which was practically touching the floor, and climbed up the branches confidently until she reached the two large forked branches that ran horizontally side by side. Cub was waiting for her and he held out a hand for her to help her up the last bit.

Once she was standing next to him, he leaned down and gave her a soft kiss on the lips. In the times when she was sitting at home doubting everything she had seen, wondering if any of it was real or just grief-induced hallucinations, she held onto these kisses because she knew they were more real than anything else.

He pulled back, stroking her face. 'Hi.'

'Hello.' She smiled up at him.

He looked out over the village. 'Can you feel it, there's a storm coming. We get a lot of storms here, big violent ones like someone is unleashing a fury on us.'

And as if he had somehow summoned it by talking about it, she watched as the clouds turned dark and rolled across the sky like they were suddenly on fast forward. Thunder clapped and rumbled nearby and rain lashed down on them, soaking them to the skin in seconds. Lightning flashed over the hills beyond the far side of the village.

'Are we going to be safe here?' Star asked, loving the sensation of the rain on her skin. It made her feel alive.

'Storms are nothing to be scared of,' Cub said, putting an arm around her.

'I'm not scared of storms, but I am worried about standing in a tree and getting struck by lightning.'

He smiled at her. 'Lightning isn't really anything to be scared of either. Not for us. It's just a magical energy in the same way that there is magic around us in the air, the trees and the water. Don't get me wrong, it will hurt a lot if it hits us, it's a powerful source of magical energy, but if you're really clever, you can control it. You can use that magical energy just for a few seconds and direct it away from you.

There have been some weather witches that have even used it as a weapon. Summon the lightning, control it to fight against others. When you start looking into our history, the real history of witches, there is some fascinating and scary stuff out there.'

The sky lit up in the cloud above them, a bit closer than the last flash.

She stared at him in wonder. 'Have you ever controlled the lightning?'

'I've been fortunate enough never to be hit by lightning. Lightning strikes on people are quite rare but lightning is attracted by great power, it feeds off it. Most of the people that have been hit by lightning are actually witches because power attracts power. But I don't think we have anything to worry about. Only twenty percent of all lightning actually makes contact with the ground, the rest stays up there in the sky.'

She looked up at him with a grin. 'Are you a weather geek?'

He smiled. 'It's something I've been studying lately. My gran tells me I have a lot of strength so I was hoping I might be able to help with the crazy weather we have here in the village. I haven't had much luck so far.'

Lightning cracked in the field below them, scorching the ground.

'That's a bit close,' Star said.

'Yeah, too close,' Cub said.

And then suddenly everything seemed to happen in slow

motion. *The sky exploded open right above them and a flash of pure white electric energy burst towards them – more specifically, her. And, inexplicably, Cub stepped straight in front of her.*

The lightning hit him square in the chest and he roared but held his arms out to the side and the lightning burst out of his hands and hit the ground and disappeared.

They stood in silence for a second. The burned smell hung in the air as did the smoke that surrounded them.

Cub turned round to face her, his hands on her shoulders. 'Are you OK?'

'Christ Cub, are you?' Her eyes raked down his body and she could see the t-shirt around his chest had a black burned hole right in the middle, the skin underneath was red raw. Tears formed in her eyes. 'Oh my god, you could have been killed.'

'I'm fine. It was a lot harder than I thought it would be to control it, but I'm fine.'

'Why did you do that?'

He dipped his head to look her right in the eye, his sea-green eyes serious when he spoke. 'I'm in love with you Seren, I'm never going to let anything hurt you.'

CHAPTER 8

S tar woke with a start, her breath heavy.

She quickly got out of bed, threw on some clothes and ran through the quiet, moonlit streets to Wolf's house. Everyone was fast asleep, all the houses in darkness as she hammered on the door. Although she could see the curtains twitching at Charles's house. She'd obviously woken him up too.

It took a few moments but then a very rumpled, shirtless Wolf answered the door.

'Star, are you OK? Come in.'

She stepped inside his lounge. 'We need to talk.'

She turned round to face him as he closed the door and immediately saw the scars across his chest and down his arms. They looked like the branches of a tree, twisting and spreading out from the impact point of the lightning.

'Oh my god.' Star stepped up and without thinking traced her fingers across the scars over his heart. The scars that proved he had saved her.

Immediately Wolf grabbed her wrist and pulled her hand away. He was furious.

'Star, what the hell are you doing? You turn up at my house in the middle of the night and start touching me. How would you feel if the situation was reversed?'

Undaunted, she couldn't help staring at it. 'It's really you, isn't it? You're Cub?'

She looked up at him and all anger faded from his face, his breath catching in his throat as he stared at her, his eyes widening in surprise. When he spoke his voice was choked. 'Seren?'

Tears filled her eyes and she nodded. It had been so long since she'd seen him. She never thought she'd see him again.

He pushed his hands through his hair, staring at her in shock. 'I can't believe you're here, after all this time. I can't believe it's you. I just... I just dreamed about that day,' he gestured to the scar.

She stared at him in disbelief. 'Me too.' She glanced down at the scar again. 'Can I touch it?'

He nodded, his anger gone. She moved forward, gently tracing the scar across his chest. 'You saved my life.'

'It was nothing.'

'You stepped in the path of lightning for me, it was

not nothing.' She frowned and stepped back. 'How is it we both had the same dream?'

'It happens sometimes when two people share a connection. I guess subconsciously we both recognised each other.'

They stared at each other, and she shook her head, barely able to believe this was all real. 'You said your name was Cub.'

'That's what everyone called me because I was a tiny little thing growing up, and they all said I wasn't a wolf, I was a cub. Although technically speaking it probably should have been Pup but Cub was what stuck. My brother Lynx got called Kitty so I probably got off lightly. I was Cub until I was a precocious sixteen-year-old and insisted I was a man now and that everyone should call me Wolf from now on. But you never told me your name was Star either. You said it was Seren.'

'It's a nickname. My parents are Welsh, they called me Seren Annwyl, which means Star Beloved, and Seren just stuck. Besides, I thought if you knew my real name, you'd get me into trouble. I was kind of on private property sitting in the tree that overhung the village.'

'I probably would have done at the start. I didn't like you being there.'

She smiled. Their first few meetings had not gone well.

'God, I had the biggest crush on you. I've had a few

boyfriends over the years but looking back nothing ever compared to the first time.'

He rubbed the back of his neck. 'Me too. I thought you were incredible. I was so in love with you. I remember you surrounded by these dancing leaves. I remember thinking how beautiful you were. You were my first kiss.'

She touched her lips as she stared at him. 'You were mine.'

They didn't move as they stared at each other.

'I used to look forward to seeing you every day,' Wolf said. 'And then one day you just stopped coming. I knew you were moving house but you never came to say goodbye. It wasn't until years later that I found out why.'

'I tried. I came back every day for two weeks before we left and I could never find the tree. It was ridiculous, I'd been coming to that tree for two years, I knew the way blindfolded, but I couldn't find it. I wanted to give you my new address so we could stay in touch but I'd walk the woods for hours and could never find the maple tree again. I even came back here years later, several times actually, just to try and convince myself it had all been real. I'd retrace my steps from my old house, into the woods, over the fallen-down tree, follow the stream until the old shack and then take the path behind and the tree should have been a bit further along the path from there. But I could never ever find it again. I wondered if I'd made the whole thing up. I was going through such a crappy time with my dad getting sick and then dying, and grief and trauma can do funny things to the mind. In the end I relegated it to one of those weird childhood memories that probably never happened and now I find out it was true, all of it. Why couldn't I find you?'

'Jessica Proudfoot strikes again. We grew up together and she had a thing for me, even back then. She found out we'd been seeing each other and told her dad, the current mayor at the time. He and the other village council members decided that it was a weakness in the security of the village if you could just climb up in that tree that overhung the village walls. They decided, probably with the mayor's help, that all of the surrounding woods were a weakness and they put wards around the village walls to stop people getting too close. When you come across a ward you find yourself walking in the other direction, without even realising it. The wards have been there for years now, and I have to agree that they give us another layer of protection from any hikers or dog walkers that happen to walk through the woods. But it meant that you could never come back and I didn't find that out until several years later.'

'They blocked me out.'

'Yes, but not you specifically, you were just an outsider as far as they were concerned.'

Star sighed. 'On my last day here, I wrote you a letter and marched up to the village gates and handed it to the guard to give to you. He said the mayor had forbidden taking any letters and when I begged and pleaded the guard said there was no one in the village by your name. I just kept wondering if any of it had been real. I kept remembering the kisses and the way you would look at me and that felt real but over the years I doubted everything.'

Wolf looked pissed. 'I never knew that. I'm not surprised by it though. My family are very wealthy and when Jessica's mum and my mum had us days apart, Jessica's dad came to my parents to ask for an arranged marriage.'

'What?'

'It was something that was very common hundreds of years ago and there was an ancient law that the mayor would have authority over such things. Traditionally, people would come to the mayor to ask permission for an arranged marriage and he would approve it if he felt it was a good and prosperous match. Jessica's dad tried to use his authority, position and this law to force my parents to promise their five-day-old son in marriage to his daughter.'

'What the hell? What did your parents do?'

'My dad punched him in the face, told him to go to hell. Apparently my parents were adamant that I would always have a choice who I married.'

'That's outrageous. I can't believe Jessica's dad would do something like that.'

'He was desperate for money. I think he saw his daughter marrying me as a prosperous match. He owed thousands in gambling debts. Over the years he was mayor, he stole thousands of pounds of village funds. I'm surprised he got away with it for so long. It all came out actually not long after you'd left and he was forced to step down and he and his family, including Jessica, were forced to leave the village. But she came back a few years ago. I didn't want to judge her for her father's actions and she was Midnight-born so I felt I had to give her a house. But she clearly hasn't changed as she has been following me around like a lovesick puppy ever since, desperate to be the mayor's wife, with the wealth and power that would afford her.'

Star let out a heavy sigh. 'God, all of this seems spectacularly unfair. I know we were young and what we had probably wouldn't have lasted, we would have grown up and moved on, but at the time our relationship meant so much to me and it deserved more than being relegated to some silly fantasy or hallucination.'

'I felt the same.'

They stared at each other and she wanted to step forward and hug him to say hello properly after all these years. She remembered those feelings as if it had been only a few hours since she'd last seen him, not fourteen years. She touched her lips again. She couldn't help remembering how incredible their kisses had been. Looking back now, the only way to describe it was ... magical. It had been innocent and sweet and she couldn't help wondering what it would be like to kiss him now, with the benefit of experience. By the way he was looking at her lips, he was clearly thinking the same.

She took a step forward and then stopped herself. What was she doing, that was in the past.

She smiled as she thought of something else. 'Why did you tell me we were going to get married?'

'That's what my gran told me. She has the gift of foresight and everyone always believes her when she predicts something.'

Her stomach dropped. 'Are you serious? How could she possibly think we were going to get married? I never even met her until yesterday.'

'I've never questioned it. She's always been right. She knew I'd been playing with you before I told her. When she questioned me about it, I was all indignant about you coming here and she told me I had to be nice as I was going to marry you one day. I never doubted what she said was true.'

'I was fourteen when we first met. How could she see my whole life mapped out in front of me?'

'I don't think she can see a whole future, I think it's the big events like marriage, children; she told me I was going to be mayor. She just knows this stuff. And I know that's a pathetic answer for how it works, but she does.'

Now a lot of what Zofia had said the day before made sense, well at least as far as Zofia was concerned.

Star stared at him. 'So what, we're getting married now? You've just accepted it. Don't I get a say in it?'

'Of course you do and no, we're not getting married. I've already said I never date anyone from the village, that includes marriage too.'

Wolf went to the cupboard and pulled out two glasses and a bottle of whisky. He poured two large shots and handed one to her. She wasn't normally a whisky drinker but it suddenly felt like this conversation needed it.

He took a big sip and so did she, feeling like there was something more.

'Listen, there's something you should know. And I'm guessing this is part of her premonition, that she knew who you were rather than knowing we were getting married.' He sighed, pushing his hand through his hair, and she wondered how what he wanted to say could be any worse. 'The village has a tradition that those that are born in the same place on the same day are betrothed.'

She stared at him in horror. 'Betrothed?'

'It's silly, it doesn't mean anything, and I have no interest in keeping that tradition just to keep the villagers happy, but if people come up to you and ask when's the big day or have you bought a dress, you'll know why. Thanks to Maggie seeing we were born on the same day yesterday, the whole village will know by now and I'll imagine they'll get very excited about it. We haven't had a wedding here for several years and a betrothed wedding, well, I don't think that has happened since I was a kid. Fortunately, everyone is distracted with the winter solstice celebrations so with any luck they'll forget about us.'

She shook her head. 'I can't believe this. I've been here just over a day and I'm already promised in marriage to someone I've just met.'

'Well technically, we were promised in marriage the second you were born here on the same day I was. And we have met before. We had two years when we were sort of dating.'

'You know what I mean. Are you really buying into this rubbish?' Star said, in exasperation.

'Of course not. I'm just saying, we're not betrothed completely out of the blue. There's a reason behind it.'

She stared at him incredulously. 'A stupid reason. I was born at half past eleven at night. Half hour later and we wouldn't even be having this discussion. How can my life be so heavily linked to yours for the sake of thirty minutes? Why is this even a thing? Who came up with this stupid tradition?'

She took another sip of whisky, it burned the back of her throat.

'I don't think someone just woke up one day and decided that those that are born on the same day should get married. The village was built on the crossing of strong ley lines and when two people are born here on the same day they share a powerful magical connection. It's said they are soul mates, bonded, forever entwined.'

'And every single time it's happened, it's ended in marriage?'

'A betrothal doesn't happen very often. Most of the population here are on the older side so there aren't a lot of young couples having children, not anymore. But yes, as far as I know, it's always resulted in marriage. No wait, there were once two girls born on the same day, and although they didn't love each other in that sense, the bond was still there which was likened to that of sisters or twins. They ended up living together with their husbands.'

'Well let's go with that then, we can have a brother-ly/sisterly friendship. If you look at me as your sister and I look at you as my brother then there will never be any romantic entanglements.'

'That's fine by me,' he said, sounding annoyed.

'Me too,' Star said, hating that she was still thinking about kissing him. They had too much history to just be friends or have a sibling-type rela-tionship. God her head was spinning with all this. Ten minutes before she'd been over the moon to find Cub again, now she was furious that they were betrothed. Back when they'd been kids, she had been happy at the prospect of marrying this boy she was in love with, but she didn't want the choice taken out of her hands.

She sat down, trying to take it all in, and took another swig of whisky. She was so tired all of a sudden. The last twenty-four hours had been the most bizarre and overwhelming of her life.

'So have you been waiting for me your whole life? You're betrothed, was this a big deal for you?' Star said, gesturing with her whisky glass.

'I hate to burst your bubble but no. You left when we were sixteen, and I missed you for the first few weeks, maybe months. Yes, I was heartbroken that we never got to say goodbye but I didn't give you much thought after that, and I certainly haven't been waiting for anyone to walk back into my life. My gran never spoke about it again after you'd left, and I never knew we were betrothed. My parents never mentioned it.'

'They never mentioned it? They never talked to you about being betrothed? Is that not a massive oversight?'

'They were probably hoping by pretending it hadn't happened that maybe it wouldn't.'

'They weren't happy about the betrothal? I thought everyone was really excited about it? I'm your soul mate apparently. Not everyone finds their soul mate during their life and here was a ready-made one for their son.'

'It was probably more to do with who I was betrothed to.'

Star felt outraged by this. 'Oh I see, me and my parents weren't good enough for you. Not wealthy enough perhaps, not in the same league as you?'

He stopped mid-drink to look at her. 'It had absolutely nothing to do with wealth. I think it had more to do with the fact that your mum was the weather witch that cursed us.'

Star had no words at all. She downed the rest of her whisky.

Finally, she found her voice. 'She... *she* cursed the village?'

'Maggie will tell you more about what happened tomorrow, or rather later on today. But from what I know of it, I'm surprised it wasn't something more than that.'

'And yet she came back here to give birth to me, she can't have hated the place that much.'

'I guess she must have known you would work out you're a witch at some point. By having you here and calling you Midnight, she gave you a way of finding out more about your past and your heritage.'

She paused. 'So there *is* a good chance I'm a weather witch too.'

Wolf weighed it up with his hands. 'Not all magic is hereditary, you may get some of your parents' powers or none, you may even have magic that neither of your parents have. But yes, it is more likely that you will inherit their abilities than not.'

'And your parents were scared I might marry you and curse you too?'

'I guess that was a concern. Historically, weather witches have not been kind.'

'Those are the ones we know about, most of the others are probably in hiding.'

'That's true.'

'Besides, I'd only curse you if you forgot to put the toilet seat down.'

He laughed and it broke the tension between them. 'Or forget to put the lid back on the toothpaste.'

'That would definitely be curse-worthy.' She sighed, her heart sinking. 'They're going to hate me, aren't they?'

He looked surprised. 'The villagers?'

She nodded, sadly. 'All my life I've felt like I don't fit in and now I've found the perfect place to fit in and they're going to come after me with pitchforks.'

'It's not like that here.'

'I don't know, they're very protective of their way of life.'

'We just need to prove to everyone how lovely you are and how you're definitely not going to curse anyone. You make cupcakes, for goodness sake, you haven't done anything horrible with your life. And your cupcakes have helped a lot of people. That's something to be admired not feared.'

She straightened her shoulders. 'That's right. I am lovely.'

He laughed. 'Modest too.'

'And if they come after me, I'll turn them all into toads.'

'Now that's the spirit.'

CHAPTER 9

S tar was woken the next day by a screech.

She sat up in bed to see a tiny owl sitting on the windowsill, tapping the glass as if it wanted to come in. She looked around in confusion and realised she wasn't in her bedroom.

Just then Wolf walked in, holding a mug of tea.

'Ah sorry, that's Mulberry,' Wolf said. He put the mug down and opened a mini fridge and took out what looked like a dead cricket. 'He's not used to finding women in my bed.' He opened the window and Mulberry started twittering as if he was talking to Wolf. 'It's OK, she's a friend.'

Star got out of bed and went to the window. 'Hi Mulberry.' She turned to Wolf. 'Can I stroke him?'

'I'm sure he would like that.'

She ran a finger over the bird's soft feathery chest and he made a noise which was almost a purr.

'He's so small.'

'He's an elf owl, the smallest owl in the world. He's native to Mexico and the very southern edges of the United States. I'm not sure what he's doing over here, whether he was brought here by another witch, but he's kind of adopted me and seems to be coping just fine with the British weather. Here,' Wolf handed Star the cricket and she offered it out to Mulberry. The owl took it gently from her fingers and then gobbled it up.

'He likes you,' Wolf said. 'He always snatches the food from my fingers.'

'Does he come and see you every day?'

'Most days. Sometimes just to check in. He's also my eyes on the village. If something is wrong, he'll come and tell me. Well, he'll try. If I can't work it out, I'll ask him to take me there or show me.'

'Does Mulberry have any magic?'

'Some. I'm not sure what use it would have but it's quite impressive to see. Mulberry, go big.'

In a puff of gold sparks, Mulberry suddenly changed to a great big eagle-type bird made entirely of fire with angry, green glowing eyes. When he squawked it was a loud ear-piercing screech that felt like it came from the depths of hell.

Star laughed. 'That's impressive stuff.'

'Like I say, I'm not sure what use it has here. I suppose if a fox tried to sneak up on him Mulberry could scare the shit out of it but, other than that, it's not much use.'

'I don't know about that, if any of the villagers piss you off, you could use Mulberry to scare them, terrorise them into behaving.'

Wolf grinned. 'Some of them definitely deserve it. But that's probably not professional. Thanks Mulberry.'

With another shower of gold, Mulberry returned to his normal size and shape.

'That was brilliant,' Star said to the owl and he puffed up his chest proudly.

Wolf turned to her, handing her the mug. 'Here, drink this. I'm just finishing off making you some breakfast. You've got time to grab a quick shower if you want. There's a clean towel in the bathroom, the blue one.'

'Why was I in your bed?'

'I put you there. We were talking about being betrothed and I went off to the kitchen to get us something to eat and when I came back you were fast asleep. I'm not surprised you were tired after the day you had yesterday. But I wasn't going to let you sleep on the sofa, so I brought you up here and I took the sofa.'

'That's very kind.'

Wolf frowned as if he didn't want her to think he was kind.

'Come downstairs when you're ready, we need to talk.'

She was surprised by his tone, it was very formal.

He left the room and Mulberry twittered something that could have been goodbye and flew off. There was something incredibly sexy about sleeping in Wolf's bed although she knew she shouldn't think like that. She had a quick wash and threw on the clothes she had been wearing the night before. She went downstairs, just as Wolf was dishing up two bacon and egg sandwiches.

'Thank you for this,' Star said.

He nodded, taking a big bite.

There was something weird between them today, something very off.

'I'm sorry for last night, for waking you in the middle of the night, for... touching you, for falling asleep and taking your bed.'

'It's fine.'

She frowned as she took a bite of her sandwich and he went back to being silent again.

'Is it though, because you're being really weird?'

He sighed and put his sandwich down. 'Star, I'm really happy to see you again after all this time, and to know you're OK.'

'But?'

'But... our history, our past relationship, our crazy

betrothal, it doesn't change anything. Nothing is going to happen between us. Not now, not ever.'

She couldn't help the little kick of disappointment at that but she knew he was right. He was going to teach her about her magic, she didn't want things to be awkward between them. And she'd just moved to a new place, she wanted to make a good impression, and jumping into bed with the village mayor a few minutes after her arrival didn't look good either.

'My role as mayor is very important, not just to me but to the people of the village. The last four mayors before me have not been good and the village has suffered because of it. In some cases, the houses, streets, supplies were not maintained and that wasn't great for the villagers. The village funds were not always spent on the right things either.'

Wolf took a drink of his tea. 'The standards of the mayors have been really bad. We had the mayor that slept with lots of other women in the village while supposedly being happily married. After him we had Jessica's dad who was only interested in his own gain and who stole tens of thousands of pounds of village funds over the next fifteen or sixteen years. That's when the village was at its worst as there was no money being spent on it in all of that time. After him was Jacob who thought being a mayor was merely a figurehead role and he spent ten months of his first and only year as mayor travelling around the world. And the last mayor before me was a racist bigot who decided that Midnight should be an exclusive club for rich white people. He started asking anyone who was not white to leave the village.'

'That's awful.'

'There was no way I was going to stand for that. I fought against it and the villagers thankfully supported me and voted him out. I say thankfully, because there's no way I could have stayed in the village if they had supported him. I can't abide racism or any kind of bullying or singling out. This village has always been for people who need it, regardless of where they come from in the world or the colour of their skin. After that I became the youngest ever mayor at the age of eighteen and I vowed I would always put the villagers first. Their happiness and safety will always be my priority.'

Star's heart leapt and she quickly swallowed the chunk of sandwich she had been chewing. 'Is this your way of saying that you don't want me here?'

He looked stunned. 'What?'

'Their safety is a priority and suddenly a dangerous weather witch who has no control of her powers turns up on your doorstep. Best to get rid of me before I unleash the seven plagues on you or murder you all in your beds.'

A smile twitched on his lips. 'I'm not sure you're the murdering kind. I think you might have missed the part where I said I can't abide someone being singled out.

This is your home, Star, and if some people don't want you here, they will have to answer to me.'

'What if none of them want me here? Once they find out who I am, or rather what I might be, some or all of them are going to have an issue with that.'

'If they ostracise you, then me and you will be leaving together as I would never want to live somewhere that wasn't accepting of all witches, regardless of their background.'

She stared at him. 'You would leave because of me?'

'For the principle of it. Although leaving would at least mean that we could date. I'd have no obligations to the village then.'

Her eyes widened in surprise. 'After your big speech, you're saying you want to date me?'

'My big speech is *because* of that. I feel we have unresolved... chemistry. There is something between us that I can't describe. Maybe it's because of our history, maybe it's because we didn't get a chance to say goodbye when we were kids so we never got proper closure, maybe it's because of our betrothal and because our connection runs far deeper than we can ever realise, but from the moment I first saw you, surrounded by those gold sparks, throwing books at me, I've felt something that I've never felt before. That's why I want to make it clear that nothing is going to happen, regardless of our feelings towards each other.'

She stared at him, she had no words at all. Her

mouth was opening and closing but nothing was coming out. It was true she had felt that connection, when he'd hugged her, when he'd touched her to show her his magic, when she'd stroked his lightning scar. There was something between them.

He picked up his sandwich and carried on eating as if the subject was closed.

She decided to poke the bear. There was something about winding him up when he was so serious that pleased her immensely.

'We could have a secret affair.'

He smirked into his sandwich. 'No.'

'We could date outside the village and then no one would know and your rule of not dating anyone in the village wouldn't count.'

'No.'

'We could have one night of crazy hot sex just to get it out of our systems, closure as you called it.'

He choked on his sandwich. He quickly drank his tea to soothe his throat. 'I have a feeling one night with you would never be enough. So no.'

'Well this is frustrating.'

'It is. Very. I'm tempted to kick you out of the village myself so I don't have to deal with this,' he pointed between them.

'But that will break your other village rule of no ostracising.'

'Yes it would.'

'Are you always such a stickler for the rules?'

He finished the last bite of his sandwich as he watched her. 'I know what it feels like to be ostracised, to be outcast because you don't fit in. My family left the village when I was eight, because my parents felt it was important for me and my brother to socialise with other children. Beyond Jessica, there were no other children in the village. The village had lost its shine and wasn't what it was so it really wasn't a hard decision for them. We moved to a small village about twenty miles from here, a little place called Bramble Hill. And my parents just did not fit in. I don't know why. God knows, my mum tried everything. But they were newcomers and the villagers did not like it. It really upset her. It wasn't as if they were using magic out in the open, they were really discreet about it, but they didn't make any friends in the four years they lived there.'

He picked up the teapot and offered it out to her but she shook her head. He refilled his own mug.

'Lynx and I had been home-schooled up to this point, most Midnight children are. Not a rule, it's just easier than a five-year-old witch telling all his mundane school mates about the magical village he lives in. So it was the first time we had been in a proper school and I hated it. I was bullied horribly. Thankfully Lynx didn't have to put up with that. Well not at first. It was just me.

As a child, I didn't have full control of my magic just like you and there were a few incidents where my parents had to quickly modify memories. But the kids knew. Maybe they didn't know we were witches, but they knew we were different. I think a few suspected what we were even if they didn't fully understand what it meant to be a witch. I was called freak, a lot. And much worse than that. The name-calling I could handle, it wasn't great but I could just walk away when they got nasty. That went on for years. But the more I ignored them, the angrier they got and the bullying got physical.'

'Oh Wolf.'

He waved it away. 'I'm sure it's nothing that most school kids don't have to deal with at some point in their lives. I'm sure you had your own bullies too.'

She nodded. 'Although it was never physical, just nasty comments, laughing at me when things went wrong. I was never hit. I hate that you went through that.'

'It wasn't great. My parents had drilled into me that I was never to use my magic in anger and I was a small kid so I couldn't stand up to them physically, so I took the full brunt of it all. They were trying to get a rise out of me to see what I would do, see what I was capable of, but I was never going to use my magic on them. Until one day they came for Lynx and I wasn't there to protect him. I was hiding from them after school and they took Lynx instead and I had no idea. They had never bothered with him before.'

'Oh my god, you're kidding.'

'God I wish I was. He was eight by this point. They took him to a field, tied him to a gate post, which they told him was electrocuted so he shouldn't move, and started aiming tin cans and stones and whatever else they had to hand to throw at him. Luckily most of them were pretty lousy shots though a few things did hit him. When I found them I was furious. They wanted a rise out of me and they got it.'

'Did you hurt them?'

'No but I scared the shit out of them. I have never seen anyone as terrified as those boys were in my life and my god it felt good.'

'What did you do?' Star laughed.

The room suddenly went dark as Wolf changed to a huge black shape that had fangs, claws and green glowing eyes. The shape filled the room entirely around her like a giant death cloud of darkness. Star laughed as the shape let out a roar that sounded pure evil. Within seconds light filled the room again and Wolf was sitting exactly where he'd been sitting before, calmly drinking his tea. 'It's a simple illusion.'

'You need to teach me that.'

'And let you scare the villagers even more than they need to be? Probably not a good idea.'

'Fair point. And that worked?'

'Oh yes and I did much worse than that. I chased those boys through the woods unleashing every terrifying horror I could conjure, wolves, demons, the greatest wind I could summon. I made the trees seemingly come alive, and the branches grabbed at them as they ran screaming past. It was wonderful. They never came near me or Lynx again. But neither did anyone else. We came back here after that.'

'And your parents didn't modify their memories?'

'Dad thought it was a valuable lesson for them. And none of the adults really believed them. Most of the children didn't either. We came back here when I was twelve and I've lived here ever since. But that's why this village is so important. Almost every one of us here has been ostracised, bullied, singled out or left out, or just treated really badly at some point in our lives because we are different. The village is a haven from all that and it's important to me that the villagers know they are safe here and will never have to face that kind of prejudice again.'

'I get it, I do, though I'm not sure why that stops you from having a life. Dating, relationships, marriage, babies. You can be a great mayor and still have all those things.'

'I do date and have relationships, well sometimes, just not with people in the village. It would muddy the waters. I don't want anyone to think I'm abusing my position and if me and the woman broke up, it would be

awkward. It's just like an employer–employee relationship, it wouldn't be appropriate.'

She finished her sandwich but she wasn't sold on
what he'd said and he clearly knew that.

He sighed, pushing his hand through his hair. 'I feel
like I owe the village so much. When Mum had her first
stroke, I was nine and the villagers of Bramble Hill
could not give a shit. She could barely walk, was having
trouble doing the most basic of tasks and no one helped
her or my dad. She managed to fight her way back to
some kind of normality but the second stroke when we
were here was much worse and every single villager
rallied round us to help. She died when I was fourteen.'

'I remember,' Star said, taking his hand. They had
bonded over their grief; her dad had died just six
months before Wolf had lost his mum.

He looked at her hand holding his and then up at
her. 'I will never forget how you were there for me.'

'You were there for me too.'

They stared at each other but eventually Wolf
looked away. 'My dad died when I was sixteen. My gran
was touring the world in her little camper van and no
one could reach her so I was left to look after myself
and Lynx alone. The villagers were amazing. I had
twenty or thirty offers from different villagers who were
happy for us to move in with them but I was a cocky,
angry teenager who didn't want to move out of my
family home and Lynx didn't want to go either. So they

helped in every other possible way. Every night there would be hot cooked food delivered for dinner. Every day, three or four times a day, someone would pop in to see how we were, or would help to clean the house and garden. They would do all the shopping. They did everything. They say it takes a village to raise a child and they literally did. They raised both me and Lynx. I have so much to be grateful for and I don't want to let them down.'

She smiled. 'You're a good man, Wolf Oakwood. But I'm pretty sure the villagers would want to see you happy. And I'm not saying you'll find happiness with me but you can't be alone for the rest of your life.'

He studied her for a moment. 'They'd probably be delighted if I ended up with you, you are my betrothed after all.'

She laughed but it was her turn to protest. 'We are not getting married because of some silly ancient tradition.'

'No, definitely not.'

She watched him looking at her. 'Then stop staring at me as if you'd like to eat me.'

He laughed and stood up. He took the plates to the sink and, with a subtle wave of his hand, they started washing themselves and stacking themselves neatly on the draining board.

He turned back to face her as the plates clattered

around behind him. 'Are you ready to go and see Maggie?'

'No, but I think I need to find out. I know I'll always be wondering about my parents if I don't. I might have made a decision years ago that I want nothing to do with them, doesn't mean I don't want answers. However hard they might be to hear.'

He nodded. 'I get that. Come on, let's go.'

She followed him out of the house and he closed the door behind him with a wave of his hand.

'Show-off.'

He grinned and they started walking down the road.

Charles was standing outside his house scowling at them. 'I don't appreciate being woken up in the middle of the night because you two are having a booty call,' he yelled, loud enough for the neighbours in their gardens to look over with interest.

'There was no booty call,' Wolf said. 'Just a problem that needed to be dealt with.'

'All night?' Charles yelled, enjoying the show.

Wolf stopped. 'Charles, Star has just arrived in the village and just found out she is a witch, that's a lot to take in and there's a lot for her to learn. As mayor of the village, I need to be supportive of that. There's no ulterior motive and I don't like you insinuating that there is.'

Charles looked suitably chastened but only for a

second. 'Well next time you want to be supportive, how about you don't do it in the middle of the night. Woke me up she did, banging on your door like the world had come to an end.'

'I'm sorry, Charles,' Star called. 'It really was very important but I promise there won't be any more late-night visits.'

Charles grunted and shuffled off to his house, his little dog following him.

'I thought you said the village was friendly,' Star said.

'Charles is the exception.'

'Sorry if me coming to your house last night will cause some gossip.'

'There will be gossip about us. I don't care about that. Just as long as there's no truth to the rumours.'

They reached the end of the road and started walking towards Maggie's house.

'Did you have a chance to meet any of the villagers yesterday?'

'I met a few when I was walking round the shops, which by the way are amazing, you've created something wonderful there. But after the Jessica incident I decided to stay in my house for the rest of the day. I started researching about witchcraft on the internet.'

Wolf scoffed. 'I wouldn't trust that to give anything accurate about our way of life.'

'I was looking at the witch trials.'

He stopped to look at her. 'Our history is filled with innocent people being killed or executed for no reason. The witch trials took place during another horrific period when many innocent women and some men lost their lives. Anyone could be accused of witchcraft for a number of ridiculous reasons. And although the witch trials ended hundreds of years ago, we will always face fear and judgement, so that's why Midnight Village is so important – so we can be free to be ourselves. But why are you worried about stuff like that? You're safe here.'

'I was worried about how the villagers would react once they find out I have all this power. One weather witch was tortured and killed by her village as they were scared she would come back and kill them all.'

'No one has ever been executed in this village. The worst thing they would do is ask you to leave.'

'And I'm almost as scared of that as I am about being stoned to death or drowned.'

'That isn't going to happen either. But you need to give them a chance to get to know you. There's a potions club tonight. I think you should attend.'

'Potions club?'

'It's kind of like a book club, there's wine and gossip and everyone sits around and makes potions. Ashley Dougan is our potions expert in the village and she leads the club. I'm sure she would be delighted to have you attend. Everyone is curious about you. Show them who you are and that you're not anything to be afraid of.'

Star bit her lip. Potions would be an interesting part of this world to learn. Especially when she had been doing some of it, inadvertently, for years by adding herbs to her cakes. 'OK, I'll go.'

'Good.' He carried on walking and she hurried to catch up with him.

They quickly arrived at Maggie's house and stopped outside.

'Are you ready for some answers?'

She nodded and he knocked on the door.

CHAPTER 10

S tar watched as teabags flew into the pot and a cake cut itself into slices which were magically served onto a plate. Maggie was sitting opposite her at the breakfast table turning one of her rings round and round her finger. Star's history was clearly a lot worse than she'd imagined and Maggie didn't know where to start.

On the table in front of them was the leather book that Star knew contained her birth record and the blood message her mum had left her. She still didn't know if she wanted to see it. But she'd listen to what Maggie had to say first.

Wolf cleared his throat and Maggie looked up at him. 'Yes, sorry.' She turned to Star, 'I, umm... I was good friends with your grandmother, Anise Blaketon,

Rose's mum. Rose was born here in the village but, when Rose was maybe five, they left. I think her dad got a good job in London so they moved up there for around ten or eleven years. Anise died when Rose was around ten and her dad turned to drink. He was not kind to Rose or her sister Tula. I think both girls fell off the rails a bit, they were always getting into trouble at school and Rose got in trouble with the police too, stealing nail varnish or cans of cider from the local shops, causing a nuisance by playing her music too loud in the park. Nothing awful, but her dad just didn't care about her and I think it was her way of trying to get his attention. Eventually her dad woke up enough to realise they were both ruining their lives and decided to bring them back here. Rose was sixteen and, although she carried the weight of the world on her shoulders, she was incredibly beautiful.'

Maggie picked up a chocolate chip from her plate and popped it in her mouth.

'William McCallister was the mayor at the time. He was quite young, probably early thirties, I think. He was married but rumour had it that he was sleeping with many of the women in the village. As soon as Rose arrived he turned his attention to her and I think she had been so starved of attention and love for so many years that she didn't turn down his advances or at least didn't turn them down for long. Within a month, maybe six weeks of them returning to the village, Rose was pregnant.'

'Oh God,' Star said. 'She was sixteen? She was still a child.'

Star thought back to when she was sixteen, trying to be cool with friends at school and college. Hanging around in a tree doing magic with Wolf. She couldn't even begin to imagine how it would feel to suddenly find out she was pregnant then when she was still a child herself.

Maggie nodded. 'Her dad was furious. He said she'd brought shame on them and the village. One night she just disappeared. At first he said she'd run away, but it soon became clear, thanks to Rose's sister, that he had kicked her out. Made the poor girl homeless, when she was sixteen and pregnant. It was awful.'

Star swallowed the lump in her throat. She'd always had so much anger towards her parents, and her mum especially, but now she understood some of what she'd gone through that anger was rapidly being replaced with an immense sadness. Rose must have been so scared. 'My poor mum.'

'The villagers did not take kindly to it. Making a teenage girl homeless is not in the spirit of Midnight, one of us would have taken her in had we known. Mr Blaketon took a lot of abuse over it and in the end he decided to leave the village himself. But not before

Rose's sister named the father of the baby. Tula made sure everyone knew that William had made a teenage girl pregnant. He denied it of course but Tula had photos of him and Rose kissing, his hand up her dress. Bert, their neighbour, even came forward and said he'd heard the two of them arguing before Rose left and that William had told Rose to get rid of it because he didn't want to be a dad. The villagers were disgusted and voted him out of office. He left the village soon after that.'

'What a dick. But how could I be Midnight-born if my mum left the village?'

'The evening of the summer solstice, Rose came back. The guards let her in, didn't see any reason not to, she had been a resident there and was Midnight-born. She said she was collecting some of her things. She was in the village for four or five hours and then left. The guard didn't see you when she went, but it was dark and she was carrying a lot of stuff. The village hall is always open so I presume she gave birth to you in there, or took you there after she had given birth to fill in the record.'

'I was dumped on my adopted parents' doorstep in Whimbles around two in the morning so that fits with the timeline. She had me here, walked out the village and left me on the nearest doorstep.'

'It took guts to come back here knowing she might

have to face her family and judgement from the villagers,' Wolf said. 'She probably had no clue that her dad and the mayor had left. But she wanted you to have a link to your home and by giving birth to you here she provided you with that. All Midnight-borns are always welcome back here. She probably knew she couldn't keep you, but she gave you a way back home.'

Star shook her head, feeling so sad for her mum. 'I hope she's OK now, that somewhere over the years she found some happiness.'

'I hope for that too,' Maggie said.

Star picked up her mug of tea and took a sip. 'But why did Tom react so badly to me being Rose's daughter?'

'Ah well, that's the next sad part of the story. Tom is William's dad. Your grandfather.'

'What? Does that mean you're my—'

Maggie shook her head. 'William was his son from his first marriage. I guess I'm probably your step-grandmother if you want to put a label on it. When William was kicked out of the village, Tom was furious and mostly he laid the fault on Rose for seducing his son.'

'You're kidding?' Star said, aghast.

'Tom is a good man, but he's blind when it comes to the faults of his son. Especially since... there's no easy way to say this but your father passed away shortly after he left the village.'

Star sat back in her chair. Her dad was a shit. Even Wolf had said that before he knew the full story. She had decided long ago she never wanted to meet her birth parents or have anything to do with them – and hearing what kind of man William was, taking advantage of a sixteen-year-old girl and then ditching her when he found out she was pregnant, hadn't changed that opinion – but it was still a bit of a shock to hear he was dead. She didn't know whether to be sad, angry, guilty that she'd thought ill of someone who had died. She didn't know how to handle this news at all.

'William's wife left him after they were kicked out. He started drinking quite heavily and one day he got in the car and went for a drive and hit a tree. Your dad didn't make it.'

'And Tom blames his death on Rose,' Star said. And by association, her too.

Maggie nodded. 'I think he will come around. You're his only living relative and he knows none of this is your fault.'

Star sighed and her eyes fell on the leather book.

Maggie slid it across the table towards her. 'I'm sure Wolf told you about the blood message your mum left for you. I'm sure she has her own side of the story to tell.'

Star let out a heavy sigh. There was still a part of her that didn't want to open this can of worms but she knew she'd always be wondering about Rose if she didn't.

'I'll leave you alone to watch it and if you have any questions afterwards you can talk to me then,' Maggie said, and she got up and left the room.

Star looked at Wolf. 'Will you stay?'

'I'm not going anywhere.'

She opened the book and flicked through the old dated pages until she came to her birth record in June and there, sure enough, right next to her name, was a smear of blood.

'How does it work? What do I do?'

'You simply touch it and you'll see the message played in front of you like watching a movie. If you decide you want a break, just let go of the page and the message will stop.'

Star nodded, took a deep breath and then placed her finger over the top of the smear of blood.

Immediately the kitchen vanished, and she could see a young girl leaning over her.

Star gasped and let go of the page.

'God I wasn't expecting her face to be so close.'

'I expect she gave you the message when she was holding you as a baby. You would have had to be there for the blood message to be given. So the message is seen from your point of view back then.'

Star nodded. 'That makes sense. She was very young. She looks like a teenage girl, not a woman, and it makes me even angrier that William took advantage of her when she was still so obviously a child.'

'I'm angry for you and your mum too. He was the mayor, he was in a position of authority, he should never have taken advantage of that role.'

Star looked at Wolf. She understood a bit more now why he didn't want to date anyone in the village. William had abused his position and Wolf never wanted to be seen to be doing the same.

She turned her attention back to the book and placed her finger over the smear of blood again. Immediately she saw the girl who was her mum. She had long black hair and her eyes had those cat-eye flicks at the corners but with bright blue eyeliner.

'It's OK, don't cry, I'm sorry I know the prick hurt, but it's just for a few seconds,' Rose said.

Star knew that Rose must have pricked both their fingers to enable her to leave the blood message.

'I just wanted you to know my side of the story. When you come back to Midnight, everyone will no doubt tell you that William was a great mayor and that I seduced him, or even that I slept with lots of boys in the village and accused him when I became pregnant when he'd never even touched me. Neither of those things are true. He wasn't a great mayor, he wasn't even a great man.'

Rose sighed and looked across the room for a second before she turned back to Star. 'The last few years, since Mum died, have been really shitty. Where Dad should have been the one to support me and Tula with our grief, he found comfort in the bottom of the bottle and took great pleasure verbally abusing us both, every single day. I suppose I should be grateful that he wasn't physically abusive but I don't feel any gratitude for the last few years.'

Rose wrapped the blanket a bit tighter around Star.

'When we came back here to live, William asked if I would give him a hand sorting out the village archives. I didn't want to but Dad said I had to as William had done him a big favour by letting us all come back to the village. Every day William and I would be working alongside each other and he was so attentive, so charming. He told me his marriage was over, that his wife didn't love him anymore and had been having affairs behind his back but they were forced to stay together for appearances. He was so complimentary and affectionate, always touching my back or my hand, or my arm. I'd only been here three days when he tried to kiss me. And like a stupid lovestruck girl, I let him. Looking back now, I hadn't had anyone treat me with love or kindness since before Mum died six years earlier. This went on for a few days, I'd come and help him here in the village hall and we would spend our time kissing in the storeroom. It felt like this wonderful delicious secret and I'm ashamed to say I loved the attention. This sexy, charming, older man and he wanted me. I'd been told for so many years that I was ugly and pathetic and no one would ever want me and William did, he couldn't keep his hands off me.'

Rose took a deep breath. 'I'd only been back here in the village a week when the kiss turned to something more. He was kissing me, touching me, saying how beautiful I was, and how much I turned him on. He asked if he could make love to me and I said yes because I was so desperate to please him. I was a virgin and my first time was a quick painful fumble inside a dirty storeroom and it was over in thirty seconds. The second time wasn't much better, neither was the third. In fact all the times we were together were pretty crap but he seemed to enjoy himself and because my self-esteem was in shreds I figured that was the only thing that mattered.'

Star watched as Rose bent and placed a kiss on her younger self's cheek and she felt tears pool in her eyes. 'Three weeks later I found out I was pregnant with you. And he didn't want anything to do with me after that. He told me I had to get rid of it. He said if I told anyone he'd deny that anything ever happened between us. It was like this switch had gone off in his head and the charming man that he'd been with me was simply a façade. He was horrible. In fact, he decided to pre-empt any action on my part and came and told my dad that I had accused him of sleeping with me and how horrified he was by the accusations. William said it was common knowledge I was sleeping with several boys in the village and that now I was pregnant and clearly trying to pin it on him. My dad was appalled and didn't want to listen to my side of the story at all. That night, he packed a bag, dragged me out to the car and drove out to the nearest bus stop. He gave me ten pounds and basically told me never to darken his doorstep ever again.'

Star was heartbroken for her poor mum. Her life had not been kind to her. She realised that the tears were falling down her cheeks when she felt Wolf's hand in hers.

Rose picked up baby Star's little hand and kissed her fingers. 'I've met someone. Dex. He's lovely and kind and he says he will take care of me and you. And there has been a huge part of me that has been so tempted. That somehow the three of us can make a life together because if we love you that's all that matters, right – that you are loved. And Dex would love you so much. And I've loved you for nine months already and I keep thinking that's all you need. But we live in his camper van and it's cold and damp. Sometimes we eat cold beans from a can because he can't afford to buy a gas canister for the stove. Sometimes we live on bread and cheese and nothing else. And he smokes a lot and not the legal kind. I've done a bit of waitressing to get some money, but I started showing very quickly and people are not interested in having a pregnant teenage girl serve their customers. Dex says we'll make it work and he promises to only smoke outside when you arrive, but I know you deserve a better life than that. You deserve to be happy and have decent food and somewhere warm and dry to spend the night.'

Rose frowned. 'And while I know that no one could ever love you as much as I do right now, I also know you will be happy and loved. I've found you a lovely couple. They aren't witches but right now I don't want you anywhere near the people of Midnight. Your dad didn't even want you to be born and my dad is a drunken bully. Plus there's the small little matter of me being a weather witch. My dad told a few people when he was drunk and they in turn told a few others and, while none of them have been nasty in the short time I was here, you could see there was a wariness, a fear, people crossing over to the other side of the street to avoid me. I worry that if I leave you in Midnight and they know you're my daughter they might fear you too. There's no way I want anyone to hurt you either emotionally or physically, though I don't think it would come to that.'

Rose paused, chewing her lip as she thought.

'I've been watching your new parents for the last few weeks, chatted to them, and while I never told them of the wonderful gift I'm going to give them, I know they will love you very much. I see your future and it is very bright. You will be loved, by your new parents, by the people you help when you're older and, most importantly, when you come back here to Midnight, you will be loved so very much. So although giving you up will destroy me and it will be the hardest thing I will ever have to do, I will do anything to give you a bright and happy future. So I'm going to give you some food now so you're full and happy and then you're going to meet your new parents.' Rose started undoing her top. 'I love you Star, so much, and I always will.'

With that the message came to an end and Star found herself back in Maggie's kitchen, tears pouring down her cheeks and Wolf sitting next to her with his arm around her.

Star was vaguely aware she and Wolf were walking towards the woods at the back of the village.

She felt numb. Her dad, a complete piece of shit, was dead, her grandad didn't want anything to do with her and she couldn't even begin to process the emotions surrounding her mum.

Wolf sat down under a big tree and she sat down next to him. She had told him everything her mum had said and she knew how angry he was. She was angry herself but the man she wanted to direct all that anger at was dead.

'Tell me what you're thinking,' Wolf said.

She shook her head. 'I honestly don't know. I feel so sorry for my mum. And those are words I never thought I'd say. But she was sixteen and my dad took advantage of her and then betrayed her, and her own dad then let her down too by taking William's side and kicking her out. She must have been so scared and felt so alone. I'm glad she found Dex – even though he doesn't sound like the sort of man I'd want for my mum, at least he was kind.'

She fell silent.

'It's still OK to feel angry with her,' Wolf said, gently.

'I can't say I'm angry, not anymore. But I keep thinking what would I do in that situation. Sixteen, pregnant, no real home, no job. I know it must have seemed so hopeless to her but I feel like I would have done anything and everything I could to keep my child. I can't imagine loving someone like she loved me and giving them up. I know she thought she was doing the best thing for me, and I was very happy with my adoptive parents, had a nice home and they did love me very much, but surely the best thing for me, regardless of anything else, was to grow up with my birth mum. I grew up feeling that I wasn't loved or wanted by my birth parents, like I wasn't enough. I wouldn't want any child of mine to feel like that. I don't know, I suppose it's easy for me to say I wouldn't have done what she did but I wasn't there. I don't know what her life was like.'

'Never judge a person until you've walked a mile in their shoes.'

'Exactly. I just feel so sad and so confused.'

They sat in silence for a while.

'Will this help?' Wolf clicked his fingers and a pot of churros and chocolate sauce appeared in his hand.

She smiled and took it. 'It helps a little.'

He wrapped his arm around her, hugging her to his chest.

'This helps a lot.'

She chewed on her churro and let out a heavy sigh. 'You need to try one of these too. They are amazing.'

Wolf helped himself to a churro. 'These are good.'

She leaned her head against his chest and he stroked her hair as if the rules he very clearly laid out that morning no longer existed or were at least temporarily paused.

'Aren't you worried about people from the village seeing us together?'

'Right now, I couldn't care less.'

She looked up at him. 'My life could have been so different. I can't regret the life I grew up with, I love my adoptive parents so much, but things would have been very different if I grew up here. I would know and understand my magic for one. And what about us, we'd have been friends from a very early age. That friendship might have turned into a deeper relationship that could have lasted a lifetime.'

'Or maybe we'd never have got together if we grew up in the same village. Maybe we only got together because we were something new and different for each other.'

'Zofia said to me yesterday, that if I had grown up here I would have been married with children by now. Given that we're betrothed, I wonder if she meant with you.'

He let out a sigh. 'That's a hard pill to swallow. The life we should have had. I've always wanted children.'

'Me too.'

She looked up at him and she suddenly wondered why they were holding back. They had been in love once. Shouldn't they be at least giving that life a chance?

But he frowned and looked away. 'You can't lament the loss of something you never had.'

She sat up. 'No of course not.'

She looked around them, needing a change of subject, and suddenly realised where they were.

'This is our tree. Why did you bring me here?'

'Our magic is strongly connected to nature and the elements. If you're outside you may be able to feel your powers more. I thought a good place to start with your training would be our tree.'

'You want to avoid anything romantic happening

between us but you've brought me back to the place we met and fell in love?'

'We are going to be tempting fate every day, working so closely together, I don't think an old tree is going to make any difference.'

CHAPTER 11

The old tree was definitely making a difference because now Star was surrounded by so many memories of meeting Wolf, being held by him when her dad died, holding his hand when he talked about his mum dying, talking for hours every day, of slowly but inexplicably falling in love with him. She remembered him showing her his magic and being so captivated by him. And now he was sitting on the branch next to hers and she was finding the whole thing very distracting. Because more than anything she wanted to kiss him again and see if that old magic was still there.

She was lying on a branch in the maple tree, just like she had as a child, staring up at the maple leaves above her. These should have turned red and fallen to the floor a month or so before but she guessed because of the weird weather the plants and trees had adapted to their new climate.

And her birth mum had done this, changed the weather for the whole village. And now Star had to learn to control her magic so she wouldn't accidentally do the same.

Wolf had made her climb up in the tree to try and re-enact the magic she had created as a child. He was waiting patiently but nothing was happening. The leaves were staying perfectly still, stubbornly refusing to even flicker let alone dance and twirl. Why had she been able to do it so easily as a child when she didn't even know she could do magic but now she couldn't even muster a spark, let alone a catastrophic Armageddon event? It would be really ironic if the villagers were scared of her when she couldn't even move a leaf.

'I don't think this is going to work,' Star said.

'What did you think about when you made the leaves dance as a child?'

'I had no idea it was me that was doing it. I just thought it was a magic tree.'

'With magic, the intent is the most important part, you have to believe it will happen, see it, know that it will. You're doubting yourself. You don't believe you can do this.'

She sat up. 'Two days ago, I had no idea I could do this or that any of this was possible. Seeing all the magic around the village, my world has changed completely so yes, it is hard to get my head round that I'm a part of all this.'

He stood up easily as if they weren't twelve feet off the ground and stepped across to her branch with grace and poise. The confidence of knowing he wasn't going to fall made her smile. If he did he could just float or fly down as he had when she'd climbed the gate. She couldn't imagine what it would be like to do something like that, how incredible it would be. She wanted to be part of this world, she was excited to learn it all.

He sat down next to her and took her hand; immediately she could feel energy buzzing through her.

'Can you feel that?'

She nodded.

'Our magic is an energy that is with us all the time, but the world around us also has an energy: the trees, flowers, the seas and rivers, the earth and the air. It's everywhere. What you can feel now is my magic, well mine and yours actually, but you can feel my magic when it's dormant, I'm not doing anything with it. But if I was to do this...'

He held his hand up and she saw the leaves ripple above her as if a sudden gust of wind had disturbed them. But she knew it had come from Wolf, she had felt his energy surge as if he had reached out to the energy that was around them.

'Did you feel what I did?'

She nodded eagerly.

'OK, I'm going to use my magic to guide yours. I won't be in control of your magic, I'm just helping you to use it. You'll be in control of it the whole time and if you want me to stop, you just need to say so.'

She nodded.

He turned his attention back to the leaves and a few broke away from the branch and floated down towards them, dancing, twirling, doing loops like some kind of aerobatic plane display.

She laughed at how beautiful it looked.

'See if you can catch one,' Wolf said.

She reached out her hand.

'Not with your hand, with your magic.'

She felt his magic surge gently through her, nudging her. It was the oddest sensation, as if tiny warm bubbles were fizzing and popping through her veins. It was lovely. But then, all of a sudden, she was acutely aware of him, as if he was inside her, a part of her, surrounding her. She could feel him, smell him, he was invading every part of her senses. Those beautiful memories were now in full high definition. And it felt amazing. She hadn't been expecting this at all, but this was his magic inside her and his magic was a part of him so it made sense that she could feel him too.

'You ready?'

She tore her attention away from the sensation of having him so intrinsically linked to her that she could feel him in her heart and soul. She nodded, biting her lip, feeling excited about what she could achieve. All of a sudden the possibilities seemed endless.

'Now take one of the leaves. See yourself reaching for it,' Wolf said.

She imagined plucking the leaf from the air and as she did she felt energy surge out from her, although it was hard to tell whether it was her magic or his or maybe a bit of both, but suddenly she knew she had control of the leaf. Her magic was controlling it. She made it sway from side to side, made it pirouette on its stem, and she laughed that she was doing this, that she had control.

Wolf's leaf continued to loop and twirl next to hers and then it moved closer to hers and, as the edges of his leaf curled round hers, they started moving together in some kind of tango. She matched him step for step, using her fingers to help direct her magic like she was controlling a marionette.

The dance was actually quite passionate, which was silly, it was just two leaves dancing, but she knew it was much more than that. It was his magic entwined with hers and with his magic bubbling inside her it felt quite intimate. She glanced at Wolf to find he was watching her intently too and she wondered if he felt that too.

She looked down at their joined hands, her leaf completely forgotten.

'I can feel you inside me,' she said.

He frowned. 'My magic?'

'No, you. And it feels wonderful.'

'It does?' He looked surprised.

'You've never touched someone else's magic before?'

He shook his head. 'Not like this. We don't do this. This is the equivalent of being invited to someone's house for dinner and going through all of their cupboards and drawers and then having a lie-down in their bed. What I'm doing to you, playing with your magic, most people would consider disrespectful and rude. It was something my mum and dad used to do. When my mum had a stroke, she struggled with her magic afterwards and my dad would guide her magic in the same way that I'm guiding yours, so I knew it was something that was possible but it's not really the done thing with people you don't know. That's why I wanted to make it clear that you have control over this and if you don't like it, I'll withdraw my magic immediately. What did you mean when you said you can feel me?'

She thought for a moment about how to describe it without making it sound sexual, especially after his big speech about not wanting anything to happen between them and her indignity over the betrothal. But the truth was that it felt incredibly intimate.

'Maybe I could show you. I could touch your magic so you know what it feels like.'

He looked unsure but then nodded. 'That's only fair, I suppose.'

She felt his magic fade away from inside her but it was like he'd left echoes of himself behind.

'How do I do this?' Star asked.

'Just reach out for me like you did when you were reaching for that leaf. See your magic flow inside me.'

She did that and immediately felt her magic connect with his. He frowned and nodded. 'Yes, I can feel your magic.' Then his eyes widened in surprise. 'Oh! I can feel you.' He shook his head as if trying to clear it. 'You're everywhere. Shit, I didn't mean to make you feel like this. This isn't appropriate at all. You need to stop before I do something I regret.'

He stood up and she could tell he was angry. Had she done something wrong?

In a panic, she quickly tried to remove her magic but she wasn't sure how and suddenly there was a loud bang like a gunshot and a flash of light and Wolf sagged and toppled off the branch head-first.

'No!' Star yelled and stretched out to catch him to stop him from falling but missed him. Without thinking she reached out with her magic like she'd done with the leaf to try and grab him and she watched in shock as the air seemed to suddenly bend around him, breaking his fall just a few inches from the ground. She was so stunned she'd done it, she let out a little yelp, staggered back a bit and nearly tumbled off the branch herself. But with the distraction, the magic surrounding Wolf disappeared and he fell the last few inches to the ground.

Star quickly climbed down the tree and rushed to his side. He wasn't moving at all. In fact, he didn't even appear to be breathing.

'Oh, god, no, please don't be dead,' Star said, shaking him. He didn't stir. She rested her cheek over his mouth to feel any breath but there was nothing. 'Shit, shit, shit. I've killed him.'

Tears caught in her throat. She knew the basics of CPR although she'd only ever practised on a dummy several years before. But she didn't know the magical equivalent, if there was one. She tilted his head back, held his nose and took a deep breath but, as her lips grazed his, he suddenly spoke.

'That won't be necessary.'

She sank back on her heels and burst into tears. 'Oh god, sorry, I thought you were dead.'

He took her hand, although he didn't open his eyes. 'Don't cry, I'm fine. Just... give me five minutes.'

'I'm so sorry.'

'Stop apologising.'

'Are you hurt?'

'No.'

'What do you need? What can I do?'

'Without meaning to sound rude, can you just stop talking, just for a few minutes.'

She clamped her mouth shut. He was still holding her hand firmly in his but, after a few moments, she felt his grip go slack, his breathing becoming heavy as if he was sleeping. His hand was ice cold though, and when she placed a hand on his chest she could feel the freezing chill of his skin through his shirt.

How could he be so cold on such a warm day? He was so icy to the touch, she was suddenly worried he might get hypothermia.

'Wolf?' she whispered.

There was no response. She knew sharing body heat was one way to keep warm so she carefully climbed on top of him, trying to cover him like a blanket, although he was huge so she couldn't do that but at least she could cover some of him. She closed her eyes and thought warm thoughts, hoping somehow that the warmth would seep into him.

'Star.'

She jolted at the sound of his voice. She looked at him and he was staring at her.

'You're awake, are you OK?'

'Yes, a little confused but I'm OK.'

'What are you confused about?'

'Lots of things, but mostly why you're lying on top of me.'

She felt her face flame. 'To try and keep you warm, you were freezing.'

'Right now, I'm hotter than the sun.'

'I was thinking of warm things.'

'I can tell.'

Tears smarted her eyes and she moved to get off him but to her surprise he wrapped an arm around her to stop her.

'I'm kidding, thank you for looking after me.'

'I don't think you have anything to thank me for, I...' All words stalled in her throat as he cupped her face and gently wiped the tears away.

Wolf let out a heavy sigh. 'I think we're going to have a problem here.'

'You mean us?'

He nodded and then he smiled. 'I saw all our memories here, as clear as day.'

'I know. I did too.'

'I still can't believe you're here, after all this time,' Wolf said softly, affection in his eyes. 'I lied when I said I didn't give you much thought after you'd left. I obviously wasn't waiting for you to come back so we could get married, but I did think about you often. I know we were only kids, but I did love you.'

His gaze flicked down to her lips and she knew he was thinking about kissing her and she was surprised how much she wanted that. Their mouths were only a few inches apart and if she leaned forward she could kiss him.

'Star, we need to talk about what happened.'

'When you fell?'

'No, when our magic connected. When you touched my magic...' he paused, clearly deliberating on what to say. 'I have never felt so turned on in my entire life.'

She blushed. 'What?'

'I wanted you in ways that I've never felt before. I could feel you everywhere but it wasn't enough, I wanted more. Is that what you felt when I touched yours? You said it felt wonderful.'

'It was.' She swallowed. 'It felt like you were a part of me, like you were inside me, in my veins, in my heart. I could smell you, feel you like you were wrapped around me. I wouldn't say I was turned on but it felt... glorious.'

'That was never my intention. I am sorry. I had no idea it would feel like that. When my dad did it to my mum, it was never a... sexual thing. It was always to help and guide her.'

'You don't need to apologise.'

'I do, I would never do something like that.'

'I know.' She bit her lip. 'I can still feel you. Not as strongly as before but you left an imprint behind.'

'I can feel you too. I think we forged some kind of connection.'

'Or reopened one.'

He frowned. 'What do you mean?'

She paused as she thought. 'I can't believe I'm going to say this when I said it was all rubbish, but do you think it felt that way because we're betrothed? Not the betrothal thing but our connection that was forged because of being born on the same day, the magic from the ley lines?'

He nodded. 'I would think that's quite likely. But then I've never done what I've just done with anyone before so I don't know.'

She let out a little sigh. 'I think we need to take this betrothal thing a bit more seriously than we thought.'

'Star, we're not getting married.'

'I'm not suggesting that, I'm not even suggesting we start dating. It's just clear that we have a connection whether we like it or not. And it doesn't have to be a physical, intimate connection, but there is something there that we should probably investigate or look into a bit more rather than dismissing it.'

He chewed on his lip. 'You're probably right, but let's not do that today.'

He looked tired and she was worried about him. 'What happened when you fell, what did I do wrong?'

'You didn't do anything wrong. When I realised how your magic made me feel when it touched mine, and how I probably made you feel, I wanted you to stop and I tried to push you out. Our magic fought against each other and yours most definitely won.'

'Oh my god Wolf, I could have killed you.'

'No, you just knocked me out. And it's not your fault. Besides, I'm guessing that you must have broken my fall, otherwise I think I'd have some broken bones to deal with now after a fall that high.'

'I somehow caught you with my magic.'

He looked at her in awe. 'Impressive stuff.'

'Well, I wouldn't rely on me doing it again, I have no idea how I did it. And quit looking at me like I'm some kind of hero. I made you feel things you didn't want to feel, forged a connection you definitely don't want and then threw you out of a tree. And for the cherry on top of my inappropriate behaviour, I lay on top of you.'

He smirked. 'I've had worse days.'

'Why are you so laid-back about all of this?'

'I'm just thinking that if the betrothal thing works out and we end up married with kids, it'll be a hell of a thing to tell the grandchildren.'

She laughed. 'We're not getting married. I don't even like you.'

This did nothing to dispel the smirk on his face. 'I don't know, you seemed very concerned when you thought I was dead.'

'Only because I thought the villagers would come after me for killing their beloved mayor.'

'They probably would too, you'd be burned at the stake.'

She felt the smile fall from her face. 'What?'

'I'm kidding. No one is going to hurt you here. Stop worrying that they're going to come after you when they find out who you are. They'll love you. Come on. I think we've had enough training for one day. Why don't I introduce you to Ashley on the way back and then you'll know where to go for potions club tonight.'

'OK.'

She stood up and Wolf stretched and stood up too and they started walking back to the village.

She couldn't help but notice the people staring at her from their gardens and windows as they walked past.

They soon arrived at a little cottage with a bright purple front door but before Wolf had a chance to knock, the door was opened and a young woman was standing there smiling. She had blonde hair in a plait down to her waist and blue eyes. She was wearing denim cut-offs and a blue t-shirt with a sparkly flamingo wearing sunglasses. And when she spoke Star realised she was American.

'I was wondering how long it would take before you brought her to meet me,' the woman said. 'Star, I'm Ashley Dougan, it's a pleasure to meet you.'

Star held out a hand but Ashley pulled her into a hug and some of her doubts and fears melted away.

'Come in,' Ashley said, stepping back to let them inside.

Star followed her in and Wolf had to bend his head to step through the door. The lounge was stunning. A simple grey corner sofa stood in the middle with an abundance of deep purple, bright turquoise and fuchsia satin sequinned cushions. There was a deep blue rug on the floor and the walls and mantlepiece were covered in coloured glass bottles of every shape and size, all catching the sunlight as it streamed through the window.

'Wow, I love your house,' Star said.

'Oh, it's a bit stereotypical for the potions lady to have all these bottles, but these aren't all potions, just some of them are. I just love coloured glass. I get some from each place I visit around the world, these remind me of my travels. Anyway, how are you settling in?'

Star let out a breath. 'It's all a bit overwhelming. I came here to escape the media and the attention and I get a whole load of attention in another way. I feel a bit like an animal in a zoo with everyone staring.'

'Everyone is bound to be curious about you. They always are with new folk, but you're extra exciting because you're a wildling. We've never had one of those before. Don't take it personally. Once people get to know you, you'll soon become old news.'

'That's what I said, she needs to give people the opportunity to meet her,' Wolf said. 'That's why I suggested she comes along to potions club tonight.'

'You'd be very welcome,' Ashley said. 'Actually you'll see that we come from all over the world, we all had very different starts in life, different journeys, different upbringings, but we are united in magic. So it doesn't matter that you didn't start your life as a witch, you are one now and magic brings us together. That and wine.'

Star laughed. 'I'll be there. Shall I bring anything?'

'Snacks are normally fully covered but if you wanted to bring something with you, you could bring some of your famous cupcakes.'

'Ah well, I promised myself I wouldn't make any more of those until I mastered my magic.'

Ashley frowned. 'Don't stop doing the things you love. Intent is a big part of magic: what do you want to use the magic for, what's the outcome? If you make cakes with only the intention of making friends, only good will come of it.'

Star smiled at that. 'OK, I'll make some chocolate ones. Only good things can come from chocolate, right?'

Ashley laughed. 'Oh absolutely. Be here at seven?'

'I will.'

She gave Ashley a wave and they stepped back outside.

'I like her,' Star said, feeling lighter already.

'I do too. Ashley has a special way with magic, she just seems to understand it so much more than anyone else. She can see it, which is very rare. She can see auras around people but she can also see the magical energies that are all around us too. She is brilliant at potions and while tonight you might not necessarily learn a lot with regards to that, as I hear wine takes precedence at these gatherings, I still think you'll have fun. And you can always come back on another day and discuss potions with her privately, when there's no wine involved.'

'I probably will. That side of things fascinates me because I think it's very similar to what I've been doing for years with my cakes.'

'I agree.'

'On that note, I need to get back and make a batch of cakes for tonight.'

'Make sure you think happy thoughts.'

She laughed. 'I will. What are your plans for the rest of the day?'

'I'm going to look more into our betrothal and the magic that surrounds it. I want to understand what we're dealing with here.'

'Oh. Good idea. Let me know what you find out.'

He nodded, gave her a wave and then walked off in the direction of the very back of the village.

She watched him go, wondering if they were able to understand the magic that was an intrinsic part of their betrothal, whether they could break it. She bit her lip as she thought back to the bond they had shared that morning because right now she wasn't sure if she wanted to.

CHAPTER 12

Wolf knocked on his gran's door and she opened it with a cocktail glass in her hand, something bright purple inside steaming and bubbling.

'Oh good, I'm glad you're here, you can be my guinea pig,' Zofia said.

'I'm not drinking that,' Wolf stepped inside.

'Oh come on, I need to find the perfect punch mix for the winter solstice celebrations.'

'Anything that colour does not look safe to drink.'

'Of course it's safe,' Zofia took a big glug of it to prove it. 'It just doesn't taste particularly good. Here, you try.'

'I'll pass.'

'You need to live a little, relax, enjoy yourself. You're always so serious. When you were little you used to love playing with your magic, you used to have fun. I can't remember the last time you had fun doing anything.'

Wolf smiled a little as he remembered how fun it had been to show Star his dark side this morning, filling the kitchen with his scary illusions. He used to love doing stuff like that with his magic as a child. But now he was an adult and he had responsibilities. Star was a distraction he could really do without.

'I need to talk to you and I'd like to keep a clear head.'

'About Star being your betrothed?'

He should be used to this by now, but it was still a little weird. He had the odd premonition here and there, obviously having picked up some of his gran's foretelling skills, but he didn't just know everything like some kind of omniscient presence.

'Yes, exactly.'

'I'm glad she's finally here, about bloody time. She should put a spring in your step and a smile on your face. Have you slept with her yet?'

'Zofia, I'm not having that conversation with you.'

She didn't like being called 'Gran' or for him to make any other reference to her being a grandparent. She wanted everyone to believe she was eternally young. She looked great for her age but having an adult grandchild living in the village with her kind of ruined that look.

'Is that a yes?'

'No it isn't. Nothing is going to happen between me and Star. She's come here for a place of refuge and now she's practically being forced down the aisle just because we were born on the same day, it's ridiculous.'

'You and I both know the betrothal runs far deeper than just having the same birthday. The connection of the ley lines is some powerful magic.'

He was beginning to realise that. He had feelings for Star that he'd never experienced before. And he couldn't even blame it on how their magic had connected earlier that day. When she'd arrived at his house the night before and touched his lightning scar, he'd removed her hand because he liked it too damned much. He wanted her hands on him, and her touching him like that made him want to power her backwards against the door and make love to her. When he'd hugged her in her kitchen on her first day, he had to stop and walk away because he wanted so much more. When she'd fallen asleep, there had been something primal deep down inside him that wanted her in his bed. Even if he then slept the rest of the night on the sofa, there was something so perfect about her lying in his bed. And he didn't get why he felt this way, so quickly and so strongly. She was a beautiful woman but he knew it was more than that – he'd been with many attractive women in his life and he'd never felt like this before. It had to be down to their connection to the ley lines and he wanted it to stop.

'How do I remove this magic?'

Zofia stared at him in horror. 'Why the hell would you want to remove it?'

'Because she should have a choice. We both should. I feel like I'm hypnotised with her, like I have no control. I can't help but touch her every time I'm with her, I need to hold her hand or touch her hair. All I can think about is kissing her, making love to her, and it's driving me mad.'

'Just give into it. If she's willing, which I'm sure she is, enjoy it, embrace it, have some fun for the first time in your life. I have no doubt at all she'll be the best thing that's ever happened to you so why are you holding back?'

'I want her to have control over this. I don't want her forced into it because some weird ancient magic is making her feel this way.'

'That's not how this works. The magic isn't brain-washing you.'

'That's what it feels like.'

'Your love story started sixteen years ago. This isn't two people being forced together, this is a rekindling of that love, this is both of you realising that those feelings never went away, they just grew stronger in all the years you were apart.'

'What if we were forced together back then because

of our connection with the ley lines? What if none of this is real?'

'Dear Gods. Why do you think you're so unlovable?'

He frowned. 'I don't think I'm unlovable. I've had relationships with lots of women over the years.'

'You've had sex with a lot of women over the years. Sometimes dinner and sex. I'd hardly call any of them a relationship. What's really going on here?'

She cocked her head, studying him, and he winced knowing she was seeing a lot more than what was on the surface. 'Ah. Worst thing your parents ever did was take you out of this village, although I appreciate the intentions were good. But when your mum had her stroke, your dad should have brought her home, we would have helped, with her and you and Lynx. Instead he struggled trying to support her and you kept the bullying to yourself. And taking you to a mundane school didn't teach you to be social and interact with other children as they'd hoped, it taught you that if you put yourself out there, you'll get bullied and ostracised. It made you withdrawn and quiet for fear of being found out. It showed you, you can never be yourself.'

Zofia frowned as she continued reading him like a book. 'There was a girl, Marie, you were ten. You asked her out and she laughed at you, she said she'd never go out with a freak like you. Bloody hell, Wolf, is that it? You were kids.' Then her face softened. 'Oh no, it was Star, wasn't it? *She* broke your heart. You told her you loved her, the only person you've ever said those words to, and she never came back. But that wasn't her fault, it was the wards the town council put around the village.'

'I know that now. She tried everything to get back to me, she even kept trying years later, every time she came up this way, and she couldn't find her way back to our tree. But I didn't find out about the wards until years after they went up, so yeah losing her did hurt, I didn't understand what went wrong between us. And I never got any closure on that.'

'You think because she never told you she loved you before then she couldn't possibly love you now. And now she's back you want to be sure if she loves you, she loves you for you, not because you're forced together by ancient magic?'

'Honestly, I'd prefer nothing to happen between us at all, it's just easier that way for both of us. But yes, if it does happen, I want to be sure she chose this.'

Zofia let out a big sigh and turned her attention back to the cauldron that was bubbling away with some mysterious liquid.

'What's in that anyway?'

'Are you asking with your health and safety hat on or because you're secretly tempted to try some?'

'I trust you not to poison everyone.'

He stepped closer; it smelled disgusting.

'It's got a lemon balm wine, an infusion of oregano

and peppermint oil, and a pinch of sage, sorrel, nutmeg and tarragon. It has blackberry and cranberry juice, orange rind and of course moonbeams and stardust.'

'OK, well that sounds fine.'

'Oh and four bottles of vodka.'

He rolled his eyes. 'Of course it has.'

He watched her stir it and waited for the pearls of wisdom she was always so quick to dispense.

'I was betrothed once.'

That was not what he was expecting. 'How did I not know this?'

'It wasn't here, it was in my old village in Poland. Dovyen, the Polish equivalent of Midnight, only much much bigger.'

'Were you betrothed to Grandad?'

'No, bless him, I was terribly fond of your grandad, he was a lovely man and a good friend, but we didn't share that incredible connection I shared with Jan.'

There was something a bit sad about that. Zofia had been married to his grandad for forty-six years and it sounded like she never really loved him. But instead it seemed like she'd missed out on the love of her life with this man Jan.

'What happened?'

Zofia added a pinch of something, which looked a bit like marigold, and poured some of the liquid into a glass.

'Jan was born in my village but moved away when

he was a baby. I didn't even know he existed until he came back when we were nineteen. Everyone was all, "Oh he's your betrothed, he's come back to woo you, how romantic,"' Zofia put on a silly girly excited voice. 'And I thought if he's here to woo me, let him. We had two months of the best sex of my entire life. What we shared was purely physical, I certainly didn't love him but if he'd asked me to marry him I'd have said yes just to have that kind of hot sex for the rest of my life. I don't know if it was our physical connection from being born on the same day or whether it was just him and his prowess in the bedroom but he was a god between the sheets and everywhere else we chose to have sex. He thought a lot of himself. The name Jan means "gift from God" and he definitely thought he was. Turned out he was giving his gift to several other women in the village at the same time.'

Wolf didn't even know where to start with that story. It was hard to picture his gran as a sexual demon, in fact it was something he would rather not picture. He took the glass off her and took a swig. It tasted as disgusting as it smelled but it burned the back of his throat and a warmth settled into him.

'So what happened to the whole soul mate thing? Destined to be together forever and all that crap?'

'I don't think being betrothed means you're each other's soul mate, if such a thing even exists. I don't think it means you will instantly love each other, it just means you share a connection. With you two both being born on the summer solstice I'd say that connection was even stronger but it doesn't mean love and happy ever after. It was quite common for children to be betrothed in my village, there were a lot of young couples and a lot of children. Many of the betrothed couples married but divorced a few years down the line when they found out they had very little in common; only some were married for life. Some never even got as far as marriage, they dated for a while, had crazy hot betrothal sex and moved on.'

'Are you saying the betrothal connection is purely sexual?'

He took another swig of the cocktail, feeling like he needed it, but instantly regretted it.

'I don't know what it is or how it works,' Zofia said. 'But I'm pretty sure it's not love. Love is too powerful to be created with magic, you know that. I'm pretty sure there isn't a magic spell, curse, charm or potion in the world that could make two people fall in love with each other.'

Wolf did feel a little better about that, though it didn't stop his rather inconvenient need for Star.

'Look, if it bothers you that much I bet it can be removed. I don't know enough about all that but I bet Ashley does. She can see magic; she will be able to see the bond that connects you. If anyone can remove it, it will be her.'

He nodded. 'Maybe I'll have a chat with her.'

'Or... just enjoy crazy hot betrothal sex, get it out of your system and move on.'

He downed the rest of his drink. He was very very tempted.

Star knocked on Ashley's door later that night feeling very nervous. She just wanted everyone to like her, was that too much to ask?

Ashley opened the door with a big smile. 'Hey, Star, come in and meet everyone. Here, let me take those off you.' She took the tin of lovingly made cupcakes and peeked inside. 'These look and smell delicious.'

'Thank you, they're perfectly safe, I promise.'

Ashley grinned and ushered her inside.

The sofa had somehow grown since Star had been in there that afternoon and it lined the edges of the room in a giant horseshoe shape. There were five women all sitting at their own individual cauldron and in the middle of the room was a table heaped high with snacks and another filled with bottles and boxes of herbs and other ingredients, which presumably were going to be used in the potions. Candles flickered and danced on surfaces all around the room.

There was a small collective cheer as the women

spotted Star and she couldn't help smiling. She recognised Maxine from the day before and the other woman who'd been was shouting at Jessica she presumed was Erin, as Wolf had mentioned her.

'Star, let me introduce everyone. Over here to your left is Nithya, she's from Goa.'

'Oh, you're the one who decorated my house, thank you so much, it looks wonderful,' Star said.

'It was my pleasure,' Nithya said.

'Did you put the photo of Michelangelo's *David* in my bedroom?'

Nithya dissolved into giggles. 'I did. It always makes me smile when I see it. I thought it might make you smile too.'

Star snorted when Nithya held up her little finger to show what exactly made her smile.

'Next to her is Darianna,' Ashley went on. 'She's from Ecuador.' Darianna smiled and waved.

'Next is Maxine and she's from Skegness.'

'Hello,' Maxine waved. 'I promise I don't have any more tomatoes on me tonight.'

Star grinned.

'And over here we have Kianga from Tanzania. She and Nithya went to the same school in Kent.'

'We were the only witches in the school, we had a lot of fun,' Kianga said.

'I can imagine,' Star said, wistfully. How lovely it

would have been to grow up with someone to share your magic with.

'And this is Erin, who is from Dublin,' Ashley finished, introducing the other woman who'd been shouting at Jessica the day before.

Star knew that Ashley was telling Star where everyone was from to prove to her that magic united them, no matter where they came from, just as she'd said that afternoon.

'Hi, hello,' Star waved, frantically trying to commit all their names to memory.

'Star brought her famous cupcakes,' Ashley said, opening the tin and clearing a space for it on the food table.

There were ooohs of appreciation as Nithya, Erin and Kianga all leaned over the tin for a look and helped themselves to one.

'Star, why don't you sit down here next to me, we're going to be starting shortly,' Ashley said.

'I don't have a cauldron,' Star said, sitting next to Erin.

Ashley waved her hand and a small cauldron floated out of one of the cupboards and sat itself in front of Star ready to use.

Star smiled. She didn't think she would ever get used to the magic in this world.

'I'm sorry about the way Jessica treated you yesterday,' Erin said. 'I promise most of the villagers are much kinder and sane. I've always thought she might be a little unhinged.'

'Well, it's good to know I'm not the only one who finds her unpleasant.'

'Where are you from?' Erin said, offering Star something that looked like a small, sticky round ball of dough. She took it and it tasted delicious.

'I grew up in the next village of Whimbles and then moved to London when I was sixteen. But I was actually born here in Midnight, although I only spent a few hours here before I was whisked away.'

Erin's eyes widened. 'You're Midnight-born. That's exciting.'

'It kind of is. But you probably know I'm a wildling, this is all completely new to me. Two days ago, I didn't even know this magical world existed.'

'That has to be scary and confusing,' Erin said.

'It is, and overwhelming and exciting and so many other emotions, my head is spinning. Can I ask you all, what do you tell your non-magic friends about your witchiness or where you live?'

'I don't really mention it, we just talk about other things rather than magic and if they want to visit I always find some excuse to put them off,' Nithya said.

'Yes, me too,' Darianna said.

Star sighed. 'My friend was due to come up here with some of my things and I had to explain it was a private village and she wouldn't be allowed in and of course she wanted to know why.'

'What did you say?' Ashley asked.

'I told her the villagers were all naturists and walk around naked all the time.'

They all burst out laughing.

'Well that would certainly make the solstice more interesting,' Erin said.

'Or traumatising. There's lots of people in the village I really wouldn't want to see naked. Although there are a few I wouldn't mind. Our mayor for one,' Maxine fanned herself.

Kianga leaned over to talk to Star, her eyes wide with excitement. 'You're betrothed to him, aren't you?'

Star smiled. 'Apparently so, we were both born on the same day, but I'm not entirely sure what that means.'

'I don't know what that means either,' Darianna said. 'You have to get married because you share a birthday? That's a bit weird.'

'It is weird, isn't it,' Star laughed. 'That's what I said, I told him I'm not marrying him because of some silly ancient tradition. Fortunately he doesn't want to marry me either so I can't see it's going to be a big deal.'

Apart from the inescapable feelings she had for him and he apparently had for her. But definitely no big deal.

'He is hot though,' Maxine said, fanning herself. 'It

wouldn't be a total hardship being betrothed to him. I'd imagine the incredible sex would make up for his grumpiness.'

Nithya snorted into her cake.

'Is he grumpy?' Star asked. 'He's only been kind to me so far.'

'I wouldn't say grumpy, he's just very serious,' Kianga said. 'He was only sixteen when he became sole guardian to his little brother and then two years later he was voted in as mayor of the village and I guess he had to grow up very quickly. His job as mayor is a big responsibility.'

'He is a bit grumpy' Maxine said. 'He wasn't impressed when I took a little nap once on the way home from potions club.'

The other ladies laughed.

'What? It was a long way home and I may have had a few too many glasses of wine,' Maxine said. 'But I still wouldn't turn down a night of incredible hot sex if he offered. He could be grumpy and bossy in the bedroom, I wouldn't mind that.'

'How do you know the sex would be incredible?' Nithya said.

'Just look at him, you can tell when a man would be amazing in bed,' Maxine said.

'I have a friend who slept with him actually,' Erin said. 'Not from the village, a few miles away, and she said—'

'Ladies, come on,' Ashley laughed. 'I don't think it's fair or appropriate to talk about Wolf like that.'

Erin coughed. 'Best sex she's ever had.' She coughed again to cover it up and everyone laughed.

Star smiled. She thought she could really like these girls.

'Being betrothed is a bit more than a silly ancient tradition,' Ashley said. 'When you are born in Midnight you forge a connection with the ley lines that run under and through the village,' she went on. 'That in itself is a powerful thing. But to share that connection with someone else is very special. It forms a bond that's stronger than anything else I've ever seen. I'm not saying that bond means love but betrothed people do tend to get married because they simply cannot be apart from the other person.'

'And because the sex is so good,' Maxine giggled.

Ashley laughed. 'That too.'

Kianga offered Star a glass of wine and she took it, gesturing with it as she spoke. 'Call me old-fashioned but marriage should be because you're in love, completely and utterly, not just because you suddenly have a shadow you can't get rid of, even if it is a damned sexy one.'

'I wouldn't liken the connection to that of a shadow, following you around, it's more like Wolf is a part of you now, and you're a part of him. Two halves of a whole,' Ashley said.

'Now that does sound romantic,' Darianna said.

'It's only romantic if we love each other, not if we're forced together by some ancient magic,' Star protested although Darianna was right, that did sound kind of romantic.

'Well, I think you should take some time to get to know each other. But the magic that connects you won't force you into doing something you don't want to do,' Ashley said.

The connection was already making them feel things they didn't want to feel. Wolf had been angry when Star had touched his magic and because of how she made him feel. She didn't want to do that again.

'You look so sad about this, being betrothed isn't a bad thing,' Ashley said.

'I know, it's just so much has happened over the last few days and Wolf has been great teaching me about my magic and introducing me to people and I don't want him to feel like this thing between us is a burden, or that it's out of his control. He never dates anyone from the village and I come along and he doesn't want any of this.'

She stopped herself from saying, *He doesn't want me*, although that was the crux of all this. And she understood that he took his job as mayor very seriously. It had been years since they had dated as kids and clearly they couldn't just pick up where they left off. And it made sense to keep these professional boundaries between them but she couldn't help feeling a tiny bit hurt over his refusal to let anything happen.

'I could see the connection you two share when he brought you round earlier. He cares for you, a great deal, but it will probably take him some time to get used to the idea, same as you,' Ashley said.

'And we've got something to cheer you up in the meantime,' Maxine said, waving a bottle of sparkling wine.

Ashley laughed. 'The girls love this potion we're making tonight. Our winter solstice festival in a few days' time is a celebration of the sun returning after the longest winter night. It's a happy time and so tonight we're making a happiness potion and one of the ingredients is sparkling wine. But let's do the other stuff first, that's the last ingredient we add.'

With a wave of her hand, little green fires suddenly flickered and sparkled to life under the mini cauldrons. A large yellow jug floated between the women and poured what looked like twinkling golden water into each cauldron.

'Our first ingredient is water from the spring infused with sunshine and starlight to welcome the sun and banish the dark.'

As the jug floated to Star's cauldron and poured the water inside, she could see it was liquid gold, sparkling and glowing in the light from the candles that danced around the room.

'OK, you have a list of herbs printed on your trays. I want you to collect a pinch of each from the jars and boxes in the middle,' Ashley said. 'Star, the girls know these herbs pretty well, but take your time to become familiar with the herbs and spices in the middle, what they smell and look like. What they feel like. It will help when creating your own potions.'

Star stood up, as did all the others. She picked up a little tray that was beside her cauldron and noticed it had little grooves and partitions similar to those of a tray an artist might use for different colour paints, although she knew these were to help keep her herbs separate before they went into the cauldron. Each section was printed with a different herb name. She noticed that, among others, nutmeg, cinnamon, marjoram, cloves, meadowsweet, lavender, lemon, geranium and rose petals were on the list. She'd worked with a lot of these herbs in her own baking.

She'd done a lot of research into the different uses of the herbs so it would be interesting to see if any of that research married up with what witches used the herbs for. Some of it must have worked in her cakes as she always got such glowing reviews, and it wasn't just for the way the cakes tasted but that they actually did the job they were intended for. However, she understood that she'd probably been adding magic to the cakes so it might not have been the herbs at all.

'I see you've added hibiscus to the list,' Maxine giggled and all the women laughed.

'Well, love and passion are two of the things that can make us happy,' Ashley said. 'But combined with the other ingredients, it will help to banish bad dreams. Can you all grab a few raspberries and orange slices too, they will help with mood-boosting and general wellbeing, and you will also need a teaspoon of local honey.'

Star moved over to the central table and looked at all the little pots and boxes of herbs. It looked like a display in an old-fashioned apothecary – apart from the large bowl of cheesy puffs that had been put on the wrong table. She picked up a few herbs and spices and sniffed them, they smelled divine. She noticed there were several pots of herbs not mentioned on her list. She spotted frankincense and myrrh, which she had never seen before. She picked them up and let the hard crystals run through her hands. She could have spent hours studying each herb, smelling and touching them, finding out what each one did, but as the others had all collected their herbs and sat back down, she quickly did the same. Maybe, as Wolf suggested, she could come back and see Ashley for some private potion tuition another time.

'First off, you want to add lemon oil for cleansing. Add five drops of that and then stir five times anti-clockwise to banish negativity,' Ashley said.

Star couldn't help but smile as she followed the

instructions. She could really love this part of magic. She might not be able to move a leaf without Wolf's help or summon or change the weather at will, but potions she thought she could be great at. She looked around the room at everyone else adding herbs, fruit and spices to their cauldrons and she wanted to laugh. The door to the magical other world had been blown off and there was no going back now, but right then Star couldn't have been happier.

CHAPTER 13

Star practically floated out of potions club and she didn't think it had anything to do with the happiness potion she had been making. She had chatted and laughed with the girls all night and, for the first time in her life, it felt like she had made some real friends. Making a potion had been brilliant and it didn't matter that her potion had ended up a slightly different colour than everyone else's, she'd had so much fun making it, she hadn't been able to stop smiling all night.

She stepped outside. It was a little cooler tonight than it had been the previous night. Not cold, but enough that she wished she'd pulled on a cardigan or a jacket.

Everyone started saying goodbye and she gave

everyone a hug goodnight before they went their separate ways.

'Oh look, your betrothed is here,' Maxine giggled and there was laughter and hushed whispers as Wolf got up off a bench on the other side of the street and walked over.

'Ladies, did you have a good night?' Wolf asked.

'We did,' Erin said. 'We had a lot to talk about.'

There were more giggles as Wolf had come up in the conversation quite a few times.

'Maybe you can persuade Wolf about the naked idea for the village,' Maxine said.

Wolf arched an eyebrow at Star and she quickly dismissed it. 'It's nothing. What are you doing here?' she asked. Surely he'd had enough of her during the day.

'I've come to walk you home.'

'Now that is definitely romantic,' Darianna said.

'Sshhh,' Kianga said. 'Let's leave them alone.'

'I'd rather stay and watch,' Maxine grumbled.

But the women all called their goodbyes and walked off up the road, until it was just the two of them.

'I think I could probably manage to get home safely,' Star said, inordinately pleased that Wolf had made the effort.

'It's dark and you don't know your way around properly yet. Plus I know how much wine gets drunk at potions club. I once found Maxine fast asleep in the top tier of the town fountain.'

Suddenly Maxine's comment earlier made more sense.

'I was quite restrained actually. I only had two glasses. I wanted to concentrate on what I was doing.'

'So you don't need me?' Wolf said.

Star looked around and, while she was quite sure she would find her way home eventually, she'd got lost twice coming over here and now it was dark and it looked very different.

'Well now you're here, an escort home wouldn't be a bad thing.'

He offered out his arm and she couldn't help smiling at the charming gesture. She slipped her hand through it and they started walking off in a direction she absolutely wouldn't have taken.

'What's with the naked idea?'

Star groaned and explained what she'd told Tig and he burst out laughing. It was rich and deep and she loved the sound of it.

'Well that's one way to put her off coming here.'

'I'm not sure. Knowing Tig, it would probably encourage her,' Star shook her head.

He studied her for a moment. 'You look a lot happier than when I left you earlier today. Did you have a good time tonight?'

'Wolf, I had the best time. Thank you for making me

go to that. The ladies are wonderful and kind and I had so much fun making the potion.'

'I'm so pleased. What potion did you make?'

'A happiness potion.' She showed him the small box she was holding with four little glass bottles inside, all containing sparkling, glowing liquids that seemed to dance and move of their own accord. 'Drinking it is supposed to bring happiness to your life.'

Wolf plucked a bottle out of the box and held it up to the streetlights where it twinkled with gold in the darkness.

'Can I try one?'

'Of course, as long as you trust me not to poison you. I don't think it will be that effective. I got confused whether I'd done six stirs clockwise or seven after I added the honey and nutmeg. And I might have added too much hibiscus and not enough rose. A pinch feels like a very subjective thing, a pinch could be a big thing or a tiny thing.'

'I don't think it would matter too much and some-times someone will add a big pinch of something because they prefer the flavour. The intent is the most important thing, just like it was with your cakes, what you want the person you made them for to achieve. A lot of it is positive thinking. If you were making a happiness potion for me, for example, you would picture me being happy, but a generic happy potion for anyone should still have the same or similar effect.'

He pulled out the cork and downed it in one. 'That does taste good.'

'That's probably the sparkling wine. What does it taste of?'

He smiled. 'Happiness.'

She laughed.

'Did you not try it for yourself?'

'No, I wasn't sure if I should. Ashley kept on talking about the person we would give it to as a winter solstice gift.'

'You should always try your own potions, you can only improve if you try them out for yourself.'

She had been desperate to try it, purely because she'd been inordinately proud of herself for making her first potion, not because she really believed it would make her happy. She took a bottle out of the box, uncorked it and drank it. It tasted really good but as she tried to describe the flavour in her head, only one word sprang to mind. It tasted of happiness. The baker in her would laugh and say happiness was not a taste, but she knew it was true.

'So what would make you happy, Star? If you could name one thing that would make you happy right now, what would it be?'

She looked up at him and smiled because she really wanted him to kiss her but there was no way she was going to say that.

An owl suddenly swooped over their heads and she had an idea.

'I want to fly.'

'What?'

'I have all this magic inside me and so far the best thing I've done with it is make a leaf dance. I want to do something really cool. I want to fly.'

He nodded and then to her surprise he took his jacket off and draped it around her shoulders. 'It's going to be cold up there.'

She frowned in confusion and she put the box in the pocket, zipped it up and pushed her arms through the sleeves. He slid his arms around her back. 'Hold on tight.'

'What?' She immediately wrapped her arms round his neck in alarm. She suddenly felt a force round her back as if Wolf had lashed a rope around her, but she knew he was holding her with his magic. 'Are we really going to do this?'

'Yes, because it will make you happy.'

Her heart leapt with excitement.

Little sparkles suddenly surrounded them and then faded away.

'What was that?'

'An invisibility charm to stop mundanes seeing us. We don't want them reporting UFOs or taking pictures of us while we're up there. This way we can go incognito. Here we go.'

She looked down in awe as he suddenly lifted them off the ground and started rising gently up into the air.

She let out an uncontrollable squeal of delight as the ground got further and further away. The houses below them became tiny little dots with golden specks which she knew were the lights on inside the windows.

An owl flew around them a few times and then off over the hills.

'That was Mulberry,' Wolf said. 'We've probably thrown him as he's never seen me fly before.'

She looked further afield and was confused how different the houses outside the village looked and suddenly realised why.

'Oh look, it's been snowing outside the village,' Star said, pointing at the snow-capped houses and hills around them. 'God, it's so beautiful. I wish we had snow in the village too.'

She could see rivers; silver ribbons winding their way through the hills. Out in the distance she could see the sea, sparkling in the moonlight.

'Star, look up,' Wolf said, softly.

She gasped as she did. The starlit sky was incredible up here, away from any light pollution, with millions of tiny crystals sparkling in the endless darkness. The moon was three-quarters full but it looked so huge and so close, she had never seen it in such detail before.

'Wolf, this is incredible. All of it. The view up there, the world below us. I've never seen anything like it. I've been on a plane at night but you don't get a proper view through those tiny windows. I've never experienced anything like this before. It's... dazzling. God you must do this every night, it's magnificent.'

'I haven't done this for years, certainly not as an adult. Flying – or rather levitating – is something I've only done out of necessity. Like helping you down from the gate or going up to my roof because a bird had got stuck up there in some cables. I don't do it for fun.'

'Why the hell not? If I could do this, I would do it every day and never ever get sick of it. I would fly all over the world, go see the Eiffel Tower at night then zoom across to the volcanoes in Iceland. The possibilities would be endless. Your magic is a wonderful gift, why not have some fun with it?'

'I feel like fun has been lacking in my life for a long time.'

'You've got to do things that make you happy, you deserve to be happy Wolf, and not just the brief happiness a potion can bring you, but always. What would make you happy right now?'

He smiled and his eyes glanced down to her lips. She knew he was thinking about kissing her.

She swallowed. 'What do you want?' she asked softly. She needed to hear him say it – after today when she'd made him feel things he didn't want to feel, she didn't want to do anything else he didn't want.

'I want to kiss you,' Wolf said.

'Is that you or the potion talking?'

'It's definitely me.'

'Well, since you've given me this beautiful gift, I can certainly do that for you.'

She leaned up and kissed him before he could talk his way out of it and it was utterly wonderful. There was a familiarity there, she knew this man, this kiss, but it was different too. Whereas before when they were kids it was sweet and innocent, this kiss was needful with the promise of so much more. His arms tightened around her back and he let out a little moan against her lips. The taste of him was incredible and she smiled against his lips when she realised he tasted of happiness.

He cupped her face, enjoying the kiss, and then tipped her head back as he moved his hot mouth to her throat, to the place where her pulse was hammering against her skin, and then lower to where her neck joined her shoulder. It was heaven.

She opened her eyes to look at the stars as he was devouring her, consuming her, and was surprised to see little sparks of gold surrounding them that hadn't been there before. It was like they were standing in a snow-globe and the glitter was sparkling around them.

'Wolf,' she whispered, not wanting to break the magic, and she definitely didn't want him to stop doing what he was doing with his mouth.

'Mmm?' Wolf mumbled against her skin.

'What's this?'

He lifted his head to look at what she was referring to and chuckled.

'That's you, your emotions. I could see it when you were scared on your first day but the sparkles were frantic then, darting around everywhere. This is... happiness. Kissing me makes you very very happy.'

She looked up at him and nodded. 'It does.'

He kissed her again, much gentler this time, and her heart soared as he gently stroked her cheeks.

She was vaguely aware, as the kiss continued, that they were slowly descending and, a few minutes later, her feet gently touched the floor and Wolf released the magic around her.

He pulled back from the kiss but he was still holding her and as she caught her breath she realised they were standing outside her house.

'Here you go, delivered safely to your door,' Wolf said, letting her go.

'Thank you, that was... incredible, all of it.'

He frowned slightly and opened his mouth to speak but she stepped up and put her finger on his lips. 'I don't want to hear how it doesn't change anything between us and that nothing else is going to happen. I have just had the most amazing, most romantic kiss of my entire existence and it's something I'm going to remember for the rest of my life. I'm going to go to bed tonight with the biggest smile on my face and replay that brilliant kiss over and over again and I don't want to have it ruined with you backpedalling away from it. So let me have this for tonight and then you can ruin my hopes of something more happening between us tomorrow.'

The frown was still there which didn't bode well, but he nodded, seemingly agreeing to her terms. 'Good-night Star.'

He bent his head and gave her the briefest of kisses on her cheek before he turned and walked away into the darkness.

She shook her head as she watched him go. He was so confusing.

CHAPTER 14

Star woke with a start, sitting bolt upright in bed, her breathing heavy. She'd just had the most vivid sex dream about Wolf that was so crystal clear in her mind she could still feel his hands on her skin, his soft lips on hers. She could even smell his wonderful spicy scent.

She shook her head, trying to clear it, taking a long cool drink of water.

Now she was wide awake and she knew she wouldn't get back to sleep, she got out of bed, threw on her robe and padded downstairs to the kitchen where Viktor was curled up in the corner.

She got out a bowl and all the ingredients she needed to make some cakes. No magic this time, just some simple apple and cinnamon cakes.

'It's the middle of the bloody night, what are you doing?' Viktor moaned, peering at her with one eye.

'I... umm, couldn't sleep.'

'Thinking about kissing the mayor last night?'

'How did you know about that?'

'I have eyes.' He stood up and stretched. 'Are you making cakes?'

'Yes. It helps to clear the mind and calm the soul.'

'My favourite cakes are blackberry and elderflower. Will you make me some of those?'

Star smirked. 'I don't have blackberry or elderflower but I promise I'll get them and make some for you.'

'When?'

'As soon as I can get hold of those ingredients.'

Viktor let out a long-suffering sigh. 'Well as you're clearly going to be making a lot of noise for the next hour, I might as well go out, but I expect my cup of tea ready for me when I return.'

'Of course,' Star said. She was tempted to do a curtsey to show how ridiculous he was but he would probably like it too much. She watched him slink out of the cat flap and turned her attention back to the cakes.

She started mixing all the ingredients, creaming the butter and sugar together first, but all she could think about was her dream. It had seemed so real. She could taste Wolf's lips as he'd kissed her, she could remember how it felt when he'd lifted her onto the table right here in this kitchen, the touch of his mouth on her throat and then on her breasts. How he'd ripped her nightie off in a desperate urgency, then pinned her to the table and made love to her. She added the egg to the flour as she remembered what it felt like to have him on top of her, his warm skin against hers as he was buried deep inside of her.

She tried to push those thoughts away. That obviously wasn't going to happen. The magical kiss the night before was probably going to be a one-off judging by the way Wolf had started to withdraw immediately after.

She added the chopped apples, poured the cake batter into muffin cases and put the tray in the oven. She washed up all the utensils and bowls, made herself a hot chocolate and went and stood outside on the decking, watching the twilight sky of dawn breaking, the birds waking up and singing their morning song, the rose gold of the first rays of sun dusting the flowers and leaves in her garden and the miles of fields behind. She felt at peace, and it was a feeling she'd never had before in her life.

She thought about the snow outside the village and how lovely it would be if it snowed here for Christmas or for the winter solstice celebrations in a few days' time.

The oven pinged to let her know that the cakes were done and she hurried inside to get them out. They were perfectly golden brown with a slightly springy top, just as a perfect cake should be. They smelled amazing too. She slid them out onto a plate to cool down and was just about to go upstairs to have a shower when there was a knock on her back door.

She looked up to see Wolf standing there. It was clear he'd just been out for a run: he was slightly out of breath, a bit sweaty dressed in t-shirt and shorts and still looked as sexy as hell.

'I was out for a run and saw your back door open and your light on, everything OK?'

'I couldn't sleep,' Star said, not wanting to tell him the reason why.

'Me neither.' He stepped inside the kitchen and she wondered if now was the time he'd give his big speech about how the kiss was a mistake and should never have happened.

He looked around at the little pots of fresh herbs she had placed on her windowsill and the flowers she had picked from the garden that were sitting in a little vase. In the short time she'd been here, she had made this place a home.

He wandered over to the table where her cakes were. He picked up one of them and smelled it. 'Mmm, apple. Any magic in these?'

She laughed. 'No, just apple cakes.'

He took a big bite. 'Wow, these are good.'

'Are they?'

'Do you never eat your own cakes?'

'Not the ones I make for other people but the ones I make just for fun I sometimes do. I just enjoy the process of making them rather than the eating of them.'

He paused as he chewed as if tasting something he wasn't expecting.

'Everything OK?'

'Yes, it's just... I'm remembering the dream I had before I went for a run. About you.'

Her breath caught. 'I had a dream about you too.'

They stared at each other and she noticed that Wolf's breathing was suddenly heavy.

'Did we... did we have the same dream again?' she asked, her cheeks flaming with heat. What could be more mortifying than him seeing her inappropriate sex dream of him? Unless, of course, she was seeing his dreams instead. Then none of this was her fault.

He swallowed the cake. 'I think we might have. Mine was a very good dream.'

'Mine too.'

They continued to stare at each other. He looked like he wanted to devour her.

Trying to distract herself from his presence, which suddenly seemed so big, she picked up one of the cakes and took a bite out of it. It did taste good but as she swallowed it she had a sudden flashback to her vivid sex dream. She glanced across at Wolf and he suddenly dropped the cake, crossed the gap between them and kissed her hard.

Holy shit, this kiss was explosive and had come almost from nowhere. She didn't know what this meant, whether he wanted to pick up from the night before or whether it was a one-off. But suddenly she didn't care why he was kissing her, only that he was. She slid her arms round his neck, pressing herself against him with a desperate urgency. He pushed her robe off her shoulders and it slithered to the floor.

He lifted her onto the table and moved between her legs to continue the kiss, his greedy hands wandering everywhere. The kiss was insanely hot, filled with passion and need, and she was desperate for so much more. He tore his mouth from hers for just a second as he ripped her nightie over her head and then he was kissing her neck, her breasts, lowering her to the table. This was just like her dream. Her skin prickled with cold goosebumps. This was exactly like her dream.

'No, Wolf stop,' she pushed against him and he looked at her, his eyes clouded with lust. She scrambled down from the table and grabbed her robe, wrapping it tightly around her. 'I'm so so sorry, this is all my fault. I never meant for this to happen, God, I'm so sorry, it was the cakes, I didn't think. This is so embarrassing. And now you're going to hate me. I would never do this, I would never want to force you into doing something you wouldn't want to do, I'm so sorry.'

He stared at her in confusion and she could see the lust clearing as he tried to make sense of what had just happened. He looked at the cakes and back at her. 'You put a love spell in the cakes?'

'No, oh my god, no I would never do that. This is horrible, I'm so sorry.'

'What did you do?'

'I...' she swallowed down the excruciating embarrassment of what she was going to say next. 'I had a sex dream about you, it was very vivid and it woke me up. I'm guessing, hoping, it was the same dream you had but I came down here and started making these cakes and I was thinking about the dream as I was making them. I forced you to kiss me and want to have sex with me, because... I guess because you were tasting my memories of my dream when you ate the cake.'

He stared at her and, to her surprise, he burst out laughing. 'You made sex cakes.'

He was laughing so hard he could barely breathe. He sat down at the table, still laughing, but quickly pushed the rest of the cakes away from him.

She stared at him in confusion. 'Why are you not angry over this? I forced you—'

He held his hand up to stop her talking, though he was still trying to suppress his laughter. 'You did not force me to do anything. I told you before that there is no magic that can make someone do something they really don't want to do. Jessica's love spell didn't work because I have no interest in her at all.'

She frowned in confusion.

'You know I want you, Star,' Wolf said. 'The reason why I was running round the fields this morning before the sun had even risen was because I had the same dream as you. I'm not sure whether I shared your dream or you shared mine but what happened here played out exactly as I saw it in the dream. The point is, the sex cake didn't force me to do something I didn't want to do, it just made me relive that dream so bloody vividly after I'd spent an hour running around the village trying to push those thoughts away. It made my need for you explode through me so fiercely there was no other option but to kiss you.'

She stared at him, her eyes wide.

'I still stand by the fact that I don't want anything to happen between us, or at least anything more. It could make things very awkward between us. And nothing is more important to me right now than teaching you how to handle your magic and I don't want anything to get in the way of that.'

'OK,' Star said. That was all she could say. She was almost stunned into silence.

'And I'm sorry,' Wolf said.

'Whatever for? I'm the one that made sex cakes.'

He smiled slightly but then frowned. 'I'm sorry for losing all control when it came to you, I'm sorry for pinning you to the table like a piece of meat when you deserve a hell of a lot more than that.'

'There wasn't a single part of me that didn't want what you did, so please don't beat yourself up over it.'

'I have never behaved like that with a woman before, I mauled you like some kind of wild animal.'

She sat down at the table with him. 'Do you think it's the betrothal magic?'

'I don't know. Maybe. But I spoke to my gran about it yesterday and she seems to think that Ashley would be able to remove it.'

'Remove our connection?' Star said. She knew that was for the best but why did that suggestion hurt so much?

'Yes, then we can just go back to our lives,' Wolf said.

She swallowed. 'Yes, good idea.'

'Get dressed, we'll go and see her.'

She stood up and went upstairs, feeling an immense sadness settle over her. She suddenly felt losing her feelings for him would be taking the biggest part of her right now.

They walked up the road towards Ashley's house, Wolf striding along at such a speed Star had to jog a little to keep up with him. He was obviously keen to get it over with as soon as possible. He hadn't said a lot since the sex cake debacle, and she wondered if he was angry although he had insisted it wasn't her fault. She wanted to get back to how things had been last night – well probably not to the most romantic most exquisite kiss of her life, but at least talking and on good terms.

'It's gone a lot colder, hasn't it?' Star said, reaching for the typical British response in times of awkwardness: talking about the weather. Although it was true, it had got colder.

'Yeah it's weird, it's normally really hot throughout December and everyone laments the lack of snow over the winter solstice celebrations.'

'It could snow, it feels like it's cold enough to snow.'

'It hasn't snowed in December for thirty years, I don't think it will start now,' Wolf said. 'Very occasionally, the curse seems to wear off a little, and we have the same weather as outside the village for a day or so, and then it's as if the curse remembers what it should be doing and we go back to the absurd weather again. But I can't see we'll have snow.'

They arrived at Ashley's house and he knocked on the door. After a few moments she answered.

'Hey, is everything OK?'

'Can we come in? We need a word,' Wolf said, all serious.

Ashley stepped back to let them in and Wolf ushered Star into the lounge which was back to normal now after the potions club the previous evening. Star smiled at how magic must have transformed the room the night before to accommodate the women and their cauldrons. She loved being part of this world and she didn't want to have to leave because things had got weird between her and Wolf.

'What's the problem?' Ashley said, dragging a pashmina off the back of the sofa and wrapping it around her.

'Can you see the bonds that connect us because of our joint birthday?' Wolf said, straight to business.

'Oh yes. I can see that very clearly.'

'Can you remove them?'

Ashley's face fell. 'Why would you want me to do that? That connection is a rare and wonderful thing.'

'It's making me do things I don't want to do,' Wolf said.

'That's not how it works. It doesn't have control over you, it can't force you to do something you don't want to do,' Ashley said.

'I've never had such a physical response to a woman before.'

Star felt her cheeks flame with embarrassment. It felt so weird to be discussing their attraction as if they were discussing the weather.

'Maybe that's because you've never met the right woman before,' Ashley said.

'I've been with lots of women I was attracted to,

this is different. The attraction is so strong it's tangible,' Wolf said.

'I can see your attraction to her and Star's attraction to you, but that's separate to the betrothal bond you share.'

'But it's because of it. I just pinned her to the kitchen table and I would have made love to her right there if she hadn't stopped me.'

Ashley rubbed the back of her neck awkwardly. 'I'm not sure I need all the details of your relationship. Why did you stop him?' she asked Star.

Star really didn't want to relive the mortification of making sex cakes. 'Because I didn't think it was fair. He doesn't want me.'

He frowned. 'I do want you, Star. Very much. And not just sexually. I want so much more than that. But I don't want to feel that way.'

'I think that probably boils down to the same thing,' Star sighed.

Ashley sat down. 'Star, do you want the betrothal bonds removed too?'

Star thought about the kiss under the stars the night before, the most incredible experience of her life. She thought about how good it felt when Wolf had hugged her and how much she'd wanted him to make love to her that morning. If the bonds were gone, that kind of thing would never happen again. But if none of it was real, then she didn't *want* it to happen again.

She nodded.

Ashley took a deep breath as she thought. 'It's not something I've ever done before or know anyone who has but I guess it's possible.' She went to her bookshelf and pulled out a large, leather-bound book with crinkled faded pages and started flicking through it.

Intrigue took over from Star's sadness for a moment. 'What's that?'

'It's a Book of Shadows. It's a place to note down all your spells, charms and potion recipes. It includes information on the different uses of herbs, spices, fruits, flowers, crystals and stones. It has the different phases of the moon, astrological events, notes about traditions and celebrations. It's generally passed down through family generations and then you add your own stuff to it before passing it on to your own children.'

'Wow, that's amazing. Can I see?'

Ashley hesitated for a moment.

'The Book of Shadows is very personal to each person who owns it,' Wolf explained. 'It contains memories and sometimes diary entries of our parents and grandparents, so it's not something we generally share.'

'Oh sorry, I didn't realise,' Star said.

'No, it's fine,' Ashley said. 'This was my grandmother's, so it is precious to me, but my grandmother was very big on sharing spells and charms with anyone who needed them. I'm sure she would be very happy that some of her magic could be used by someone else.'

Ashley passed her the book and Star could feel the weight of its importance. She could also sense the magic contained within the pages as if the book was somehow alive. She turned the pages and smiled at the beautiful cursive writing and that several people had added their notes to the book over the years.

'Maybe you could come back at another time and Ashley could explain more about her Book of Shadows then,' Wolf said, gently.

Star nodded and carefully handed the book back; she knew she could spend hours looking through it and it would never be enough.

'And I'm more than happy to share mine with you too,' Wolf said.

'Thank you, that's very kind.'

Wolf smiled at her and it was so easy to believe in the affection he had for her in his eyes.

'With regards to your issue,' Ashley said, making Star remember that they were there to break the bond that Wolf didn't want. 'I think as the magic was created on the summer solstice when dark triumphs over light after our longest day it would be easier to break on the winter solstice when light triumphs over dark. Then when the new year starts the following day, it will be a clean start for the both of you.'

'That's two days from now,' Wolf said, clearly wanting a quick fix.

'Yes, but there are things you can do in the meantime in preparation for it. Tonight is a full moon, which is a very powerful time in the different phases of the moon.'

Star knew Ashley was explaining that for her benefit, not Wolf's.

'You need to take a swim naked in a moonlit lake, to cleanse yourselves of any unwanted magic. I suggest you go together and, if you want to be extra thorough, you should wash each other as a symbol that both of you wish to be rid of the magic that binds you.'

Star stared at her. 'You want us to wash each other, in a lake, naked, under the moonlight? Isn't that tempting fate just a little?'

'Many cleansing rituals involve bathing in a moonlit lake. It's symbolic not sexual,' Wolf said.

'Right, so my hands stroking over your wet, naked body, your hands on mine, not remotely sexual at all?'

Wolf cleared his throat and turned his attention back to Ashley. 'Do you have any other suggestions?'

'Yes, but they are all equally as important. You need to do them all, the connection between you and the ley lines is very powerful. Tomorrow morning, you need to go to the beach and take a swim in the sea for the first sunrise after the full moon. The salt water has great purifying and detoxifying properties and the high tide at sunrise will help with cleansing the energy around you.'

'And I guess we have to be naked for that too?' Star said.

Wolf smirked.

Ashley frowned. 'Of course not. Although nudity is something I would encourage in all cleansing rituals, it is optional. Tomorrow night you should take a bath together, fully clothed if you wish. Use lavender, bergamot, eucalyptus and peppermint oils. And you can also use this.' Ashley moved to the shelf and, after a moment of perusing the bottles, picked up a tall pink glass bottle. 'Five drops of that. No more. Then at sunrise on the day of the winter solstice I want you to burn white sage and paint the ash across each other's heart. At sunset I want you to build a fire, write a list of all the things you are attracted to in the other person, read it out loud to each other and then burn the list. If everything goes to plan with my part and yours, at midnight on the evening of the winter solstice, the bonds will be broken for good.'

Star chewed her lip. Was this for real? Ashley had just described three days of romance and by the end of it she and Wolf were supposedly not going to be attracted to each other anymore. How was that going to work?

'I can see you're doubting this, but everything I've

said are basic cleansing rituals, aren't they Wolf?' Ashley said.

'I have heard of things like this before but normally to detox the spirit and the soul, not to remove betrothal magic. But then I've never heard of anyone removing betrothal magic before so I guess these things have their merits.'

'Cleansing the spirit and soul is all part of the magic we need to remove the bonds. We can use banishing spells but I'm guessing you don't want to go that far?' Ashley said.

'Absolutely not,' Wolf said firmly.

'What's a banishing spell?' Star asked.

'It's a spell you use to remove someone toxic from your life permanently. Effectively you would be banished from the village,' Wolf said.

'Well that would solve all your problems if I'm not here.'

'No, this is your home. I don't want to get rid of you, I just want to stop feeling like I have no control with you.'

'All of this will help,' Ashley said. 'My part will be the hardest and I can't guarantee it will work as I've never done anything like this before but what you do over the next few days will help.'

Star wondered if their part might actually be the hardest.

'OK, we'll do our part,' Wolf said. 'Thanks for your help.'

Star stood up. 'Thanks and if you don't mind I will pop back at some point and we can talk about the Book of Shadows and potions?'

'You'd be very welcome.'

Star and Wolf stepped outside. It was colder and Star shivered a little. Wolf took off his jacket which she'd only given back to him that morning and wrapped it around her shoulders. 'You need to start wearing a coat.'

'Sorry, I wasn't expecting it to be cold, not after the hot weather of the last few days.'

Wolf looked up at the darkening sky above them. 'It is really weird. I wonder if the curse is wearing off. After all, it's thirty years since the curse was placed on the village, and a lot of curses have time limits.' He looked at her. 'You didn't try to summon the snow again, did you?'

'No, of course not. I'm not even sure how I did it in the first place, *if* I did it.'

Wolf didn't look entirely convinced. 'Right, let's go back to mine and I can teach you some more about magic.'

'Should we perhaps try to keep our distance over the next few days? Do the rituals as Ashley said but not spend any more time with each other than that? Then we won't be tempted to kiss each other or make sex cakes for each other.'

Wolf smiled. 'Don't beat yourself up over that. I suspect the dreams are coming from me and you're seeing them, so this is my fault not yours.'

'Well you can't control your dreams. And what makes you think last night's dream was yours?'

'It had the same clarity as one of my premonitions. A premonition dream and a normal dream are very different. But when I keep revisiting that dream in my head, it had that reality that my premonitions always do.'

'Did the premonition show me stopping you?'

'No, but the premonitions can change.'

She thought about this for a moment and then smiled. 'When you say you keep revisiting that dream in your head, how often are you revisiting it?'

He pulled the collar of his jacket tighter around her. 'I think I'll be revisiting that dream every damn day for the rest of my life. But to answer your question about whether we should avoid each other: no. Your training is important and I'm sure we can restrain ourselves for a few more days until the bonds are lifted.'

He gestured towards his house and they started walking.

'Do you really think we can restrain ourselves when we have to do all these romantic things together? Wash each other in a moonlit lake, watch a sunrise on the beach and go for a swim – that's practically a date. Then we have to take a bath together, rub hot ash over each other's bodies. If we make it to the winter solstice without anything else happening between us it will be a miracle.'

'I think we just have to try to be professional about it. Remain detached. Wash each other in the same way you might wash a pair of boots. It doesn't have to be sexual.'

'It's nice to know you'll be thinking about a pair of old boots tonight when you're washing me.'

Wolf was silent for a moment. 'Honestly, it's going to take every ounce of strength and determination I have to not think about that dream while I'm washing you, to not think about how good it felt when I pinned you to the table, and it will take more strength than I have not to think of that incredible kiss last night.'

They were both quiet as they walked along the streets.

'There is another option, you know?' Star said.

'To the cleansing rituals?' Wolf asked.

'Yes. You're so convinced these feelings have come from the magic surrounding our betrothal and the ley lines but it could be because of our past, our friendship, our relationship.'

'That thought did occur to me too. And my gran said the same, she said our love story started sixteen years ago and it's that reconnection that we're feeling now. A reawakening of those old feelings. Although I never dreamed about pinning you to a table when I was fourteen or even sixteen.'

'We were kids, we wouldn't think of stuff like that.'

Wolf opened his front door and let her go in ahead of him, closing the door behind him. 'If these feelings are real, then they will still be there when the bonds have been broken.'

'And then what? You still don't want a relationship with anyone in the village.'

'If these feelings between us are still here on Saturday, the day after the winter solstice, I would be willing to give things a go between us.'

'You would be willing?' Star said, in exasperation. 'Thanks very much.'

He shook his head. 'This is why I never have relationships. I never know the right things to say. Let me rephrase that. If we still have these feelings on Saturday, I would like to take you out for dinner and then after, if *you* are willing, I'd like to bring you back here and make love to you in my bed.'

Star had no words at all. She swallowed. 'I would be very willing.'

Suddenly Saturday couldn't come soon enough.

CHAPTER 15

Star flopped back on the sofa, letting out a huff of frustration. Nothing was working. Wolf had asked her to move several things in his house, big things, little things, and they hadn't moved an inch. He'd talked to her about reaching out for the objects in the same way she had reached out for him the day before but she just couldn't do it. Now she'd spent the last half hour trying to control the flame of a candle and she couldn't even do that. It seemed she could only do magic if Wolf was there to help guide her powers but he obviously didn't want to go inside her again and she certainly didn't want to ask him.

Wolf suddenly burst out laughing and she scowled at him.

'I'm sorry, I've been keeping that laughter in all morning. You're trying so hard, you're also concentrating too hard, your face is all screwed up like this when you try to do any magic.'

He did a squashed gurning face and she laughed. 'I do not look like that.'

'I should get a mirror for you next time.'

'That will really put me off if I see myself doing that.'

Wolf wiped his eyes as he laughed. 'Oh, I haven't laughed like this in a long time.'

'I'm glad I amuse you.'

'You do. You light me up like a firework. I'm loving teaching you and just being with you because you make me smile so damn much.'

The smile grew on her own face at that lovely compliment.

He cleared his throat as if he hadn't meant to say that and stood up. He moved over to a chest of drawers and brought out a small black leather box.

He offered the box to her and sat down next to her. 'This is for you.'

Star opened it and inside was a pendant with a dark green triangle-shaped stone that glittered in the light. It looked like it might be some kind of crystal. It was beautiful.

'This was my mum's,' Wolf said. 'I told you before that she struggled with her magic after her stroke. Well, one day this blue battered horse-drawn caravan pulls up outside our house and this witch knocks on our door. We'd never seen her before or since, I don't even know her name, but we knew she was a witch. We didn't tell her anything about Mum's stroke or that she couldn't use her magic anymore, but she knew. She gave my mum this amulet, told her to use it whenever she wanted to use her magic, to hold the amulet and tell it what she wanted to do and the amulet would do it. Well, to be clear, the amulet used my mum's magic to do her bidding, but it helped.'

Star shook her head. 'I can't take this, this is your mum's. I'm sure it's hugely sentimental for you.'

'It is. I used to wear it a lot after she died. Not to focus my magic, but because a magical artefact like this, it leaves echoes of the person who used it imprinted on it. So I could feel her when I wore it. But it wasn't really my mum's, she was merely a caretaker. It came into her life for a short period before it was time to be passed on to the next person. It's had lots of owners over the years and a lot of history. Actually some of the people in the village knew more about its history than I did. Apparently it's been in my family for generations and it was always given as an engagement gift by the oldest son as a symbol of his love.'

She frowned. 'And you're giving it to me?'

'The use of it changed over the years. At some point it was charmed to be a conduit for someone's magic, a long time before it came to my mum. Although everyone still refers to it as the engagement emerald.'

'It's an emerald? Then I definitely can't take it. It could be worth something.'

'I have no doubt it is worth a lot of money, but its true worth is in its history, in the people that wore it, who gave it as a gift of love, or the people who gave it as a gift of kindness to help other witches with their magic. I haven't thought about this amulet for many years, but last night I had a dream, before that *other* dream, that my mum was here chatting to you and she took off the amulet and gave it to you. I know she would want you to have it. I was reluctant to do so because everyone in the village will associate it with an engagement gift for my betrothed but it's right that it should come to you now for however long you need it. Just maybe keep it under your clothes so the villagers won't have any more ammunition to add to their gossip.'

Star held it up to the light and sunlight streamed though it like a prism. 'It's beautiful. Why don't you wear it any more?'

'I keep my mum in here,' Wolf pointed to his heart. 'And because every time Jessica would see me wearing it, she could never keep her eyes off it, staring at it with pound signs in her eyes, asking to borrow it, asking to touch it, saying she needed it to use with her magic.'

'And you never let her?'

'Hell no, I didn't want her to taint it or steal it and sell it, which is probably more likely. She'll freak out if she sees you wearing it. In fact, wear it on the outside of your clothes, that will really piss her off.'

Star smiled. 'You're a cruel man.'

'She deserves it. Try it on.'

She hesitated and he took it from her and fastened it around her neck. Instantly, his fingers against her flesh caused goosebumps to erupt across her skin.

Straightaway she could feel the warmth of the emerald and the echoes of the magic contained within. The most recent magic was Wolf's. Whether he used the amulet to guide his magic or not, he had still used it. Although the strongest magic she could feel must have come from his mum because she could also sense some of her feelings entwined with her magic too.

'I can feel some of the echoes of the people who wore it before me. Your mum's is very prominent. She loved you very much.'

He frowned. 'You can feel that?'

She nodded.

'I never felt that when I wore it.'

'Maybe you couldn't separate her magic from her feelings because all of it was a part of her, so you just felt her. I can sense the different parts of her, and her love for you and Lynx was a massive part of who she was.'

He stared at her. 'Thank you for sharing that with me.'

'It's your history, you're entitled to know it.'

He cleared his throat and looked away.

'Is this too weird, me having this connection to your mum in this way? Do you want me to take it off?'

'No, it's fine. Let's do this. OK, try bending the flame of the candle,' Wolf said. 'Touch the amulet, close your eyes and picture what you want to happen and then open your eyes and watch it bend.'

'Really?'

'It's that simple. Eventually you'll be able to do it without touching the amulet, you just need to wear it and think about what you want to happen. And after a few months, you probably won't need the amulet at all and you'll be able to pass it on to someone else that needs it. You'll know when you meet the person.'

She closed her eyes and let out a deep breath. She held the amulet and could feel its warmth. She visualised the candle bending and then opened one eye. She laughed to see the flame had bent clean in half so the tip was now touching the wax.

'See, you did it,' Wolf said, looking extraordinarily pleased with her. 'Now see if it works on other things.'

Star glanced around the room to find something she could move. Her eyes fell on the crystal ball and she smiled. She held out her hand for it, just like Wolf had on the first day, closed her eyes, held the amulet and visualised it zooming into her hand. She didn't even have time to open her eyes before she felt it hit her palm. It was such a shock she nearly dropped it and had to catch it with her other hand to stop it hitting the floor.

'Don't worry, it's not expensive,' Wolf laughed.

'I can't believe it's so easy,' Star said. 'The amulet does all the work for me.'

'It's your magic Star, it's just using the amulet to focus it.'

'What else can I do? Can I fly?'

'You can practise, but promise me you will only do it indoors unless I'm with you. If you levitate outside without proper control of your magic then you could fall out of the sky.'

'Oh no, that would be bad,' Star smirked at his doom-mongering.

'Just keep to small stuff for now, don't run before you can walk.'

She nodded reluctantly.

'OK, we need to go, it's time for the winter garland ceremony.'

'The what?'

'We start decorating the village for the winter solstice a few days before. It's mostly evergreens, similar to how mundanes decorate their homes for Christmas just without the garishness.'

'Excuse me, we are not garish in our celebrations of Christmas.'

'*You* are no longer part of that *we*, but I've seen many mundanes with plastic Santas flashing away in their front gardens, enough lights to compete with Blackpool illuminations, moving reindeer, inflatable snowmen, and one village, not far from here, had giant underpants hanging above the street. And as for the solstice tree, I've seen fairies, dragons, Christmas puddings with googly eyes, cats, dogs, parrots, turkeys, cars, trains, horses, wine glasses and a whole host of ornaments that have no place on a winter solstice tree let alone in the Christian celebration of Christmas.'

'You're so grumpy,' Star laughed. 'Christmas is for celebrating however you see fit. And what's wrong with spreading a bit of joy and humour with a big flashing inflatable Santa or a walking talking Rudolph?'

'Thankfully, most people here are a lot more sedate and tasteful when it comes to the winter solstice celebrations. We have greenery, branches, berries, winter flowers. The hanging of the winter garland is the start of our celebrations. There's a big group who've been busily making the garland over the last few weeks and will hang it around the village green. The whole village will come out to see it so it'll be a great opportunity for you to meet and chat to more people.'

'Well, lead the way.'

Star grabbed a big red blanket from the back of the sofa and wrapped it around herself like a shawl.

'I'm not sure you should wear that,' Wolf said.

'You'll get it back later, and I promise I'll wear my own coat from now on if it continues to be this cold.'

'But—'

'And at least this way you get to wear your own jacket.'

Wolf shrugged. 'OK, sure, why not.'

Star felt sure she could see a smirk on his lips.

They left the house and started making their way towards the village green. Star could see lots of people were already gathering or making their own way towards the centre of the village.

Some people were nudging each other and pointing over in Star's direction and she understood that she was a novelty and something interesting but after a while she realised they were pointing and getting more excited about the blanket than her.

'OK, what's the deal with the blanket?' Star said.

'What do you mean?' Wolf said, innocently.

'People are very excited that I'm wearing it.'

'Oh that. Yeah, it's a love blanket.'

'A what?'

'It's a gift given to newlyweds. Supposedly a couple will consummate the marriage on it, or under it, and it brings luck and happiness in their marriage. It was given to my parents on their wedding day. I have no idea if they consummated their marriage on it but it was always something very special for my mum.'

'I'm wearing a consummation blanket?' Star said.

'It's been washed several hundred times in its life, you don't have to worry, it's clean.'

'I'm not worried about that, I'm worried that everyone here knows this is a consummation blanket.'

'Love blanket.'

'It's a sex blanket. And I'm wearing it like a trophy, like a hunter wearing the pelt of the animal they've killed. They're all going to think we're doing it and this is my way of letting the whole village know.'

'I don't care what they think.'

'What happened to presenting a professional image to the villagers?'

'There will always be gossip in a village this size, some of it true, some of it wildly exaggerated. You just have to ride it out until the next bit of gossip comes along to take the attention away from you. We're betrothed, we're spending all this time together, people will talk whether you're wearing a sex blanket or not.'

Star grunted her disapproval, but he had a point. 'You could have warned me.'

Wolf smirked. 'I did try.'

Just then Jessica came over. While others were whispering their comments about Star wearing a sex blanket, Jessica had no such scruples.

'What are you wearing?' Jessica laughed as if they were friends and she was teasing her but, after what happened in the shops the other day, Star knew there was an undertone of nastiness. 'You might as well have a big neon flashing sign saying I'm shagging the mayor.

I don't know what everyone must think. You must be so embarrassed, Wolf.'

'Why would I be embarrassed?' Wolf said, without missing a beat. He slid an arm around Star's shoulders. 'We're betrothed, what do you think we've been doing?'

Star looked at him in shock but the expression on Jessica's face was priceless. It was a look of pure horror.

'You mean you two are actually sleeping together?' Jessica said, her voice dripping with revulsion as if Wolf had just told her he liked to wash himself in pig filth.

'The last few days have been the best of my life,' Wolf said, staring at Star as if he was head over heels in love with her.

If this was what he wanted she might as well play along. 'Mine too, it's been... heaven.'

Jessica just stared at them in disgust and dismay. Her eyes suddenly fell on the amulet Wolf had given her.

'You gave her the engagement emerald?' she said, spitting the words out with venom.

'You do know what the word betrothed means, don't you Jessica?' Wolf said.

'But you're not seriously going to marry her, are you? You've only just met and now because of some silly tradition you're going to marry her. That's ridiculous, only a fool would do that and I never took you for a fool.'

When Wolf spoke his voice was low and angry. 'You

need to be careful how you speak to me. I am the mayor of this village and your place here is already hanging by a thread after that stunt you pulled with the love potion. Now *that* was ridiculous.'

Star had never seen Wolf pull rank before, it was quite impressive to see.

'And the derogatory way you've just reacted to me being involved with Star is an insult to her and I won't stand for that.'

She watched Jessica backpedal immediately.

'Of course, sorry, I just didn't realise you two would get engaged so quickly. It seems so out of character for you.' Jessica narrowed her eyes at Star as if she had forced Wolf into a relationship because of some witchy magic. While that wasn't a million miles away from the truth, it wasn't Star's magic that was doing the forcing. 'I'm very happy for you, for both of you.' She moved forward to give Wolf a congratulatory hug but he side-stepped her and with his arm at Star's back he ushered her towards the village green.

Star could see what people meant about him being grumpy; when he was angry he was clearly not to be messed with, but she quite liked it.

'A lot of people are going to think or say the same as Jessica,' Star said. 'She just has the brass to say it to our faces.'

'In the rudest way possible. Let them talk, but if I

hear one bad thing said about you, they will face my wrath.'

Star giggled. 'What are you going to do, chase them all through the village with dark demon-shaped shadows?'

'If need be.'

They approached the village green and the impressive fountain that looked like a giant cauldron.

'That is a fantastic fountain,' Star said.

'It was built in honour of Ashley's grandmother who knew everything there was to know about potions. When she died, she left a massive hole in the village. This seemed a fitting way to pay tribute to her,' Wolf said, manoeuvring their way through the crowds to get to the front. 'OK, stay here for a moment, I just need to give my big speech.'

Wolf moved off towards the centre of the green.

Kianga and Erin were standing nearby and they beckoned Star over. Kianga linked arms with her when she got close.

'I'm glad you're here,' Erin said. 'The garland ceremony is one of the most impressive celebrations the village takes part in. Everyone should see it. The garland is a symbol of hope, light and unity but it's also a great example of what can be achieved when we work together and use our magic as a team, not as individuals.'

Star liked that.

A man arrived next to Erin and when she saw him her face lit up and she hugged him. Erin started talking to him and Kianga waved her hand in front of herself and Star and the chatter of the village green suddenly went silent. Even though Star could see that everyone was still talking and laughing around them, it was as if the plug had been pulled on all the sound in the world.

'I saw something I probably shouldn't have last night and I've been dying to talk to you about it. I love looking at the stars and I was looking through my telescope when I saw you and Wolf up there in the clouds, kissing.'

Star looked around, not wanting anyone to hear.

'No one can hear us,' Kianga said. 'Not even Erin. I haven't told anyone what I saw, and I won't. It's just that when we spoke about Wolf and your betrothal last night you said that nothing was going to happen between you so it was a bit of a surprise. But tell me to bog off if you don't want to talk about it, I won't mind. I'm just excited for you and I've been bursting with excitement all day. From what I briefly saw, before I turned the telescope away, it looked like the kiss of two people very much in love.'

Star let out a sigh because she did want to talk about it with someone. 'It's complicated – the feelings I have for Wolf are not like anything I've felt before. And I think he feels the same. I'd love to believe it's nothing more than an instant connection, that love-at-first-sight feeling, but we both feel it might be because of the betrothal magic. We don't know if it's real. We've asked Ashley if she can remove the bonds that connect us and she thinks she can do it on the night of the winter solstice. After that, on Saturday morning, whatever feelings we have, we'll know are ours.'

She didn't tell Kianga about Wolf's plans for Saturday night if their feelings were still there.

'Oh, I totally understand that. You want to know if it's true love. I don't know much about betrothal magic, but I spoke to my bibi last night, my grandmother in Tanzania, and asked her if she knew and she said her sister, Farida, was betrothed in the same way. We chatted about the magic for a while – I do love learning new things – and I asked about whether you had a choice or whether the magic would make you fall in love. It turns out Farida never married her betrothed, they didn't even date, she couldn't stand the man. He was absolutely vile. Farida told Bibi that she was always aware of the connection whenever they were near each other, like she could feel when he had entered a room she was in even if she couldn't see him, and that sometimes she could feel a magnetic pull that made her want to get closer but her hate for him would always override that. Not once was she ever tempted to kiss him, or let him touch her. That connection you share – the betrothal bond – is a shared energy, but it's not love. If you love him, that's all you, not some weird old ley line magic.'

Star smiled at that. She hoped Kianga was right.

'So if you still have feelings after the bond is removed, will you two date?' Kianga said, her eyes wide with excitement.

'Probably, maybe,' Star said. 'I think so. If the feelings are mutual.'

'How wonderful,' Kianga looked out over the green, but there was still no sign of any magical garland. Wolf was chatting to a few men on the green, they were obviously waiting for something. 'Oh my god, have you ever had witch sex before?'

'What?' Star was startled by the sudden turn the conversation had taken.

'Sex with another witch?'

'Not that I know of.'

'Trust me, you would know. It's the most wonderful thing in the world. Where I grew up on the outskirts of Kent, there weren't too many witches around, so I ended up dating mundane boys, which was fine and lovely and completely normal. The first time I had sex with a witch, my god, it was... magnificent. I'm so excited you get to experience that for the first time with Wolf.'

'Surely it's just like regular mundane sex?' Star said.

'Believe me, there's nothing mundane about it,'

Kianga giggled. 'Sure, it starts off the same but that moment when your magic combines, it's exquisite.'

Star thought about it for a moment. 'Yesterday, Wolf was helping me with my magic and he used his magic to guide mine. Is it like that? That felt nice.'

'He did that?' Kianga said, in surprise. 'That's kind of intimate.'

'It was, I don't think he realised how it would make me feel.'

Kianga shook her head. 'It doesn't feel like that. Guiding your magic is kind of like this.' She picked up Star's arm and gently moved it back and forth. 'I'm in control of your arm but you can take back control at any time. I'm not being forceful with it. When your magic connects during witch sex it's like... two lightning bolts slamming into each other, becoming one.'

'You're making me nervous now.'

'Oh no, you'll enjoy it. I promise.'

Erin looked over at the two of them talking and frowned. Kianga waved her hand and the noise from the village returned in an almost deafening wave.

'Are you doing that weird secret bubble again?' Erin asked Kianga.

'Kianga was just warning me about witch sex,' Star said.

The man next to Erin coughed into his drink.

'I wasn't warning her, I was telling her how incredible it is,' Kianga said.

The man leaned round Erin to talk to Star. 'You've never had sex with a witch?'

'Be kind. She's a wildling, she only discovered she's a witch herself a few days ago when she came here,' Erin said.

The man's face cleared in surprise. 'Wow, really? I bet that caused a few problems for Wolf.'

The man smirked into his drink as he said this and Star frowned at the pleasure he seemed to get from that.

'Wait, why are you talking about witch sex? Are you and Wolf going to have sex?' Erin asked.

The man choked and spluttered on his drink, gasping for breath, and Erin patted him on the back.

The man finally caught his breath. 'If you've fixed your sights on my brother, you'll be very disappointed. He never dates or sleeps with anyone in the village. Or has any fun of any kind.'

'Brother?' Star said. 'You're Lynx?'

'The very same,' he stretched out a hand and she shook it. 'I'm just back to celebrate the winter solstice with family and friends and to keep an eye on my brother.'

'I'm Star Brightheart.'

'So is he training you?' Lynx said.

'Yes, or trying to.'

'I figured he would take on that responsibility. And he spoke about me?'

'We talked a lot about his childhood, you, your parents.'

'He doesn't talk about that with anyone,' Lynx studied her with fresh eyes.

'Did you know they're betrothed?' Erin said.

His face grew suddenly serious. 'What?'

'Apparently so,' Star said.

'So you've come back here to, what, stake your claim on him?'

'No, not at all. I had no idea about any of this, witches, magic, what it means to be betrothed. Trust me, I'm as surprised as you about all of this.'

Just then Wolf started speaking, his voice magically projected so everyone could hear him.

'People of Midnight,' Wolf said, and the noise died down immediately. It was clear everyone here respected him. 'Thank you all for coming to our annual garland ceremony. The winter solstice is our shortest day and our longest night, after that the days get longer and therefore this is a celebration of the sun and light returning. The evergreens such as ivy, holly, yew, juniper and pine are used in our celebrations and our garland as a symbol that life continues through the winter.'

Star smiled that this explanation was probably largely for her benefit; everyone else here would already know all about the winter solstice.

'The garland has taken many weeks of work and

everyone here in the village will help to light it up. Can we have the garland please.'

There were cheers and claps from all the villagers as a team of men and women walked out onto the village green magically floating a long, thick garland of greenery. This thing was huge, easily a hundred metres long, and it was beautifully decorated with flowers and berries. The team floated the garland up so it rested on the tops of the lampposts that surrounded the village green and formed a complete circle.

'Everyone will create a ball of light now to adorn the garland,' Kianga whispered. 'Wolf will go first as he is the mayor, then any descendants of the village founders, then everyone else.'

Wolf formed a ball of light in his hands and floated it up to rest on top of the garland. Jessica, Lynx, Tabitha, Ezra and a few others then formed balls of light too, which floated up to join Wolf's light on the garland. Then slowly everyone else started joining in as well.

Wolf moved over towards Star as little balls of light floated through the air from each of the villagers. He smiled when he saw Lynx and came over to give his brother a big hug.

'Lynx, it's good to have you back,' Wolf said.

'I think I came back just in time, I hear you're betrothed,' Lynx nodded his head in Star's direction.

When Wolf looked over at her, his gaze was filled

with pure warmth. 'It's been an interesting few days. Come round to mine this afternoon and we can catch up.'

'I will.'

Wolf patted his brother on the back and returned to Star's side, his hand on the small of her back. 'Will you put a light on the garland too?'

'I don't know how.'

'Just hold the amulet, close your eyes and imagine a ball of light forming in your hands.'

Star did as she was told as the last few villagers sent their orbs of light up onto the garland. She opened her eyes and smiled to see a little orb of light sitting in her hand. Still holding onto the amulet, she floated it up to sit on the garland but, as it touched the green leaves and flowers, the garland burst into flames.

CHAPTER 16

The flames quickly spread around the area she had touched with her orb. People gasped and screamed and others ran forward, shooting water from their hands. Within moments the fire had been put out but it left behind a smouldering pile of ashes. Most of the garland was thankfully still intact but an area of about three or four metres was completely destroyed.

Everyone fell silent.

'Oh my god, I'm so so sorry, I don't know what happened. I'm sorry, I'll fix it,' Star said.

'You can't fix that, love,' said a man standing next to Wolf. 'No magic in the world will fix that.'

'I like it,' said Zofia. 'Winter solstice is about acknowledging the dark of the winter but celebrating the light of the longer days. Now we have light and dark in our garland.'

There were a few murmurs of agreement.

'You ruined it,' spat Jessica from across the green. 'Weeks of hard work and the start of our winter solstice celebrations has been completely ruined.'

There were a few more murmurs of agreement and one man shouted out, 'Yes exactly.'

Star recognised him as one of the men who had brought the garland in and he had every right to be upset.

'What were you thinking?' Jessica went on. 'You should never have put an orb on the garland if you don't know what you're doing with your magic. Someone could have been killed.'

A few more people were nodding and agreeing.

Jessica was rallying a mob again and it made Star feel really uneasy. Before, when Jessica had been trying to gather support against Star for her role in what had happened to Cleo Walsh, it had been about an incident that had taken place far away from the village, and, as Wolf had said, no one really cared. But this had happened in front of everyone. It had ruined the garland ceremony that everyone had been so looking forward to. Now it was a lot easier to highlight how dangerous Star was because she was so clearly unknowledgeable about her magic.

'OK, everyone calm down,' Wolf said. 'It was an

accident, we've all made mistakes with our magic at some point in our lives and I expect a little more understanding. Most of the garland is fine, nothing has been ruined. Go back home and continue your preparations for the solstice.'

He turned and took Star's arm, guiding her away from the green. But before they'd taken a few steps, Ashley stepped up to talk to Wolf and, with a wave of her hand, she must have created that secret sound bubble around her and Wolf – it was quite clear the two of them were angrily talking but Star couldn't hear a word of it.

Mulberry landed on Wolf's shoulder and it seemed even the little owl was angry too, squawking and flapping his wings. For a second Star saw him glow with fire but Wolf shook his head and Mulberry returned to his normal colour.

Other people began to disperse and walk away, shaking their heads sadly at the state of the garland. Star saw Jessica come over to Lynx and start talking to him, gesturing in her direction.

The conversation between Ashley and Wolf had clearly come to an end. Wolf took Star's arm again and practically marched her back to her house. The door opened with a wave of his hand and as they went inside the door slammed behind them.

'You're angry?' Star said in surprise.

'Oh I'm livid.'

'I'm really sorry but—'

He moved towards her, his hands suddenly on her shoulders. 'This isn't you, you didn't do this, and even if you did I wouldn't be angry at you.'

'What do you mean, I didn't do this?'

'I told you before that some witches are good with water, some are good with fire, and that some witches can simply look at something and it will burst into flames. Jessica is one of those witches.'

'What?'

'Jessica is a fire witch, that's her strength.'

'You think Jessica did this?'

'Oh, I know she did, I just can't prove it.'

He strode off into the kitchen and started pacing back and forth. She followed him in and could feel him buzzing with an uncontrollable rage.

'Ashley saw it too,' he said.

'She saw Jessica do it?' Star took the love blanket off and folded it up, putting it on the kitchen table.

He shook his head. 'She can see magic, she can see the threads, the colours of different spells and charms. If twenty people all cast twenty different spells and if you could freeze the magic as it was coming out of them, she could walk along the line and say exactly what spell each person was going to do based on the shape and colour of it. Fire magic is very different to the magic used for lighting an orb. It's red and angry and hungry. She saw the fire magic touch the garland, she saw where it came from, but she can't be a hundred percent sure it came from Jessica. Jessica was there in the area where it came from but so were lots of other people. Now Ashley and I both know it was Jessica but we can't categorically prove it. Even Mulberry was angry. He kept pointing at Jessica and squawking. He wanted to change into his firebird to teach her a lesson but I told him no. Though maybe I should have let him.' He continued to pace back and forth like a caged animal. 'I'm going to make her pay for this. I will.'

Star wanted to help him, do something to calm him down. She spotted one of the bottles of happiness potion so she grabbed it and passed it to Wolf. He took the cork out and downed it in one. He sighed heavily and sat down.

'This helps a little.' After a moment he looped an arm round Star's waist and pulled her onto his lap, leaning his forehead against the side of her head, breathing her in. 'This helps a lot.'

She sat there feeling his breathing slowing down, becoming more steady. She didn't say anything about Wolf's lack of professionalism; after seeing how quickly the mob could be rallied, she needed this too.

She turned her head and kissed the top of his and he looked up at her, stroking her face.

'She'll do it again,' Wolf said.

'I know.'

'She wants to turn the villagers against you and I

can't protect you from that. I promise I won't ever let anyone hurt you, not that I think it will ever come to that, but I can't protect you against people not liking you.'

'Then I'll just have to prove to everyone how likable I am. They can't all hate me because of a little accident.'

'No, but I don't know what she'll try next.'

They sat there in silence for a while.

'Would you like a change of subject?' Star asked.

'Yes please, because right now I'm thinking of all the horrible things I could do to Jessica to give her a taste of her own medicine.'

'Kianga was talking to me about witch sex.'

A smile appeared on his lips and it grew across his face. 'Go on.'

'She said it was very different to mundane sex.'

'Yes it is.'

'Wolf, you can't just say that with a big grin on your face and not give me any more information. As far as I know I've never had witch sex, I feel like I need to be more prepared.'

'You would know if you'd had witch sex.'

'Wolf!'

'OK, OK. When you have mundane sex you might share a connection with the other person, it might be an emotional connection if you love them or a physical connection if the sex is good. But with witch sex, you share a magical connection too. When a witch is angry or sad or happy their auras are stronger, that's the magical energy that surrounds them. You saw it last night when we were kissing, little golden sparks of happiness. Now you have your aura, I have mine and they never connect. Doesn't matter what we're doing, they won't connect. Even when I used my magic to guide yours yesterday, that's just my magic touching yours.' He motioned with his hands, sliding one palm against the other. 'When witches have sex, the auras connect in ways they don't ever do at any other time. It's not just a connection, it's two forces of energy becoming one. And it's incredible.'

'I have to say, I'm a little bit nervous about Saturday night now. *If* we have sex.'

'*When.* When I make love to you, not *if.*'

She smiled and stroked his face. 'You don't know that. You might hate me once the bond has been removed.'

He shook his head. 'I know how I feel. I can't see how that could possibly be taken away from me. We'll go through all the rituals because I want you to have a choice, I don't want you to come here and be forced into this weird magical relationship.'

'I have a choice. Kianga said her great-aunt was betrothed and she hated the man. Nothing ever happened between them because she chose not to. I have a choice, Wolf, and I choose you.'

He stared at her for a moment and then reached up

and kissed her, cupping the back of her head with his hand.

God this kiss was everything. It was too much yet nowhere near enough. Star wanted to feel his skin, feel his body against hers. She started undoing the buttons on his shirt and he let out a little moan of need against her lips. She dipped her head and kissed at the hollow of his neck then up his throat to where his pulse was hammering against his skin.

'Star, we need to stop,' Wolf's voice was strangled.

'Why?' She continued her kisses.

'Because it doesn't feel right.'

'Funny because it definitely feels right to me.'

She moved her mouth back to his before he made any more protests and after a few moments she felt his hand slide up her bare thigh under her dress. He hooked a finger through the waistband of her knickers and pulled them down her legs then threw them across the room. He moved his hand back between her legs and when he touched her she moaned against his lips.

Oh, his fingers were wonderful. Instead of floundering around in a cursory attempt at foreplay, he knew exactly where to touch her, his thumb applying the exact right pressure, his fingers doing magical things inside her. She arched against him and that feeling was suddenly building inside her like a rocket about to explode which surprised her, she'd never orgasmed so quickly before in her life. She pulled back slightly to look at him, his breath was heavy against her lips and she knew he was getting as much enjoyment out of this as she was. And then she was falling, spiralling, her head thrown back, shouting out words and noises that didn't even make sense.

He pulled her chin gently back towards him and he kissed her hard as she tumbled into the abyss. But as the feeling started to subside she was suddenly desperate for more and the way he was kissing her he obviously felt the same.

He pulled back slightly. 'Do you have any condoms?'

'No.'

He swore.

'But I'm on the pill if that makes any difference.'

He swore again and moved her off his lap. He snatched the love blanket off the table and arranged it haphazardly on the floor then came back to her, kissing her hard and desperate. The fact that they were going to have sex on a love blanket suddenly added another layer to this.

He moved his hands to her bum, hauling her closer to him and she could feel how much he wanted this. He slid his hands down to the hem of her dress and started easing it up over her waist.

Suddenly there was a knock on the door and Wolf froze.

'Just ignore it, they'll go away,' Star said.

'Star!' Maxine shouted through the letterbox. 'It's me and Darianna.'

'Fat chance of that with Maxine,' Wolf muttered.

'We know you're in there. Claudia said she saw you and Wolf go inside so open up. Unless you two are doing it then feel free to tell us to sod off,' Maxine giggled.

Wolf opened his mouth, probably to do just that, but Star clamped her hand over it. 'Don't you dare.'

'We just want to make sure you're OK,' Darianna said.

Wolf sighed with frustration and stepped back from Star. 'There are good people here, even if their timing is awful.'

He quickly started doing up the buttons of his shirt, and straightening his hair. Star grabbed her knickers and pulled them on and, once she'd made sure that Wolf was decent, she ran to the door.

'Hey,' Star said, trying to calm her breathing and wondering if her friends could tell she'd just had the best orgasm of her entire life.

'Are you OK?' Darianna said.

Wolf squeezed past her. 'I'll pick you up at half eleven tonight.'

Star nodded.

'And just so you know this... conversation isn't finished, not even close. We're going to finish off what we were just talking about tonight.'

Star didn't dare speak because it would only have come out as a whimper of need.

Wolf discreetly waved his hand at his side and out of the corner of Star's eye she saw the love blanket leap up off the floor, fold itself neatly and place itself on the table.

'And bring a blanket, it might get cold,' Wolf said, leaving no doubt in her mind which blanket he wanted her to bring.

'I will.'

He nodded and turned his attention to Maxine and Darianna. 'Thank you for coming and checking on her.'

With that he walked off, leaving Star a quivering jelly of need.

'Come in,' Star said, stepping back to let them inside the house. She walked down to the kitchen, sweeping a critical eye over the room to make sure any evidence of debauchery wasn't to be seen.

'Don't beat yourself up over what happened,' Maxine said, sitting down in the exact chair Wolf had been sitting in a few moments before with his hand up her dress.

Star moved to the sink and poured herself a glass of cold water, gulping it down to try to cool her thoughts. She turned round to find Maxine and Darianna both staring at her.

'Sorry, can I get you both a drink?'

'Water's fine,' Darianna said.

'I'm OK,' Maxine said. 'You're taking this very well. I thought you'd be a blubbering mess.'

'What Jessica did was unforgiveable,' Darianna said.

'So you know she started the fire?' Star said, passing Darianna her glass of water.

'What? No way,' Maxine said.

'I was talking about stirring up all that shit, being overly dramatic over a little accident, but you think she started it?' Darianna said.

Just then Viktor waltzed through the cat flap. 'She definitely did it. As a cat I can see people's auras a lot easier than when I was a human. I could see her aura changed to red just before the garland caught fire. That and her stupid smug face.'

Star nodded. 'Ashley saw the fire magic come from the same side of the green that Jessica was standing on. We can't prove it's her but we know it is. We pissed her off because she was being shitty about me wearing this apparent love blanket, which I had no idea about when I pulled it on. So Wolf pretended we were properly betrothed and that we'd been sleeping together just to annoy her and that was her revenge.'

'That's horrible,' Darianna said. 'And then rallying people to get them to hate you.'

'She wants me gone. She's had her eye on Wolf since they were young and she's still holding out hope that one day he will fall in love with her.'

'Everyone knows she has a thing for him, it's a bit embarrassing for her really,' Maxine said.

Star suddenly felt bad for Jessica. To be in love with a man for so long and never get anywhere with him or have any closure must be torture. And yes, Star did think that part of that attraction for Jessica was Wolf's wealth and position but no one would hold onto a torch for this long if it was just about that. There were probably thousands of other wealthy witches out there that Jessica could have set her sights on. And then for Star to waltz in here and scoop him up in a matter of minutes must be really galling. If the shoe was on the other foot Star would probably be pretty disappointed too, although not enough to make her want to sabotage someone's home. Maybe she could talk to Jessica. She couldn't tell her that nothing was going on between her and Wolf because after what happened here in the kitchen, and the thinly veiled promise of what would happen tonight, something was very definitely happening between them. But maybe a conversation would help – even if she had no idea what she would say.

'Maybe she's lonely,' Star said. 'Does she have any friends here?'

'Oh god no, she's a bitch to everyone,' Maxine said. 'She thinks because she's one of the founders' descendants that she is above everyone else. She also has her sights set on being mayor one day but that's never going to happen. Even if Wolf stepped down, she would have to be voted in and no one's going to vote for her after the way she's behaved over the last few years.'

Star sighed. Jessica really had made her own bed and was now having to lie in it.

'What are you going to do?' Darianna said.

Viktor jumped up onto the table. 'I can scratch her eyes out.'

He lifted a paw and the claws shot out as if they'd been fired from a gun.

'I don't think that will be necessary,' Star said.

'I can do it while she's asleep, one swipe of these bad boys and those eyeballs will come tumbling out.'

'That feels like a slightly over-the-top reaction,' Star said.

'We could curse her,' Viktor said, clearly not to be deterred. 'Force her to confess or her head will explode.'

'Again, it feels a bit extreme.'

'Spoilsport,' Viktor said.

He jumped off the table and disappeared out of the cat flap again. Star only hoped he wasn't going to take revenge into his own hands... or paws.

'Will you tell everyone that she started the fire?' Darianna asked.

'I have no proof but there's a few of us that know and if we casually mention it to a few others, word will soon get around. Even if people don't believe it, the seed will be sown for the next time she tries to pull a similar stunt. In the meantime, I'm going to try and make some cakes for everyone in the village to apologise for my little accident.'

'But you have nothing to apologise for,' Darianna said.

'But most of the villagers don't know that, most of them think I'm some reckless wildling that ruined their garland ceremony.'

'That's a tough crowd,' Maxine said. 'And you do know that there's nearly seven hundred people in this village, that's a lot of cakes.'

'Then I best get started.'

'Can we help?' Darianna said.

Star thought about the forgiveness she wanted to put in each cake and shook her head. 'But you can gather me some flowers and leaves if you really want to help. I'm going to attempt to fix the garland too.'

'You do know that took weeks to make?' Maxine said.

'Yes, but that was for the whole thing. I'll only be making a few metres' worth to swap out the burned bit. How hard can it be?'

Lynx was already waiting for Wolf when he got home. Sitting on his sofa, feet up on his coffee table, one arm behind his head, he looked totally relaxed.

'Hey,' Lynx said.

'Comfy?' Wolf said, shutting the front door behind him.

'Always. What's going on with your witch?'

Wolf flopped down on the sofa next to his brother. 'She didn't set fire to that garland.'

'I know that.'

Wolf sat up to look at his brother. 'You know?'

'As a fire witch myself, I can feel whenever someone else uses fire magic. It's like goosebumps on the back of your neck and that feeling came from Jessica's side of the green. Although I can't be sure it was her as there were a few other fire witches over there, the fact that the other fire witches looked as shocked as everyone else when it happened and Jessica was the one shouting the loudest about it after it happened, I'm pretty sure it was her.'

'I thought that too and Ashley saw it coming from her side of the green, though again, she doesn't know who it came from.'

'Jessica came up to me after, telling me that Star had bewitched you and I needed to get rid of her if I wanted to save you. She's got it in for your witch.'

'She's not my—' Wolf stopped what he was saying. He could hardly deny anything was going on after what had just happened in Star's kitchen. He couldn't even blame sex cakes this time.

'So what's going on, has she bewitched you? I mean, I'm not entirely sure that's a thing. Surely there's no magic in the world that can make you fall in love with someone?'

'No, there isn't. Well not to my knowledge or that of anyone else I talk to about it but...' Wolf let out a heavy sigh. 'But the betrothal is not just some silly tradition. It's a powerful connection forged because we were born in the same place on the same day.'

'And you're worried that connection might mean an attraction that you don't have any control over.'

'I don't have control of it. She's like a drug I just can't get enough of. I've nearly made love to her twice now in her kitchen. I have an insatiable thirst for her that I can't quench. I want to be with her all the time. She's the last thing I think about when I go to bed and the first thing I think about when I wake up and then I spend the night dreaming of her. It's ridiculous. I've asked Ashley to remove the betrothal bonds but she thinks the best time to do that would be on the winter solstice and in the meantime that attraction is getting deeper and deeper.'

Lynx was staring at him like he didn't know who he was and Wolf could totally relate. He didn't know the person he was when he was with Star either.

'I know, it's crazy. I've never felt like this before. It's

been a long time since anything has made me smile and laugh like Star does. It's been a long time since I've been truly this happy. And it scares me.'

Lynx suddenly burst out laughing, which wasn't really the sympathetic reaction Wolf had been hoping for.

'Dear Gods, I never thought I would see the day. You're in love with her.'

'No, no, no. This is... it's not that.'

Lynx was still laughing. 'It is. I'm sorry but it is. What you're describing is love. Trust me on this. I don't care what magical energy is connecting you, it's not going to feel like that. You've never felt this way before because you've never been in love before. Apart from that girl you used to hang out with in the woods when you were a kid and I don't think we can really count that. What was her name, Seren, was it?'

Wolf let out a sigh. 'Fun fact about Star. She was adopted by mundanes, which is why she didn't know she was a witch. Her adopted parents were Welsh.'

'Right?' Lynx clearly had no idea where he was going with this.

'Did you know the Welsh word for Star is Seren?'

The smile fell from Lynx's face as the penny dropped about what Wolf had just said. 'It's her. Star is the girl you used to play with in the woods?'

'Yep.'

'Oh, that explains everything. You never ever got

over her. And now she's back, of course you're going to have complicated emotions with seeing her again. But if she makes you so damn happy why not just enjoy it?'

'There is the ethical standpoint you're conveniently forgetting. I don't want to force her into doing something she doesn't want to do.'

'In the times when you've been with her, intimately, was there any part of you that thought she didn't want this? When you look into her eyes, do you see fear or confusion?'

'No, not at all. She wants me as much as much as I want her. And everyone I speak to about the betrothal magic says it's not going to force us to do anything we don't want. Did you know Gran was betrothed?'

'Was she? To Grandpa?'

'No, some guy in the village she grew up in. They slept together for a few months and moved on. But she said she never felt she was forced into anything.'

'There you go, so what are you scared of?'

'What if it's not real, what if I spend the next few days falling further and further in love with her and it comes to a crashing end on Friday night?'

'Love is a risk. Forget about magic and betrothal bonds for a moment. Love is always a risk and it's scary for anyone, witch or not. What if she doesn't feel the same way, what if it ends. Couples have been worrying over that for thousands of years. But if you don't do anything, and if when the magic ends there's nothing there, you will regret for the rest of your life that you didn't have this time with her. This time now will give you the closure you never had when she left before. Take this happiness, you deserve it, even if it's only for a few days. But you know in your heart that these feelings are much bigger than any bonds that hold you together. You have to trust in her feelings too.'

Wolf sighed. He only hoped Lynx was right because losing Star when she was right here working alongside him every day was going to be more devastating than it was before.

CHAPTER 17

Star looked at all the flowers and leaves the girls had gathered for her. Maxine and Darianna had roped in Kianga and Erin to help with their quest. Nithya had gone off to spend the solstice with family, but she'd already heard about the disaster with the garland and texted her support. Although a text wasn't going to help Star sort out this mess.

She'd spent several hours making mini chocolate yule logs and she'd probably be making the rest well into the night so there was one for every member of the village. She had thought forgiving thoughts as she made them and then decorated them with icing shaped like berries and green leaves with extra forgiveness sprinkled on top. But she really wanted to fix the garland too but she had no idea what she was doing.

'How do we stick all these flowers and leaves together?' Star said.

'I'm no florist, but don't they use things like Oasis foam to put flowers in when they do flower arranging?' Erin said.

'We don't have that,' Star said. 'Is there some magical way to join them together?'

The girls looked blank.

'If there is, I don't know it,' Kianga said.

Maxine was scanning the internet for ideas. 'This one lady uses a pool noodle for a flower arch.'

'Yeah, sadly we don't have that either.'

'What about good old-fashioned string? I attended a wreath-making workshop once and the man there was just lashing the greenery together in small bunches and then adding each bunch to the wire frame,' Darianna said.

'I feel like we need something in the middle to attach the leaves to as we don't have a frame,' Star said.

'Oh, when I was little we used to make guys for Bonfire Night,' Maxine said.

'What's a guy?' Darianna said.

'Guy Fawkes supposedly was plotting to blow up the Houses of Parliament many hundreds of years ago and his plans were thwarted. So we celebrate it every year by having bonfires and fireworks. Kids make these life-size Guy-Fawkes-doll-type things from paper and old clothes and burn them on a big bonfire,' Maxine said.

'Sounds a bit barbaric,' Darianna said.

'It is a bit, but England has many weird festivals. There's a village not far from here that does a worm charming festival every year, people travel from all over the country to charm worms from the ground. There are prizes for the team who can charm the most worms, I think.'

'OK, I'm definitely going to see that. I bet I could win,' Darianna waved her fingers and a little bit of sparkle appeared out of the ends.

Star laughed. 'I feel we're going off on a tangent here, how does making a guy help us?'

'Well, we'd get an old pair of leggings or trousers, tie off the feet and stuff the legs with newspapers. If we do that then we have a base to attach flowers and stuff round the outside,' Maxine said.

'Great idea,' Star said. 'I have some old pyjama bottoms upstairs I could sacrifice.'

She raced upstairs and dug around in her drawers, pulling out two pairs of pyjama bottoms. One set with unicorns on them, the other with cactuses that, randomly, looked like penises; she wasn't sure whether that was deliberate or accidental on the part of the designer. But no one would see them underneath the leaves and flowers. Once the legs were stuffed, they could tie the two waist ends together and that should give her a base long enough to replace the burned area of the garland.

Star heard raucous, loud laughter from the kitchen below her, squeals of delight and horror. Maxine was no doubt regaling the others with some tale of drunken debauchery.

She went back down to the kitchen, showing off her pyjama bottoms like she had found a fabulous treasure, and stopped in horror. The girls were all tucking into her tin of sex cakes and howling with shock and laughter.

'Oh my god, no, stop eating,' Star said, running forward to stop the car crash that was happening before her eyes. She grabbed a half-eaten one from Darianna, but Maxine held hers out of Star's reach.

'There's no way I'm giving this up. I feel like I just got invited to the hottest porn show ever.'

'No, no, no!' Star said, reaching for Erin's who gladly gave hers back.

'I really didn't need to see that.' Erin clamped a hand over her eyes and laughed. 'Nope, I can still see it.'

'You made porn cakes,' Kianga said, laughing so hard, tears were rolling down her cheeks. 'This needs to be a new line in your cake-making services, they'd be very popular. Oh, if you could tailor the images to your clients' own sexual fantasies – a hot night with Chris Hemsworth for example – people would pay a small fortune for that.'

Even Viktor was faceplanting a cake, clearly eating it with great relish.

'Viktor!'

He looked up with cake crumbs all round his mouth. 'When you get to my age you've been there and seen and done it all and you certainly don't let a bit of sex get in the way of damned good cake.' He shoved his face back in the cake again, noises of pleasure could be heard as he devoured it.

Darianna was fanning herself. 'I'm not sure if I can ever look you in the eye again. Did that actually happen?'

'It was a dream I had,' Star said, feeling her cheeks burn with mortification. 'I got up and made these cakes because I couldn't get back off to sleep and I thought about the dream while I was making them and inadvertently put that sex scene in my cakes. I'm so embarrassed you ate them and saw Wolf...'

'Mauling you like a wild animal on the kitchen table,' Maxine said. 'Good lord, I said he would be hot in bed. I wasn't expecting that.'

'It was just a dream, it didn't actually happen,' Star said, failing to mention it nearly did after Wolf had eaten one.

'I can't believe you had a sex dream about our mayor,' Erin said.

'I can't control what I dream about. Once, when I was drunk, I had a dream about dancing with a six-foot cabbage. I can't stand cabbage. I don't think the dream means anything.'

'Only that you have a crush on him,' Maxine said.

'They're betrothed,' Kianga said. 'They have a connection that none of us really understand. Even Star doesn't understand it. It's only natural she'll be thinking about him. Although, perhaps not like that,' she dissolved into giggles again.

Star watched her friends laughing uncontrollably and felt the smirk touch her lips. There was only one way she could escape this with a scrap of dignity. She sat down at the table, grabbed a cake and took a bite and the sex scene flashed before her eyes. 'It was a damned good dream.'

They all laughed again, even louder, and Star couldn't help laughing too.

Star stood looking at the garland in dismay. She and her friends had spent some time tying leaves and flowers to the stuffed legs of her pyjamas, and she had been quite impressed with it when it had sat on her kitchen table. They'd carried it to the village green and, with a bit of magic, had hung it from the lamps to cover the burned area, but it looked awful. Even with their magic it was hanging limply and in comparison to the beautiful arrangement of the rest of the garland, it looked like a five-year-old had grabbed a few branches and tied them to an old sack with some string. What was worse, little bits of the pyjamas were visible through the gaps in the foliage. She just hoped no one looked that closely as they would see some rather odd-shaped cactuses peering through the leaves.

'I like it,' Maxine said. 'It's unique.'

'I think... for the time we had, we did OK,' Erin said, diplomatically.

'I think it's lacking what the rest of the garland has,' Kianga said honestly. Even Darianna didn't look impressed.

Star chewed her lip nervously. What if people took offence at their pathetic attempt?

Someone moved next to Erin to have a look and Star glanced over and saw Lynx. He was clearly very unimpressed with their replacement garland too.

'I'm not sure that's any better than the burned area,' Lynx said, tilting his head to look at it.

'Hey!' Erin said, indignantly.

'Did you have something to do with this?' Lynx said.

'Yes I did,' Erin said.

'In that case it's the most beautiful garland I've ever seen.'

'Good answer.'

'Well, as this has definitely not ticked the box in

terms of asking for forgiveness, I better get on with my forgiveness cakes,' Star said. 'Thanks for all your help.'

She waved goodbye and started walking back towards her house but she was surprised when Lynx fell in at her side.

'Hey?' she said, in confusion.

'So this must all be a bit strange and overwhelming. You come here, find out magic is real and that you're betrothed. I'm sure it's not the quiet respite you were hoping for.'

'I... don't think I've ever been happier. I never really fitted anywhere before, always the odd one out. Now I finally feel like I belong somewhere and I've made some great friends. Everyone here is just like me, we were never really happy living a mundane life and now we can be free to be who we are. But I'm sure you're not asking about my mental wellbeing.'

'Well, my brother is a little bit smitten with you.'

'The feeling is very mutual.'

He stopped her with his hand on her arm and she turned to look at him. 'I think he's concerned you won't feel that way once the bonds have been lifted.'

'I know he's worried about that.'

'I just wanted to say that when the bonds have been lifted, if you don't feel the same as you do now, maybe consider that Wolf may still have these feelings, so please be kind.'

Star smiled at his concern. 'There have been times

since I've come here when I've thought, is this real? When I see a hundred-metre garland floating with magic; when Kianga blocks out all the sound so we can have a conversation with no one hearing us; when Ashley magically makes her sofa and lounge so much bigger than it really is; when Wolf flew me up into the clouds last night just to make me happy, I've wondered if I'm just having the most amazing dream. But when Wolf kissed me up there beneath the stars I knew that was more real than anything I've experienced in my life. When I look at the magic around me and start doubting it, the one thing I know for sure is real are the feelings I have for your brother.'

Lynx studied her for a moment then broke into a huge grin. 'Good answer.' He nodded with approval. 'I think you might just be the best thing that's ever happened to my brother.'

With that he walked off and she watched him go. It seemed she had impressed at least one person in the village, beyond Wolf and her new friends. Now she only had approximately seven hundred others to impress and she hoped her chocolate forgiveness yule logs would do the trick.

Wolf looked up at the sky as he walked through the streets. It was decidedly grey rather than the bright blue they normally had in December and the clouds were heavy as if it might snow, which was a bit of a worry. He felt sure, if it did, the villagers would connect the dots with Star's arrival and the weather changing and he didn't think it would be in a good way.

He was surprised actually that no one had expressed concerns about her being a weather witch. He was pretty damn sure Maggie would have remembered that Star's mum was the weather witch who cursed them and if Maggie knew, then she would have told the whole village. But not one person had spoken to him about it, which was odd. There were only a handful of people living in the village thirty years ago who were still living here today – Maggie and Tom, Charles, Esther and Lizzie, and his gran – so it was strange that none of them had mentioned it to him either.

He saw Maggie in her garden, without Tom; Wednesday was his day of playing golf at a nearby mundane golf club, or rather winning at golf, which conveniently Tom did every time.

Wolf wandered over to talk to her.

'Hi Maggie,' he said.

Maggie turned off her hosepipe and waved at him. 'Dreadful business at the garland ceremony this morning and rumour has it Jessica set fire to the garland, not your Star.'

He was glad that rumour was circling. If Maggie had heard it, she would be sure to tell others. Anything that would take the attention off Star would be a good thing.

'I heard that rumour too, but I have to say without proof there isn't really a lot I can do. It wouldn't be good to spread those kinds of rumours and tarnish someone's name if it's not true.'

'Of course not,' Maggie said, her eyes wide with feigned innocence.

Wolf suppressed a smirk. Telling Maggie not to tell anyone was a sure-fire way to make sure *everyone* was told.

'Listen, I was just wondering what you told people about Star after you'd met her?'

'That you two were betrothed, which is terribly exciting. I can't remember the last time we had a betrothal wedding.'

'You didn't tell them anything else?'

'Like what?'

'I don't know, the stuff you told Star, about who her mum is and the affair between Rose and the mayor.'

'Oh no, I don't concern myself with that kind of gossip,' Maggie dismissed it.

'Maggie, you and I both know you love that kind of gossip.'

Maggie's face grew serious. 'Why are you asking about her mum?'

He narrowed his eyes because her tone of voice was protective.

'As you said, Star is my betrothed and I don't want her to get hounded out of here because... of who her parents were.'

If Maggie didn't know Star's mum was the weather witch who cursed the village, he absolutely wasn't going to tell her.

'I think you better come in for a cup of tea,' Maggie said.

He frowned in confusion and followed her inside.

She directed him to sit down at the kitchen table and bustled about making a pot of tea. After a few moments she placed the pot in the middle and sat down opposite him.

'I presume you're asking whether I told everyone that Star's mum was the weather witch that cursed this village?'

He nodded. 'That's exactly what I'm asking.'

She paused while she added sugar and milk to her cup.

'I never told you that my mum was a weather witch.'

Wolf sat back in his chair. He had not been expecting that.

'And no, those powers were not passed down to me.

I can't even raise the wind or spray water from my hands like some of you air and water witches so there's no chance at all of me being able to control the weather. I lived in a witch village in France with my mum and she never told anyone what she could do. She had spent most of her life moving on, being shunned for her special powers, so she'd learned to keep quiet about it. One day there was a great fire in the village where she lived and it spread quicker than anyone could stop it. So my mum summoned a great torrential rainstorm to put it out, which it did. She saved the village and the very next day the whole village marched up to her door and forced her to leave. She barely had time to pack. One man had a shotgun and told her if she didn't leave he would kill us both.'

'Maggie, I'm so sorry.'

Maggie picked up the teapot and poured out two mugs, and Wolf noticed her hand was shaking.

'He stood in the doorway while Mum threw everything into boxes and suitcases and pointed the gun at me the whole time. I was six years old. Our own kind and we had been threatened by the people who should have been more understanding about her magic. We'd been ostracised, banished. All of our friends turned against us. I will never ever forget that feeling.'

She took a long sip of tea and stared into its depths for a moment. 'I was very close to Rose's mum, Star's grandmother. And when Rose was born and her parents discovered she was a weather witch, they decided to keep it a secret from everyone in the village. I swore I would never tell a soul after seeing the treatment my mum went through when I was little. But I always wondered what would have happened to her if more people had found out. Would she have been threatened and made to leave just like my mum had? Of course, after Rose left and the curse was placed on the village, a lot more people found out too and there were a lot of people that took the attitude of, thank goodness she's gone, which was just horrible. She was a sixteen-year-old kid.'

Maggie opened a tin of cookies and offered Wolf one, but he shook his head.

'So when Star came here and I realised her mum was our weather witch I knew I had to keep it quiet. If Star is too, and people find out, I think a lot of people won't want her here.' She took a bite of her cookie. 'Is she?'

'I don't honestly know but that is my concern too. History books show that people are not kind to weather witches. She has a lot of power, more so than anyone I've ever met, so there's a really good chance she is.'

'And she has no control over her powers, people are going to be even more concerned about that.'

'I know.'

'Fortunately, it's been so long since Rose left, and so many people in the village from that time have either died or moved on. Most of those here just know there was a weather witch that lived here at some point and she cursed us with crappy weather. They won't make the connection between her and Star.'

'That's what I'm banking on too,' Wolf said.

'Unfortunately that cow, Jessica, has been sniffing around. Yesterday she asked to see the records of the year you and Star were born and as those records are public record, I can't say no. As far as I know there's nothing written down to say that Rose was a weather witch but there are diary entries from the town clerk at the time, even a little local newspaper. If she starts digging into them, it might reveal everything. If Jessica is looking for dirt on Star, I don't think it will take her too long to find it.'

Wolf swore under his breath. Accidentally setting fire to a much beloved garland was nothing in comparison to having a weather witch here with the potential to destroy the whole village, at least in the eyes of some of the villagers. He wanted to protect Star but how could he protect her from suspicion, fear and even hate?

CHAPTER 18

S tar was waiting anxiously in the lounge for Wolf to come and pick her up for the evening's cleansing ritual. She had no idea what the night was going to hold. As Wolf had clearly talked to Lynx after they'd nearly had sex about how he was still concerned that her feelings were real, he'd probably talked himself out of finishing what they'd started like he'd promised.

There was a knock and she ran to open it, wondering if she should greet him with a kiss hello.

She opened the door and couldn't help smiling at the sight of him standing there. And she could see it all over his face, a desperate attempt to be professional and his need to be with her were raging an internal battle, but as a big smile spread across his face she thought the latter might have won.

'God, you're infectious. Come on, let's go before I say to hell with the cleansing rituals and just take you to bed instead.'

'I'd be OK with that.'

'I know you would.'

She grabbed the love blanket.

'I'm not sure you'll be needing that,' Wolf said.

'I'll bring it just in case.'

'You're going to be the ruin of me,' Wolf said, but he took her hand as he led her out to the car and it made her smile so damn much.

He opened the door for her and she slid inside, bubbling over with excitement. He went round to the other side, got in and drove down towards the gate which magically opened to let them out.

'So we're going to treat this cleansing ritual professionally then,' Star said, still unable to suppress the smile on her face. 'No hanky-panky.'

He smiled. 'You're getting a lot of pleasure out of my torture. Regardless of what happens tonight, I still want to go ahead with the cleansing rituals and the breaking of the bond so we both know that whatever is left is real. Jessica told Lynx that she thinks I'm bewitched and I feel like I am, I have never ever felt the way I feel about you and it's getting stronger every day. So we're going to do this cleansing properly.'

'And then?'

'Star, we're washing each other naked in a moonlit lake, neither of us are getting out of that alive.'

She burst out laughing.

He glanced over at her. 'I can see the excitement sparking out of you.'

She looked down at herself and could see a pale gold glow with little sparks of lightning arcing out of her like a solar flare.

'This is incredible, I've never had this before. It only happens around you.'

'I like it, I've never made a woman glow before.'

He pulled into a very narrow road barely wide enough for his car and at the top a gate magically swung open to let him through. High hedges lined the narrow drive as they bumped along a gravel track.

'Where are we going?'

'This land is owned by the village but I'm the only one allowed to come here. I come here at every full moon to collect moonlit water for potions and a few times a month when the sun is the highest in the day to collect sunshine water.'

'Wait, we're going to bathe naked in a lake that everyone uses for their potions?'

'It's a lake fed by a geothermal spring and a small waterfall from a river up on the moors. I'll gather the moonlit water before we go in. By the time I come up here again to gather more water our... nakedness will have been washed out to sea.'

'OK, good. I don't want anyone to drink a moonlit potion and get a flash of us naked in the lake.'

Wolf laughed.

The hedges cleared and below them, nestled into the hillside, was a lake covered with the silver of the full moon.

'This is beautiful,' she said, softly.

'It is.'

They parked up by the side of it and got out. It was a small lake, probably more of a pool, and at one end there was a short waterfall pouring off the rocks about six foot above the surface, the water sending silver sparks into the air as it splashed into the pool.

Wolf went to the back of the car and Star spread out the blanket by the side of the lake. Just in case.

He came back with two huge canisters. He unscrewed them and dipped them into the side of the lake, filling them with the silvery water.

'Is that enough for the whole village?'

'Probably only a quarter of the village make their own potions. Everyone else will get their potions off them. But most people who use moonlit water in their potions will only use a few drops so this will last a long time.'

He replaced the lids on the canisters and carried them back to the car. He came back to her and took both her hands in his.

'The lake is enchanted. It's a powerful place. It's

heated by a geothermal spring from below and beneath that the ley lines that cross under our village run right underneath the lake. It is entirely possible that once we wash each other the bonds will be broken, so this could be the last time we feel like this for each other. The other rituals are probably more symbolic than magical, but this could very well do the job.'

Star smiled and took his face in her hands. 'I'm not worried. These feelings I have for you are real. I feel that with every fibre of my being. I have no reason to believe that your feelings for me are any less real. But if you're concerned we'll never get a chance to ignite this fire between us, we could make love now and wash each other after.'

He kissed her wrist, lingering his hot mouth over her pulse which made her heart go into overdrive. 'Very, very tempting.' He trailed his mouth down to her palm, his eyes on hers the whole time. 'Lynx says we should just enjoy ourselves for the next few days and then if it ends at least we had this time together rather than fighting to keep apart.'

'Lynx is a very very wise man and I'm not fighting to keep us apart, only you are doing that.'

'I'm trying to be respectful so you don't feel I'm taking advantage of you while we're under the influence of betrothal magic.'

'Which is lovely but you already know I want this. Is there another reason you're holding back?'

He looked away over the lake and she knew immediately that there was.

'Is it because you think your feelings will be gone by Saturday and you don't want to lead me on?' Star said.

'No. It's not that. I mean, of course I don't want to do anything to hurt you but I'm fairly confident my feelings will still be there.'

She remembered what Lynx had said about being kind to Wolf if her feelings were no longer there. 'You're worried I might be leading you on, that this is just sex for me?'

He looked at his watch. 'Let's go for a swim. We have a few minutes before midnight and before we have to start the cleansing ritual.'

He started stripping off and she couldn't take her eyes off him. He was gloriously strong everywhere; his legs, arms, the muscles in his back, even his bum was muscular. He dived into the lake in one beautifully exquisite, graceful movement, disappearing under the water.

She quickly undressed and stepped into the shallows, wading out up to her chest before Wolf re-emerged.

'It's really warm,' Star said.

'That's the spring pumping water from below. The other side of the lake is colder as it's fed by the river and the waterfall. Want to see behind the waterfall?'

'Oh sure.'

They swam closer and she could feel the water get colder. Wolf dived under the surface to get through the waterfall and she saw the shadow of him reappear on the other side. She followed suit, feeling the water pound on her back as she swam under the spray. She lifted her head out of the water and Wolf helped her to stand up on a ledge, although they were still fully in the water. She wiped the water from her eyes and gave a little gasp as she saw tiny little orbs of gold moving about near the rocks at the back.

'Fireflies!'

'Yeah. No magic needed for these little beasties. They're magical enough on their own.'

'They're beautiful. Is it common that they're around in December?'

'The curse has impacted on a lot of the animals and insects in the area. This area is owned by the village so it's subject to the same weather patterns. The glow worms emit this light to attract a mate and then they lay eggs, something that should happen in the spring and summer months. The warmer weather at this time of year has confused them but if the female lays eggs outside of the village parameters it's unlikely they will survive.'

'Oh no, that's sad.'

'Hopefully they'll have the good sense to stay where it's warmer. Although the weather even inside the village has been so much colder than we're used to at this time of year.'

'Is that because of me?'

'It might be. It's hard to know.'

She turned back to face him. 'It's safe to say that my arrival has caused a lot of disruption in the village and not necessarily for the better.'

'My life has been infinitely better since you arrived.'

'Despite being bewitched, whatever that is?'

'Because of it.' He frowned slightly, stroking her face. 'I don't think you're leading me on or that this is just about sex for you. I just feel that it might mean something different to you than it does to me.'

'I think you just have to trust me that I'll still be here when all this is over.'

He nodded and then looked at his watch. 'It's time. Let's go back to the warmer area.'

They swam back through the waterfall to where the spring was bubbling away and got to a place where they could stand. She stood up and his eyes took her in, greedily.

'You know, with the fireflies, in this country anyway, it's the females that light up, not the males. They dazzle their mate. You... you shine like a diamond. You are dazzling.'

She smiled. 'You're pretty spectacular yourself. How does this work then?'

He cleared his throat, obviously trying to focus. 'We

just scoop water onto each other and rub it across each other's skin, like this.'

He scooped some liquid up in his hand and poured it over her shoulder, then he stroked the water down her arm. She swallowed at the gentle intimacy.

'Let me wash you first,' Star said.

She scooped up the water and was surprised to see it sparkled in her hand. She poured it over his chest and it glimmered on his skin.

'You're so beautiful,' Star whispered. She started massaging the water into the scars on his chest. 'I remember that day so vividly: the lightning, you saving my life, the smell afterwards of burning flesh, but probably the thing I remember the most is you telling me you loved me. No one, outside my parents, has ever said that to me. I walked out of the woods absolutely buzzing with what you'd done and what you'd said and then I never saw you again. And the worst thing was, I never said it back, I was in so much shock over the lightning strike that I didn't even realise I hadn't until later. But of course I loved you. I loved you so much and I think a part of me has always loved you. And now you're here and those feelings I felt for you back then are flooding back and I think I'm falling in love with you all over again.'

She looked up at him. His breathing was heavy, his eyes dark and he bent his head and kissed her hard. She immediately kissed him back. The connection was instant, like flicking a switch. His kiss was urgent, desperate, and she knew nothing about this was a lie.

He pulled her against him and she relished the feel of his hard body against hers. His greedy hands were everywhere, devouring her body, making her whimper with need.

He lifted her and she wrapped her legs around him as he carried her to the side of the lake, still kissing her, and then laid her down on the blanket. Then he was over her, kissing her, touching her, making her body hum for him.

He kissed her neck and very slowly trailed his mouth down her body, across her breasts, making her gasp, and then slowly down across her stomach and suddenly he was kissing her right there between her legs.

She gasped, arching up towards him. But he was relentless, giving her exactly what she needed until she was screaming and writhing in absolute mindless pleasure.

He leaned back over her, kissing her hard.

Her breathing slowed as the feeling faded, and he pulled back slightly.

'Are you ready for witch sex?' he grinned.

Her breath hitched in anticipation. 'You're making me nervous.'

'There's nothing to be scared of, you'll enjoy it. But we can stop now if you want.'

She shook her head. 'I want this, I want you.'

He bent his head to kiss her again and she stopped him.

'Wait, do you have a super-powered penis or something?'

He laughed, loudly, the vibrations travelling through her body. 'I promise, it's nothing like that.'

He kissed her, easing slowly inside her, and she wrapped her arms and legs around him. His kiss was divine and, for a while, everything was just perfect, as he moved slowly against her and she started to relax, enjoying the feel of his skin against hers, his touch, the little sensations of bliss as that feeling started to slowly build again inside her.

He pulled back to look at her, his eyes locking with hers, and suddenly a feeling of fire and ice slammed into her, wind roared across the lake and even the ground trembled slightly.

'Wolf.'

'It's OK, don't worry. It will pass.'

The air around them was suddenly filled with a bright golden light which made even Wolf jump a little. There was a golden cage of light like a forcefield surrounding them, but inside there were giant orbs of light floating around.

'Bloody hell,' Wolf muttered.

'It's beautiful,' Star whispered.

Wolf rolled so she was on top, and she sat up so she was astride him. 'What is this?'

'It's us, our powers combining,' Wolf said as he stared at the light in awe. 'Touch it.'

She tilted her head back and looked at the golden cage, a thousand lines interconnecting, knotted and twisting. The orbs were floating around inside, sometimes bouncing gently off the cage walls, sometimes bouncing off each other.

'Will it hurt?'

'No.'

She reached out a finger to touch the walls and felt a warm burst of happiness seep through her.

'Oh Wolf, this is lovely. Is this what witch sex is normally like?'

'Nothing about this is normal. Touch the orbs,' Wolf insisted.

She gently touched one of the orbs and an incredible feeling washed through her, something she couldn't quite define at first and then she suddenly recognised it for what it was. She felt loved. It was one of the most beautiful, exquisite experiences of her life.

She looked back at Wolf. 'I feel what you feel, for me. You need to feel this.'

He sat up, wrapping one arm round her waist to keep her from toppling off him. He reached out a hand and one of the orbs settled in his palm and the biggest smile spread across his face.

He cupped her face and kissed her hard, then slid his hands down to her hips, pulling her tighter against him. She started moving against him and the orbs drew in closer, surrounding them, dusting their shoulders, brushing against their hair. It was magnificent, there was no other word for it. But as that feeling of complete and utter love consumed her, his feelings for her, that was the thing that sent her roaring over the edge.

CHAPTER 19

S tar woke wrapped in Wolf's arms as they lay in his bed. It was still dark outside and he was trailing his fingers up and down her spine.

'We have to get up if we're going to do the sunrise swim in the sea.'

She snuggled down in his arms. 'Let's miss that one. I'm perfectly, blissfully happy right now. A freezing cold swim in the sea does not sound appealing.

'I know but what if I treat you to a full English breakfast afterwards? There's a little beach café right on the sands and they're always open early for all the surfers. The breakfast there is amazing and it helps that it's run by a witch.'

Her stomach gurgled at the thought of bacon, eggs and sausages for breakfast. 'I could be tempted by that.'

She looked up at him, stroking her fingers across his chest. 'I'm sorry last night didn't go according to plan.'

After lying on the blanket, kissing and cuddling for a while, Star had insisted they tried the cleansing ritual again. They'd spent a grand total of a minute washing each other under the stars before he'd ended up making love to her right there in the pool. Then he'd brought her back to his house and made love to her again in his bed. It definitely had not gone to plan.

He smiled. 'Sometimes the best things happen when you throw your plans out the window. I have zero regrets about last night.'

'We did manage to wash each other for a little while before... other things got in the way. Do you feel like the attraction between us has reduced a little?'

Wolf laughed. 'Do I feel less attracted to you after the best sex of my entire life? Last night was incredible even before you lit up the sky like floodlights at a football match. Even before our powers combined in the most magnificent, brilliant way possible, I was having the time of my life. And even now, I can feel that connection between us and it's burning brightly. So no, the attraction did not reduce at all. In fact I'd say it's probably a hundred times worse,' he kissed her. 'Or better.'

She smiled against his lips and sat up. 'What time is it anyway?' She grabbed her phone to see it was just past six o'clock. 'Urgh.' She noticed she had a text from Tig and opened it.

TIG:

> Have you seen the hot mayor
> naked yet?

Star laughed. 'My friend Tig wants to know if I've seen you naked yet. This lie is going to keep catching up with me.'

'Telling the truth will be even more complicated. But at least you can answer her question honestly. Take a photo of us together.'

Star lay down and Wolf wrapped an arm around her, she snuggled into his chest and then held the phone up. She took a photo of their heads and shoulders, she wasn't about to share any nudity with Tig, but it was very clear they had shared a night of passion, her hair was like a bush and Wolf looked sexily bedraggled too. She looked at the photo. They looked so in love with each other. She attached it to a text and sent it to Tig. Despite the early time, the replies were instant.

TIG:

> Oh my god.

> You look so happy.

> This is so exciting.

> I need all the details.

Star smiled. She couldn't really explain they had first made love by the side of an enchanted lake while trying to cleanse themselves of unwanted magic but she could certainly tell Tig how happy she was. She'd text her later.

'Right, come on,' Wolf said, getting out of bed and taking his beautiful naked body off towards the bathroom. He waved his hand as he left the bedroom and the duvet was rudely snatched off her.

She laughed and rolled onto her back. Life was never going to be the same again. And if this thing between her and Wolf didn't work out, her sex life would be over because there was never going to be another man who could make her feel the way that Wolf did.

The beach was deserted. The café had just opened behind them as they stared out at the horizon but the surfers had yet to make their way out of their beds, which was where Wolf thought he should be, with the woman he loved wrapped in his arms.

He wasn't entirely sure what was the point of continuing with these cleansing rituals now after the night before. It was probably counterproductive to wash each other in a moonlit lake to remove the magical bonds and then make love by the lake and in it. And after he'd felt Star's feelings when their magic connected, he'd been left with no doubt at all that she was feeling the same as he was. But he also knew it was crazy to feel this way so quickly and, after being raised in a village that had its own weather, separate to that of the rest of the world, he realised that with magic, anything was possible. So removing these bonds was the only sure-fire way to confirm their feelings were real, for him and for her.

The icy wind roared round them and the waves were crashing on the beach. Tiny flakes of snow were starting to fall but were whipped away in the wind before they could touch the ground. It was bleak and the smell of fresh hot coffee was already wafting out invitingly from the café. The horizon had a sliver of gold; they were probably minutes away from the sun making its appearance.

'You know, it would probably be just as effective if we dipped our feet in the sea at sunrise. I don't think we need to go for a full-body immersion,' Wolf said.

Star laughed, her dark hair flying in the wind behind her like ribbons.

'You know Ashley wanted to encourage nudity in every cleansing ritual. It's more effective apparently.'

To his utmost surprise, she stripped off all her clothes and ran naked into the waves just as the sun peeped above the horizon and he'd never seen anything as spectacular in his life.

He could hardly chicken out now. He stripped down too, waded out into the shallows and then as a big wave rode towards him he dived into it. The cold penetrating his skin was a huge shock. He surfaced and found Star bobbing about in the waves, her arms above her head in some kind of sun salutation yoga pose. The sun painted her wet skin with a layer of gold. She was enchanting. He swam over to her and gathered her in his arms, kissing her hard, and she laughed against his lips as she wrapped her arms around him.

A big wave crashed over them, knocking them off their feet, but he held onto her tightly as they landed back on the beach.

He pushed her hair out of her eyes. 'Are you OK?'

She looked up at him with a smile. 'Of course I am, I'm with you.'

Another wave crashed on their legs.

'I think that's enough,' Wolf said.

'I agree and you owe me breakfast,' Star said.

Star sat looking out of the window of the café as the sun rose spectacularly over the waves. The breakfast was delicious, probably the best cooked breakfast she'd ever had.

'Did you say the owner of the café is a witch?' Star said, dipping her bacon in her egg.

'Yes she is. You'll meet her shortly, I'm sure. She's an old friend.'

'Did she make breakfast with magic, it's amazing?'

Wolf laughed as he wiped his toast around the beans. 'I wouldn't be surprised.'

'And what a great location for a café. That view is incredible. I do wonder whether Ashley has just set up a load of romantic date moments for us to take part in so we fall in love with each other rather than out of love.'

'That thought had crossed my mind too, but these cleansing rituals are all stuff I've heard of before, so there's some credibility to them. Although I've never heard them being used to remove the bonds of love.'

'I don't think anything can remove the bonds of love. This might remove the betrothal magic but our feelings for each other are completely different to that. I feel that in every bone of my body.'

Wolf took her hand. 'I think that too. I guess we'll find out tomorrow at midnight.'

'How's my favourite man?' said a female voice from behind Star and she looked up to see a woman in her sixties bearing down on Wolf for a hug. He stood up and hugged her. It was quite a surprise; Star had never seen Wolf be affectionate with anyone, apart from her and Lynx.

'I'm doing good Beth, how are you?'

'Business is good, and I'm engaged to that fine young thing,' she nodded in the direction of a man who looked so beefy he could have been a bouncer or a bodyguard. He was waiting on tables and was probably younger than Star.

'Ah I'm happy for you, you deserve someone nice in your life.'

'And I see you're dating too,' Beth said, her eyes lighting up like a Christmas tree.

Star wondered what Wolf's reaction would be to someone knowing they were together. She had the feeling he didn't want anyone in the village to know.

'We are,' Wolf said, smiling at Star. 'It's very early days but I have a good feeling about us. Beth, this is Star Brightheart, Star this is Beth Winters.'

'Hello, lovely to meet you,' Star said.

'And you. I've never known Wolf bring a woman here before.'

'Do you come here often?' Star asked Wolf.

'Not as often as he should,' Beth said.

'It's one of my favourite places,' Wolf said. 'I used to surf down here when I was younger, now I just come here for some peace and solitude. But I don't get here as often as I'd like.'

'Well, maybe this might help you get down here more often,' Beth said. 'I'm selling my house.'

Wolf sat up straight. 'The Pearl?'

Star watched him curiously.

Beth nodded. 'I could never live there after Jim died. Too many memories of him growing up there. But I couldn't let it go either. I'd rent it out, or family members would stay there, and it was always open to witches if they needed it. I'd put food in there and change the sheets if anyone stayed over, kept it clean, but it wasn't my home anymore. But since I've moved in with Julian and we're getting married, it finally feels like I can let it go. You always said you wanted to live there.'

'That was a very long time ago.'

'Do those hopes and dreams really change?'

'The dreams don't but responsibilities do.'

Beth rolled her eyes. 'If you want to have a look, the house is open to witches, it always is.' She turned to Star. 'Maybe you can encourage him to take more time for himself. It's good to see him smiling. I almost never see that anymore.'

Star smiled. 'I will try. This breakfast is wonderful and this place is lovely, what a great view.'

'Thank you. It's built in honour of my son James. That's why it's called Jim's Place. He always wanted to have his own café one day. He had this little shack at the back of the beach and he'd sell burgers and sausages, but the café was always his dream. He died out there in the surf.'

'Oh my god, I'm so sorry,' Star said. 'I didn't realise.' Her heart broke for Beth; she could think of nothing worse than losing a son or daughter.

'It was a long time ago. Twenty-eight years actually. He was only seventeen. The power of nature is not something any of us can fight against, not even the most powerful witch. But I decided something good must come out of it. So I opened the café right here, living out his dream but also so I can keep an eye on all the other surfers.'

'There hasn't been a fatality or serious injury on this beach in twenty-eight years,' Wolf explained.

Star stared at him and back at Beth in confusion. 'You... you protect them?'

'Yes, I don't want another mother or father or anyone else to lose a loved one. I can't protect every surfer in every part of the world, but this was one of the most dangerous beaches in the UK and now it's not.'

'But... how?'

Beth looked at her in confusion.

'Star is actually a wildling, she came to my village a few days ago, completely unaware she was a witch. I've been teaching her to use her magic but there's still a lot of things she doesn't understand about our world,' Wolf said.

Beth's eyes widened in shock. 'How did you get to your age and not know?'

'I was adopted by non-witches. Although they found out I was a witch very early on, they were scared of magic and tried to dismiss anything weird that happened as just my imagination. You get told enough times that something isn't real, you start to believe it.'

'What a confusing and frustrating upbringing for you.'

'Yeah. So this is all so new to me. How do you protect all the surfers?'

'It's quite complicated really and quite simple at the same time. It's a good luck and safety charm I devised, which is simple enough but I have to make sure it gets to all the surfers and swimmers. I created this ward, a type of energy field at the gate up there, and I charge it every morning when I arrive to open the café. Everyone who walks through the gate is protected with a luck and safety charm while they're in the water. Some witches don't like it, they think it's interfering with fate. They take the attitude that if it's your time then it's your time and that I shouldn't get in the way of that. But there are so many witches in the world that use their magic for their own gains, why can't I use mine for something good?'

Star nodded. 'I think it's wonderful. So we were blessed with luck and safety when we came onto the beach this morning?'

'Yes you were, which probably explains why you didn't get hurt when you were out there doing some weird naked early morning swim.'

'Cleansing ritual,' Wolf said.

'Ah, I did wonder. What magic are you trying to cleanse yourself of?'

'Now that is complicated.' He looked at Star, his eyes locking with hers. 'But it's safe to say it didn't work.'

Star smiled. 'So when we leave here, do we leave the good luck behind?'

'Hard to say really, but I would like to think you'd take a little bit of luck with you.'

'That's good, I think I need some of that today.'

The door opened and three young surfers came in.

'I better go,' Beth said, then she looked at Wolf meaningfully. 'I'll see you again soon.'

'I promise,' Wolf said.

Beth hurried off to greet the surfers.

Star stared at her breakfast as thoughts swirled round her head.

'You OK?' Wolf said.

'Yeah, I was just thinking, I have all this power and I want to do something good with it too. She has dedicated her life to saving lives on this beach and I want to do something to help people as well.'

Wolf smiled. 'I think that's a lovely idea but you're trying to run before you can walk. There's so much you need to understand about magic before you can do something like that. And you have helped people, thousands of people have benefitted from your cakes. There's no reason why you can't continue doing that now.'

'Apart from the fact that everyone thinks I deliberately poisoned Cleo Walsh and no one will buy my cakes ever again.'

'Start afresh then. Sell the cakes under a new name or sell magic chocolate bars instead.'

Star thought about that. She'd got so much pleasure from making cakes, it would be a shame to give that up. 'That could work, but it doesn't feel in the same league as Beth.'

'Don't underestimate the power of your cakes. You've helped people get the job of their dreams, you've helped people move on after their husbands or wives have cheated on them. You've given someone the courage to fight a fear. You've healed a broken heart. As someone who had their heart broken once, I would have given anything to take that pain away. Focus on what you can do right now. Saving lives can come later.'

She frowned. 'Who broke your heart?'

He smiled sadly. 'It was a long time ago.'

She pondered his evasiveness for a moment before letting it go. 'Do you want to tell me about The Pearl?'

'It's the house there on the cliff.' Wolf gestured to the house behind him and Star could see a white house with large windows overlooking the beach. 'It has steps leading down into a tiny secluded cove and when the tide comes in, that cove is only accessible from the house. The cove also has some really cool rock pools. Lynx and I would come down here a lot when we lived outside of Midnight. The village we lived in was filled with those bullies and after Mum had her stroke, she didn't want us in the house watching her struggle with basic tasks so we came here often. It was a twenty-minute bike ride and then all this freedom.'

He took a drink of his tea. 'We were playing in that cove one day and we didn't see the tide come in. When we realised, the only way to safety was to climb up the steps to The Pearl. A storm came in and the house was open so we went in. We knew straightaway that it was a witch's house and that we were safe there, it had that feeling. There are many witches' retreat houses around the country that will let in a witch in times of need and we figured it was one of those. It was also very obvious that no one was living there. So we started coming back there regularly. It was like our own little sanctuary. We started taking board games and playing them in the lounge, and food started appearing in the fridge for us to eat, which we stupidly thought was the house providing food for us. We had no idea that Beth knew we were there every day and that she was providing the food. I didn't even meet her until I was much older and that's when she told me. She knew we needed this little haven and so she let us keep coming there. The door was always open, food always waiting for us, sometimes some new puzzles and games were waiting for us too. I have very fond memories of that place.'

'Well let's go and have a look, even if it's just for old times' sake.'

Wolf turned to look at the house. 'OK.'

They waved their goodbyes to Beth and crossed the short distance across the cliff to the house. The door was open as Beth had said it would be and they stepped inside.

'Is she not worried about burglars?' Star said.

'It's only open for witches,' Wolf said as if that explained the complete lack of security. Maybe it did.

As Star moved into the house, she could feel happiness here; every corner, every inch was filled with joy and love and laughter.

'This is a happy home.'

'Really? I've always thought it was a bit sad and lonely,' Wolf said.

'Can you not feel the happiness here? There are children here. I can feel their laughter and mischief.'

'You mean ghosts?'

'No, more like echoes. Maybe it's you and Lynx I can feel. Maybe it's just because it's a witch's home, I can feel its history in the same way I could when I put on the amulet. I have never walked into a house before and just felt so much happiness and contentment.'

She looked around and everywhere was painted white or cream. The sofas were bright blue, the only spots of colour in the place, but as she stepped further into the lounge the view of the beach and the sea stretching out to the horizon was the most impressive thing in the room.

'This is beautiful,' Star breathed softly. 'I can see why witches would come here for a place of safe haven. If I was ever in trouble, knowing this place was here to escape to would be a comfort.'

'If you're ever in trouble, you can come to me. I would look after you.'

She smiled.

Suddenly she heard a child's laughter and she turned to see a little girl of maybe three or four with long bright red hair, sea-green eyes and dinosaur dungarees running through the room, laughing uncontrollably as she clutched her toy T-Rex. She ran into another room and Star left Wolf staring out of the window at his memories and followed the little girl into the kitchen. She stopped dead as the little girl was suddenly picked up and thrown over the shoulder of a man who looked exactly like Wolf, except Wolf was still standing in the lounge looking out of the window, she could see him. She turned back to the kitchen and saw the other Wolf stomping round the kitchen like a monster or probably a dinosaur as the girl squealed and giggled in delight as she hung upside down over Wolf's shoulder. He was growling and roaring and looked happier than she'd ever seen him. Movement caught her eye and she looked over at the back of a woman with long red hair, making a sandwich. The woman turned slightly and although Star couldn't see her face she could see the woman was heavily pregnant. She looked back at Wolf standing in the lounge and when she returned her gaze to the kitchen again, it was empty, the sound of laughter gone.

She stepped back in shock and slammed into Wolf. She whirled round to face him.

'Are you OK? You've gone as white as a sheet.'

'I'm fine, are you ready to go?'

'Oh sure, if you want.'

Her mind was whirling as they walked back to his car. They got in and Wolf turned the heating on.

'Are you OK?'

'Your premonitions, when you see them, how do you see them?'

'What do you mean?'

'Are they in your head or only in dreams or what?'

'Oh, sometimes in dreams. Sometimes I can be walking down the road and it's acted out right in front of me and I have no idea it's not real until it fades away. My gran doesn't see premonitions as such, it's more a case of just knowing. Although I asked her yesterday how this whole thing with Jessica would play out and she didn't know, which has got to be a first. Did you... did you see something in The Pearl?'

She nodded numbly. 'I think you need to buy that house.'

'I can't buy a beach house. I have responsibilities to the people of the village, I can't just drop everything and swan off to the beach every weekend. People need me.'

'Your responsibilities shouldn't be twenty-four seven. Your role as mayor shouldn't be all-or-nothing. You have your own life to lead and there's no reason why you can't do both. There's a whole world out here for you to enjoy. Have you even been on holiday since you became mayor?'

'No, being mayor is too important.'

'You can't let life pass you by, you need to grab hold of it, embrace it, the good, the bad and the ugly. Wring every little moment of joy out of it.' She couldn't tell him what she had seen because she couldn't get her head around it but this house was an important part of Wolf's future, if he was willing to accept it. 'Trust me on this, you're going to be very happy in this house.'

'Did you see us?'

'I saw you and you were so happy.' Her voice choked because she knew the little red headed girl had been Wolf's daughter. And it was reasonable to assume that the red-headed woman was the girl's mum, pregnant with Wolf's second child. Tears pricked her eyes. She had been so confident that what she shared with Wolf was real but what if it wasn't? What if she had just glimpsed a future she wasn't part of? Wolf hadn't looked any older than he did now in the premonition. So if he had a three- or four-year-old daughter, he would need to conceive her soon. What if releasing the betrothal bonds meant he was finally free to pursue a relationship with someone else? Maybe even the woman who broke his heart.

She tried to be rational about this. The woman could have been a friend, a relative, a neighbour. She might not have anything to do with Wolf, she just happened to be in *his* home, making a sandwich in *his* kitchen. She swallowed, was she just clutching at straws? Or could the little girl have really been Star's? Her heart leapt at that thought. Both she and Wolf had dark hair, and she knew that the red-headed gene was one that could miss a generation or two, but she wasn't sure how common that was. Was it possible she'd just glimpsed her future as well as Wolf's? Or was that as unlikely as hoping the red-headed woman had simply been a neighbour?

She pushed the image of the little girl away for now. 'We should get back. I have a whole village to deliver some forgiveness cakes to and maybe, with a bit of Beth's good luck, people might be more willing to take them.'

'You have nothing to ask for forgiveness for,' Wolf said, scowling.

'I know that, but most of the villagers probably don't. Besides, I need to do something to get them on my side. Once they find out I'm a weather witch it'll be pitchforks at dawn.'

'Do you mean pistols?'

'Let's hope it won't come to that.'

CHAPTER 20

Star had already delivered her yule logs to a few people in her road, who were most appreciative of the gesture, but now she had to deliver one to Maggie and Tom. While she was quite sure Maggie wouldn't hold what happened at the garland festival against her she wasn't sure the same could be said for Tom.

Unfortunately it was Tom who answered the door. Her heart sank.

'Oh it's you,' Tom said, gruffly.

'Hi, umm... Is Maggie in?'

Star knew that was the cowardly response. She would have to talk to him at some point, she certainly couldn't avoid him forever.

'No, she isn't.' He paused. 'But maybe you best come in. There are some things I need to say.'

'Oh, I need to—'

'It won't take a moment,' Tom said.

She sighed and stepped inside.

He closed the door and then she followed him down to the lounge. He gestured for her to take a seat and sat down opposite her.

'I wanted to say I'm sorry for how I reacted the other day,' Tom said.

'Oh.' Star hadn't been expecting that.

'I love my son. He was my world and nothing can ever prepare you for losing your only child and it's not something I'll ever get over either. I have a lot of anger about how the villagers pushed him out, which I think ultimately was responsible for his death. To meet the daughter of the woman who caused all that, at least in my eyes, was a bit of a shock.'

He picked up a glass paperweight and turned it round in his hands a few times, watching it as the different colours caught the light.

'He had faults, of course he did. I knew he was sleeping with lots of women behind his wife's back. I didn't like it but sometimes you learn when to keep your mouth shut and mind your own business. How he conducted himself was nothing to do with me. But then when the rumours started circling about how he'd got your mum pregnant I couldn't believe it, I didn't want to believe it. Rose was a child and that was a low bar even for me. I asked him about it but he denied all knowledge of it and I believed him. For the past thirty years I've always blamed your mum for making up vicious lies. I believed that his life unravelled because of the lies and that was the thing that caused his death.'

'And now?' Star said.

He glanced over to a framed photo on the other side of the room and she followed his gaze to a picture of a young man with dark hair. Presumably her dad. She couldn't see him clearly from where she was sitting and she wasn't sure if she wanted to. Star swallowed down the anger she had for her dad and the way he had taken advantage of her mum. It wasn't her place to convince Tom of the truth and he probably didn't want to hear it anyway. But she was hopeful that while she and Tom would probably never be close, maybe one day he wouldn't blame her for his son's death.

'You look like him. There is no denying you're his daughter,' Tom said.

Star looked at Tom. She hadn't been expecting that.

'And now I have to reconcile in my head that not only did my son lie to me, that I believed those lies for the last thirty years, and that I blamed and hated your mum for his death when she was the innocent one in all of this. But I also have to reconcile that my son had no moral code and treated your mum appallingly. I suppose I have to look at my own parenting if my son thought his behaviour was acceptable and it's going to take some time to get my head around all of that.'

'I don't think you can blame yourself for anything your son did. He was an adult and he made those decisions himself.'

'Still, I'm certainly not innocent in all of this. I spent years hating your mum and I regret that now.' He let out a heavy breath. 'I'm not a touchy-feely man. I'm never going to be the kind of grandad that shares his Werther's toffees and sits by the fireplace telling his grandchildren stories but I'd like to get to know you.'

Star gave a small smile. 'I'd like that too.'

He nodded. 'Do you play chess?'

'I can learn.'

'Well maybe sometime you'd like to come round and we can have a match. Maybe start catching up on the last thirty years?'

'I'd really like that.'

He nodded again and stood up.

She took two of the yule logs out of the tin and placed them on the table. 'I'm giving these to all the villagers to apologise for what happened with the garland.'

'I think most of the village knows it was Jessica who did that, Maggie will make sure of that.'

'Well, enjoy the cakes anyway.'

She went to the door and he opened it for her. 'I'm glad you're here, Star.'

'I am too.'

She gave him a wave and walked up the road.

Star knocked on a bright pink front door and smiled when she realised it was Zofia's house.

'Hello my dear, come in, come in. I'm still perfecting this solstice cocktail for tomorrow. You can try some. How are things, how are you settling in? How is everything with you and Wolf?'

Star smiled at all the questions.

'I'm loving being here, I've made some lovely friends, and I love learning about my magic. Wolf is a very patient teacher.'

'I'm sure he is, but I wasn't asking about his teaching skills, as you well know.'

Star grinned. 'And I'm not going to kiss and tell.'

'Ah, so there is a kiss to talk about?'

'Wolf is the most incredible man I've ever met but that's all you will get from me.'

Zofia tutted and handed Star a glass of bubbling blue liquid.

'What is it?'

'Drink it and find out.'

'Is it a truth potion?'

Zofia laughed. 'It's not that.'

Star took a cautious sip. 'Oh it tastes good.'

'What does it taste of?'

Star took another drink. 'Success, happiness, confidence. And gin.'

'You have very discerning tastebuds. Now I hear that your birth mum left a blood message for you. That must have been weird for you.'

'It was. I've always wondered what she looked like and whether I took after her. Although I was just speaking to Tom and apparently I look a lot like my dad, which is slightly disappointing.'

'Your dad was an ass. But looking like him doesn't mean you're like him. You weren't even raised by him. The person you are now has been shaped by your adopted parents and your life experiences, not genetics. You have your own strengths and weaknesses. You're a good person, I see that.'

Star sighed. 'He took advantage of my mum, she was only sixteen and he charmed her, took her virginity in a cupboard and then betrayed her when she found herself pregnant. She must have been so scared finding herself alone and pregnant at that age. In the message she said she was living in a van with a nice man called Dex and she gave me up because that wasn't the life she wanted for me. I'm not sure how I feel about that. But I can't help wondering where she is now and if she's OK.'

Zofia tapped her lips for a moment and Star wondered if there were some wise words coming her way.

'There is a way we can find out,' Zofia said.

'There is? A way I can talk to her?'

Zofia shook her head. 'For want of a better word, it's a way you can spy on her, for a very short time. You can see what she is doing right now. It's a tiny window, probably ten seconds at most, which obviously doesn't tell you a great deal of information about her life, but it might help a little to see where she is and what she's doing.'

'How do we do it?'

'You need to think carefully if you want to do it. What would you like to see in an ideal world?'

'I'd like to see her happy.'

'Really? That might hurt you to see that she dumped you and went on to have a happy life. I wouldn't judge you if there was a tiny part of you that wanted to see that she was miserable and regretted abandoning you every single day.'

Star shook her head. 'While there's a part of me that will never understand what she did when she gave me up, she wanted me to have a good life, a better life. Her intentions were good even if it's something I don't think I could ever do. I want a good life for her too. She had such a shitty start in life with her mum dying, her dad treating her terribly, my dad taking advantage of her, finding herself pregnant and alone; I hope life has been kinder since. While ten seconds isn't really enough to determine that, it will give me something.'

'If you're sure?'

Star nodded.

Zofia waved her hand and a small cauldron floated out of one of the cupboards. A flash of green lit a fire underneath it. She waved her hand again and a large flask floated from the cupboard and poured a silvery liquid into the cauldron.

Star took a step back as a little gold knife flew into Zofia's hand.

'This is a blood connection. I need a drop of your blood to forge that connection between you and your mum.'

'You're going to stab me?'

'That's a little overdramatic. It's a pinprick, I only need one drop.'

Star held out her hand and Zofia examined it and obviously found something she liked the look of. 'You ready?'

Star looked at the knife and closed her eyes. It looked very sharp. She nodded her head.

It was only a second of pain and, just as Zofia had said, it was more like a pinprick than a slice from a knife. When she opened her eyes, she watched Zofia squeeze one tiny drop of blood into the cauldron. But anyone would have thought that Zofia had cut off an arm as the silvery water immediately turned as red as if gallons of blood had poured in there. The water turned gold and then silver and, as Zofia chanted some words softly under her breath, the water appeared to go solid as if made from a mirror.

'Think about your mum and look inside.'

Star took a deep breath and peered inside the cauldron. There was her mum, older and wiser, probably; her hair was a lot shorter. She was sitting on a beach near an open fire with a group of people, one of them a man who had his arm around her mum's shoulders. Rose was laughing loudly at something someone else was saying and Star couldn't help smiling. She looked happy and, while it was just a tiny snapshot into her life, Star felt some relief from that.

The mirror suddenly wobbled and the image dissolved into the liquid again. Her mum was gone.

Star sat back.

'Well?'

'She was happy.'

'And that's good?'

Star nodded. 'It is. She deserves to be happy.' She swallowed a lump of emotion that seemed to stick in her throat from seeing her mum. 'I should go, I have hundreds of cakes to deliver. Thank you for this.'

'Anytime. And I mean that – if it helps, you can come back and do it again.'

'Thank you.'

Star took out one of her chocolate yule logs, gave Zofia a wave and left feeling suddenly a lot lighter.

So far delivering the cakes had gone quite well. Not only had it been lovely to introduce herself to all the villagers but, to Star's surprise, most of them believed that Jessica had been guilty of the fire not her. Clearly the rumours had spread quickly. But, worryingly, a few people had asked if Star was a weather witch and Star didn't know how to respond to that. She had feigned innocence at first, claiming she didn't even know what that was; being a wildling had some advantages. When others had asked, she'd simply said that she didn't know, which was the truth.

She knocked on one door and, after a few moments, a lady in her eighties came to answer it. Her eyes lit up when she saw Star.

'Lizzie!' the woman yelled. 'The new girl is here. Lizzie!'

Another octogenarian came up from the lounge. 'Esther, why are you screaming so loudly? What could possibly be so exciting that you need to scream that loudly?' Lizzie said, leaning heavily on her walking stick. She spotted Star and her face lit up too. 'Oh my.'

'See, that's what I was screaming about,' Esther said.

'Come in, come in,' Lizzie said, and then turned to her friend. 'Why did you leave her on the doorstep?'

'Well I didn't know if you wanted her in the house, seeing as she might strike you down with lightning,' Esther said.

Star bit her lip nervously as she was ushered inside.

'Don't be so ridiculous,' Lizzie said, leading the way back to the lounge.

'If you wanted to strike her with lightning, I wouldn't mind,' Esther whispered as Star walked past her.

The lounge was covered in scuba diving memorabilia. Photos of Esther and Lizzie in the sea or on a boat wearing wetsuits, air tanks and face masks sat alongside photos of some impressive looking shipwrecks. There was some artefacts around the room which had obviously been found on wrecks too.

'Sit down will you, you're making the place look untidy,' Lizzie said, directing Star to a black leather sofa with the end of her walking stick.

Star sat down. 'I won't keep you long. I just wanted to introduce myself and give you one of these chocolate yule logs.' She opened the tin to show her beautifully decorated yule logs. 'I know the yule logs are a big part of the winter solstice celebrations. I've added cinnamon for good luck, and lavender for peace and happiness. I've also added a tiny bit of rosemary to banish negativity. I've decorated it with holly, a tree that stays green in the darkest of winter, and orange slices to celebrate the sun returning,' she rattled off her little prepared speech.

She had done a lot of research into the yule log and hoped it would pay off. 'I'm also hoping that in this season of joy and merriment, you might find it in you to forgive what happened with the garland.'

'This is very kind,' Esther said. 'But there isn't anything to forgive. Jessica started that fire, we all know that.'

'Well that's what I've been told, but there's no proof of that. But Wolf said my orb of light was just like everyone else's so I'm not sure how it could have possibly caused a fire,' Star said.

'She did it, mark my words,' Lizzie said. 'She's been sniffing round trying to find information about your mum. She knows all about the affair between your mum and the mayor and she was going on about the apple not falling far from the tree. But I told her, just because your mum was a weather witch didn't mean you were too.'

Star's heart sank. That would be just the ammunition that Jessica needed.

'I have to say, I probably shouldn't have said that, she looked like she'd won the lottery with that news. But I thought everyone knew that your mum was a weather witch – a few people have been talking about it over the last few days.'

'It's OK, people will find out soon enough, with or without Jessica's help.'

'Are you one?' Esther said, excitedly.

'I don't know. I can only do the bare basics with my magic right now. I have no idea if I have the abilities to control the weather and how to do it if I did.'

'A weather witch who has no control of her powers is a very dangerous thing,' Lizzie said.

'We don't know that she is one,' Esther said.

'We don't know that she isn't.'

'I should go,' Star said, taking out the yule log and placing it on a napkin on their table. 'I hope you enjoy the yule log.'

She got up and left, leaving Esther and Lizzie squabbling over whether she was a weather witch or not.

The next house was Charles's. She didn't think she'd get a good reception there but she squared her shoulders and knocked on the door.

Charles answered it after a few moments, his little dog Frankie barking incessantly at his heels.

'Yes?' Charles snapped, scooping Frankie up.

'I just came by to give you a Christmas yule log.' She was about to launch into her spiel but figured Charles was a man of few words, so she cut to the chase. 'In the hope you might forgive me for what happened to the garland.'

'Well you didn't set fire to it, did you, silly girl. I was standing next to Jessica when she did it and I felt it. I'm a fire witch too and you can feel when someone uses

fire. I told her I knew she had done it and she threatened to kill Frankie if I told anyone.'

'Oh Charles, that's horrible.'

'Oh, I've got my own back, nasty little bitch. No one
threatens Frankie and gets away with it. So I cursed
her.'

'You... You did what?'

'Oh, this one's a good one. She's so vain, obsessed
with her looks, that one is. She has this mole on her
neck. It's tiny, about the size of a peppercorn. She hates
it. When she was younger she tried to blast it off with
magic, she left a tiny scar on her neck because of that.
Anyway, every time she does something nasty, that
thing will grow a tiny amount. If she's mean again it
will grow a tiny bit more. It will only shrink if she starts
being nice.'

Star stared at Charles in shock; she didn't know
whether to love or hate this idea. Poor Jessica could end
up with a mole the size of a watermelon on the side of
her neck if her reputation was true.

'I'm not sure that's a good idea,' Star said.

'I didn't ask for your permission, did I?' Charles
snapped, snatching up the yule log and slamming the
door in her face.

Star sighed but as Wolf's house was right next door
she figured she'd go and say hello, keep him abreast of
the latest situation.

She knocked on his door and he answered it while on the phone.

'I'll call you back,' he said into the phone and hung up on whoever was on the other end before they got a chance to protest. 'You OK?'

'Yes, just...' she gestured to his neighbours, wondering where to start.

He took her tin of cakes off her and placed it on the hall table, then opened his arms for her. She immediately stepped up and hugged him and he wrapped his arms around her, holding her tight.

Oh, she needed this so much. Every doubt and worry melted away as he held her in his arms.

After a while she pulled back slightly and looked up at him and he stroked her hair from her face.

'What's happened?'

She told him about her conversation with Tom and seeing her birth mum, albeit briefly, and Wolf hugged her again.

'And there's good news and bad news from my other neighbours. Bad news is that quite a few people know I might be a weather witch and they are understandably nervous.'

'I know, a few people have mentioned it to me. Apparently Jessica is taking great pleasure in telling everyone so I'll take any good news you can throw at me right now.'

'We may have found a weird ally in Charles.'

'What?'

'He's cursed her.'

'He did what?'

'Every time she's nasty, the mole on her neck grows.'

Wolf's face showed a battle between disapproval and amusement, and amusement won out.

'Well the next few days are going to be interesting.'

'That's what I thought. Right, I have to go and finish my deliveries, thank you for this.'

'Anytime.' He gave her the sweetest kiss on the lips.

'I'll see you at the tree ceremony shortly.'

'Yes, I wanted to talk to you about that. Jessica is going to try something, the bigger the audience the better. So I'm going to tell everyone in the village that I've blocked your powers. That way, if she tries to set fire to the tree or do something else with her powers and blames you, everyone will know it's not you.'

'Can you do that?'

'Yes but I'm not actually going to do it. I can't think of anything worse than losing my powers. They are a part of you and I would never take them away from you. No one will know your powers aren't blocked but at least it might deter Jessica from trying anything.'

'OK, sure. Got to try anything right? OK, see you soon.'

She gave him another brief kiss, grabbed her yule logs and headed off. She had one more street to deliver to, so she walked out of Wolf's road and into the last one. She knocked on the door of the first cottage and her heart hit her shoes when Jessica answered.

'What the hell do you want?' Jessica said.

Star made her decision that while Jessica was absolutely not going to get one of her delicious yule logs, perhaps now would be a good time to chat to her.

'I came to talk. You obviously have an issue with me. I came to see if we can work it out.'

'My problem with you is you've obviously done something to Wolf to make him besotted with you. You come in here, spot the richest, most powerful man in the village and you swoop in. I don't know what it is but when I figure it out I'm going to expose you for the gold-digging whore you really are.'

'Whoa Jessica, say what you really mean. I understand your concern for Wolf when he's acting so out of the ordinary but to say the motive is money and power is a bit of a stretch. We're betrothed, I've been sucked into this relationship as much as Wolf has,' Star said, knowing Jessica wouldn't believe for one second that they both had fallen head over heels in love with each other. 'We have feelings for each other and we don't know if it's because of the betrothal bonds that connect us. We've asked Ashley to remove the bonds and then we'll see what remains. I wouldn't do that if I was just after his money.'

This seemed to throw Jessica; she clearly hadn't

known they'd asked Ashley to do that. While she floundered around for some clever retort Star took the time to find the mole that Charles had referred to. She spotted it on the side of Jessica's neck. Charles had said it was the size of a peppercorn but it was a bit bigger than that now, maybe the size of a small pea. Perhaps it was the gold-digging whore comment that had made it grow bigger or maybe she'd done something else.

'The apple clearly doesn't fall far from the tree though, does it,' Jessica said, clearly having recovered herself. 'Your mum was a slut who slept with the mayor and now you're doing the same.'

Star took some grim satisfaction from seeing the mole grow fractionally from that comment.

'I also know your mum was the weather witch that cursed this village. I think the villagers will be very interested to know that little fact. People have been pissed off with this curse for years. Do you really think they're going to welcome you with open arms?'

'I don't think we can judge me on my mum's actions. Your dad was stealing money from the village for years and no one is accusing you of being a thief. Wolf still let you back in the village because it was your dad that did the crime, not you.'

'How dare you?' Jessica said and not for the first time Star wondered if Jessica was just a little bit unhinged. Anyone else who'd been reminded of their dad stealing thousands of pounds would have been embarrassed or contrite, but Jessica was outraged. 'That money was his right. He worked his arse off for this village for sixteen years and they never paid him enough. And then they kicked him out. What the hell kind of thanks is that? When I'm mayor, I will be welcoming him back to the village with a full parade in his honour.'

Star had to swallow down the bark of laughter that bubbled in her throat. Jessica was insane. If she pulled on an oversized rabbit head and danced down the street naked, she wouldn't be surprised right now. And there was clearly no reasoning with her either.

'OK,' Star said, slowly. 'I'm going to go.'

'I'm going to ruin you. By the time the mundanes celebrate Christmas, you'll be out of here and I'll make sure you'll never be welcome back.'

Star gave her a polite smile and walked on to the next house. Well that was enlightening, she thought, that and a little bit scary.

CHAPTER 21

A big tree had magically been placed in the middle of the village green but right now it was devoid of any decorations. Star had been looking forward to this celebration the most out of all the winter solstice preparations. Decorating a tree for Christmas had always been one of her favourite things to do at this time of year so she was glad she would still get to do it for the winter solstice. Around the outside of the green were lots of stalls and stands, some of them serving various foods and drinks, others set up for making decorations for the tree.

Wolf was standing next to the tree, greeting people as they came onto the green, and as he finished chatting to one couple, his eyes suddenly found hers as if he knew exactly where she was.

She smiled at him and the look he gave her was pure warmth.

'I don't think I've ever seen him this happy before,' Lynx said as he joined her on the outskirts of the green. 'Whatever you're doing, keep doing it.'

'He makes me happy too,' Star said.

'Oh please,' Jessica muttered as she barged past them.

Lynx watched her go. 'What did you do to rattle her cage?'

'Well I thought it was because she was in love with Wolf and I stole him from her, at least in her eyes. But now I think it's been a big ploy to become mayor herself. If she marries Wolf she would have a lot more authority and then if something were to happen to Wolf she would be the natural replacement as she had already been the mayor's wife and she's a descendant of one of the founders. I think she's playing some long game here. She told me that the first thing she'd do when she was mayor was invite her dad back into the village.'

'The one that stole tens of thousands of pounds from the villagers? I can't see that being a welcome idea. And what do you mean, if something were to happen to Wolf? Did she threaten him?'

'No. I'm speculating about her motives. She didn't say anything about harming Wolf, maybe being the wife of the mayor would be enough to give her that authority. But she definitely has ulterior motives for wanting Wolf to marry her and I don't think it's to do with love. I've clearly ruined her plans.'

'I'd watch your back if I were you,' Lynx said.

'I know. I tried to talk to her calmly earlier, it did not go well.'

Just then Wolf started addressing the crowd.

'People of Midnight, thank you for coming to our tree decorating ceremony. It's the part of the winter solstice celebrations I look forward to the most,' he said.

Star smiled.

'I know you're all eager to get started but I just wanted to say a few words before you do. As a precaution, and with Star's full blessing, I have blocked her powers just for the ceremony. That way we can relax knowing there won't be any little accidents with our tree.'

There was a bit of laughter around the village green.

'Like you, I have heard the rumours it wasn't Star that started the fire on the garland,' Wolf went on and several people looked over at Jessica, who looked completely unabashed. 'Several fire witches have told me they felt the fire magic come from the opposite side of the green to where Star was, and some of you have even told me who you think it was that started the fire. Now I have spoken to this person and she has denied it was her and without any concrete proof I have to believe her. I also can't believe that anyone would be so nasty and cruel as to try to frame Star for something she didn't do. That is not the ethos of the village – we welcome everyone, regardless of their backgrounds. And although we've never had a wildling before, I expect that all of you will welcome her and treat her with fairness and kindness. But at least we know today, that if there are any other fires, they haven't come from Star.'

There were murmurs of discontent. People either weren't happy that Jessica had got away with it or they weren't entirely happy with the presence of a wildling, one who was possibly even a weather witch, the most dangerous and powerful of all the witches.

'Come on, Jessica did it, we all know that,' Charles suddenly shouted.

'If there was even an ounce of proof, I'd be out of here,' Jessica called back. 'This is nothing more than a vicious rumour put about by someone who wants to save her own neck.'

There were more murmurings.

'Lack of proof doesn't mean lack of guilt,' Charles shouted back. 'Anyone watching the garland ceremony with half a brain would have seen that the orb Star placed on the garland was light not fire. I was standing next to you at the time and I know it was you who produced that fire magic.'

'Well it's your word against mine, old man. Who are

they going to believe, a confused, doddering old fool or me, a well-respected descendant of one of the village founders?'

Star watched the mole grow a little bigger at that comment.

'Maybe it was you that produced the fire magic,' Jessica went on.

'OK, enough,' Wolf said and his voice had enough authority for Charles and Jessica to both fall silent. 'We're here to celebrate the winter solstice and I won't have these accusations and insults ruin the day for everyone else. If you have a problem with someone in the village then you need to come and see me and we'll discuss it in private. For now, everyone, I hope you enjoy your day.'

People started moving off to the stalls, muttering disappointment at having their entertainment thwarted. Star got the impression that this kind of thing never happened in Midnight.

A few people did go over to talk to Wolf, obviously unhappy about something. Star decided to explore the stalls. The idea was that everyone would make decorations and then place them on the tree. Although it was clear there would be no toilet-roll Santas or cotton-wool snowmen being made today.

Kianga took her arm. 'What are you going to make first?'

Star smiled that Kianga had taken her under her

wing. 'I don't know, why don't you show me around some of your favourites.'

'I do all of them. I could spend the whole afternoon here and it wouldn't be enough. This kind of thing is right up my street. A lot of the decorations will be natural elements, including fruits and vegetables for the animals to eat – in that way we are giving back to nature. This stall is making popcorn and cranberry garlands. It's quite simple, just thread the string through the popcorn and dried cranberry pieces, but it's a bit fiddly. The squirrels, birds and rabbits love those and the end result looks great.'

But before Star could linger at the popcorn stall, Kianga was whisking her on to the next stall. 'This one is making sprays of herbs and flowers, you choose the herbs for what you want out of the year to come. Lavender is for luck and happiness, rosemary for banishing negative energies, roses are for love. I think you definitely need to make a spray with roses today,' Kianga wiggled her eyebrows mischievously. 'Bay leaves are for success, yarrow is for healing, chamomile for comfort. I'm sure you know all this from your baking – you used herbs in your cakes too, didn't you?'

'Yes, but some of your herb uses are different to the ones I know so I'd be very interested in doing this and getting to know the various herbs and spices in the real way.'

'Did you use flowers in your cooking?'

'Some. Lavender mainly, rose too, sometimes I'd use marigold or violets.'

'Flowers have meaning too and all of these have a place in our spells and charms. I'm sure Tabitha would be happy to talk through with you what each one of the herbs and flowers means before you make your spray for the tree.'

Star watched for a moment as some of the villagers selected their herbs and flowers for their own sprays, somehow intrinsically knowing which herb did what. It had taken her years of research to know which herbs and flowers to use and which parts of the plant. Even now, after a few short days in the village, she'd found that many of the herbs had different purposes to those she'd been using them for all these years. It really did show that the magic had been in the intent; it had been her who had made the cakes magic, not the herbs and spices.

'Come on, the next stall is my favourite,' Kianga said, ushering her on.

At the next stall were dried slices of orange, grapefruit, lime, peaches, apricots, pears and apples. The smell was amazing.

'We're going to make fruit garlands,' Kianga said, excitedly. 'These are really easy to make, we just get some twine and these big needles and thread the slices of fruit onto the twine. They look so pretty once they're finished and the smell is out of this world.'

Star threaded the twine onto the needle and then started poking an orange slice onto the twine. 'Does fruit have meaning too?'

'Oh yes, of course, everything in nature does. Oranges represent the sun and, as the winter solstice is a celebration of the sun returning, you'll see a lot of those on different stalls today.' Kianga was silent for a moment while she focussed on threading the twine through a slice of pear. 'Of course, it has other meanings too. The orange is also a symbol of fertility.' She waggled her eyebrows again. 'Maybe next year might bring the gift of a baby.'

Star laughed. 'One step at a time.'

Although if her premonitions were to be believed, a child featured in Wolf's not too distant future. She just had to hope that was her future too.

Wolf watched Star as she made sprigs of herbs and flowers to hang on the tree, laughing and chatting with Kianga and Erin. She made him smile so damn much.

'So, definitely not in love?' Lynx said as he stepped up by Wolf's side, eating a bag of popcorn and nuts.

'Oh I think I definitely am.'

Lynx let out a bark of laughter. 'See, I told you. And

she's smitten with you too. All you have to do now is not screw it up.'

'I don't think it's me who will screw it up.' He gestured to Jessica. 'I may need to leave.'

Lynx looked at him in alarm. 'What? This is your home. Why would you want to leave?'

'Because there's a good possibility that Star is a weather witch and Jessica has taken great pleasure in telling everyone that. A few people have expressed their concerns to me and if it comes down to a vote whether Star stays or goes, I don't think it will fall in her favour. If she goes, I'm going with her.'

Lynx stared at him in shock.

'I know it's very early days in our relationship and who knows, once the betrothal bonds have been removed, I might not have any feelings towards her at all, but I can't live here if they turn against her. That's not the village that I've tried to create. I've worked very hard to make this a place that welcomes everyone. If they throw her out, it means it's not the kind of place I can live in anymore. And being with Star over the last few days has made me want more than the life I lead. She told me that if she could fly and master the invisibility charm she would fly all over the world, visit every little corner of it, and there was a time when I wanted that too. What we have is a gift and it's wasted. Every day I wake up here and deal with village life and stay within these walls because it's safe and I'm not sure I want a safe little life anymore.'

'I totally understand that. You've been mayor almost twenty-four seven for twelve years – you need a break at least, if nothing else. But you know if you leave, Jessica will somehow take your place. I'm not sure the village will be a safe place under her care.'

'I'd have to make sure someone suitable took my place. Do you fancy it?'

'I don't do any kind of responsibility, you know that.'

'There are other founders here, I'm sure one of them would step up. Maybe Ezra, he's done such a good job managing Stardust Street, I'm sure he would make a great mayor.' Wolf felt something wet and soft touch his cheek and he looked up.

'You know the easiest option would be to kick Jessica out before she causes any more trouble,' Lynx said.

Wolf's heart sank as there were little gasps around the village. 'It might be too late for that.'

Fat fluffy snowflakes were floating softly to the ground and everyone seemed to realise it all at once, looking up at the snow as it danced and twirled around them. Some were regarding it with joy – snow for the winter solstice would be extra magical – but others were eyeing it with worry.

He glanced over at Star and she was looking at it

with a big smile on her face but as the murmurings of worry grew louder her face changed and for the first time he saw real fear in her eyes.

He moved closer to her. Although he was sure it wouldn't come to violence, he also knew he would destroy anyone who tried to hurt her.

Suddenly a scream sounded out across the green and he knew it was Jessica. This was what she'd been waiting for, a perfect excuse to incite panic and terror in the villagers.

'She did this, she brought this upon the village,' Jessica shouted. 'Everyone knows her mum was the weather witch that cursed this village and now she's come here to finish us off. We all know weather witches can harness the lightning as a weapon, she'll kill us all. We need to get her out the village now before it's too late.'

'Oh shut up,' Wolf snapped and everyone fell silent and with good reason. He had always been professional in every matter that had arisen in the village, never lost his temper, always been calm, but he'd had enough. 'You're being irrational. Star is not going to kill us. If anyone knows anything about curses, you will know that almost all of them have some kind of time limit. As Star's mum deliberately gave birth to her in this village, giving her the name Midnight so she could find her way back here one day, it would make sense that her mum set the curse to come to an end when Star came here to live. And if anyone knows anything about controlling the weather, you'll know it takes a lot of concentration. Star has been making decorations all morning, not standing here summoning the snow. And can I remind all of you that Star's powers have been blocked for today so she couldn't have done this even if she wanted to.'

There were mutterings around the green.

'You would defend her. Do the villagers know you're sleeping with her?' Jessica said as if playing her trump card. 'Do they know she has cursed you in some way to fall in love with her?'

'That's rubbish.'

'You've been compromised. You're thinking with your heart not your head, and putting us all at risk because of it. You should have kicked her out the second you found out she was a weather witch. But you put your own... needs ahead of everyone else's. You're not fit to be mayor anymore.'

'That's ridiculous,' Ashley said. 'Wolf is the best thing that's ever happened to this village.'

There were some cheers of approval, which Wolf was grateful for.

'He is entitled to have a relationship with anyone he chooses, being mayor does not mean he has to live the life of a monk,' Ashley said.

'Not if that means our lives are in danger,' Jessica said.

'Oh grow up,' Maxine said. 'Star is about as dangerous as my left bum cheek.'

Wolf saw Star smile at that comparison.

'Is she a weather witch?' Esther called out.

'We don't know,' Wolf said. 'I've been teaching her the very basics of how to use her magic, we've not tried to control the weather at all. There is still so much for her to learn.'

'I'm not sure what's worse, a weather witch with full control of her powers or one with no control over it,' Lizzie said.

'We don't even know if she is one,' Erin said.

'And there's a good chance she's not,' Kianga said.

'My mum is a weather witch,' Star said. 'There is a good chance I am too.'

Wolf scowled at her. She didn't need to give them any more ammunition.

She stepped forward and took his hand. 'It's OK, we both know there's a possibility I am and we need to be honest about that.' She addressed the villagers. 'I understand that you're concerned and even scared that I could hurt you and no one should feel like that in their homes. I know what it's like to be hounded out of my home and be frightened to answer the front door. You have a right to walk around the village and not be scared about getting struck by lightning or worry about losing your home in a hurricane I might somehow cause. This village is supposed to be a place of safety for all of you and if I've taken that away from you then I will leave. I have loved my time here over the last week, getting to know some wonderful people and being introduced to this amazing world of magic, but this is not my home, it's yours and I will leave if you want me to.'

'Oh boohoo,' Jessica said. 'Get the violins out. No one wants you here. And I demand a vote on whether you should be kicked out.'

Wolf's heart sank. As a descendant of one of the village founders she had the authority to demand a vote on any decision for the village and he had to carry it out.

Mulberry landed on his shoulder, flapping his wings and twittering angrily, and for a second there was a flash of fire among his wings. Wolf shook his head. Unleashing a huge angry firebird on Jessica was not the way to handle this, as much as he wanted to. Mulberry flew off and Wolf knew the little owl was furious with her.

'Jessica!' someone shouted in alarm. 'What's happening to your neck?'

Wolf looked over and could see the mole on her neck had suddenly grown to the size of an apple. Clearly the last few minutes of nastiness had taken its toll.

Jessica grabbed her throat and her eyes widened in fear. 'She did this to me. You little bitch.'

The mole grew even bigger until it was now the size of a large mango.

'She didn't do it, I did, after you threatened to kill my dog,' Charles said. 'No one gets away with threatening Frankie. Every time you do or say something nasty, the mole on your neck grows. I only started the curse this morning and look at how nasty you've been in one day. I thought we might have a few weeks before it grew this big, but I clearly underestimated what a horrible, evil little cow you are.'

'You piece of shit, I'll get you for this.'

The mole grew again, forcing Jessica's head to bend to the side.

'Charles, stop, you're going to break her neck,' Star said.

'Or maybe her head might explode,' Charles said, rubbing his hands together with glee.

Star ran forward. 'Jessica, you just have to be nice and it will shrink.'

'I'm not being nice to you, you gold-digging whore.'

The mole grew to the size of a watermelon; it was now bigger than Jessica's head.

'You don't have to be nice to me, just be nice. Pick someone here, anyone, and say something nice about them,' Star said.

Jessica looked around the village with desperation.

'Dear Gods, even when her life depends on it, she can't be nice,' Lynx muttered.

'Charles, this is enough,' Wolf said. 'You've made your point.'

'I can't reverse the curse, only she can do that,' Charles said.

'Let's start with an apology for threatening Frankie,' Star said urgently. 'Surely you can manage that.'

'I'm sorry,' Jessica muttered. 'I'm sorry for threatening to kill your dog.'

The mole shrank a fraction.

'Do you have anyone else you could apologise to?' Star said.

Wolf thought the list was probably a mile long.

'Maggie, I'm sorry I insulted your tree ornament earlier. Constance, I'm sorry I said your solstice cake was disgusting.'

The mole shrank a little bit more but Jessica's head was still at a dangerous angle.

'Charles, please,' Star said.

'Fine, I may have put a back door in the curse. Get her to tell the truth about the garland and all of this will go away.'

Star turned back to Jessica. 'Did you set fire to the garland yesterday?'

'Of course not, that was all you and your dangerous weather witch magic.'

The mole started growing again.

'OK, OK, I did it. I set the garland on fire because I

wanted to get rid of Star. I wanted everyone to hate her as much as I did.'

There was suddenly the sound of a large pop and green pus exploded everywhere around where Jessica was standing. For one horrible moment Wolf thought her head had actually exploded but then he saw her face and clothes all covered in pus. The mole had gone.

Everyone stood in shock as they stared at Jessica and Wolf wondered if there were ever pictures drawn to record this moment in the village history, how on earth they would depict this. Jessica was visibly shaking. She'd been scared by that, even though she would never admit it.

He cleared his throat. 'Jessica, as you have admitted to deliberately causing property damage and to inciting hatred to another village member, I'm afraid you will have to leave. Pack your things and I will send security to escort you out shortly.'

Jessica was too stunned to speak, or maybe too afraid to after what she had endured, and she started walking off the green. But her silence was only temporary.

'My demand for a vote still stands. If I'm going, I'm taking her with me. And you'll all thank me for it, you mark my words.'

With that she walked off the green in the direction of her house.

There were a few cheers and claps from the crowd

but then everyone turned back to Wolf to see what would happen next.

Wolf let out a heavy sigh. 'A formal vote has been demanded by one of the founder descendants. As part of our village rules, we have to carry that out. Two boxes will be left inside the town hall for forty-eight hours. You're voting whether you want Star Brightheart to leave the village. Vote yes if you want her to leave, vote no if you want her to stay. Now our celebrations have been ruined for long enough, so please go back to your decorations.'

After a few moments people went back to their tables and stalls, all talking between themselves about what they'd just witnessed.

Star gave him a sad smile and came back to him. 'It's the right thing to do.'

He took her in his arms, not caring what any of the villagers thought. If it was the right thing to do why did it feel so wrong?

CHAPTER 22

Wolf waited at the gate as Eric, one of the guards, escorted Jessica towards him. She didn't have a car so he was quite surprised to find out she intended to walk down the drive to catch a bus from the nearby village. She was just taking a suitcase of clothes, which was floating along behind her. The rest of her stuff would be packed up for her and sent on to wherever she was.

'You'll be sorry for this,' Jessica said as she drew level with him and the guard opened the gate.

'I don't think I will. You've gone too far this time. You've never fitted in here, always looking out for yourself instead of others, being nasty to people, but this was a new low even for you.'

'And what about what Charles did to me?'

'You threatened to kill his dog. I would be furious too if you threatened someone I love.'

'Like your little *witch*, you mean. Don't tell me you love her, that's the most ridiculous thing I've ever heard. She's been here five minutes. Pretty soon that curse or whatever she's done to you will break and you will realise what a complete fool you've been and then you'll be begging me to come back.'

'You're so deluded. She makes me happier than I've ever been in my life. I don't care if that makes me a fool.'

'Well she better watch her back. One day, when she least expects it, I'll be there and she'll regret the day she ever crossed my path.'

Wolf felt the anger suddenly bubbling inside him. 'Is that a threat?'

'What are you going to do? You're so straightlaced, live your life by the book, never step a foot out of line. You might look big and intimidating when you're angry but what are you really going to do?'

'If you go anywhere near Star, you'll soon see how angry I can be.'

Jessica had the audacity to laugh. 'Goodbye Wolf. You missed out big time turning me down.'

She started walking down the driveway, floating her suitcase behind her.

Mulberry landed on his shoulder, twittering angrily, his wings flashing with fire for just a second.

Wolf looked down at the little bird and then back at Jessica.

'Go big Mulberry,' he said, softly.

Mulberry flew off his shoulder and hovered in front of him to look at his face to see if Wolf meant it.

'Go big.'

Mulberry didn't hesitate. He suddenly changed to his big angry firebird and, with a screech of death, flew after Jessica.

She turned round to see what the noise was and her eyes widened in horror as Mulberry flew towards her. She quickly turned and ran down the driveway but Mulberry was close behind, letting out another ear-piercing screech.

Wolf took a deep breath and unleashed his full darkness on her. Shadows of black monsters joined in the chase as did a pack of snarling wolves, the trees either side of the drive grabbed at her clothes and hair as she ran screaming past, her suitcase clattering to the floor as the magic she'd created to carry it was suddenly forgotten. She tried to shoot fire over her shoulder at her pursuers, but shadows were tricky things to destroy. The shadows roared, Mulberry screeched and Jessica screamed all the way down the driveway until she was out of sight. Only then did Wolf release his darkness. After a few moments, Mulberry, in his majestic firebird form, swooped back up the drive towards him, doing a few somersaults as he did before he turned back to his little old self and settled on Wolf's shoulder.

'Good job Mulberry.'

Wolf turned to go back through the gates to find Eric, who must have watched the whole thing unfold.

'Remind me never to piss you off,' Eric said.

Wolf grinned. 'That felt too good. Make sure she gets her suitcase.'

He walked back into the village. He had better things to do with his time than spend it tormenting Jessica.

'What will happen to Charles?' Star said as she lit a few more candles around the bathroom. She'd read up on cleansing rituals and candles played a big part in them. It was an added bonus that they made the bathroom look romantic and that the light of the flickering flames across Wolf's naked wet skin was sexy as hell.

They'd run the bath with all the added oils just as Ashley had said and added five drops of potion from the mystery bottle but, with the way Wolf was looking at her, she was fairly sure this cleansing ritual would be as successful as the others in removing any feelings they had for each other.

She climbed in the bath with him and sat down in

his lap. He wrapped his arms around her and kissed her shoulder.

'I don't know. Surprisingly there are no rules about cursing other members of the village, although there should be. I've told him in no uncertain terms that he's never to pull a stunt like that ever again. He says it was a joke and that he didn't think it would get that far, so I don't think I can really kick him out for a joke that went wrong.'

'Apparently Viktor helped him with the curse too. He suggested it yesterday but I didn't take him seriously. Apparently, Viktor then went off to find someone who would take it seriously.'

'Why am I not surprised Viktor had a hand in this? I'm as guilty as they are for that curse. You told me that Charles had cursed Jessica and I did nothing because there was a huge part of me that wanted to see her get her comeuppance. So maybe I'm not fit to be mayor after all.'

'You know that's rubbish, you know you've done amazing things for this village. You gave the village Stardust Street. That gave people jobs, money, somewhere to go, a place to visit for relatives. And you can see that everyone respects you, not just for that but for the way you handle everything with such professionalism and commitment. Don't let one unhinged individual make you think otherwise. This was all a big plan to eventually become mayor herself so of course Jessica tried to discredit you.'

'And take you down with me.'

'She had it in for me from the moment she found out we were betrothed. She'd been trying to get you to fall in love with her for years and I swoop in and manage that in a matter of days.'

'Seconds more like.'

She smiled and kissed him.

'I am so sorry this has turned out the way it has,' Wolf said. 'With the villagers deciding your fate.'

'It's only fair. I'll be gutted to leave but no one should have to live in fear. And I understand they're scared or worried about having a weather witch among them. History doesn't paint weather witches in a good light. You've worked hard to make sure this is a place where people feel safe and I don't want to take that away from them. I don't want people to feel like they need to leave the village because of me. And, while Jessica forced our hand, it would have come out eventually.'

'If you go, I'm coming with you,' Wolf said.

'What? No. This is your home and your role here is really important. I would never want to take you away from that. And you have no idea how you will feel for me after tomorrow night.'

'It doesn't matter. Even if we want nothing to do with

each other after tomorrow, I don't want to live some-where where the villagers get to pick and choose the kind of people they want living with them. Everyone should be welcome. This is how I became mayor in the first place – because I fought against someone who wanted to handpick the right kind of people for his village, or rather the right colour people, in his eyes. If we vote you out, where do we draw the line? Will they be voting out Kianga next, or Nithya? Ashley isn't British, should we kick her out too? I can't live somewhere like that.'

She smiled and stroked his face. 'You're a good man.'

'We can get a place nearby. I mean, you'd get a place and I'd get a place. I'm not suggesting we move in together but if we lived close by we could take some time to get to know each other. And even if we don't want a relationship after tomorrow, I want to continue teaching you how to use your magic. I don't want you to be alone. And if you get a place near the village, maybe Ashley and Kianga and the others will agree to have potions club once a week at your house instead of Ashley's so you can still see them too.'

She smiled that he had thought of that.

'We'll get you a place with a big kitchen so you can continue making your cakes or chocolates. It's impor-tant that you do something that makes you happy,' Wolf said.

'What about you? What makes you happy, what would a happy future look like for you?'

'I don't honestly know. There's a part of me that feels like I need to take some time to get to know who I am, outside of being mayor. I was eighteen when I became mayor and I don't know anything beyond that. I've always wanted a family, children. I don't know what the future holds for us, but I'd be lying if I said I hadn't thought about that future with you.'

She felt so touched by that and she loved that he'd thought about a future together with her; it gave her so much hope. But she couldn't stop thinking about her premonition. What if the only way he got that future was by her letting him go so he could find happiness with someone else?

'Wolf, I don't know if the future I saw at The Pearl, your future, includes me.'

He frowned. 'What did you see?'

She swallowed the lump in her throat. She couldn't tell him about his daughter because she didn't want to give him false hope. What if being with her meant he never got that future?

'Was I with another woman?'

She frowned. 'There was another woman there. There was no indication that you were with her in the romantic sense. You weren't kissing or hugging her. She was just there in the kitchen of The Pearl with you. Making a sandwich.'

He looked amused by this. 'Are you jealous about me making a sandwich with another woman?'

'She was making the sandwich, you were... doing something else. The sandwich isn't important. And I'm not jealous. It's just that you were really happy in my premonition and if she's the one that brings you that happiness then I want that life for you.'

'Who was she?'

'I couldn't see her face. She had long red hair.'

Wolf shrugged. 'She could have been anyone. My cousin, Tilly, is a redhead. Maybe it was her. But if you're worried I was playing happy families with someone else you don't need to be. I'm head over heels in love with you, Star. There could never be anyone for me but you.'

All doubts and fears went out of the window with those words. They'd talked about having feelings for each other but he'd never said those words to her, not since she'd arrived in Midnight, anyway.

She felt the smile spread across her face. 'You love me?'

He grinned. 'Completely and utterly.'

She kissed him and after a few moments she knelt up and shuffled round so she could straddle him. His hands round her back, holding her close, stroking up her spine were heaven. He moved his mouth to her throat as he slid his hand between her legs.

She gasped, tilting her head back to give him access,

and gripped the back of his neck as his fingers did wonderful things. How was it that he knew the exact place to touch her, as if he knew her body better than she did? He moved his hot mouth lower across her breasts and she let out a noise that was filled with need. Within seconds she was tumbling over the edge.

She tilted his head back up and kissed him hard. She knelt up and, with his hands at her hips, he guided her down on top of him and she moaned against his lips at the feel of him inside her. She stroked his face, relishing the feel of his stubble under her fingers as she kissed him.

She pulled back to look at him. 'Do you think it will always feel this good between us?'

He smiled and stroked a finger through her hair. 'Always.'

The room was suddenly filled with that golden bright light and the warmth of his magic connecting with hers was like a blanket filled with complete and utter love. As that feeling exploded through her she knew there was never any coming back from this. If it all ended tomorrow, she knew she'd never get over him.

CHAPTER 23

Star woke up sprawled out on top of Wolf's chest. Outside, there was a glistening blanket of snow sparkling under the early morning sun. The perfect way to start the winter solstice.

She looked up at Wolf who was gazing out of the window with a contented smile on his face. Noticing she was awake, he stroked her hair.

'Hey,' he said, softly.

'Happy solstice.'

He grinned. 'I think this might be my happiest solstice yet.' He checked his watch. 'We better get up. We have the procession of light shortly, which you have quite the starring role in, and then dinner with family and friends.'

'I love the irony of me being part of this procession

to show all are welcome and then half the village voting me out by tomorrow.'

'I think it's a good thing that you have the starring role as the newest member of the village. It will serve as a reminder that when we celebrate that all are welcome that includes you.' He got out of bed. 'I'll be back in a second.'

He walked out of the room and came back in with what looked like a small log that was made up of dried leaves. He placed it in a metal bowl and set fire to it.

'What are you doing?' Star asked as smoke started to fill the room.

'Burning the white sage as Ashley told us to,' he said, staring at the swirls of smoke.

She couldn't help feeling a kick of disappointment that they were still doing these cleansing rituals. She knew that the whole point of them was so they would both know their feelings for each other were real, but the night before he'd told her he loved her and now this morning he was burning sage to rid himself of any attachment to her. She'd be lying if she said it didn't hurt a little.

The sage leaves burned quickly so soon there was only a bowl of smouldering ash. She stood up and moved to stand next to him.

'So what do we do?' she said.

'We just smear the ash over each other's hearts.'

'Fine, let's get on with it,' she said and Wolf looked at her in concern.

He dipped his fingers into the ash. 'It's warm but not hot so it shouldn't hurt.'

She nodded and he wiped his finger gently over her heart, smearing the ash into her skin.

She repeated the gesture on him.

'Are we done? Can I have a shower now or do I need to wear this ash on my body all day?'

'No, you can have a shower. The ritual is complete. Are you OK?'

'I'm fine,' Star said and walked off to the bathroom. She got in the shower and let the water soak into her skin, dipping her head under the spray.

A few moments later, Wolf joined her, kissing and touching her as if he never wanted to be parted from her, and she let her sadness wash away. This time tomorrow they would know for sure if these rituals and whatever Ashley was going to do to remove the betrothal bonds had worked. They would either still be head over heels in love with each other or have lost each other for good so she knew she had to make the most of whatever time they had left. She turned round in his arms and kissed him hard.

Everyone was waiting around the outside of the green and lining the main streets as Wolf fastened the holly crown to Star's head.

'Don't be nervous,' Wolf said.

'I'm not, just hoping they won't be poking me with their pitchforks as I walk past.'

'They won't do that. The winter solstice is a happy day, they just need to remember what these traditions stand for.'

He handed her the red yule candle.

He stepped back to address the crowd. 'Thank you all for coming to our winter solstice procession. I want to wish you all a very happy solstice.'

There were murmurings around the green as people wished each other a happy solstice or a joyful Yule.

'As the newest member of the village Star will carry the yule candle up the street to the oak tree and be greeted by the village member who has been here the longest, who happens to be my lovely gran. Zofia will light Star's candle and join with her, as will the rest of you on the walk back to the green. Remember, we do this to show that all are welcome in our village, young and old, regardless of their backgrounds.'

'Less of the old,' Zofia shouted, and everyone laughed.

Wolf smiled and gestured for Star to start walking.

Star walked up the main street and as she went people formed little orbs of light in their hands to guide her way. People gave her encouraging smiles as she walked past which was nice.

She reached Zofia and, to her surprise, Zofia gave her a big hug. 'Welcome to the village.'

Star smiled. 'Thank you.'

Zofia waved her hand over the candle and lit it, then took Star's hand and they walked back down the main street. Star smiled to see that everyone followed them. Symbolically, it was a welcome to the village. She just hoped that everyone remembered that when they voted whether they wanted her to stay or go.

'Are you sure it's OK if I come to your family solstice lunch?' Star asked, as they approached Zofia's door.

'Of course. Our solstice celebrations are always noisy and chaotic, there's lots of family and friends. You will be more than welcome,' Wolf said.

Star had been expecting a quiet family meal with Wolf, Lynx and Zofia. She hadn't realised the whole family would be there. That kind of put a stop to her plans to talk to Zofia at some point about her future.

'I hadn't realised you had a big family living here.'

'Oh no, there will be people from the village there, friends of Zofia. She likes to entertain. There'll also be a few family members from outside the village that have come to stay for a few days.'

Wolf opened the door and let her in ahead of him. Straightaway Star was surrounded by the noise of maybe twenty or thirty people all drinking and chatting and having a good time. It was quite clear there wasn't going to be a formal sit-down meal either, as a banquet of food was laid out on long tables on one side of the room and people were just helping themselves to whatever they wanted.

A few people looked over at Star curiously as she walked in with Wolf but there wasn't any animosity. Most of the people she recognised from around the villager but there were a few people there she hadn't met before, she wondered if all of those were relatives of some kind. As an older man with a splendid red waistcoat decorated with suns accosted Wolf for a chat, Lynx swooped in with a big hug and then escorted her to the food table.

'There's plenty of food to choose from, just help yourself. Did you bring cakes?' Lynx eyed the tin in her hand.

'I brought sunshine cake pops.' She showed off the cake pops she had hurriedly made that morning which had been beautifully decorated with holly leaves and orange segments shaped out of royal icing. 'They're chocolate orange flavour as I know oranges seem to be a big factor in the solstice celebrations, and there is also the essence of happiness.'

Lynx took one and shoved it into his mouth whole. 'Tastes good to me.' He took the tin off her and placed it on the table and started guiding her around the room. 'Let me introduce you to a few people to start with. This is Tomaz, my uncle's husband,' he pointed to someone with a fantastic beard, which had the kind of perfect wavy curls Star had never achieved in her own hair. She shook his hand. 'Tomaz is an absolute demon in the kitchen and most of the food here today has been cooked and lovingly prepared by his fair hands.'

'Nice to meet you, I'm Star.'

'And you. Did I see you come in with Wolf?' he eyed Lynx mischievously.

'Yes, yes, she came in with Wolf,' Lynx said. Rolling his eyes and fishing his wallet out of his pocket, he handed Tomaz twenty pounds. 'Tomaz has the gift of foresight, though his gift is, shall we say, a little wonky. Some premonitions come true, some do not, some are completely bonkers. And at the summer solstice, Tomaz told me that Wolf would be in love by the next solstice which I did not believe but Tomaz was adamant it would happen so we had a bet that I'm very glad to lose. Let me introduce you to some others before Tomaz swindles me out of more money.'

'Pleasure to meet you Star,' Tomaz said, gleefully pocketing the money.

Lynx ushered her on. 'The food that Tomaz cooks is on the red plates and bowls, it's delicious. The food on the blue bowls, I wouldn't touch with a barge pole unless you want to be sick for a week after. Aunt Edith hasn't a clue about keeping food fresh or using it while it's in date. Her fridge-freezer packed up three or four years ago and she flat refused to get herself another one. Wolf even offered to pay for one for her but said she likes the old-fashioned method of keeping her food in salt water. Honestly, how she hasn't killed herself with food poisoning is anyone's guess.' They approached an elderly lady dressed head to toe in pink velour. 'Aunt Edith, hi, I was just telling Star about your delicious sausage rolls. Interesting pastry though, what did you use?'

'Oh banana skin, it adds a wonderful texture to it,' Aunt Edith said.

'Oh yummy,' Lynx said. 'I'll have to check that out.'

He ushered Star on, probably because Aunt Edith's plate was piled high with suspect-looking food and he didn't want to be offered any. 'Oh, this is my cousin Tilly. Tilly, this is Star Brightheart, Wolf's better half.'

Tilly grinned and embraced Star in a big hug. 'I've heard all about you, I'm so pleased we get to meet.'

Star smiled as she hugged her but couldn't help feeling a tiny bit disappointed. Tilly was definitely not the redhead she'd seen in her premonition. Tilly was tall and willowy, while the woman she'd seen in her premonition was a lot shorter.

'Star!' a voice called out across the room. 'Come and get yourself a hot cider.'

Star turned round to see Zofia waving at her from the kitchen.

'Oh, looks like you've been summoned,' Lynx said. 'Good luck.'

'Come and find me later,' Tilly said, 'I want to get to know the woman who stole my cousin's heart.'

'I will,' Star said.

She made her way to the kitchen where Zofia was stirring a bubbling cauldron.

'You wanted to talk to me about your future?' Zofia said, throwing a few more herbs into the cauldron.

'How could you possibly know that?'

'That's the way my brain works. But despite what Wolf tells you about my omniscient gift, I don't know everything. Your future is not clear to me, not right now. When you arrived here in the village, I could see your wedding as clear as day. You got married at the spring equinox, it was a bright sunny day, flowers everywhere. I can't see that anymore.'

'We don't get married?'

'I didn't say that, just that it's a bit grey. Getting Ashley to remove the betrothal bonds has damaged that future, even if she hasn't done it yet. The wheels have been set in motion. But what has happened over the last few days has written a new future.'

'A good one or a bad one?'

Zofia shook her head. 'I don't know. I see two or three different futures. One where Wolf is crazy happy and one where he is miserable and bitter for the rest of his life and I'm not sure which part you play in either of those futures. I think a part of that is because you haven't decided your future yet. I see a future with you living here but I also see you leaving the village, soon, maybe in the next few days, and honestly I wonder if that's not a bad thing.'

'You think I should leave, that Wolf would be happier without me?'

'I don't know and I've never felt like this before, so uncertain. But the last few days I can't seem to see anyone's futures with any great certainty and it's a bit of a worry. You have such great power and I think you're confounding me and I wonder if you're confounding Wolf too.'

'You think I've bewitched him in some way to fall in love with me?'

'Oh honey, I like you. I really do and I have no doubt at all that what you feel for him is genuine because you would leave in a heartbeat if you thought it would make him happier. And I think you've already considered that.'

'I have. Zofia, I saw a premonition of my own, of

Wolf's future. He was so very happy. I want him to have that future even if that doesn't include me.'

Zofia smiled. 'That shows real love. I can feel how much you love him. I know you're not here with any malicious intent but with your power you have great influence. You've seen the effects of that in your cakes: fixing a broken heart, helping to ease anxiety, giving people confidence to get a job. It's not the herbs or the delicious topping, it's the power of your influence. There's a part of me that wonders if because you love him you want him to love you and therefore he does.'

Star gasped. 'No!'

'I don't know if that's true or even possible. Love is a powerful magic all of its own. A few days ago I would have said there isn't a magic in the world that could make someone fall in love if they didn't want that. But then I've never met someone with so much power as you before.'

'But how do we know for sure? We asked Ashley to remove the betrothal bonds and we've been doing all these cleansing rituals to make sure our feelings for each other were real. What else can I do?'

'I think that old proverb, "If you love something set it free. If it comes back, it's yours, if not, it was never meant to be," couldn't be more true in your case. You need to let him go. The betrothal bonds will be removed tonight at midnight. That might change everything. And then I think you use your influence in the same way you would help anyone in his position: you give him clarity of mind, you help him to make the best decision to give him a happy life or whatever else it is you would do for someone in his situation. Give it to him in a cake if need be, or a drink. And then I think you need to leave for a few days to let him realise what a life without you is like. You'll soon know if it's meant to be.'

Star sat down, rubbing the ache in her chest at the thought of leaving him, which only got worse when she thought about causing him any pain. But Wolf had been adamant from the start that they needed to know this was real, he had been committed to doing all the cleansing rituals and he'd been the one to ask Ashley to remove all the bonds. If letting him go was the only way to know for sure, then she had to take the chance that he'd never really been hers at all.

CHAPTER 24

It was just past eleven at night as Wolf and Star sat in front of the fire in her cottage. This morning she'd been thinking of asking him to skip this ritual but now she knew she had to go through with it. She could already feel her heart breaking inside as she wrote the list of things she loved about him on a piece of paper. Wolf was writing his own too and taking a long time over it. It was hard to believe that all those feelings could be gone by tomorrow.

Wolf put the lid back on his pen and looked over at her. She added a few more things to her list and then put her pen down too.

'So we just read them out to each other and then burn the list?'

'Yes, that simple,' Wolf said. 'Shall I go first?'

She nodded, although she wasn't sure she wanted to hear this.

He cleared his throat. 'I love your determination to learn your powers, I love how you scrunch your face up when you're concentrating on your magic. I love your kindness. Even yesterday, when Jessica was being so vile to you, you still wanted to help her. I love how you've dedicated your life to helping others by making your cakes. I love that you want to do something good with your magic like Beth does for all those who surf on the beach. That kindness is a rare and beautiful thing and I love that about you.'

Star felt tears fill her eyes and fall down her cheeks.

'I love that you're putting the villagers' needs above your own, that you're prepared to leave to keep them happy and feeling safe,' Wolf went on. 'I love that you were so honest about the possibility you're a weather witch rather than hiding it. I love that you tried to replace the garland with pyjama bottoms stuffed with leaves that are shedding every day. I love that you made sex cakes. I love your optimism, your zest for life, your spirit of adventure. I love that you've made me fall in love with magic again. I love how fun it feels to just be around you, how you make me laugh so much.' He swallowed. 'I love how happy you make me, that being with you makes me feel truly alive for the first time in my life. I love you so much it fills me up to the very top.'

Star was sobbing by this point.

'Hey, don't cry,' Wolf said, bringing her into his arms. She clung onto him, crying into his chest. 'Why are you crying?'

'I just don't want this to be over. I don't want to tell you all the reasons I love you for you to throw them in the fire. I want you to keep these reasons with you always. I don't want to lose you.'

'You're not going to lose me. Did you not hear this big long list of things I love about you? Those feelings are not going to go at the strike of midnight. This is not some Cinderella story where I forget who you are and how you make me feel after twelve o'clock. This love I have for you is forever.'

She pulled back. 'I want you to hear my list. I want you to really listen to it because if it all ends tomorrow, if you no longer love me, I want you to know that you are loved. No matter what happens, you need to know that.'

'Star, you're panicking over nothing. I know you love me, I sure as hell know I love you. The only reason I wanted to go through all these cleansing rituals is because I wanted you to feel like you had a choice. You come here and are faced with a world of magic you don't understand, and you start having these feelings for me and I for you and I wanted you to know that there is no magic in the world that can make you feel like you're in love, that these feelings from both of us are real. And I suppose, in the beginning, I wanted that confirmation too, that before I gave you my heart I'd know all of this was real. But it's too late for that. I've already given my heart to you. I can't take that back.'

But she could. She could make him fall out of love with her.

'In fact, let's forget this stupid ritual,' Wolf said. 'I don't need it.'

'I do,' Star said. 'I need to know that you'll truly be happy with me. You say there is no magic in the world that can make you love me, but what about the magic of a weather witch? You don't know what I'm capable of – hell, neither do I.'

'*If* you are a weather witch, then you can summon the rain, create storms, make it snow, harness the lightning, make the sun shine every damn day, but you can't make someone love you. That's not in your power, that's not in anyone's power.'

'Look, let's do this, let's finish what we started and then tomorrow we'll know for sure.'

'Fine,' Wolf said, clearly exasperated. 'Read me your damn list.'

Star picked up her piece of paper although she didn't really need it to know all the ways she loved him. 'I love that when we were kids, you were the one to hold me when my dad died. You didn't even like me at that point and you held me tight in your arms while I cried and snotted all over your shirt. I gave you a little piece of my heart right there and then and, every day for the next two years, you took a little bit more.'

She took his hand. 'I loved the magical world you showed me – even if there was a part of me that doubted any of it was real, I thought you were the most magnificent person I'd ever met. I love your fierce need to protect me, even from a lightning strike. Now, knowing you as a man, I've fallen in love with you all over again but I love that there is still a little boy in there that wants to have fun with his magic. I love your commitment to the village and the villagers, that you only want what's best for them. I love that you stood up to racist bullies at the age of eighteen. I love that the villagers have so much love and respect for you. I love your enduring patience when teaching me about my magic. I love that you gave me the most romantic, most incredible kiss of my life up there in the stars. I love that when you make love to me, my love for you shines out like a beacon. I love that with you I'm the happiest I've ever been in my life.'

Wolf stared at her in shock and then leaned forward and kissed her hard. She kissed him back, clinging onto his shirt, afraid to let him go.

He moved his mouth to her neck and she closed her eyes, relishing the feel of his lips against her skin, but then she pushed him back gently. 'You need to go. I can't do this with you tonight. It's nearly midnight and I can't make love to you and then watch the love fade from your eyes. We need to burn these lists, you need to go home, and if you still love me tomorrow when you wake up, you come and find me.'

'It'd be easier if I stayed here until after midnight then you can see for yourself.'

'Please, I don't want to be holding your hand or kissing you at the point when you realise you don't love me. I can't bear to see that love turn to hate if you think I've tricked you somehow. Give me your list, let's burn them both and set you free and then you need to go home.'

He handed her the list and she moved towards the log fire. She hesitated to throw their lists in. This felt more symbolic than any of the other cleansing rituals. This was literally throwing away their love story. She quickly grabbed her phone and took pictures of both the lists and then texted hers to Wolf so he would always have it. She quickly followed her text with the photo of them in bed together that she'd sent to Tig because she wanted Wolf to see the love she had for him in her eyes when he read the list. Then she threw both lists into the fire. The paper curled at the edges and within seconds both pieces of paper were gone, sending a thin plume of smoke up the chimney.

'You need to go,' Star said, looking at the time. It was quarter to midnight.

He didn't say anything as she quickly ushered him to the door.

He stepped outside and turned round to speak to her but she stepped forward and kissed him. She pulled back slightly. 'If you wake up tomorrow and realise that you don't love me and you never did, please know that I never meant to hurt you, that's the last thing I would ever do. And know that I will always love you. Always.'

She kissed him again and he held her tight and, as she kissed him, she held onto the amulet and gave him clarity of thought so his actions were not clouded by love or lust or any kind of magic. She gave him the courage to walk away from false feelings and sent him the determination to find the thing that made him the happiest in the world.

He stepped back from her and looked at her in confusion and she wondered if it was already starting to work.

'If you still love me, come and find me tomorrow,' she repeated, hoping somehow he would know how to find her.

He took another step back and then another and then he turned and walked away and didn't look back. She stepped back inside and closed the door, leaning against it as she cried for the man she'd just lost, the man she loved with all of her heart.

She finally understood what her mum had gone through when she'd given Star away. Star's happiness was more important than her mum's love for her.

Wolf's happiness was more important to Star than staying with him for her own happiness.

After a while, she went back into the lounge, held the amulet and waved her hand over the candles and the fire, extinguishing the flames. She heard the village clock chime midnight and knew she had to leave in case Wolf came back. He needed to have a few hours at least to find that clarity without her being there to confound him. She grabbed her bag, which she'd packed earlier, and went out to the car, magically closing the door behind her. She drove down to the gate and the guards waved her through.

She made her way through quiet country lanes, concentrating on the journey and not her heart breaking into a thousand pieces, until she saw the sea glimmering as she drove down the hill towards it. And there was The Pearl, almost glowing in the light from the moon.

She got out of the car, grabbed her bag and walked up to the door, hoping it would be unlocked to her as it was for all witches. The door opened easily and she stepped inside. She didn't bother with any of the lights, welcoming the darkness, and as she sat down on the sofa she let the tears fall.

CHAPTER 25

olf woke the next morning and his thoughts immediately turned to Star. He'd had a moment of clarity the night before. When he sat down to write the list of everything he loved about her, he'd looked over at her, her hair falling over her face as her head bent over her own list, and he'd wanted to smooth her hair out of her face. He had been filled with a desperate need to kiss her, to taste her, to touch her. He wanted to show her how much she meant to him by making love to her, not by writing a damned list. He wanted to feel her hands on his skin, he wanted to see her body react to his touch as if only he could make her feel that way. He wanted to see the love for him in her eyes. He wanted to feel that glorious moment their powers merged together, not just because their connection was so magnificently brilliant it took his breath away, but because at that moment he could feel the love she had for him and it filled him up to the top.

He'd looked down at his piece of paper and wondered how he could put that need for her into words and he'd suddenly realised that none of that was love. It was desire and need and passion and lust but it wasn't love.

Looking back over his short but wonderful relationship with Star, he knew his list had to be real, not a list clouded with lust or desire but the things he really truly loved about her. And once he started writing he couldn't stop. It had been quite cathartic actually. With all his fears about their feelings not being real, as the long list of why he loved her poured out of him, he knew every single one of those reasons were true and he didn't need any cleansing rituals to confirm that.

He loved her and, now the betrothal bonds had been removed and there could be no more doubt, he needed to go and tell her.

He quickly washed and dressed and then had an idea. There was something he could give Star that would prove that he loved her and wanted a future with her. He quickly made a phone call and then made his way to her house. But as he walked up her road, the bottom fell out of his world when he saw her car had gone and tracks in the snow leading up the road.

He found himself running and he burst through her door.

'Star,' he called but he didn't need the silence to know she had left, he could feel it.

He wandered through the rooms. All her stuff was still here and it was clear she had departed in a bit of a hurry; their drinks glasses and dinner plates from the night before were unwashed. He went upstairs to the bedroom and her clothes were on the bed as if she had grabbed a few items and left.

What the hell had happened?

He quickly grabbed his phone from his pocket and the first thing he saw was the photo she had texted him the night before with her long list of the reasons why she loved him. He read through it, his throat raw with suppressed emotion. It wasn't possible for her to feel these things at a quarter to midnight and then, as soon as the clock struck twelve, those feelings had vanished. He couldn't believe that. He looked at the other photo she'd sent him of the two of them together. She looked like someone who was completely in love. None of this made any sense.

He dialled her number but it went through to answerphone.

He walked back downstairs, numb with shock. Why would she just leave and not talk to him?

Just then Viktor walked in through the cat flap.

'What did you do?' Viktor demanded. 'I saw her

leave last night. She seemed to be in an awful hurry. Crying too. I liked her. If it was you that hurt her, I'll curse you as well.'

'I didn't do anything, I love her, I would never do anything to hurt her. Did she talk to you about why she was going or where?'

'I only saw her as her car roared past me.'

'What time was this?'

'The clock had not long struck midnight. Maybe ten minutes past, but it wasn't long after you left.'

Ten minutes past midnight. So the betrothal bonds had been lifted and Star had clearly realised she didn't love him after all. Ten minutes later and she'd run.

Wolf was chopping wood in his front garden, but heaving the axe into the wood and watching it splinter wasn't doing anything to dispel how angry he was.

After everything he and Star had been through for the past week, how could she not have the decency to tell him she no longer loved him, that she'd never loved him? How could she just run away rather than face him to tell him the truth?

'Hey!'

He looked up to see Lynx watching him warily from the end of his drive.

'I've just heard that Star left. Want to put that axe down so we can talk about it?'

Lynx, with his positive, laid-back approach to life, was the very last person Wolf wanted to talk to about this but he sank his axe in a piece of wood and gestured for his brother to follow him inside.

'I can't believe she left,' Wolf said.

'What happened? Did you two have a row?'

'You'd think, wouldn't you. You'd think that we must have had a blazing argument and she's stormed off. But the last words she said to me were that she loved me, that she would always love me. We were doing these bloody cleansing rituals like Ashley told us to and this last one was to write a list of all the things we loved about each other and then to burn it. Look at the list she wrote about me.'

He passed Lynx his phone to show him the photo of Star's list, giving him a moment to read it.

'How can she feel like that for me and then half hour later all of that is gone? I thought that what we had was forever.'

Lynx passed the phone back to him. 'She loves you. Why would you doubt that?'

'Did you miss the part where she left?' Wolf said in exasperation. 'Ashley's final part of the magic to remove the betrothal bonds was lifted at midnight last night. Ten minutes later Star left.'

'Come on. This is the woman you love, does that

sound like something she would do? Even if she no longer loved you, don't you think she would come and talk to you?'

'And yet here we are,' Wolf said.

'So if you can get past your own bruised ego for a second, let's think why she would do that.'

Wolf glared at Lynx and then looked back at Star's list, thinking back to the night before. She'd been almost panicking, desperate for him to know how much she loved him. He suddenly remembered something.

'She was scared that the strength of her magic could inadvertently make me fall in love with her. She said she didn't want me to think she'd tricked me into loving her and hate her because of it.'

'Well that sounds much more likely than her running because she doesn't love you anymore. She's seen you when you're angry and she doesn't want that wrath turned on her.'

'She's not scared of me. She's scared of seeing me and no longer seeing my love for her.'

'Or that,' Lynx said. 'Her magic is such an unknown energy, no one really knows what she can or can't do. I can understand she's scared by it and mostly the impact it can have on others.'

Wolf nodded. 'She was so upset to find out she'd been making magic cakes for all these years influencing people with her magic and with no real control over it. She used her magic for good but it could have gone very wrong, which it did when she nearly killed Cleo Walsh.'

'How did she manage that?'

'By pouring hate into her cake.'

'Dear Gods,' Lynx muttered.

'And now she's scared she's influenced me for her own gain. But why on earth would she think that?'

Lynx looked awkward for a moment.

'You know something. Did you say something to her? Did someone else?'

'She was talking to Zofia for a long time yesterday in the kitchen at the solstice celebration. When she came out she looked devastated.'

Wolf swore. This had the markings of his grandmother's interference all over it.

'I need to talk to her.'

'Go easy on her, I'm sure she was acting in your best interests.'

'If she's lost me the woman I love then she will be the one to see my wrath.'

He stormed out of the house.

On his way to see Zofia, Wolf stopped in to see Ashley to ask her about the betrothal bonds. He knocked on the door and she answered with a big smile on her face.

'Hey Wolf, you OK?'

'Not really, can I come in?'

'Of course.'

She stepped back to let him in and he walked into the lounge. 'Did you manage to remove the betrothal bonds last night?'

'Oh, I completely forgot all about that,' Ashley said.

'You forgot to remove the bonds?' Wolf said, incredulously. After all the work they'd done with the cleansing rituals and she hadn't done the most important part. Not that it mattered, he knew his feelings for Star were real, but how could he prove it to her if the betrothal bonds were still there?

'Oh no, I removed them. I thought it would have to be done at the winter solstice but apparently not. I did it straight after you came to see me to ask me to remove them. Didn't take me long. It was a lot easier than I thought it would be actually. Only took about ten minutes.'

'That was three days ago.'

'Well, yes.'

'Why didn't you tell us?'

'Oh, with all that stuff with Jessica starting the fire at the garland ceremony and all the drama with the snow at the tree decorating ceremony, I just completely forgot to tell you. And then I saw you all loved-up together and I figured that it didn't matter. I told you the bonds of your attraction were far stronger than the betrothal bonds and now they're even stronger. I can see that.'

'But we did all those cleansing rituals.'

'And I'm sure taking a bath with the woman you loved was such a hardship for you. The cleansing rituals wouldn't have got rid of your love for each other. Nothing can do that. It would have only got rid of unwanted magic.'

'So the last few days, these feelings we've had for each other, they were all real? There was definitely no magic involved?'

'No, not at all. You love each other and that shines brighter than any magic.'

Wolf sighed.

'What's wrong? Isn't this what you want?'

'Star thinks the power and strength of her magic has made me fall in love with her. She ran last night.'

Ashley's face fell. 'She left?'

Wolf nodded. 'I don't know how I can prove to her it's real. She told me that if I still loved her today after the betrothal bonds were supposedly lifted at midnight to come and find her but I don't know if it's enough. She has to trust in my love, trust in us, and I don't know if she can do that.'

'Well now I feel bad that you were doubting the love you had for each other all this time because you thought the betrothal bonds were still there. I thought you would have known it was real.'

'I did. I thought she did too, but then Zofia told her something and it made her doubt everything. She put this idea in her head that her weather witch magic could change the way I feel. I'm furious with Zofia but I'm angry at Star that she could doubt what we have, that she ran without talking it through with me first.'

'Star was trying to protect you from her. I think just telling her you love her will probably be enough. I'm sure she's waiting for you.'

Wolf nodded. 'I don't even know where she is. I guess she might have gone back to London.'

Ashley smiled. 'Love is a powerful thing. I'm pretty sure if you listen to your heart, you'll know exactly where to find her.'

Wolf nearly rolled his eyes at the ambiguous message of hope but then all of a sudden he knew exactly where Star was. She'd even told him when they were at The Pearl together that if she was ever in trouble knowing that was there as a safe haven would be a great comfort. He'd told her at the time that she could always come to him if she was in trouble but then what did he expect when he'd spent the last few days doing cleansing rituals to remove their love? How could she trust in that when he'd seemingly been so keen to get rid of it?

'I need to go.'

He hurried out of the house and immediately saw Zofia running towards him.

'Wolf, I've made a terrible mistake, I'm so sorry.'

'What the hell did you do?'

'My magic, my premonitions of the future, it all went on the fritz when Star arrived. I couldn't see anything clearly anymore and I thought if her magic could inadvertently cause that maybe it had also caused you to think you were in love with her too.'

'You've ruined everything. She's the best thing that ever happened to me and you've taken that away from me.'

'I am sorry. I've never been in love. Your grandad was a friend, with Jan it was purely sex. I never had what you and Star had. To watch you fall for her so quickly, and so hard, it worried me. She was scared for you too.'

'After you put these bloody stupid ideas in her head.'

'No, before that. She had a premonition.'

'I know. She saw me with some red-headed woman making a sodding sandwich. Don't tell me she ran because of that.'

'Since she's gone I can see more clearly. I can see what Star saw. Her premonition was about a child.'

He stared at her in shock. 'What?'

'She saw you and your daughter playing together and you were so happy.'

Wolf felt like he'd just been hit by a bus.

'Your daughter has beautiful red hair, just like the

red-headed woman she also saw. Red-headed woman, red-headed child, it was easy to assume that the little girl was yours and the other woman's. Star wanted to let you go so you could have that future. And yes, thanks to me, she thought her magic may have influenced you to love her and she left so you wouldn't be influenced by her anymore, but she was already worried that staying with you would stop you having that future. I just put the nail in the coffin and you don't know how sorry I am for that.'

His heart thundered against his chest, his head was spinning. 'I... we... Star and I, we have a daughter together?'

'I told Star I could see two possible futures for you, one where you were crazy happy and the one where you were miserable for the rest of your life. Right now, that still stands. If you can persuade Star your future is together, your daughter will be born before the next turn of the Wheel of the Year.'

'She'll be born within the year?'

'Yes.'

'I need to go.' Wolf turned to run for his house and then stopped. Conjuring a quick invisibility charm, he flew up into the air.

CHAPTER 26

Star stood at the window of The Pearl looking out at the sea and the snow, the waves crashing onto the rocks reflecting her mood.

She'd spent the whole night crying. If she'd thought it felt bad when the doors to her life as celebrity cake-maker slammed shut, it felt even worse slamming the door shut on her relationship with Wolf.

She kept hoping that he would turn up and tell her he still loved her but, as it was now mid-morning, she had to accept he wasn't coming. She had set him free and now he didn't love her anymore.

She felt broken.

She wandered through the different rooms and all the happiness and love and joy she'd felt on her previous visit had gone and she didn't understand why. She'd felt the presence of children here and that was gone too. The house was now filled with sadness, bitterness and anger and that didn't make any sense – unless the feelings in the house were representative of the mood of the people in it. But that didn't explain why she'd felt children here and now she couldn't.

She walked into the kitchen hoping to see her premonition again so she could know she'd done the right thing. If Wolf was still happy then this heartache was worth it but there was nothing here.

A thought suddenly occurred to her. Had she caused this? What if the presence of the children she'd felt hadn't been echoes of the past but the future? Had running away taken this future away from him? Had she been his future and now she'd ruined that by leaving? Had she really seen *her* daughter running through here and now she no longer existed?

The pain to her chest was instant and brutal and she curled up in a ball. She couldn't breathe with the thought that she had lost her daughter, that bright beautiful future, and that she had destroyed it because she hadn't trusted that Wolf's love was real. She moaned into her hands. What had she done? She knelt like that for too long, wondering if she could change things if she returned or if the hurt she'd caused Wolf was too much for him to take her back.

But suddenly it was like a switch had been flicked and she felt the happiness and love flood through the house again. She lifted her head in confusion and the house was filled with premonitions, echoes of her future, Wolf bottle-feeding their son, their daughter taking her first steps, their son floating up to one of the cupboards to get a snack, their children having a water fight, shooting water from their hands, and she and Wolf there for it all. She stood up as the echoes faded and vanished, but she could still hear the happiness and laughter ringing in her ears. She couldn't help smiling. Her future had changed and she suddenly knew why.

Wolf was coming to get her.

She ran outside expecting to see his car coming down the road towards the house but the road was empty. Suddenly he landed hard on the ground in front of her, sending a cloud of snow up into the air, but before the flakes had settled she ran forward and he gathered her in his arms and kissed her hard.

She felt the tears pour down her cheeks. 'I'm so sorry,' she mumbled against his lips, although he was kissing her so ardently she could barely get a word out. 'I'm such an idiot.'

Without taking his mouth off hers, he scooped her up in his arms and carried her into the house. 'I have to say I'd expected to have to do a lot more persuading to get you to come home with me. I had a big speech planned to convince you of my love.'

'I don't need to hear it. I know you love me. I risked everything when I left. I was such a fool.'

He sat her down on the sofa and perched in front of her on the coffee table, taking her hands in his. 'No, you weren't. You were trying to protect my future. You saw my daughter and a red-headed woman and thought I could only have that life without you. I have no idea who the woman is but the little girl is ours, not mine.'

'I know that now, I saw her, I saw us all, a family. But I love you so much I couldn't bear the thought of you missing out on that happy future with your daughter. I was so scared that I had used my influence to make you love me. As Zofia pointed out, I had been using my influence for years when I made my cakes, changing people's frame of mind to make them face fears, or get over a broken heart. What if I had inadvertently influenced you? So last night I used my magic to try to set you free, to give you clarity of mind, to help you seek out the things that make you really happy.'

'And here I am, more sure than I've ever been that you are my future and that I love you with all my heart.'

Fresh tears filled her eyes. 'I should have talked to you, told you about your daughter.'

'Our daughter and I wish you had but I think Zofia was right, although I'll never tell her that. The only way for you to know I really love you was to leave, to let me have that space away from you to know my own mind. I just wish you'd told me the plan.'

'I'm sorry, I never meant to hurt you. But would you have let me go if I had told you?'

He smiled. 'Probably not. I don't blame you for any of this. How could I ever expect you to really trust in my love when I had been so hellbent on removing the bonds from the beginning? It's not the most romantic start to a relationship. Part of that was to protect you, but part of it was to protect myself. I was devastated when I told you I loved you as a child and you never came back. I know that wasn't your fault but there was a huge part of me that was scared to put my heart on the line again. But you crashed back into my life in all the best ways and, as much as I tried to fight it, my heart was yours almost from the second you arrived here.'

She leaned forward to kiss him and then, with his mouth on hers, he half stood up and fought his way out of his coat before kneeling on the sofa and rolling her back so she was under him.

'Wait, we can't make love on Beth's sofa.'

'It's our sofa, I bought it this morning.'

'You bought her sofa?'

'I bought the whole house.'

She let out a bubble of laughter. 'Oh well, I guess we can.' She pulled off his jumper and t-shirt in one go and ran her hands over his chest. 'I can't believe you bought it.'

He unzipped her jeans and pulled them off unceremoniously, he was obviously in a bit of a hurry. 'You told me to.'

'Yes but you were all, "My responsibilities are to the village and—"'

He leaned over her, looking her right in the eye. 'My responsibilities are to you. My priority is you. Always will be. And our daughter.' He dipped his head and kissed her belly.

'I don't think she's in there yet.'

'She could be. Zofia said she arrives within the year.'

Star laughed and then the laughter died in her throat when she saw Wolf was serious.

'A year?'

He studied her face. 'We can take more precautions, try to push it back but—'

'No, I've already messed with fate once, I won't risk losing her again. She'll be here when she's ready and we'll just have to make the most of our time together until she comes.'

'Agreed.'

He pulled her jumper and shirt off, quickly removed her bra and knickers and then kissed her hard. She slid her hands down his back and then round his waist, unzipping his jeans and pushing them and his shorts off his bum and down his legs.

He sat back up to wriggle out of them.

'Why did you buy the house? Did you envisage it being some kind of sex shack for me and you to sneak away from the village and have hot rampant sex? Because I like the sound of that.'

'Partly. You said I was happy here and I can't think of anything that would make me happier than spending time with you here. I wanted time to get to know you properly. The village has been my entire world for too long. But you're part of my world now and I want time away from there to explore this new world with you in it. But also so I have a place for me. I need time for myself, a place where I can just be me and not the mayor and find out what that looks like.'

She laughed. 'You bought yourself a bachelor pad. Oh, you're going to be so disappointed.'

He leaned back over her, sliding his hand up her leg, and she gasped as he touched her in the exact spot that made her weak.

'How could I possibly be disappointed with this?'

She had no words as he drove her wild with pleasure. As she tried to catch her breath as she came down from her high, he gathered her legs round his hips and slid carefully inside her.

'You'll come home with me after this?'

She shook her head.

He frowned, opening his mouth to protest, but she cupped his face, placing a thumb over his lips.

'I love you so much. Wherever you are, I'll be there too. We may live in the village because your work is there and my friends are there but this will always be our home. Let me show you what I saw before you arrived.'

She held onto the amulet and thought about the premonitions she'd seen, casting them onto the wall for Wolf to see. He stared at the life laid out in front of them, a life filled with love and laughter, he watched their children playing, and a big smile spread across his face.

He turned back to look at her and she let the premonitions fade away. 'How could I be disappointed with that?'

'There's no time for quiet contemplation and reflection in that life.'

'But it's a life filled with happiness.'

She smiled and kissed him and he started moving against her, taking her higher. He pulled back to stare at her and this time when the light exploded out of her, it was no longer a cage that surrounded them but a beam of warmth that filled every inch of every room.

CHAPTER 27

Star walked hand in hand with Wolf up to the town hall to see what fate the village had in store for her. It was funny that being kicked out of the village had been the most worrying thing a few days before, but so much had happened since then. Now, knowing her future with Wolf, she wasn't too bothered about the result anymore. She would be sad to leave the village when it was such a place of wonder and magic. She knew she could learn so much from the villagers if they let her stay and she'd made some lovely friends but she knew she'd keep in contact with them if she did leave. She had a very happy life in front of her, with or without the village, so it was a win-win either way.

Quite a lot of people were gathering outside to hear the result and Star smiled to see the potions club had turned out, all giving her smiles of encouragement as she walked past.

Lizzie and Esther were there and Star couldn't help wondering if they were here to make sure she went.

Maggie was waiting for them on the steps with the two sealed boxes in front of her. Wolf had already warned Star that it had to be done formally.

Wolf nodded to Maggie that they were ready to proceed and he put his arm round Star. Kissing her forehead, he whispered in her ear, 'Wherever you go, I go.'

She smiled. She didn't want to take him away from his job but she did admire the principle of it. She also knew he had his formal resignation in his pocket, which didn't bode well for how he thought this would turn out.

Maggie cleared her throat. 'As a descendant of one of the village founders demanded a vote, as per the village rules, it has been done. You had forty-eight hours to cast your vote and all votes are final and cannot be undone. You were either voting "Yes" you want Star Brightheart to leave or "No" if you wanted her to stay.'

She unlocked both boxes and ceremoniously removed the lids ready for counting.

'Oh my. We've never had that before.' She cleared her throat, clearly remembering the pomp and ceremony. 'The vote is unanimous. Everyone has voted Star can stay.'

416

Star's heart leapt in her chest. 'I can stay?'

'Are you sure?' Wolf said, clearly as much in shock about the result as she was.

Maggie nodded and turned the boxes on their sides. The 'Yes' box for Star to leave was completely empty, while the other box had hundreds of bits of paper in.

The small crowd cheered and some of them started making their way back home as the entertainment was clearly over.

Star found Lizzie and Esther among the stragglers. 'You voted for me to stay?'

'Esther reminded me that I started a fair share of my own fires when I was little and learning my magic. It wouldn't be fair to judge you on any of your mistakes,' Lizzie said.

'Thank you. It means a lot that I can stay. I know I will learn so much more from being here.'

They nodded and walked away. Ashley and the members of the potions club came over to give her a hug and so did Lynx. Then Zofia came over to hug her.

'Welcome to the family, my dear,' Zofia grabbed her shoulders. 'I am sorry for what I said. I know I nearly ruined everything. But you belong here and you belong with Wolf – I can see that now.'

'You were only doing what you thought was best,' Star said. 'And honestly I think we needed to do it so there would never be any doubt again.'

Zofia smiled and turned away.

'Zofia,' Star called after her. 'I have to ask. Who is the red-headed woman I saw?'

Zofia grinned. 'Well that's a story waiting to be told. But she's not someone who has any bearing on your relationship.'

She walked off and Star turned to Wolf in confusion. 'What does that mean?'

'It means our happy ever after is set in stone and nothing or no one will ever change that.'

EPILOGUE
ONE YEAR LATER

Star put her chocolate yule logs with added happiness in a tin and added that to the box of sunshine cake pops that had been such a big hit the year before. This year, to celebrate the winter solstice, she'd also made a dark chocolate cake infused with moonlight with silver sprinkles on the top.

Moonlight, stardust and sunshine cakes had become very popular with her new following. She'd set up a new Instagram page called 'Witchy Cakes and Bakes' and had taken photos of her delicious cakes sitting next to a bubbling cauldron or a witch's broom or even a few cobwebs and spiders for added spookiness and people had loved it. But it was the photos taken of her cakes with Mulberry – and sometimes Viktor if she could persuade him to sit still for long enough – that were her biggest hits. She still made cakes for anxiety or a broken heart, or whatever her clients needed, but she was very clear about the added magic and, whether people believed it or not, they were still eager to buy them.

The old story of her 'attack' on Cleo Walsh had withered and died within a few weeks of last year's winter solstice, especially as Star was no longer in the public eye or could even be found. By the time Star had started Witchy Cakes and Bakes a few months later, no one even remembered what had happened or who she was, although she was always careful not to share her face or name on social media just in case.

She turned round to see her beautiful husband watching her and she leaned over and kissed him.

She had married Wolf at the spring equinox, just as Zofia had originally foreseen, not to fulfil any prophecy but just because there didn't seem any point in waiting. They both knew that what they had was forever and, as the seasons had all returned to normal now, the equinox seemed a beautiful time to do it. They hadn't got married in the village though, as Zofia had originally predicted, because Star's adopted mum wouldn't have been able to attend, so they'd got married in the gardens of The Pearl instead. And although her mum knew about witches and magic, all the witches invited to attend had been instructed to be on their best behaviour and not to do magic in front of the non-magic folk. Tig had come too but still in the dark about Star's magic, she was more disappointed that everyone was fully clothed than anything else.

'You're amazing, you know that, right?' Wolf said, in between his kisses.

'Why?'

'Because you gave birth a month ago and you've been in here making cakes all morning.'

'But I did have magic to help me,' Star said. She waved her fingers and a little gold magic flickered from her fingertips. Wolf had insisted he helped as well but his baking skills were not his strong point and he had no idea how to add things like happiness or success to his creation. Besides, she was happy to do it. Wolf had been right, making cakes had been such a big part of her life for so long and she enjoyed it so she was glad she had found a way to keep doing that. She even had a cake shop on Stardust Street which had become very popular with the villagers and their visitors.

She leaned down to kiss Blaze, snuggled up in the papoose that Wolf was carrying. Blaze was snoring softly and blissfully unaware what was going on around her. It was actually her due date today but she had been super excited to come into the world and surprised them both by coming four weeks early while they were spending one of their many weekends at The

Pearl. She had arrived at sunrise with just the two of them there, which turned out to be a good thing as she was literally glowing when she came out, her magic shining from her in a blaze of glory. Any non-magic doctors would have freaked out if they'd been there to see that. Blaze was perfect in every way, already curious and inquisitive about the world, already making her toys fly above her head as she lay in her cot. Star would often lie awake just watching her, in awe of how perfect and beautiful she was with her head of bright red curls.

They had spent most of their time at The Pearl since she'd been born, with Wolf taking some well-earned paternity leave, and it had been utter bliss, just the three of them. They'd come back to Midnight a few days before to enjoy the solstice festivities.

'Right, we better go before Ezra blows a gasket over us being late,' Wolf said.

'He's doing a wonderful job as your deputy mayor. He's super organised and efficient and if he gets a little stressed sometimes when things don't go exactly to plan at least he gets things done. And he really cares about doing a good job.'

'He is. It makes taking some time off or a weekend off here and there a lot easier knowing I have Ezra here to handle things.'

'It probably wouldn't hurt to tell him that occasionally.'

Wolf grunted. 'I suppose.'

Star smiled and shook her head. Ever since they knew Blaze was on the way, Wolf had been training Ezra up to cover for him and, as much as Wolf needed someone to pick up the slack when they were away, she knew it was hard for him to hand over the control of the village when he'd been in charge for so long.

She pulled a hat on over Blaze's head. 'Is she going to be warm enough out there? It's cold enough to snow.'

'I'll be thinking warm thoughts throughout the procession.'

Star smiled, knowing her daughter would be toasty warm if that was the case.

Viktor jumped up onto the counter next to the tins of cakes. Although his house had always been Aurora Cottage and Star now lived with Wolf in his house, Viktor had started spending a lot more time with her here than with the new woman who now lived there. Star didn't know whether to be honoured by this, as he still always carried an air of disappointment and disdain whenever she was around, but it seemed he was quite partial to her.

'You can't have those,' Star said. 'They're for Zofia's solstice party.'

'Why am I never invited to these gatherings?' Viktor said, pawing at one of the tins in the hope he could pop open the lid.

'You don't like parties... or people. I'm sure it's not really your thing,' Wolf said.

'But I'm sure you'd be very welcome,' Star said. 'Providing you didn't sit there all afternoon with your face in the cakes.'

'Then there's no point in going if I'm not allowed to eat cake.' Viktor turned around so his back was towards them.

'I did make you this,' Star said, opening a small box and pushing it towards him.

Viktor turned round and looked at the box suspiciously. He sniffed the air and his eyes lit up. 'Blackberry and elderflower?'

'Just for you,' Star said.

Viktor faceplanted the cake and noises of pleasure could be heard as he snaffled it. She'd take that as a thank you.

'Right, let's go,' Star said.

They stepped outside and started walking, hand in hand, towards the village green. Frost twinkled on the ground and in the trees, and lights sparkled in the windows as they walked past. There was even the scent of toffee apples, oranges, cinnamon and chestnuts in the air and Star wondered if Ezra had arranged for that Stardust Street scent to be spread everywhere in the village. Little orbs of light were floating above the streets, guiding the way towards the green.

'My life has changed so much in the last year,' Star said. 'I've discovered the wonder of magic, met some incredible people, built a successful cake-making business, fallen in love, got married, had a baby. It's been the happiest and best year of my life.'

'For me too,' Wolf said, kissing her hand. 'Life has been perfect. The only thing that could make it more perfect is if it snowed for Blaze's first winter solstice.'

Star laughed.

They approached the green and some people who had yet to meet Blaze were obviously curious and looking over in their direction.

Ezra spotted them and came rushing over to talk to them.

'Wolf, are you sure you don't want to take the lead for the procession of light? It doesn't feel right that today of all days I should be the one that addresses the village. People might think I'm getting ideas above my station.'

'I think you absolutely should be the one that addresses the village,' Wolf said. 'They need to know that, despite me being back, I'm still on paternity leave and you are very much in charge. It makes sense that the most important person in the village starts the procession and right now that is you. Besides, I have to help Blaze with her part in the procession of light today.'

'Yes of course but Star can always take Blaze or you can take her after you do your speech—'

'Ezra, you're doing a great job. You've really become someone I can depend on over the last year and I know the villagers feel the same. They can rely on you and I'm sure they would appreciate a word from you today.'

Ezra just stared at him in shock.

Star smiled and nodded. 'Knowing you're here, taking care of things, has meant we've been really able to relax after Blaze was born. And Wolf wouldn't leave just anyone in charge.'

'No, of course not,' Ezra said, clearly still stunned to get a compliment.

'We'll see you up there,' Wolf said and started walking up towards the green again, leaving Ezra staring after them like a rabbit in the headlights.

'See, I bet that felt good,' Star said.

Wolf smiled. 'Yeah it did.'

They joined the crowd around the green and found Lynx who gave them both a hug. As if sensing her important moment was here Blaze suddenly woke up, looking around her curiously.

Ezra stepped out onto the green and scanned around as the last few stragglers joined the crowd.

'People of Midnight,' Ezra said. 'Welcome to our procession of light. I'd like to wish you all a happy solstice and a joyful Yule.'

The villagers wished everyone around them a happy solstice.

'The newest member of our village, the lovely Blaze, will now walk to the oak tree, with a little help from her dad, to be greeted by the member of the village that's been here the longest, Zofia Oakwood. Zofia will light the candle carried by Blaze and officially welcome her to the village.'

Ezra gestured for Wolf to come forward. Obviously Blaze was too young to wear a real holly crown so Ezra had kindly made one of wool. Who knew knitting was also part of Ezra's repertoire. He placed it gently over her head and handed Wolf the yule candle.

He started walking up the street and Star watched as people lit the way with orbs in their hands just as they had done when she had taken part in the procession of light the year before.

Wolf reached his grandmother and Star saw Zofia bend and give Blaze a kiss on the cheek before lighting the candle.

But Blaze clearly wanted to get in on the act and, as the candle flickered to life, she emitted a glow stronger than any of the other orbs of light.

Star laughed, as did all the other villagers.

Wolf and Zofia started walking back down the street towards the green and everyone followed them.

Star looked up to the sky and closed her eyes for a moment. When she opened them, fat flakes of sparkling snow were gently falling from the clouds. Everyone clapped and cheered and Star couldn't help smiling at what she'd done.

Wolf rejoined her, a big smile on his face as he bent his head and kissed her. 'Happy solstice.'

'I think this one might just be my happiest.'

ALSO BY HOLLY MARTIN

The Midnight Village

Sunshine and Secrets at Blackberry Beach

The Wishing Wood Series

The Blossom Tree Cottage

The Wisteria Tree Cottage

The Christmas Tree Cottage

Jewel Island Series

Sunrise over Sapphire Bay

Autumn Skies over Ruby Falls

Ice Creams at Emerald Cove

Sunlight over Crystal Sands

Mistletoe at Moonstone Lake

The Happiness Series

The Little Village of Happiness

The Gift of Happiness

The Summer of Chasing Dreams

Sandcastle Bay Series

The Holiday Cottage by the Sea

The Cottage on Sunshine Beach

Coming Home to Maple Cottage

Hope Island Series

Spring at Blueberry Bay

Summer at Buttercup Beach

Christmas at Mistletoe Cove

Juniper Island Series

Christmas Under a Cranberry Sky

A Town Called Christmas

White Cliff Bay Series

Christmas at Lilac Cottage

Snowflakes on Silver Cove

Summer at Rose Island

Standalone Stories

The Secrets of Clover Castle (Previously published as

Fairytale Beginnings)

The Guestbook at Willow Cottage

One Hundred Proposals

One Hundred Christmas Proposals

Tied Up With Love

A Home on Bramble Hill (Previously published as Beneath the Moon and Stars

For Young Adults

The Sentinel Series

The Sentinel (Book 1 of the Sentinel Series)

The Prophecies (Book 2 of the Sentinel Series)

The Revenge (Book 3 of the Sentinel Series)

The Reckoning (Book 4 of the Sentinel Series)

STAY IN TOUCH...

To keep up to date with the latest news on my releases,
just go to the link below to sign up for a newsletter. You'll
also get two FREE short stories, get sneak
peeks, booky news and be able to take part in exclusive
giveaways. Your email will never be shared with anyone
else and you can unsubscribe at any time
https://www.subscribepage.com/hollymartinsignup

Website: https://hollymartin-author.com/
Email: holly@hollymartin-author.com
Twitter: @HollyMAuthor

A LETTER FROM HOLLY

Thank you so much for reading *The Midnight Village,* I had so much fun creating this story and creating a wonderful new location in Midnight Village and all the magical ingredients. I hope you enjoyed reading it as much as I enjoyed writing it.

One of the best parts of writing comes from seeing the reaction from readers. Did it make you smile or laugh, did it make you cry, hopefully happy tears? Did you fall in love with Wolf, Star, Viktor and Mulberry as much as I did? Did you like the magical village of Midnight. I would absolutely love it if you could leave a short review on Amazon. Getting feedback from readers is amazing and it also helps to persuade other readers to pick up one of my books for the first time.

Thank you for reading.

Love Holly x

ACKNOWLEDGEMENTS

To my parents, my mom, my biggest fan, who reads every word I've written a hundred times over and loves it every single time, and for my dad, for your support, love, encouragement and endless excitement for my stories and for cooking celebratory steak every publication day

For my twinnie, the gorgeous Aven Ellis for just being my wonderful friend, for your endless support, for cheering me on, for reading my stories and telling me what works and what doesn't and for keeping me entertained with wonderful stories. I love you dearly.

To my lovely friends Julie, Natalie, Jac, Verity and Jodie, thanks for all the support.

To the Devon contingent, Paw and Order, Belinda, Lisa, Phil, Bodie, Kodi and Skipper. Thanks for keeping me entertained and always being there.

ACKNOWLEDGEMENTS

To everyone at Bookcamp, you gorgeous, fabulous bunch, thank you for your wonderful support on this venture.

Thanks to my fabulous editors, Celine Kelly and Rhian McKay.

To all the wonderful bloggers for your tweets, retweets, facebook posts, tireless promotions, support, encouragement and endless enthusiasm. You guys are amazing and I couldn't do this journey without you.

Thanks to Kerry Murphy for all the witchy help and the advice about the winter solstice.

To anyone who has read my book and taken the time to tell me you've enjoyed it or wrote a review, thank you so much.

Thank you, I love you all.

Published by Holly Martin in 2023
Copyright © Holly Martin, 2023

978-1-913616-48-9 Paperback
978-1-913616-49-6 Large Print paperback
978-1-913616-50-2 Hardback

Cover design by Dee Dee Book Covers

Made in the USA
Coppell, TX
12 November 2023

24144513R00256